This is the Day

DANIEL BLYTHE

First published in Great Britain in 2007 by
Allison & Busby Limited
13 Charlotte Mews
London W1T 4EJ
www.allisonandbusby.com

Copyright © 2007 by DANIEL BLYTHE

The moral right of the author has been asserted.

Extract on page 415 by Philip K Dick in 'How To Build A Universe That
Doesn't Fall Apart Two Days Later', in *I Hope I Shall Arrive Soon*
(Doubleday, 1985), is used by permission of Scovil Chichak Galen Literary
Agency, Inc., New York, NY, USA

A CIP catalogue record for this book is available from
the British Library.

10 9 8 7 6 5 4 3 2 1

ISBN 0 7490 8164 3
978-0-7490-8164-5

Typeset in 11/16 pt Sabon by
Terry Shannon

Printed and bound in Wales by
Creative Print and Design, Ebbw Vale

DANIEL BLYTHE was born in Maidstone in 1969 and educated at Maidstone Grammar School and St John's College, Oxford. He is the author of the novels *The Cut* and *Losing Faith*, as well as the non-fiction books *The Encyclopaedia Of Classic 80s Pop*, *I Hate Christmas: A Manifesto for the Modern-Day Scrooge* and *Dadlands: The Alternative Handbook For New Fathers*. He is married and lives on the edge of the Peak District with his wife and two young children.

For further information and to contact the author, see *www.danielblythe.moonfruit.com.*

DEDICATION

*To my happy family,
Rachel, Elinor and Samuel,
for their love and support.*

ACKNOWLEDGEMENTS

*With special thanks to my agent,
Caroline Montgomery at Rupert Crew Ltd,
for ten years of dedication, inspiration
and perspiration.*

PART ONE

Faking It

'No man is rich enough to buy back his past.'

Oscar Wilde

Mrs Felicity James-Wallace, MA (Cantab.)
Head Teacher
Millmount Hall School
Beeches Lane
Cherford
CR3 6AS

21st June

Dear Mrs James-Wallace,

I am writing in acknowledgement of your letter of the 19th to confirm that we are happy to accept the revised fee rates for the coming academic year.

We realise that the extension of the music suite has been an undertaking with many unexpected costs and that some of the expense must devolve to parents.

I confirm that we will be keeping both Ben and Isobel at Millmount Hall, and would like to thank you and your staff, as ever, for your dedicated work. Tom and I look forward to meeting you again at the next Parents' Evening or at the Garden Concert.

Yours sincerely,

Ella Barclay

Ella Barclay (Mrs)

From: Tom Barclay <tom@appletree.uk.net>
To: Andy Barclay <andybee@bravemail.com>
Date: June 21, 11:37 PM
Subject: would you believe it

Andy mate,

Christ, guess what. Bastard school has put the
fees up for next year. Some crap about the
music block having cost more than they expected.
I think we're going to make a stand about it.
We're not the kind of people who just agree to
these sorts of demands. But they've got us over
a barrel, because we're not bloody well going
to withdraw them, are we? Yes, I know your
brood have gone to the Lycée with the locals,
but you should see some of the state schools up
here. Believe me, you wouldn't wish them on
your enemies' kids, let alone your darling
nephew and niece. Anyway, hope you and Gabrielle
are keeping fine and that you'll have the
generator back online soon. Your story about
Madame Dufresne, the goat and the coffee is
brilliant. You should write one of those books.
See you again before long.

T.

CHAPTER ONE

Would Like To Meet

Tom had never been unfaithful to his wife. For one thing, he hadn't realised it was going to be so bloody difficult.

Strike One: girl in the pub, three months ago.

'Go on, then,' Jeff said, 'talk to her.'

'I only said I *could* fancy her,' Tom muttered, glowering. 'If I wasn't a boring, married git.' He felt hemmed in by all the students with their squawky laughs, and he could taste the smoke in the air. Giving up was hardest in the pub. And Jeff, sympathetic but unrepentant, always had a cigarette between his fingers.

'She looked over at you,' Jeff told him, eyes showing wry amusement from behind rimless glasses. 'Just then.' Jeff gestured with his pint of Old Thistle.

'Oh, don't be a tosser,' Tom muttered, but he couldn't resist a glance.

She had a black bob, teased-up eyelashes and carmine lips and was sipping from a vase of lager. She caught his eye – just long enough. He risked a longer look. Pink streak in her fringe, stud in her nose, Strokes T-shirt stretched over the cupolas of her breasts, glossy leather skirt. He realised, with a sinking heart, that she had to be a decade younger than him. A vast chasm.

Tom looked back at the amused expression on Jeff's face. 'Like I said. I could talk to her.' He took another slurp of his pint. His shoes were sticking to the floor as if they'd encountered the trail of a large gastropod.

'Oh, well.' Jeff shrugged, sighed contentedly and leant on the bar. 'If we're just talking hypothetical, then I'm having a bloody affair with Cherie Lunghi, sunshine. Have been for years.'

'Who?' Tom felt disconnected, irritable.

'Cherie Lunghi. The bird from the coffee adverts. You know, used to shake the beans at old Gareth Hunt in a seductive way.'

Tom glanced at the girl again. She was in animated conversation with her friends, and was laughing, showing advert-bright teeth. 'Uh-huh.'

'Yeah. Point is, if you're only ever going to *talk* about chatting up someone other than your dear, darling wife, who, I have to say, I admire and respect and would almost certainly shag myself if she weren't taken—'

'OK, *too* much information, Jeff.'

'—then you might as well decide that you're having it off with Favourite Celeb Totty, yeah? This is real life, Thomas. Get your fucking tank engine in gear, mate.' Jeff laughed, long and hard.

Tom enjoyed having Jeff as a friend, because Jeff was the brash, bold, sweary and shameless version of himself. Jeff had left his wife ages ago and had taken up with a younger woman, a lovely Spanish girl who he was now bored with and two-timing.

Tom and Ella still went out, children permitting, in the old groups from their Saturday nights, but mostly Tom saw his friends and Ella saw hers. It was odd, sometimes, having a friend like Jeff, with whom all he did was drink, chat, play pool and do pub quizzes. With other friends, he and Ella did films, theatre, dinner, walks. But Tom and Jeff were happy enough in the Rowan, chatting about life and testing each other on Eighties pop trivia.

'I'm too old for this sort of thing,' Tom protested.

'Thirty-seven isn't old, mate.' Jeff looked almost affronted. 'Christ, it's the best time of your life! You can fancy a woman *and* her daughter without being either repelled or imprisoned.'

'I see. You've told Inez you fancy her mum, have you?'

'Don't go there. Come on, get a grip. What about Little Miss Pert?'

Tom smiled weakly. 'Look, she's – OK, but what the hell would I to talk to her about?'

'Start with her taste in music.'

'Er, no, I don't think so.'

'Well… I dunno, you run a homeless charity. She's probably a right-on sort. See if that impresses her.'

'Jeff, young people aren't right-on any more. She's probably into clubbing and dropping E's and…and texting and stuff.'

'I'll give your Appletree Project ten quid if you'll go and talk to her.'

'That's not fair. That's bloody emotional blackmail.'

'Twenty quid, then. Twenty smackers for Appletree. That'd

get one of your homeless buggers off the street for a night or two, wouldn't it?' And Jeff grinned, taking a deep drag on his cigarette.

You had to admire him, Tom thought bitterly. He knew what he was doing. 'No, I can't, mate. I've lost the knack. I don't even remember what I said the night I chatted up Ella.'

'Jesus, Tom. It really is time to live a little.' Jeff wrinkled his nose. 'Hang on, what about Lol's stag weekend? That Irish bit?'

'No, she approached *me*. And I spent most of the conversation being sick in the bogs, remember? Not that it seemed to put her off.' Tom didn't like the feeling of being backed into a corner, and was getting defensive now. 'All right.' He took a preparatory gulp of his Guinness. 'You make it thirty pounds. And you have to come into the office and deliver the cheque in person.'

'Only too happy to. I love to support our local charities.'

'Like hell you do.' Tom took another gulp of Guinness. With its warmth in his veins, and the memory of the girl's eye contact, he felt better. 'OK, OK. Let me think of an opening line.'

'Try spilling her drink,' Jeff said. 'Offer to get her another.'

Tom gawped at him. 'Are you *mad*?'

Jeff shrugged. 'It's what I do. That's how I first got talking to Inez. It seemed to work.'

Spilling her drink. Right.

A few more minutes' discussion of the logistics of this, a bit more Guinness, and now he was flexing his fingers, eyeing up his path between the jostling youngsters. He was picturing the pleasant thought of Jeff, Nature's biggest cynic, having to give thirty pounds towards the education of the homeless.

The girl was tucking a strand of hair behind one ear in a very cute way.

Here I go, Tom thought, and allowed himself to swing slightly from side to side as he approached, arms and legs loose. Just right for catching a top-heavy vase of lager. It was on the table in front of the girl, and she was still talking excitedly to her friends, using both hands.

Two metres away.

One.

Zero.

Oh, yes.

He flicked round, caught the glass with his jacket and swung towards the table with a melodramatic gasp, just in time to see the glass rolling, empty, and a waterfall of lager cascading into the girl's leather-clad lap.

'*Shit!*' She leapt up, began frantically mopping at her skirt with a handkerchief. Lager dripped from the edge of the soaked table, and one or two of the young men were muttering, wiping drips from themselves, giving Tom belligerent stares.

'Sorry,' said Tom. 'Um…gosh, I'm so sorry.' He ran a hand through his hair. The pungency of the spilt drink wafted up towards him and he felt genuinely embarrassed.

The girl looked Tom in the eye, but her expression was somewhat angrier than he had been expecting. 'You clumsy *wanker*!' she spat.

'Come on, Lise,' one of her girlfriends said. 'It was an accident, the guy said sorry.'

'Let me get you another,' Tom said, fishing out his wallet

and giving her a reassuring grin. He hoped he wasn't blushing too much. 'What was it?'

The girl sighed, rubbed again at the skirt. 'No, no, it doesn't matter...' She waved a hand.

'No, really.' Tom waved his wallet and half turned towards the bar.

'I said don't worry.' The girl didn't even look up from her frantic cleaning.

Having come this far, he couldn't blow it. He was thinking of Jeff having to write out that cheque. 'Look, come on. Tell me what it was and I'll get you another one. It's the least I can do.' He gave his most endearing smile and delivered what he thought was the ultimate, winning line. 'I insist,' he said.

The girl straightened up, hands on hips. 'OK,' she said, her expression slightly pitying. 'Since you *insist*.'

Tom held the smile, waited expectantly with his fingers on the ten-pound note.

'It was a patent leather Karen Millen skirt,' she said. 'And they don't make this line any more, so you're not going to get me another one. So please, just fuck off and don't bother. All right?'

Strike Two: the woman from the council.

'The Directorate finds it very difficult,' she said, smoothing her black cotton trousers, 'to fund non-vocational opportunities.' She peered at him over her slender glasses.

A spectre of a smile there, Tom thought. Like she's saying, let's get down to the more serious stuff, like you asking me if I'm free for lunch one day. Or a drink, today. The old plastic clock on the wall told him it was nearly half past three. (The

Countdown theme tune bounced through his head, as it always did. *Daddum, daddum, diddly-doom.* He hoped he'd remembered to set the video timer.)

'Absolutely,' he said, nodding seriously and pressing his fingertips together. 'I understand. Thing is, er, Geri...'

The thing is, you're the first attractive woman to walk into the shabby, rented offices of the Appletree Trust for several months. And I'm not listening to what you're saying because I'm looking at the way your dark hair curls as it nuzzles your slender neck, and I'm thinking about pinning you to a bed in some hotel room, breathing on that neck, pressing my lips to it and marking my territory with a mottled red bite that leaves you squealing, panting and damp beneath me.

'Yes?' she said, her voice level.

Tom shifted his chair forward to make sure his erection was concealed beneath the desk. He smiled, spread his hands. 'We've always prided ourselves at Appletree on our flexible arrangements with educational providers. Yes, it's important for our client base to gain employment, but it's just as valid for them to achieve a sense of self-worth. And part of that comes with valuing education – not just as a means to an end, but as a way of improving yourself and as a desirable... commodity in itself.'

She smiled, leant forward with her chin on one ivory finger. 'Go on.'

'Lots of the people we see, they didn't make the most of school. Many of them ran away at fifteen and have been living on the street ever since. We owe them more than just giving them a bog-standard, twenty-week course in IT just because that's what the Directorate will fund. We owe them more than a piece of paper that'll get them some McJob that they don't really want. We owe them...' Tom lifted his hands up, trying to symbolise the sum of human knowledge held in an invisible crucible. 'The cadence of the French language, the grace of Fermat's Last Theorem, the thrill of Shakespeare's soliloquies. Beauty, ugliness, passion, fire, love, hate... We need to show them that learning is fantastic. That it's *fun*.' He paused, pressed his fingers together. 'That is, if we don't run out of money first,' he added.

There was a long pause. Tom was aware that he was perspiring and panting slightly, and that his cock, through his trousers, was nuzzling the underside of the desk.

'Yes,' said the girl uncertainly. She made a note on her clipboard. 'OK.'

Tom glanced through the glass separating his office from the busy main area, an upper floor of a converted warehouse which was home to the desks of his young, dedicated team. They were yapping efficiently into their Eighties phones (not retro, just old) or tapping away on their begged-and-borrowed PCs. Someone was making coffee. Nobody seemed to be looking over in his direction.

'What do you say?' Tom asked, and gave her his most winning smile.

She blinked behind her glasses, in a way that made Tom want to go over and rip her austere little black jacket open. He imagined the silver buttons pinging, hitting the walls like shrapnel as the pair of them crashed to the floor in a tangle of sweaty limbs.

'Perhaps,' she said tentatively, 'we could start them with the computer course in September, and see how they get on?'

Tom sat back in his seat. 'Yes,' he said in weary resignation, 'that'll be fine.'

'I will refer your comments to the Directorate, though.' She sounded as if she might mean it. 'I mean…you never know.'

'Oh, yes,' said Tom, nodding. 'You never know. They might decide tomorrow that the one thing they've always wanted to do is to run a course in Elizabethan Drama for homeless kids, just for the hell of it.'

'Well,' she said diplomatically, 'they *might*.'

'Yeah. And those pigs had better watch out for the cranes, that's all I can say.'

She frowned, looked up, peered over her glasses again in a way that made him imagine her sitting there, wearing nothing but those smooth black frames. 'I'm sorry?'

Tom flapped his arms. 'Oink. Oink.' The girl still looked blank. 'Pigs might fly,' he said, sighing. 'A joke,' he added lamely.

'Oh,' she said. 'Yes.' She snapped her folder shut and stood up to leave. 'Well, I think that'll be all for now.'

Tom managed to make a discreet adjustment before standing up. They smiled, shook hands.

'Rest of the day busy for you?' Tom asked, scratching one ear.

She shrugged, smiled. 'Not really. You were my last meeting.'

'Great. Fancy a drink?' He was astonished at how casual he made it sound.

She smiled on one side of her face, glanced at the sunlit, grimy cityscape outside the office for a second, as if to say: *Out there? In the proper world? Where we don't have an excuse to be together?*

'I don't think so,' she said, snapping her briefcase shut. 'I told my girlfriend I wouldn't be late tonight.'

And as she turned on her heel and left the office, he was sure that she winked mockingly at him.

'Oh, *dear*,' said Jeff with a sigh, that Friday in the Rowan. 'Oh, dearie, dearie me.' He turned to one of the young barmen, who was washing glasses beside them. 'Hey, Mickey. You'll never guess what. Tom here tried to chat up a Sister of Sappho. A drinker from the furry cup! A fucking muff-diver!' The barman grinned and chuckled along with Jeff.

Tom buried his face in his pint. 'For God's sake,' he hissed at Jeff, 'don't *tell* everyone, mate.' He looked furtively from side to side. Nobody was taking any interest, he realised, in the conversation of two ordinary thirtysomething blokes in jeans and casual shirts. 'And you don't have to use derogatory language, Jeff. Can't you just say she was a lesbian?'

'Oh, don't come over all *Guardian* Society section. Where's the fun in that?... Listen, don't take this the wrong way, mate, but I don't think you're cut out for infidelity.'

'Really?'

'Nah. Now, your Ella, she's quite a woman. Why don't you just accept your lot and throw yourself wholeheartedly and whole-bollockedly into the nuptial bed?'

But he was, Tom thought moodily, that was the thing. He and Ella had excellent sex. It was like a well-oiled machine. Pinball in your favourite arcade, knowing exactly what to tweak, precisely when to tilt. Ka-pow. *Ding*.

'Or alternatively,' said Jeff, with one of those heavy sighs which indicated he was about to say something half serious, 'why don't you just leave her?'

'*Leave* her? Why on earth would I want to leave Ella? She's fabulous.'

'But you said to me the other day that things...aren't the same.'

Tom winced. He had said that, hadn't he? Tom's unguarded moments sometimes came back to haunt him, although Jeff probably knew him well enough to let him get away with them. 'OK. Maybe I did.'

'You said they haven't been right since—'

'Yeah, all right, enough!' He held up a hand. 'The truth is, some people get divorced because they... I don't know, because things aren't fairytale-perfect any more. They can still talk to each other, still get on, but for some reason they decide to end it. That just seems stupid to me. When you think of all the upheaval...you have to be *convinced* that you'd be totally, utterly better off afterwards. Otherwise...nah.'

Jeff nodded thoughtfully, didn't add anything. Tom appreciated that about Jeff – he usually knew when it was his turn to shut up.

'Anyway, we get on great,' Tom went on. 'We have a laugh. We like the same stuff. Every Wednesday we open a bottle of Sauvignon Blanc and watch *ER* together.'

'God, it sounds sickeningly blissful, mate.'

Well, maybe, thought Tom.

In fact, he had worked out, in front of the shaving mirror one night, Ella was 76 per cent perfect. He had marked her, in categories, out of ten – being realistic and not starry-eyed.

It was what *Top DVD* magazine did. It marked every

release with a series of scores for Script, Direction, Plot, Entertainment Value, Music and more, then totted them all up for an overall percentage. In *Top Wife* magazine, he reckoned, Ella would have got: Kindness 7, Sexiness 8, Bed Performance 10, Tits 7, Arse 8, Easy-goingness 5, Humour 8, Coolness 6, Lovability 9, Beauty 8. Total, 76 per cent. He didn't feel guilty about the low mark for Easy-goingness, because she could be a stubborn cow at times, but that was part of her attraction. And although she had a great sense of humour, he lopped off a couple because she just didn't get *Monty Python*. Sat there stony-faced through every single video.

So, 76 per cent. That was bloody good. Amazing, in fact. If it was a GCSE result, it would be an A-star performance. And he'd not had a wife before, so he'd gone from zero to 76, almost overnight. He couldn't argue with a relationship that only missed total perfection by 24 percentage points.

'You've been married fifteen years, mate. *Fifteen years*. People get less than that for armed robbery.'

'I know. And mostly, it's been fine.' Tom shrugged. 'She's the best wife I've ever had,' he added with a grin.

'I can't quite get a handle on it, Tom. You've no complaints, and yet you *still* want to play away?'

'OK. It's like this. You don't stop fancying people just because you're as happy as a pig in shit. You just stop wanting to...to do anything about it.' Tom took a sip of his pint. 'For a while,' he added.

'So what is this? Round two of the seven-year itch?'

'No, nothing so trite. I just wonder... Look, technically, so far, I haven't ever been unfaithful to Ella.'

'That won't wash. It's not for want of trying.'

'But that's what I mean. Maybe these two in three marriages that work – or one in two or whatever it is these days – they only work because people are faithful by default. They never get in the position where they *could* be shagging someone else. Or if they do, then they're too shy to take it further.'

'Almost profound.' Jeff held up his glass. 'At least, it seems that way after three pints of Old Thistle. Just out of interest, mate – how would you feel if the lovely Ella was getting rooted by someone else?'

Tom blinked. It was a question out of left-field. Not like Jeff to see the alternative point of view so clearly. He drained his glass and thumped it down on the bar.

'I'd be bloody furious,' he said. 'Of course.'

'And I assume she'd react the same way,' offered Jeff with a knowing smile.

'Well, yeah. Which is why, if and when I ever find some poor unsuspecting creature to enter into a dalliance with me, Ella's never going to know.'

'Right,' said Jeff. He waved at the glasses. 'Same again?'

Strike Three: the familiar face, last Thursday, at the Multicultural Awareness Forum.

At first, he hadn't been sure he knew the girl. He stared at her as he hovered by the buffet, his mouth full of an over-spiced pakora. (Why, he grumbled to himself, did *every* voluntary-sector event wheel out the same old stuff for lunch?) The girl, blonde hair in a bun, was engaged in eager conversation with a middle-aged Somali woman.

Tom watched them carefully, and took another pakora.

It had to be vegetarian, of course, it always was – but that didn't mean it always needed to be liberally doused in cardamom and cumin. At *lunchtime*, and in June. At times like this, Tom fought an urge to go and fry a large rump steak ostentatiously in the nearby kitchen. He sometimes felt he just hadn't been born with the right genes to be a charity manager, and that someone was waiting, poised to strike, ready to pick him up the second he slipped.

He caught the eye of his friend and she grinned, gave him a half-wave which he returned.

Name, name... Alison, was it? No, Alice. A little chubbier, but otherwise not much different. And it was *good* chubby – all in the right places. (He and Jeff agreed fervently that they liked women who actually looked like women: curvaceous, voluptuous, sensual. There was nothing worse than a 'scrawny bint with no tits', as Jeff so eloquently put it.)

When he and Alice finally got a chance to chat, there were only five minutes to go before the afternoon workshops, and Tom got his questions in quickly. She met his gaze with a twinkle and a big, genuine smile. Yes, she remembered him; that conference on Futures Of Non-Vocational Learning, wasn't it? In Leicester? But then someone was tapping a glass, asking people if they could possibly make their way to the workshop rooms. Tom was in Workshop One, but she was in Workshop Four. He seized the moment, asked her what she was doing afterwards.

And that was how they'd ended up sitting in a small, quiet pub just off the ringroad, one he'd only been in a couple of times before.

So he sipped his Guinness, and watched her as she lifted her half of lager to her lips, and he decided that in the fanciability stakes she qualified as an 'OK'. She wasn't someone he'd have crossed the room for, but now – talking cheerfully, with no awkward silences and no interruptions – he decided he liked her bold, sapphire eyes, her wispy hair and her enticing curves. Alice had a nervous laugh and a slightly desperate edge, he thought, which normally he'd have found a turn-off – but right now he was starting to think it was just what he wanted.

So, she'd come down from Edinburgh especially for this Forum? Oh, how interesting. Staying in a hotel? Hmm, very interesting. Him? Oh, he lived here. Living in a city with a lot of regeneration money being thrown at it, he explained with a wry smile, meant that you got to go to a lot of courses without running up hotel bills. Bit right-on, though, all of it. They had a complicit smile about that. They ordered more drinks, and some crisps.

Tom went to the Gents and phoned Ella. He told her that the conference had been incredibly dull and that he was dying to get away, but he'd been asked to do some networking in the bar and he couldn't really say no. She understood. The children were already in bed. She told him not to worry.

He thumbed the phone off with a smile. To himself. In the mirror.

The second drink slipped by in a blur of did-you-knows and do-you-thinks and what-do-you-imagines. By the third pint, they were talking about themselves. He mentioned the family, kept it brief. She mentioned an ex-boyfriend, didn't keep it brief. There was obviously a chip on the shoulder there, he thought with an inward sigh, as he nodded and sipped and nodded and let his eyes glaze over for five, ten, fifteen minutes while she detailed this bastard's exact shortcomings. Oh, really, he said. How awful. Still, you're shot of him now.

And then there was a fourth drink, and the pub was darker and fuller, louder and smokier, and the Guinness had stopped tasting of velvet and started tasting of yeast, and he knew he should really have some water.

He felt warm, excited, reckless inside. Alice was resting her chin in one hand and was grinning stupidly at him. Last orders rang and she waggled her eyebrows. Gosh, she said, haven't we been here a long time? And then, staggering, gliding or drifting, they were on the pavement, in the warm night air, in the glare of the ringroad traffic, and she leant up to kiss him.

Not on his mouth. Beside it.

Her warmth and her perfume slipped away from him before he realised what was happening, and his arm, which had been circled around her hips, clutched empty air. She was doing a comedy wave at him. Uncertainly, he did one back.

'I thought,' he said. 'I thought, um, we. Could.' And he cleared his throat.

'I know,' she said, and shrugged and blew him a kiss. 'I'd have liked to as well. It's lonely in the hotel. Bottom line is, though, you're married, and I ain't that kind of girl.'

And a big, dark taxi opened up for her like a guardian angel, enveloping her, sealing her off and bearing her away.

Luckily, she was gone before he could open his mouth for the riposte he had started to form. *But you must be.*

'Face it,' Jeff said, as they gathered their coats under the eye of an impatient barmaid. 'You're just too bloody *uxorious*, mate.'

Jeff had heard the full story of the unattainable Alice, but only after he had made Tom accurately tell him the 1983 line-up of The Cure.

Tom thought he ought to know what 'uxorious' meant. He was sure it had been on *Countdown*. By the time he had got the words together to ask Jeff, though, he was aware of a thump on his arm and glimpsed his friend being swallowed up by the swishing doors of a bus.

At home – once he had eased his angry bladder and sluiced his mouth with water – Tom looked the word up in the dictionary. He had to focus so hard on the swirling letters that they made his head pound with pain.

There it was in black and white. Well, fuzzy grey and white. The definition. It made him smile, and it made him wonder.

No, that wasn't him, he had to say. Sorry, Jeff. A pity – but no.

He turned the bedside light off, and lay awake beside Ella.

No good. He couldn't sleep.

Downstairs, he made a pot of tea and flicked to the local radio phone-in. Always good for a laugh. The calm and collected Janie Jones, maintaining her poise, fielding the problems and rants of the drunk, the lost and the insane of three counties, coolly interspersing them with the weather, the adverts and Simply Red.

'—*feel that we should send them somewhere else?*' the husky-voiced Janie was murmuring. '*I mean, the thing is, Kevin, they are citizens like you and me. How would you feel if someone wanted to move you somewhere else? It isn't that simple. Let's have some music from Sting, then we'll go to another caller.*'

Good old Janie, he thought. She can even make asylum debates sound sexy.

Back in bed, still head-poundingly, limb-achingly, frustratingly awake, teasing a mild erection (which came to nothing), he watched the black sky fade, fragmenting into crusts of cloud as the dawn tuned itself in.

CHAPTER TWO

What Not To Wear

'Ladies and gentlemen,' said Ella to her reflection, 'as you approach Cherford Castle from the west incline, you look across the Causeway at the splendid façade of the Gloriette.'

Ella narrowed her eyes to slits, then opened them wide, staring herself out in the bedroom mirror with her hands clasped behind her naked body. The June heat moistened her flesh, but she enjoyed the sheen of her tanned skin. It felt comfortable, and was not unattractive.

Her eyes prickled. She blinked.

'Its magnificent state today,' she went on, 'is the result of five years of painstaking work, for which we have the members of the Foundation to thank.'

And at this point she would turn, she decided, and open her eyes and mouth seductively as she nodded her thanks towards the Chair of the Foundation.

Her accent entranced them. It was chocolate-box Home Counties on the surface, until she got to a tell-tale word – like 'castle', which she rhymed with 'hassle'. Sheffield steel, but tempered in the fires of Middle England. Some called it Yorkshire Posh.

'Entering the keep through the gatehouse, you glance to your left and notice the impressively restored fortifications of the fifteenth-century Barbican.'

Ella raised a quizzical eyebrow and idly clasped her hands over her breasts. She allowed herself a little smile at their warmth and firmness. She placed a thumb over each nipple, enjoying the tautness as they puckered, the electric current between breasts and loins. She allowed herself a dirty, inviting smile. Often, she thought, I wonder who on earth the miserable, saggy bitch in the mirror is. But some days, I could quite happily fancy myself.

She put her head on one side and let her dark fringe fall over one eye, as she often did when trying to engage the attention of a group of speakers. It always worked.

'You may also have noticed,' she began again, curling her mouth around each word as if murmuring sweet obscenities to a lover, 'that the fortifications of the fifteenth-century Barbican have recently benefited from extensive restoration. This work was undertaken with the aid of a generous grant from the Heritage Lottery Fund.'

But some days, she reflected grumpily, I don't even like myself.

In the spattered mirror she saw a wife, a mother, attractive but a little untamed. Crow's-feet crinkling her eyes, that double exclamation mark above the bridge of her nose. Hips had a good shape, but would never again be girlish, not after two children.

Attractive but a little untamed. The untended garden, wild and natural.

'Not going to win any prizes,' she said ruefully to her mirror image, 'but at least I'll blend in with the environment.'

With an efficient hoist and clip, she contained her body in two pieces of black cotton. Serviceable chain-store underwear – today was not a day for Agent Provocateur or La Perla. She sheathed her legs in black tights, smiling. What was it Tom called tights? 'The devil's invention', that was it. She could hear him now. She could summon his image, standing behind her, hands spread in a gesture of despair.

'Who the hell wants to see women in *tights*?' he was saying. 'They're the sort of thing incontinent pensioners wear, for God's sake, not good-looking women in their thirties.'

'Know a lot of incontinent pensioners, do you, darling?'

He was on Transmit. 'What's wrong with stockings? They've just been fetishised, that's the bloody problem. You're conditioned to associate them with male fantasies. You think we're all imagining, I dunno, someone like Anne Bancroft on that poster for *The Graduate*.'

'Yes, dear, of course we do.'

'Whereas we're just wanting our gorgeous wives and girlfriends to celebrate their loveliness, that's all.'

'You're so sweet, love. How many wives and girlfriends did you have, at the last count? I want to keep track.'

'I mean, yes, I can see they – what? Oh, yes, yes. Ha-ha... I can see they don't keep all the bits in as efficiently, but that's the price you pay, isn't it? That woman on that programme the other night was saying it.'

'Was she? Oh, well, it must be right, then.'

'That programme, you know. The one with those poor sods who get a makeover before going on their dates. *Fashion isn't about comfort*, she says, *it's about looking good*. That's a woman talking. A woman. Not one of us, one of *you*.'

'One of *us*. My goodness. You must keep watching these lifestyle programmes, Tom. They're obviously giving you a remarkable insight into what makes us tick.'

'Well, you know. I like to keep up.' A mere breath-pause. 'You're always moaning that I don't take enough interest in your clothes.'

Yes, Ella thought, that was Tom all over, capable of complimenting and insulting a woman in the same conversation – often in the same sentence – and then looking slightly irritated and saying, 'What? What is it *now*?' if you brought it up.

She grinned, winked at his photo on the dressing table. He'd always been a little pompous, although that had been part of his initial appeal, all those years ago. He'd seemed sensible, a grown-up among the boys. The other students had their stupidly trendy haircuts and their ridiculously fashionable clothes, but Tom's style, or lack of it, had been more her scene: baggy jumper, faded jeans, black hair ruffled into untidy spikes. He had the same haircut now – the same one he'd had since he was about ten, as far as she could tell. Although his temples were slightly greying, he didn't look in danger of losing clumps of hair yet, which was a blessing (too many men went for a skinhead at the first sign of receding). The edges of his eyes were etched, like hers, but they still held that sparkle of mischief.

A wriggle and a zip later, and she was in a black cotton pencil skirt. A plain cream top and her black jacket and knee-length leather boots completed the look. Sober and businesslike, but with enough hints of sex – in the creak of the boots, in the curve of the skirt – to keep them interested.

Because they always were. For all her unflattering horticultural metaphors, Ella knew that she was desirable. And she usually had a mesmerising effect on balding businessmen with pots of money to throw at Heritage. At least, she hoped so. She assumed that was why she'd been picked for the job.

The big speech wasn't for a couple of weeks yet, but Ella had taken to practising the attitude in front of the mirror. She swivelled, plumped her breasts up a little. And then she allowed herself a broad, lovable white grin – albeit, she noticed ruefully, with that one damned wonky incisor, the bastard almost at forty-five degrees these days.

'Ladies and gentlemen,' she murmured. 'The façade is the result of one fuck of a lot of restoration work. But, I think you'll agree, not bad for a thirty-eight-year-old mother of two.'

Tom, rubbing his eyes, pulled another desk drawer open. He needed those papers urgently, and now he couldn't remember what he'd done with them.

Maybe Ella had tidied them away. She used to do things like that, when she'd been off on maternity leave. About an hour before he got in, he reckoned, was when she started her household frenzy, so that when he walked in the door she'd give the impression of having been slogging at it all day. (He only twigged because a woman at work told him she used to use the same trick with her husband.) Ella would be frantically polishing, hoovering or dusting, too busy to acknowledge him with more than a brief kiss and some instructions. A screaming child would need to be fed, some washing fetched or a light bulb replaced. Sometimes she would have pinned up a list for him. And things which he had left in specific places – for specific reasons – were now hidden in drawers and cupboards.

'What are you *doing*, Daddy?' said a small voice at chest-height.

'Just a minute, Izzy.'

As he located the folder he needed, Isobel began tugging on his trouser leg. 'Dad? What are you *doing*?'

Tom grabbed the papers, squatted down so that he was level with his seven-year-old daughter's perfect brown eyes. He tried to ignore the little clicks his body gave these days, and the ache in his limbs from a night of frustrated dozing. He ruffled her curls. 'Yes, Izzy-bizzy?'

'Dad, you're so *sad* when you call me that,' said Isobel, a scowl creasing the dough-smoothness of her face. 'That's a baby name. Mum said she wouldn't call me that any more.'

'Sorry, darling. What is it?'

She shifted gear, as she could, from feisty minx to simpering princess. 'Can I have the Zillah Zim Magic House for my birthday?' Isobel asked. Tom raised his eyebrows, prompting her. 'Please?' Isobel added – an afterthought as usual.

'Well, we'd agreed you were having a computer. Ben hogs the other one so much, after all.' Her brother, away for a few days on Scout camp, wasn't there to defend his supposed profligacy.

'Yes, but I want the Zillah Zim Magic House as *weee-eell*,' Isobel explained patiently, folding her hands demurely behind her back and swivelling on one foot. Her voice lowered to a breathy whisper and her eyes flicked from side to side, not quite meeting Tom's gaze. 'It's got a dressing-up room. And everything.'

'Ah. A dressing-up room. Every girl should have one, of course.'

'*Please*, Daddy,' said Isobel, and she lunged forward, throwing her arms around his neck and planting a soft, wet kiss on his stubbly cheek.

You little madam, he thought. In ten years' time the guys just aren't going to stand a chance. Still, it'll be good for me – she'll probably never have to pay for anything herself.

'We'll see,' he said, kissing the soft, dark curls with their autumnal scent of apple shampoo.

Zillah Zim – every little girl in the land knew her. A pink-haired sorceress, TV icon and purveyor of jaunty pop, she had implanted herself into the national consciousness. Her image shone from countless books, dolls, CDs, DVDs, T-shirts, bowls, mugs, socks, shoes, hats, keyrings, nightshirts, toys, games, balloons, notepads, cereals, chocolate bars, yoghurts, birthday cards, trading-cards, mousemats and anything else which could be stamped with the silver double-Z (double-*zee*) logo and the beaming, scrubbed face of the actress who played Zillah. They had been restrained, knowing Isobel could well be into something else in a year's time. Ella, though, who pounced on anything with supposed educational value, hadn't been able to resist the Official Zillah Zim CD-ROM ('Magic with words and numbers!') which had turned out to be all flashy graphics with little content.

'I'll tell you what,' Tom said at the table, as he pushed a

bowl of cornflakes under his daughter's nose. 'Why don't you try saving up? Put aside a bit of your pocket money in your piggy bank every week.'

Piggy bank, he thought, ruefully biting into his toast. Which decade am I in? Isobel and her brother Ben each had an ISA, untouchable until they were eighteen. Ella, in her more wine-soaked and cynical moments, referred to these savings as 'the beer-and-drug fund'.

'I haven't got a piggy bank,' said Isobel through a mouthful of cornflakes.

'Would you like me to get you one?'

She nodded. The big, theatrical, emphatic nod of the seven-year-old. 'Yes, please,' she said indistinctly.

'Then you could put, say, fifty pence a week in. You could save up.'

You hypocritical bastard, said the Angel Of Conscience who squatted on his shoulder. How long did you 'save up' for that box-set of *The Prisoner* you got three months ago?

'Save up?' said Isobel with a frown.

'Yes, you know. If there's something you really want, put money aside for it, a bit a week. It soon grows. Look, you know how Mummy and I planted the plum tree in the garden?'

Isobel nodded, her eyes wide and serious. She knew all about the plum tree.

'Well, it took a while, but it started to produce fruit. And we've had lovely plum crumbles and jam as a result of something we did. Thinking ahead, Izzy. Money doesn't grow *on* trees, but it can grow *like* trees.'

Oh, very good, very Responsible Dad, sneered the Angel of

Conscience. I'd like to see you explain, right now, how this applies to that Contour chair you put on the credit card last month. Or that impulse buy in HMV – the entire Paul Weller back catalogue. Good God, even the Style Council's *Confessions Of A Pop Group*.

'OK,' said Isobel.

Tom paused with a slice of toast halfway to his mouth. 'OK?' he repeated in disbelief. 'So, if I get you a piggy bank, you'll do it?'

He hadn't actually expected the Bizzy to take up the idea so readily. He was used to the children ignoring him.

'Yes, Daddy,' said Isobel. She put her spoon neatly in her empty bowl and gave her father a gap-toothed grin. 'Daddy,' she said, 'am I good?'

'Izzy, you're very good. You're a specially good girl.'

'Daddy?'

'Yes, darling?'

'Please may I have fifty pence a week more pocket money?'

'Oh, my stars,' Ella groaned. 'Look who's in this morning.'

She was leafing through the tour roster in the minimalist, pine-and-chrome Estates Office of Cherford Castle. Formerly a stable block, the Estates building was set apart from the main Keep and fortifications. It was half a mile across the moat, beyond the flower gardens and the maze. If she wished, Ella could view most of the Castle grounds from the huge, tinted window on the south-facing wall of the office.

Janet, the senior guide, looked up from the rack of radio-links. 'Parkfield Comp?' she hazarded, smiling at Ella over half-frame glasses.

'Parkfield Comp,' Ella agreed grimly. She tossed the roster aside with a sigh. 'Good God. Hide the valuables. Put newspaper down in the Banqueting Hall.'

'Some of them are good kids, Ella,' Janet said with a wry, indulgent smile. 'They're not all thieves and drug addicts. And it can't do them any harm to be exposed to a day of history.' The radio spat static. 'Aha, working at last!'

'No, no, I suppose not.' Ella was light-headed, sipping the morning's first coffee on an empty stomach and just getting fired up by its kick. 'All the same, though...bloody *Parkfield*.'

Everything was in order. Immediately in front of the Estates Office, the ducks were waddling across the terraced green slopes, picking over the fingers of bread already left by the early-morning strollers. Ella let her gaze wander across the moat, where the morning sunlight was smashed into glittering fragments, and then beyond, along the elegant Causeway to the honeyed stone of the Castle. The ground-staff vans in their distinctive green livery skimmed the skirts of the estate. The stewards were taking up their positions at the Gate-Tower – she could just see them if she squinted.

'Ready for the Gawpers,' Ella said softly.

She was happy at Cherford Castle, although she often wished she could love the visitors as much as she loved the fifteenth-century (ha-ha) house and its exquisite gardens.

Her favourite time of day was just before eight when she arrived on the estate, flicking her pass at the barrier and descending, often through filigrees of morning mist, into an uninhabited wonderland, haunted by the cries of moorhen and mallard. Then, for an hour at least, it was as it should be; the place was pure, and so was Ella. She would pace the echoing office, fuelled by filtered water, her skin still tingling from the morning's micro-granule exfoliation. And then they arrived – the Hordes.

In her interview, Ella had acted the part of someone who was Good With People. In truth, she didn't care for them at all: the sweaty mums, the stained, grouchy kids, the tattooed and paunchy men who had to be asked to put their shirts on. Then there were the cackling old biddies who peered at their brochures and would stop you to ask the same three questions: Where are the toilets? Where's the restaurant? and Did Henry the Eighth actually come here, then? And then there was the time they'd foolishly held the outdoor concert during the World Cup and all the Gawpers had come armed with portable TVs as well as their usual picnic paraphernalia.

Ella couldn't exactly place when she had become a snob. She tried not to be, but it was hard.

Last week, a man with about ten earrings had guffawed at the size of the bed in the King's Chambers, bellowing across the room, 'That 'Enry, 'e were a randy old git, wernee? Coulda got all eight of 'is bleedin' wives in there at once. Chop the 'ead off one, move onna the next.' Ella had been in the Bedchamber at the time, but she merely shuddered and didn't take the man aside for a brief history lesson. It wasn't difficult, surely, to get the number right? *Divorced, beheaded, died, divorced, beheaded, outlived.* It was a mantra that everybody learnt, wasn't it?

'Three buses in the car park already,' Janet was saying, pinning on her badge as she headed out of the door. 'I'm going to head down there.'

'OK. See you later.'

Ella retreated to her desk, smiling and nodding at other staff who were just arriving. She was always one of the earliest. She popped her head into Admin as she always did, said hello to the secretaries, exchanged some comments about last night's television.

In her office at the end of the building, she glared at her full in-tray. She slumped back in her chair for a second or two, thought about making a cup of coffee, glanced at her watch, decided it wasn't long enough since the last one.

She slid her desk diary out. Meeting with Sir Nigel at 2 p.m. Security review panel at 4 p.m. That would drag on, so she could count on getting out at six at the earliest. Tom would collect Izzy from school at about five – thank God for supervised prep, she thought, reminding herself for the hundredth time that Millmount Hall was worth every penny – and with any luck he'd shovel something nutritious down her before braving the traffic again for Brownies.

Bookmarking the desk diary was one of those forbidden objects. A family photograph.

She frowned for a moment, wondering how it had got there; the picture had to be about five years old. The happy, reddened, sand-dusted faces of Ella and Isobel. She smiled at her own wind-blown hair, at how much blacker it was, how much more voluminous; and at Izzy's chubby, innocent face with its unruly tangle of brown curls. They were both holding spades up at the camera, crossing them playfully like swords.

She shoved the picture back in her diary, slammed it away in the drawer. She fielded five telephone calls, sent six emails, then deleted three emails offering her free XXX lesbian porn, cheaper car insurance and something in Japanese. She then made a brief call to Timothy, the senior IT technician, and asked if he could take another look at their anti-spam software.

Ella drummed her fingers on the desk. '*Parkfield*,' she said grimly, out loud.

She glanced at her watch. The tour would be under way by now. Something inside her was dying to see those kids, to see how they reacted to this place.

Everyone knew Parkfield – the name sent a shudder up every middle-class parent's spine. The place had been all over the national news last year when its new geography block was torched in the first week of term. The sort of place, she was told, where the teachers didn't take their cars unless they wanted them to end up as scrap.

Ella knew places like that. She knew them better than most of her friends.

She took a decision. She clipped her radio to her belt, grabbed her keys and left her desk.

On her way out, she briefly touched her forehead, then her stomach, before tutting at herself and stopping before she could complete the action. Force of habit, she thought irritably. What was it the boys at church used to say? *Spectacles, testicles, wallet and watch.*

'Just doing a walk-round in the Keep,' she announced, putting her head round the door of the admin office. 'Buzz the com if you need me.'

CHAPTER THREE

Skin Deep

He had tried three times, and he had failed three times. Locking his car outside Appletree's premises that morning, Tom was deep in self-examination.

He and Ella hardly ever entertained at home now. This was mainly because, at some point in the evening, he would watch Ella getting volubly stressed in the kitchen, having refused any offers of help with a vulpine snarl, and he would casually stroll over to lend a hand and murmur something like, 'Getting your whisks in a twist, love?' and Ella would tell him cheerfully to fuck off, and he would tell her, equally cheerfully, to fuck off herself. They would spend the evening pointing out each other's shortcomings across the room, loudly and amusingly and with brandished wineglasses.

When everybody had gone, though, he would slap her bottom or she would pretend to knee him in the balls, and they'd somehow turn it into a drunken embrace and fight their way upstairs, ripping each other's clothes off. Giggling and whispering their way past Ben's room and Isobel's room, they would collapse on the bed and have vigorous, filthy, gorgeous, uninhibited sex. The kind of sex he thought married people just weren't allowed to have any more. The kind they never had when they were sober.

The previous night, when Jeff came round to see if he wanted to pop to the Rowan, Ella had been snoozing contentedly in front of some old Audrey Hepburn film on cable. She didn't even notice him go.

'The thing is,' Tom said, over their second pint, 'it's about guilt. I mean, you won't understand, not having kids, but – you can't win. If you work all the hours God sends to provide for them, you're feeling bad that you're not spending enough time with them. And if you work flexi to be with them, you should see the funny looks you get. Women actually stopped talking to *stare* at me when I wheeled little Izzy into toddler group. And all the time I was there it was like they were thinking, "Why isn't that bloke at work? What a waster. I'm glad he's not *my* husband." I mean, they were perfectly nice, smiling and everything, but I could feel it. Strained.'

'Didn't they appreciate that you were doing your bit?' Jeff asked.

'Not round here, mate. Men do cars, work and football. Ladies do baking, children and book groups. It's like 1973 sometimes. You see, what women want,' Tom put his pint down and tapped the table with both hands, 'is for us to have a great, well-paid job which gets us out of the house, but *not for too long*. And – what a fucking coincidence! – it's what we'd all like too. Problem is, there aren't any.' He drained his glass. 'I'll get them in,' he said, and headed unsteadily towards the bar.

Over their third pint, Jeff said, 'You know, it's great how we can share stuff. And it's not like we're a pair of poncey New Men or anything, like those tossers from that Men's Group you went to.'

Tom shuddered. 'Don't remind me.'

'It just shows we're proper mates, doesn't it? We can *tell* each other things. We don't *have* to talk about cars and sport all the time like...' Jeff nodded in the direction of some familiar faces at the bar. 'Well, like that lot over there.'

'Hmmm. Don't delude yourself, Jeff. I come out with you to make myself feel good. And especially, today, to tell you this great theory about marriage I've just worked out.'

Jeff grinned. 'That's the thanks I get for all the advice I give you.' He wagged a finger. 'The happily married are the *least* qualified people to give advice to the single.'

'Mmm, yes. Remind me again, why did you get divorced?'

'Unreasonable behaviour,' said Jeff.

'Yours, I take it?'

'No, hers.'

'What did she do that was so unreasonable?' Tom asked.

'She wouldn't let me shag other women.'

'You know, sometimes, Jeff, it worries me when I think you're being serious.'

Jeff sighed, placed his pint carefully on the table and folded his arms. 'You mentioned something about a great theory?' he prompted.

'About marriage,' said Tom. 'It's...well, it sort of encapsulates it for me. Tell me what you think.'

Jeff leant back, twirling his glasses with a mixture of indulgence and mockery. 'Go on, then.'

'Imagine that you're a big fan of pasta. Proper Italian pasta. You think it's God's gift to the gastronomes of the world.'

'Right,' said Jeff uncertainly.

'Well, being married is like having pasta every night.'

'It is?'

'Yeah. And, the thing is, it's bloody *great* pasta. Fresh, home-made, quality stuff, none of your dried gubbins out of a bag. You're in heaven, because you think pasta is the best thing ever. You can't get any better than pasta.'

'OK, go on.'

'One night, you have, say, fettucine with a crab and mushroom sauce, fennel and garlic, with a Caesar salad and a sun-dried tomato foccaccia bread.' Tom was warming to his theme. 'The next, you might have penne, with a spicy pepper and tomato sauce and garlic-and-marjoram croutons. And a nicely chilled bottle of Frascati with it. The next night—'

Jeff held a hand up. 'All right, Nigella. I get the point. Go on.'

'Until one day, you look down at your gorgeous vermicelli lightly tossed in Parmesan and unsalted butter. And you think – *bugger this, I could really murder a curry.*'

There was a pause. Jeff took a thoughtful sip of his beer. 'Is that it?' he asked.

'Yes.'

'This fucking culinary metaphor is your great pronouncement on the paradox of marriage?'

'Yes,' said Tom. 'It's good, isn't it?'

'Well,' said Jeff, and he took another sip of beer. 'Um,' he added. 'Maybe you should send it in to a women's magazine. They'll print anything.'

'They wouldn't want it. Too close to the truth.'

'Have you *seen* the stuff they publish? On page 25, "Be Curvy And Happy! say our full-figured readers". Followed by twenty pages of size 8 clothes, modelled by spiky flat-chested bints with a bucket just out of shot. So come on, then, how long did it take you to think up your great analogy?'

'Er, well, I thought of it lying in bed the other night.'

'Hmmm. OK, so here's the thing. Here's a question for you, John Thomas, you and your big pasta-versus-curry theory.'

'Mmm?'

'Do you go out for your chicken jalfrezi,' Jeff asked, 'or do you get a takeaway in?'

A good question, Tom thought now in the echoing brick-walled office, leafing through the messages marked 'For Urgent Attention'. Good, but academic – because Karen Millen Girl had told him to fuck off, Geri the council woman preferred her own kind, while curvy Alice from the conference had followed her *morals*, for Christ's sake.

He flicked through the messages in a desultory fashion. Routine stuff. Steering committee, wanting a copy of some minutes or other. Social workers, needing to set up some client visits. And a bloke called Phill Janowitz from Centrespace, the visual arts project, wanting to talk to him about Appletree's Art group doing some murals. How little, Tom thought bitterly, do I care about bloody murals right now?

He threw them all aside, leant back in his chair and sighed.

'Thomas,' he said out loud, thumping the arms of his chair, 'it's getting embarrassing. You have to do better than this.'

There were so many beautiful young women in the streets

and shops. He passed them every day. Some of them were so smooth, so glossy, so *casually* gorgeous; he could hardly believe how effortless they made it look. Ella seemed to be continually plucking, tweaking, scrubbing, toning, cleansing or moisturising. She was always either smearing on an unidentifiable substance from Body Shop or sluicing it off, pencilling an eyebrow or buffing a nail.

His wife was beautiful, of course, but in the way that a restored Victorian house was beautiful: the brass was polished to its former finery, the period floor tiles were lovingly cleaned until their old colours came through, and there had been a bit of underpinning work on the subsidence. The doors squeaked and it was draughty in winter, but that was part of the charm. The nubile girls who haunted his vision, meanwhile, were more like minimalist, soulless show homes: everything gleamed in chrome and pine, gas hobs sprang into life at a fingerclick, taps gushed at the touch of a button.

He still found it so hard to believe. A not-bad-looking, intelligent and reasonably witty guy like him couldn't even have a bloody affair – and in twenty-first-century Britain. A place where, if you believed the colour supplements, sex-starved vixens were on the rampage for married men, lecherous succubi ready to ravish men senseless and drain them of every last drop of semen, the air crackling with raw oestrogen as they sniffed out their helpless prey.

It wasn't even as if he was being fussy.

'What are your criteria?' Jeff had asked him. 'Able to steam up a mirror?'

'Oh, very funny. Under forty. No dykes and no mingers.'

'What about Christians?' Jeff pointed out with a flick of

ash. 'You've got to discount Christians. More trouble than they're worth.'

'Well, they sort of exclude themselves, don't they?... Actually, I'm prepared to be flexible on the under forty thing.' He paused, reflected. 'Well, and the dyke thing, actually,' he added. 'If she's, you know, partial to a new experience.'

'Yeah, dream on, John Thomas, dream on.'

If something didn't come up soon, he thought moodily, prodding at his keyboard, he was going to have to start advertising on the Internet.

'Walk, don't run!'

A man's voice, young but commanding.

Ella frowned, tilted her head. She was at the foot of the Great Staircase, listening to the babble on the upper corridor. She knew they would be nearing the end of the tour. She folded her arms, set her feet apart, stood and waited.

Inhaling the old, clothy, woody smell of the place, her breath loud in her ears, she stood as still as the suits of armour. Guardian of the Castle Keep, she thought.

Here they came, streaming down the stairs.

'I said *walk*!' That voice again.

She narrowed her eyes. First impression – a lively, chattering bunch of teenagers. They didn't look like vicious thugs. They had hideous blue sweatshirts, some of them tied like belts or neck-scarves. The boys seemed to be competing to see who had the shortest hair and the girls to see who had the shortest skirt, neither of which surprised her. She was astonished, though, at the number of earrings, eyebrow-studs and lip-rings on display – it was as if she'd wandered into some sort of piercing convention. They were all carrying Cherford Castle workbooks, and some of them were actually writing in them.

'Quietly down the stairs! Get yourselves assembled there at the bottom, please.'

Ella was still looking for the source of the male voice. It had to be a teacher, but she couldn't see him yet.

About thirty kids, she estimated. At least half of them were chewing. The smell of sweat and hormones, not quite masked with deodorant, was in the air.

The stares she got ranged through interest, suspicion and outright hostility. Ella almost cracked a smile, but she remained impassive just in time. She knew those looks. Knew them well.

'Hey, I said *quietly*, guys! C'mon.'

Three teachers had come into view – first a middle-aged man and woman, then a man in his twenties, the one who had spoken. He seemed to be in charge, but was little more than a boy himself, Ella thought. He wore a scuffed denim jacket, white T-shirt, black jeans and cowboy boots. His hair was brownish, tousled into gelled spikes and streaked with highlights, like...the name of a young pop star drifted into her mind and out again. His lean, malleable face sported a hint of stubble, and something metallic in his left earlobe caught the light. He looked more like a Brit-Art star or a young TV producer than a teacher, she thought.

He nodded affably to Ella. She smiled back, folding her arms and leaning against the cool stone.

'OK, OK.' The teacher-boy, she noted with some respect, only had to hold his hands up for the babble to subside. 'Now, you've all had a chance to go round, and ask the guides questions, yeah? And to look at the exhibits? So, you should have filled in most of the questions in your workbooks?'

Oh, no, she thought, closing her eyes as he continued to speak. He does *that* thing. Upspeak. Raising your voice at the end of the, like, sentence? Like it's, y'know, a question? Ben had started doing it – she had threatened to cut his allowance unless he stopped. It was either symptomatic of the fundamental uncertainty surrounding every statement – the tone of a generation too terrified to commit to any cause – or it was the result of watching too much *Neighbours*. Ella rather suspected the latter.

'Napping on the job?'

Her eyes snapped open. He was leaning beside her, a mocking smile on his stubbly face.

'Certainly not,' she said. 'I was deep in thought.'

'Glad to hear it. Wish some of this lot would do a bit more of that.' He nodded towards the horde, who were being marshalled out by the other two teachers. He held out a hand. 'Matt Ryder. I'm head of history at Parkfield?'

'You are? Well, hello.' Ella straightened up, suddenly remembering to be professional. 'Ella Barclay. Senior Visitor Manager. I hope you've had a pleasant morning.' How old was he, she wondered – twenty-four, twenty-five? His handshake was firm and warm and, involuntarily, she inhaled his scents. Something pepperminty, a male muskiness, smoke. Hand-rolled, she thought? Yes, there was a tobacco pouch peeping out of his pocket. She had a brief twinge of longing for her smoking days.

'Yeah, it was cool,' he assured her with a boyish grin. 'I think they, ah, learnt a lot?'

'Oh, good. Year Ten, are they?'

'That's right.'

'If you don't mind my saying,' Ella ventured, 'you're awfully young to be a head of anything.' She blushed, realising how stupid and patronising that sounded. 'Sorry. Oh, God. What I mean is, I suppose you must be terribly good.'

'Not really,' Matt Ryder said with a self-deprecating smile. 'I think it's, like, one of those jobs nobody else wanted?'

'Oh. Surely not. It must be very fulfilling?' (Oh, fuck, she thought, he's got me doing it now. It's bloody catching.)

'People don't exactly clamour to work at our school. It's got, like, a bit of a reputation in the city.'

'Yes, I...heard about your geography block.'

'That wasn't our kids.' Matt's eyes were bright, angry, and he had moved a couple of centimetres closer to her. 'The people who did that came from outside the area, yeah? Only they never caught them, so they, y'know, can't prove it.'

'Ah. How unfortunate.' They exchanged a rueful smile. 'You're not like the teachers I remember,' she added, wondering where the hell this bold, unprofessional conversation was coming from.

'Oh, sure, I know. You're gonna tell me they were all crusty old sods in tweed jackets with elbow-patches, who gave kids the slipper if they stepped out of line, yeah? Well, things have changed.'

She felt an odd sensation – a mixture of outrage and amusement. 'Actually,' she said, folding her arms as she did when she was arguing with the children, 'I wasn't talking about my schooldays. I meant, when I was one of *you*. I used to be a teacher, before I got into Heritage.'

'Oh, right.' Matt Ryder raised his eyebrows at her for a second. The signal was both impudent and endearing. 'Where did you, like, teach? Roedean or somewhere?'

She looked him up and down. Not an attempt to wrong-foot her, just a genuine assumption. I must sound posh these days, she thought.

'No,' she said, 'actually, it was the Isis Girls' School. In Oxford. I taught English and History... Years ago, though.' She paused. 'When I was about your age.'

Below the belt, she thought.

'Aaaah...' Matt Ryder smiled smugly. 'So I was sort of right, then.'

'Sort of right? What do you mean?'

'Nice, posh fee-paying school for young ladies. Hey, that's...kind of young to be at such a top school. Oh, no, wait...' Matt held up his index finger. 'What I mean is, you must have been terribly good at it. Right?'

'Right,' she said. Their smiles synchronised for the second time.

'Better get back to the gang,' he said. 'Hey, nice meeting you?'

'Likewise. Hope the kids enjoyed it.'

'Yeah, great. They loved the interactive room.'

'Oh, good.'

Well, everyone liked that, Ella thought. Hands-on, simulation stuff with scale models of the Castle, recreations of the battles with computer graphics, touch-screens showing the Castle's gory history.

'Any...other highlights?' Ella called out.

Matt Ryder paused at the door. 'I'll let you know,' he said, and winked.

She stood at the door and watched the school party heading off down the drive towards the Gate-Tower and the coach park beyond. She was aware of Janet breezing past, looking amused.

'What?' Ella said.

'Nice young chap, that teacher. Very dishy.'

Ella laughed out loud, almost relieved to hear such an old-fashioned word. 'Yes, and young enough to be my son.' Well, he would be, she added in her head, if I'd been a very stupid little teenage slapper indeed.

She headed up the Great Staircase, taking one last look over her shoulder, and began her familiar stroll through the designated route, along the balcony, into the Armouries, heading for the spiral staircase. She was still grinning broadly when she came back down ten minutes later, and heard Janet's radio crackling urgently.

Ella stopped, steadied herself on the banister, and turned as she listened, with mounting incredulity, to the actual words which the guide in the Banqueting Hall was saying on the radio to Janet.

'You're sure?' Janet was saying, her mouth pressed close to the radio. 'Listen, Ella Barclay is here with me now, I'll—'

She nodded, waved a hand. 'I've got it.'

And a second later, Ella had turned to face the door again, and this time she was running.

Outside, she broke the rules, hopped over the chain and took the short-cut across the smooth lawn. Sod the heel-marks, the groundsmen could shout at her later.

She flicked her radio on. 'CC-3 to CC-10. Urgent response, please. Over.'

There was a flurry of static, then the reassuring voice of Mike, the head of security. 'CC-10 responding. What's the flap, Mrs B? Over.'

She was breathless as she ran. 'Mike, I'm heading...from the main keep entrance...down towards the Gate-Tower. Tell me...if that coach from Parkfield School...is still within the perimeter...over?'

More crackling, more impatience. She scurried under the shadow of the Gate-Tower, dodging the pushchairs and the blue rinses, narrowing her eyes against the bright June sun as she emerged on to the drawbridge.

She was still trying to take in what she had heard on the radio. *The Cadmus Bronzes.* The thieving little shits. Right under her very nose, as well.

'Mrs B? They're driving up to the barrier now, over.'

'Lock it down. Don't let them leave. Don't let them *move* till I get there, over.'

'Yes, Mrs B. Over.'

'Thank you, Mike...CC-3 out.'

Tom's finger hovered over Delete. He was wondering if he needed the email from Phill Janowitz at Centrespace, who was still very keen to meet up and talk about the Appletree artists' group doing an exhibition for them.

'The guy would have a double-L, wouldn't he?' Tom muttered. 'Very arty-farty. Probably gay.' He jotted the name on his Post-it pad.

He had to make notes of everything, these days.

'Don't forget you're taking Isobel to Brownies, love,' had been Ella's parting shot to him as she swept imperiously out, and while he was again rummaging in the bureau for some more months-old paperwork.

Things always needed doing. Certainly it was a big and beautiful house, shining with the lustre of modernity and money – polished beechwood floors, terracotta-painted walls, glazed blue vases, books neatly ordered on pine shelves. They had a girl called Beth in to clean twice a week, but Ella always pre-empted her. Tom would have quite happily let Beth attack every encrusted coffee cup, wodge of fluff and muddy footprint, but Ella, who had never really done the Domestic Goddess thing, would go mad if she was expecting visitors. She'd crank herself up into a frenzy of dusting, tidying, surface-swabbing, tutting and muttering.

He knew why. Her mother.

Maggie, who disapproved of women doing anything other than staying at home with children, saw a grimy household as the mark of an inferior woman and the hiring of a cleaner as an admission of defeat. She usually tended to prod behind the television or peer at the mantelpiece, saying something like, 'There's an awful lot of *dust* behind here, Ella. I'll just give it a going over,' and would then march off to the kitchen, returning with Pledge and yellow dusters. Ella's mum, Tom knew, could also be relied upon to rearrange their dried herbs into alphabetical order, or to grab a wet cloth and start wiping out cupboards. 'You shouldn't let standards slip, Ella,' Tom heard her say once. 'Just because you're a Working Mother. I worked, you know. And I kept a tidy house without all these machines to help, too.' And Ella shook her head in despair.

'Mother, you did *two mornings* a week helping out at Mr Beech's shop. And you only had me. It's hardly the same.'

And when Ella found little surprises waiting for her – teabags allocated a new home, plates stacked by size in the cupboard – she would snarl 'My *mother*,' in the tone most people reserved for phrases like 'tax return' or 'politicians'.

And the house was never quite perfect – there was always a dripping tap, a loose fuse, a dud bulb. Tom sorted those out, and phoned local firms for anything involving the deeper workings of gas, electricity or water. He didn't trust himself with those.

He also got help in for anything he found too menial or boring. He'd once taken a day off work just to paint the bathroom, but hired a decorator instead. Ella, quietly fuming, asked what it had cost, and Tom told her a price which was about three-quarters of the real one. He had been sure to pay the man in cash, in case Ella checked the bank statement.

In the office now, he reached for the Delete key, then withdrew his finger.

'What the hell,' Tom said. 'Might be worth a laugh.'

He spared the message from Phill Janowitz, and made a note in his diary to visit Centrespace.

Matt Ryder knew one thing. It was something to do with that woman, Ella. She was there again, just the other side of the barrier – immaculate in her dark suit, talking to two big guys in green shirts with the Castle logo on.

Matt asked the driver to let him off the coach. Ignoring the catcalls, whistles and thumps on the windows, he jumped down and strode across to the bleached gravel beyond the barrier. Behind him, Cherford Castle rose above the trees, sturdy and honey-gold against a cobalt sky.

He saw her turn towards him. She was definitely a good-looking woman, he thought. Smart, tailored suit, and were those designer boots? Probably. Very sexy. Gorgeous hair, sleek and black. The odd strand of grey, but that was fine. Snub nose. Big, authoritative eyes with cute little crinkles at their edges. Proper laughter-lines. A face that knew what it was doing and where it had been. She wasn't smiling now, though.

He folded his arms, grinned. 'Hi there! We meet again so soon.' He tried to sound jaunty. 'What have we, um, got, then? Bomb scare?' He checked her name-badge again. Ella Barclay, that was it. Like the bank. How could he forget?

'Mr Ryder,' she murmured. 'I think it might be a little more serious than that.' He saw her exchange a look with the two muscular guys, and noticed that they took a respectful step backwards without her needing to say a word to them.

'Really?'

'Mr Ryder. Let me explain, and perhaps we can sort this out.'

'OK,' he said.

He liked her voice, he decided. Soft, but cool and authoritative. And what was her accent? Posh, but with the odd northern vowel in there. Something flashed into Matt's mind, and he realised he was thinking of a line from his favourite novel, *The Great Gatsby*, about the voice of Gatsby's love-icon, Daisy. There was that telling, haunting phrase Fitzgerald used, about Daisy's voice.

Yeah, of course. Ella Barclay's voice was *full of money*.

'About twenty minutes ago,' she said, 'Janet Bridge, our senior guide, received a message from the duty guide in the Banqueting Hall. The message informed us that two matching statuettes, pieces of great value to the Castle's collection, are missing from the table where they usually stand.'

Matt frowned. He could feel his forehead beginning to prickle with righteous anger. 'Oh, yeah?'

'Yes. They're known as the Cadmus Bronzes. They're exquisite pieces of metalwork, depicting a key scene from Greek legend; the transformation of Cadmus, founder of the city of Thebes, and his wife Harmonia into serpents, after he—'

'Yeah, yeah. Spare me the *Antiques Roadshow* bit, right, and cut to the chase? You're saying, like, one of my kids has nicked them?' Ella didn't answer. 'Well? Aren't you?'

Ella closed her eyes, held up a forefinger. 'It's rude to interrupt, Mr Ryder. If you will allow me.'

Patronising cow, he thought.

'Together,' she went on, 'the Cadmus Bronzes are worth several thousand pounds. They were left to the Castle as part of a legacy by the last owner but one, Lady Galloway, and they've been in our collection for twenty-five years. If we report these items as stolen, it would be a PR nightmare. It wouldn't look good for us, or for whichever light-fingered so-and-so was eventually caught with the Bronzes shoved into a rucksack. So, let's get this sorted out privately – shall we?'

For a moment, he was too angry to speak. He could hear the blood rushing in his ears, feel the sun pounding down on his exposed head.

'I see,' he said. 'You, um, want me to go back in there,' he jerked a thumb towards the coach, 'and ask everybody to turn out their bags and pockets, right? Is that what you want?'

She smiled serenely. 'If that's what it takes.'

'You don't think it might have been somebody else?'

Her answer was crisp, sounded rehearsed. 'Your tour was given special dispensation to go round early, Mr Ryder. Visitors don't normally enter the Castle until 11 a.m., and we hadn't let any other parties into the Banqueting Hall at the time when the Bronzes were reported missing.'

'You're accusing one of my kids, basically.'

'Oh, Mr Ryder, let's not get this out of proportion, please. As you said, I could quite legitimately ask every pupil on that coach to disembark right now and, one by one, to open up their bags for inspection. I'm choosing not to use that authority.'

Her radio crackled with some impenetrable, static-crushed message.

'So what are you saying?' Matt asked.

'I'm asking you, because you know the members of your party, to sort this out with tact and discretion. I'd like the person responsible to *volunteer* to return the Bronzes anonymously in the next half-hour, and if they do so, no action will be taken. And then, perhaps, we can leave it with you as an internal disciplinary matter.' She tilted her head slightly, as if sizing him up. 'Does that sound fair?'

Before he could answer, Ella's radio crackled into life again. This time, a fragmented message was just about audible. 'CC-5 to CC-3, come in, please. Over.'

Matt nodded at the radio. 'Hadn't you better get that?'

She gave him a cold, hard stare for two seconds, then unclipped her radio and stepped a few metres away from him, in the shade of the oak trees, to take the call.

'You're sure about this?' Tom asked in horror, looking up from the letter. '*Absolutely* sure?'

Patrick Newlands – independent consultant, lifeline and saviour of the Appletree Project on more occasions than Tom cared to remember – nodded sadly. 'I'm afraid so,' he said. 'They can't go on funding you for ever, you know. It was always going to be a short-term thing.'

'Yes, but...we thought the renewal would be a shoo-in?' Tom sank back, as the full horror of the situation washed over him. 'The bloody council... I mean, we can get scraps from other places, but if they cut their funding now, Appletree is just dead.'

'I'm afraid so.' Newlands rubbed his moustache, looked uncomfortable.

'They seemed so positive! What went wrong?'

'I've no idea. Perhaps you said something to upset them?'

'That isn't funny, Patrick.'

He thought back to the girl Geri, with her departing, mocking wink, and decided that he detested her. Surely no one would be so shallow? Maybe they would. Politics – sexual included – drove everything, and politics basically came down to not upsetting people.

'You know your options,' Newlands said, unclipping his briefcase. 'The Board are going to put an emergency stratagem in place. I don't need to tell you, but...' He shrugged, handed Tom a slim, stapled document. 'I've put together some recommendations for cutbacks, to give the charity another year or so. It's all down in writing for you, so you get a chance to see it before they do.' Newlands waved a hand. 'A little irregular, but consider it a favour, old chap.'

Tom smiled warmly. 'I'm grateful. Thank you, Patrick.'

'Well, don't thank me. You know what I think. You should have got out last year when things were good.'

'This charity employs ten people, including me,' Tom said. 'Look at those guys out there.' He nodded at the glass partition. 'They never stop. They're all part-time, but they put the bloody hours in because they know it *can* make a difference.'

'I know. I'm sorry, Tom. We always knew this day was going to come, sooner or later.'

Tom was thinking aloud. 'You know Tash and Neil over there?' Patrick Newlands nodded. 'They stayed still seven o'clock the other night, just to get one of our guys his references done in time. We pay them peanuts, and yet they did it because they didn't want to let this client – this *person* – down.'

Patrick Newlands spread his hands. 'Nobody wants to let people down, Tom, old man. I'm on your side, you know I am.'

Tom nodded grimly. He didn't think it had quite hit him yet. 'OK, up front, Patrick. I thought we'd kept a grip on the money?... So go on, tell me. Just how big is the cliff we're about to drop off?'

And when the answer came, Tom sank back into his chair, feeling a numbness gripping him, and knew that he had to be going very, very pale.

* * *

'Shit!' Ella snarled, kicking off her shoes. 'Don't ask me about the fucking awful day I've had. Just *don't ask*.'

She hurled her bag against the wall as Isobel came running up the hall for a hug. Ben, more coolly and warily, sauntered behind, taking a reluctant peck on the cheek from his mother and then hiding behind his fringe.

'Mummy, Mummy, can I go and see It-Girl at the Arena?' Isobel asked breathlessly. 'Chloe and Sara and everyone are going.'

'We'll see. Who's everyone?'

'*Ev*-eryone, Mummy!'

Ella was too tired to think. She smiled wearily, ruffled Isobel's hair and kissed her again, then slumped at the kitchen table.

'They grow up too fast,' said Tom, leaning against the kitchen door with a glass of white wine in his hand. He looked, Ella thought, as if it wasn't his first of the evening. 'My dad thought thirteen was too young for me to see Echo and the Bunnymen.'

'You went anyway,' said Ben, from somewhere deep in the fridge.

'Course I did, mate,' Tom admitted with a wry grin.

Ben slammed the fridge door shut, emerging with a Bounty bar. 'Hey, seventy pence, Mum.' He rattled the battered blue collection box which sat permanently on the table.

Ella's head was pounding. 'What?' she snapped. She was aching to tell Tom about her personal disaster, her total embarrassment. She wanted their son to disappear, to go and play a stupid computer game or something.

'One S-word, that's twenty, and an effing, that's fifty,' said

Ben smugly. 'You said yourself, we all have to do it the same. Didn't you?'

Ella sighed. 'We ought to introduce mitigating circumstances,' she muttered, pulling the change from her purse and shoving it in the charity box with bad grace. 'There you are. Every little helps, I'm sure,' she added. She immediately felt guilty for her sarcastic tone, especially as Tom scowled at the comment.

Upstairs, she ripped off her crackling, tight clothes, splashed some water on her tired eyes. She tugged a comb through her hair, pulled on a stretchy red top saying 'Star' (which she worried was a bit too young for her these days) and her comfy jeans. Better. More human now.

Downstairs, Ben had disappeared, taking a football magazine through into the lounge. Isobel was in there too, playing her It-Girl CD and ignoring her brother's sardonic comments.

'Well?' Tom said, offering the wine bottle.

She smiled, sat opposite him at the kitchen table. 'What a day. Jesus. And I'm invoking his name in proper lapsed-Catholic style, so don't go charging me for blasphemy.'

Izzy was singing along to It-Girl's last Number One. '*And bo–oy, boy, you wind me uuuuup / And boy, I'm neee-ver drinking / Outta your lovin' cup…*'

It-Girl, Ella remembered, were teenagers. They were intelligent, well-spoken young women, the only serious rivals for Zillah Zim when it came to getting primary-school girls to part with their pocket money. They were harmless, and yet they disturbed her. Here they were, brash and bright, in the living room with her seven-year-old, encouraging her to want crop-tops and navel-rings (no bloody *way*) and getting her to sing about boys, lovin', gettin' it, doin' it right and whatever else was in the trite lyrics of the bloody song. God, Ella thought, I feel *old*.

Tom, she noticed, was not quite looking her in the eye as he poured her a full glass of the Soave. 'I've watered the plants,' he said. 'They were looking a bit needy, in this heat.'

'Oh, shit. We've been neglecting the garden. What about...?'

'The plum tree?' He smiled, and their eyes briefly met in complicity. 'Relax. It's fine... Ella, I need to tell you something.'

'I know, you've bought the kids some presents.' She had seen them upstairs: a pink piggy bank for Isobel and a football tankard for Ben. 'They're nice, Tom. From that pottery place on Broad Acres, aren't they?'

'Yeah. That wasn't it, though.'

'Ohhhh.' She pulled her fingers down her face, stretching her eyelids, and let her hands fall on the table like wilting petals. 'Well, let me go first. Please? This woman who's just started working as a guide, right, she calls Janet on the com this morning and says that she can't see the Cadmus Bronzes anywhere. These two little figurines, really valuable. Old heirlooms from Lady G, remember?'

'You gimme that shout, say work it out, / But I knowwaddit's all a – bout...'

'So I see this party of reprobates from Parkfield Comp has just barged through, and I think, aha! Time to nip something in the bud and get a bit of kudos for acting detective.' Ella winced, shook her head. 'Bad move,' she said. 'Very bad move.'

She could hardly bear to think about it now, and it almost gave her a physical ache in her stomach to recount the story to her husband for the first time.

'So what happened?' Tom asked.

She told him how she had stopped the coach before it left the perimeter; about the confrontation with Matt Ryder; about how reasonable she was, how firm but fair. How she had felt totally on top of the situation.

'And then,' she said, pausing for a gulp of wine, 'and then, I get a call on the com, saying, guess what? The fucking Cadmus Bronzes – *don't even think about it* – haven't been nicked at all. They're away being cleaned. Apparently there was a memo. Which I never got, thanks to our crappy email system which needs a total fucking overhaul. Of course, nobody would expect the new guide to know. All she knew is that the Bronzes were there last night and then, after those kids went through, they were gone!' She sank back in her chair. 'Mother of God,' she said, relishing the expression more than any of her other profanities. 'I feel like such an idiot, Tom... Sir Nige was *not* happy. I managed to sweet-talk him eventually, but nobody will be surprised if the school puts in a formal complaint.'

'I shouldn't worry. It sounds as if you handled it diplomatically.'

'That's not how young Matt what's-his-face saw it. The teacher.'

Matt Ryder.

Ella remembered his name perfectly, but wasn't sure why she affected not to.

'Well, as I say, I wouldn't worry.'

Tom sounded dismissive, she thought angrily. No, of course he wasn't. He was trying to be kind, trying to help by playing it down. She felt she ought to tell him what she had been building up to.

'Tom,' she said, 'listen to me. We were talking about my stepping the hours down, yeah? Spending more time with the kids. I hate the fact that I can never meet them from school. I don't feel like a mum, I feel like a bloody...video. Or a hologram.'

'You could never be a hologram,' he said. 'Not with magnificent tits like those.' And he let his fingertips brush her right nipple.

'Stop it, you randy sod.' She slapped his hand, tried not to laugh. 'I want to have a serious conversation.'

'Sorry.'

'Er, hello? My face is up here.'

'What?'

'Tom, I'm well aware that I'm not exactly flat-chested. It's probably why you married me, darling. But would you like to talk to me tonight, and not just to my breasts?'

'Dunno. I'll have to ask your breasts how they feel about that.'

It was their usual repartee, but she wondered, briefly, if Tom was delivering it a little distractedly today, as if he didn't really care. She shrugged it off.

'I just think,' she went on, 'you know, after days like this, I find myself asking why the hell I bother with the place any more. The staff are ungrateful. I hate the bloody visitors. Yes, Sir Nigel thinks I'm wonderful, but he totally takes me for granted. And it's obvious the stress is just freaking me out.'

'Don't be silly, Ell.' He gave her a reassuring smile.

They were talking softly in the dimly lit kitchen, sharing a bottle of wine like in the old days, their heads down and close and their fringes almost touching.

'No, really. I'm not being silly. Six months ago I wouldn't have gone off the deep end like that. Putting two and two together and making... Jesus, not even five. Making *ten*. I felt so stupid. If I can have a bit of distance from the whole thing, then maybe it'll do me good.' She felt fired up, reckless with the wine in her veins. 'Hell, maybe it would be good to cut free altogether for a while. Perhaps I should just resign.'

'You don't want to do that,' Tom said quickly, glancing up at her and then down again at the tabletop.

'Yeah, yeah. I know, love. You're going to tell me how great I am at my job. You always do when I have a crap time.' She allowed herself a deep, shuddering sigh and drained her wineglass. 'OK, your turn.'

'What?'

'Well, I've wittered on enough,' she said. 'Tell me the thing you wanted to tell me.'

'Oh,' he said. 'Oh, it...doesn't really matter.'

He looked distracted, she thought. Poor darling. I bet Izzy's been nagging him about that Zillah doo-dah thing again.

'Base four,' said Ben, suddenly re-emerging into the kitchen. Tom and Ella sprang apart, like illicit lovers surprised by a mutual acquaintance.

'Benedict, we were having a private conversation!' Ella snapped.

She knew he hated having his full name used, but

sometimes she just felt like reminding him of it. She had power over him then.

'Don't mind me,' said Ben moodily, heading out towards the hallway.

'What do you mean, base four?' Tom called after him.

'Two and two,' said Ben's voice distantly as he headed upstairs. 'It does make ten, if you're working in base four.'

'Boy's got a point,' said Tom admiringly, leaning back. 'There's your solution. You're right and everyone else is wrong. Cheers,' he added, and poured them each another glassful.

'Cheers,' said Ella wearily.

She didn't feel much like this one, or the next one, or the one after that. But, after Izzy and the exuberant It-Girl had both been put to bed, she lost count and stopped caring.

And later, she leant on the bedroom door and watched Tom snoring for once. She knew the stupor wouldn't last; he'd be up for the loo in an hour and then would be pacing restlessly. But for now, three people's breath sang softly in the walls of the house and only Ella, moodily gulping the dregs of the wine, was awake.

She looked fondly at the picture on their dressing table. Both children in their Millmount Hall uniforms, Ben's dark fringe ordered for once and the Bizzy's wild curls almost tamed under her hat. Ella smiled sadly. Her boss, Sir Nigel, proudly displayed pictures of his sons and grandchildren in silver frames on his desk. He could do that. Showed he was a caring family man as well as the boss of one of England's biggest tourist attractions. Ella didn't have that luxury. With the family on show, she was a Mumsy.

She shuddered as she remembered that awful time, only a couple of months back. She had left Tom gently holding the shoulders of a sweating, shivering Ben as the boy vomited unendingly into the toilet; some awful stomach-bug or other. She'd gone away and left them to it, because she had the Policy Review meeting at nine and nobody else could chair it. And Tom had made two calls – one cancelling his appointments, the other to ask Sara's dad to take Izzy to school – and he had stayed, had dealt with all the mopping and the flushing and the Pepto-Bismol. Of course, the next morning Ben had been bouncing around, bright-eyed, shovelling Weetabix into his mouth as usual. But it had been a day, a whole day, when her son needed her and she hadn't been there.

She could expect a few more of those, especially now she was paying for a fuck-up.

Of course, Sir Nigel pretended it wasn't a fuck-up. He'd been reasonable, just asked her to follow up with the school and make sure things were smoothed over, maybe offer them a freebie or two. (Or had that been her idea?) But they would be watching her hawkishly now, and those who didn't like her – and there were a few – would be loving it.

The telephone rang.

She checked the clock. Ten-thirty. Oh, yes, the news would just have finished, so she knew who it would be.

'Hi, Mum.'

'Hello, love. Isn't it terrible?'

'Yes, Mum, it's awful.'

She didn't know what was, but it would be some murder or conflict which had just been given prominence on the TV news, and which would have led her mother to wonder if she was going to be garrotted in her bed that night.

'So how are you?' Ella asked.

'Well, I thought I'd give you a call, you know. It's been a while. I thought maybe you'd gone away and not told me.'

'I know. Sorry. We've been busy.'

'Mrs Wells down the road, her family pop up every day. Until I told her, she didn't even know I had any grandchildren.'

'Well, it must have been a nice surprise for her,' said Ella, slumping back into her chair.

Dropping constant hints about how little she saw her daughter had to be her mother's most irritating habit, Ella reflected. Well, that and the way she always addressed birthday cards to 'Mrs T Barclay'. Maybe that was how you used to do things, but no way was she a mere ancillary to Tom as Maggie had been to her husband. Ella would make pithy comments about her name not being Theresa or Tina, but they were always deflected.

'I worry about you and Tom, you know. Stuck in Cherford, miles away from everyone. There's some lovely houses being built here, down Waterside Avenue. Four bedrooms, big garages. They'd be just right for you and the family. I've got some brochure thing-gies to show you next time I pop up.'

It was hardly a 'pop', but her mother was notorious for making the trip without phoning first. On one occasion, Maggie's visit put paid to a pre-planned afternoon of sex – Ella and Tom had delivered the children to friends' houses and had just made it to the bedroom, charged with hormones and giggling like teenagers, when the doorbell rang.

'Mum, we are not *stuck* here. We live in Cherford because we like it.'

'Well, I don't know why. Just think, if you lived here you'd have a ready-made babysitter, and you and Tom could go to the pictures whenever you liked. And I could pop round and take you shopping in town. We'd be just like a proper family.'

'And we'd both have a three-hour round trip to work, and so would the children to school, we'd never see our friends and we wouldn't know anybody.'

'Well, that's rubbish. You could get jobs here. There's always something going at the Tourist Board, and Tom could do…his thing, I'm sure. We've got lots of homeless here. What *is* his job title, love? You did tell me, but I'm not quite sure I understood it. Is he something to do with that *Big Paper* thing-gy they sell on the streets? I'm not quite sure how I feel about that. They do *accost* you when you've got your shopping and a bus to catch.'

'Mum—'

'I mean, you hear of some of them who've got expensive flats and cars all paid for and just do it for money to get drugs. And, well, I'm not racist, but a lot of them seem to be these immigrants or asylum seekers or whatever we're told to call them these days. Anyway, don't be silly, you'd know lots of people here. Only the other day, Samantha Bickerdyke's mum was asking after you in the Co-op. Samantha's had another boy, Kieran. Her fourth, isn't it? Jackie's so proud, you should have seen her.'

As was often the case when talking to her mother, Ella felt she had wandered into the middle of a Women's Institute meeting where nobody had introduced her. 'Mother, I don't know who the hell Samantha... Bickerstaff is.'

'Bicker*dyke*, love. Samantha Wallis as was. She married Johnny Bickerdyke from Bob Mason's garage. You surely remember Bob and Betty *Mason*. Her with the operation. She had to go into hospital for an anagram.'

Ella had a bizarre mental picture of Betty Mason, whoever the hell she was, watching *Countdown* while wired up to the machinery.

Her mother's malapropisms could be amusing if Ella was in the mood. Maggie's last trip on a motorway had involved her being 'stuck behind a big arctic lorry'. She also still told people that her late husband's last days in hospital had involved him wearing 'that cafetiere device'.

Ella sighed. 'I still don't have a bloody clue who she is, Mum.'

'Don't be coarse, Ella. You *do* remember her. She lived down Hadwell Close and you went to school together. Her mum was deaf as a dodo. She came round our house that day your dad was mending the hall bulb and he fell off the ladder and twisted his ankle. We had ravioli with slices of cucumber, then Instant Whip. I had to take it up to him in bed, on a Silver Jubilee tray.'

Ella processed this deluge of information. 'Mother,' she said, 'that was in 1978.'

'Well, there you are, you go back a long way. And you know Kerry Morton still lives down our road. She was your best friend for a while. I've always been upset you let Kerry drop.'

The vaguest memory of a Kerry Morton stirred in her mind. Hadn't they been to see the Human League together? Or was it Culture Club? Anyway, if it was the girl she was thinking of, she'd gone to work in Tesco, saying she hated being stuck in fuckin' school 'cos it was a fuckin' prison, and had celebrated her new-found liberty by getting pregnant five times over by three different men. The idea that she had 'let Kerry drop' almost made Ella want to laugh out loud. Friends didn't always want to be bloody well Reunited.

'Anyway,' her mother went on, 'I don't want to monotonise your time. But I'll just say I've made Isobel a nice cardie for school. It'll get chilly in the autumn.'

She had to thank her, of course, even though the Millmount uniform had never included cardigans. And then she had to talk about a dozen other things, and listen to the litany of strangers from her home town and their ailments, family feuds and disputes with neighbours.

'You *know* who Beryl Shankland is, love. Don't be silly. She lived in the Porters' house down Westway Green – well, before it was the Porters', of course, when Alfred was still at the Post Office. You used to go round on Thursday after Brownies and she'd give you toffees for having clean hands. Don't tell me you've forgotten *her*? She's always asking how you are, stuck there miles away.'

It was chilling. Her mother would, in many ways, have preferred it if Ella had never gone to university – if she had become a Samantha or a Kerry, sagging and contented, surrounded by slack-jawed children. She wanted her married to a local boy, living just round the corner in a pebble-dashed townhouse. Trundling a double buggy between Boots, Woolies and 3C ('Charlie's Cut-Price Clothes, great for all the family') with Maggie in tow to point out the bargains.

Trapped in the same miserable, gum-encrusted High Street she'd longed to escape from all those years.

But she *had* escaped, she reassured herself as her mother prattled on. And she'd done what she needed to do, created her perfect life.

She just wished, sometimes, that she could be sure it was so perfect after all.

Tom half heard Ella talking to her mother and noted, as he always did, the way her accent slipped from its moorings. Not just her accent but the way she *spoke*, the way she used her mouth. She didn't open it properly, as if she were trying to pout and grit her teeth at the same time. Her vowels normally had a fruity fullness and her consonants clicked like soldiers standing to attention, but with her mother, Ella lapsed back into the way Tom imagined she had spoken when living 'at home', as Maggie called it: sullen, casual, hardly moving her lips. Her greeting, rather than her usual breezy 'Hello-ooo!', was a grudging 'Hey up' (which Tom loathed; it sounded so *northern*). 'It isn't' and 'I haven't' became 'tint' and 'ant'. And then there were the odd, clunky words she used, even with him. Those strange verbs and nouns reeking of soot and cabbage. They crackled in her sentences, slipping through like interference on the TV.

He can see her at the worktop in their first kitchen, framed by late Eighties painted-wood cupboards and a hideous floral border. They have been living together for just a few weeks.

She's saying, 'Shall I mash?'

Tom, looking up irritably from his newspaper, pictures his wife with a saucepan of potatoes and a fork, and sees her instead with the teapot. 'Mash?' he repeats incredulously. 'Mash? You don't *mash* tea. You'd end up with a frightful mess.'

Ella sighs, folds her arms and rolls her eyes. 'Oh, right. Don't tell me. That's something else people supposedly don't say?... What's your word for it, then?'

Tom gazes into the distance, thinks for a minute. 'Well, there isn't one. You just say "make a cup of tea". That's all.'

Although born less than two hundred miles apart, they are often divided by a common language. This happens every so often; Ella will try to convince him that a roll is actually a 'breadcake', that a kerb is a 'coursey-edge'. Then there are the convoluted arguments concerning what constitutes a 'tea', when you have your 'dinner' (as opposed to your lunch) and where, if at all, you would fit in 'supper'. Tom's trump card here is that, if a man asks a woman for a date, he'd look a bit silly asking her out to *tea*.

'I don't know. I feel sorry for you.' Ella shakes her head and fills up the kettle. 'The poverty of your language.'

Tom rustles the paper and hides behind it. 'It's like calling a spade a... I don't know, a *diggitybob*, or something, and then asking me what my word for spade is, when it's *spade*. I'm convinced you make half these things up,' he adds. 'Just to annoy me.'

In the depths of the night, she heard him being restless.

'Are you awake, Tom?'

Silence.

'Tom, will you wake up if I ask you for sex?'

'I'm a bit too tired.'

She giggled, nuzzled closer to him and reached across his thighs. She was pleased, and not surprised, to find an unyielding hardness.

'Bloody hell. Someone's not tired. What have *you* been thinking about?'

'Wouldn't you like to know?'

'Probably lesbians, I expect. It's usually lesbians, isn't it?... Still, waste not, want not.'

And Ella flipped herself over, rolling her thighs on to her husband's face, her mouth descending to meet his taut, eager erection.

CHAPTER FOUR

Artistic Licence

Tom couldn't miss the Centrespace Gallery. Its ugliness made it beautiful.

Towering above the quayside in the Cultural Quarter, it was a cathedral of art, like a cooling tower of blue glass packed into six jostling parabolas of white concrete. It reminded Tom of that mountain from *Close Encounters*, mixed in with some crazy Oscar Niemeyer tribute thing going on.

He was cautious on the translucent steps, and when he stepped through into a blood-red lobby, his heart sank.

'Hi, can I help you?' The voice belonged to a chubby young man in blue glasses. His hair was bleached fridge-white and his multi-pierced earlobes jangled like keys.

'Um, yeah, hi. Tom Barclay from Appletree? Phill Janowitz said I could drop in. It's about the homeless people's arts project.'

'Oh, yeah. Come on through, Tom, I'll get you a drink. Cuppatea?'

'That'd be great. Milk, no sugar. Thanks.'

'Have a walk round the exhibition area if you like.'

Beyond the lobby was a hall filled with giant canvases covered with swirls of bright paint. Cheerful men on stepladders were fixing them to the walls; the air was filled with the whine of electric drills and the pungency of newness. Tom looked down at the floor, which shone with seamless royal blue paint like the sort used for the decks of yachts. He let his eye travel the full length of the gallery, right to the round window at the end which looked out over quayside cafés and restaurants.

You could sleep fifty people in here, he was thinking. He tutted, told himself not to be a philistine. After all, it had pictures in, of a sort. He had dreaded finding the usual suspects: the eviscerated shark, or some bloke flicking a light switch on and off. In comparison, this stuff was positively traditional.

'Like it?' said a voice behind him.

He turned round. A curvaceous, red-haired woman in her thirties was giving him a big smile, offering a hand.

He shook her hand, smiling back. He gave the woman the brief once-over. Good teeth, nice tits, sultry green eyes. 'Yeah, I'm...just waiting for Phill,' he said.

'Well, looks like you've found me,' she said.

'I'm sorry?'

'Phillippa Janowitz. Phill with a double-L, for short. I'm the External Projects Curator.' She said '*pro*-jects', with a long 'o'.

'Oh, I...' He laughed. 'I see. Phillippa.' They shook hands. Her accent was odd, Tom thought; like American but with an odd twirl to it, almost south-west English.

Her skin glowed and her jade eyes had a feline slant to them. Her layered bob of hair shone like copper, except for two curves of ash-blonde which parenthesised her face. Hoops of gold hung from her ears, a silver ankh dangled between her splendid breasts and she sported olive nail varnish. Chunky bangles chimed on her arms, while a cheeky dolphin-tattoo peeked out from under the low neck of her top.

'It's Tom, right?... So, you're the guy who gets people off the streets?' she asked. The bleached man brought them each a mug of tea, and they sat down on orange bucket-chairs by the wall.

Tom nodded his thanks. 'Er, well, Appletree is part of the process. We work with other charities and Social Services to deliver an education-based programme of re-integration for young homeless people... God, I sound like our corporate report. Sorry, I usually speak in something closer to English.'

Phill Janowitz laughed, pushing back her hair with a clank of bracelets. The deep richness of her laugh made him tingle.

'Well, that sounded pretty good,' she said. 'Yeah, I looked you up on the Internet.' (She pronounced it 'Innerned', he noted.) 'Shazia Bell at one of the hostels recommended you to us. You know Shazia?'

Tom nodded. 'We've worked together.'

He'd placed the accent, now – Canadian, of course.

'We're looking for something really striking,' Phill went on, 'really different, for one of the upstairs galleries. Something with a bit of an angle, a conscience. So, I'm looking around and I hear from Shazia that your A-level group have done some fantastic work.'

'Yes, they had an exhibition at the Civic Hall last term. It went down well.'

Phill smiled, nodded. 'So I heard.' She raised her eyebrows

at him. 'We thought they could do a group mural, depicting some aspects of their lives. You know, kinda bring it home to people.'

'Sounds great,' Tom said, nodding enthusiastically. 'Of course, if you want a really crazily contemporary installation that everyone's going to talk about for years to come, you could open the gallery up as a dormitory and let two dozen of our clients sleep there. Might win a prize.'

Phill's eyes gleamed, and her mouth fell slightly open. 'Mmmm,' she said, and Tom watched her tongue moisten her glossy lips. 'Wow, that is...*edge*. That is so totally outside the box. Contemporary and contentious. It's brilliant.'

Their gaze held for a couple of seconds. Phill's face cracked into a smile, then so did Tom's.

'I'm serious!' said Tom, opening his eyes wide at her.

'You are *so* not serious.' Phill gave a rippling giggle, and then her cheeks flushed and that laughter was flowing again.

'No, you're right. I'm not. But it's what some people might think of doing.'

'I can see I'm gonna have to watch you,' said Phill Janowitz, and crossed her legs neatly as she took a sip of her tea. Over the top of the steaming mug, her eyes were full of wickedness.

'I think,' Tom said, 'that a mural would be a great idea. Let's talk about it. I'll get Roger and Serena, the tutors, to come down and have a chat with you...'

They talked more, sorted out some details and some practicalities, discussed potential dates and flipped through diaries. Tom liked this: the briskness of business, the feeling of doing something positive without having to be sitting in an office doing it. And a touch of flirtation as the icing on the cake.

He'd never have got this, he reminded himself, in the dull recruitment firm where he'd first found himself after graduating. The voluntary sector had its compensations – not least the fact that it was full of women.

'Thank you,' he said. 'I think that'll be really good. A bit of a boost, given our financial disasters right now.'

He had subconsciously shifted into 'trying to impress' mode. He was worrying unduly about his tired eyes and the grey in his fringe. For the first time since he was ten, he wanted to wear a badge with his age on.

Phill smiled in sympathy. 'Hey, these things go in cycles. I mean, we were trying hard to keep afloat for a while, before this new money from Europe and the Arts Council came along.' She held a finger up. 'I know what I meant to say... I'd like you to come along to this, if you can.' She pulled a bright orange flyer off a nearby table and gave it to him.

Tom looked at the flyer. It was blank, except for a black circle in the middle, about the size of a digestive biscuit, inside which small orange letters announced:

zeroes heroes
art to challenge the *mind* & lift the *spirit*
sequenced chain of installations @ centrespace surround gallery
www.centrespace-arts.org.uk

On the back, it gave a date and a time for the private opening.

Tom nodded, folded the flyer thoughtfully in two. It sounded dreadful, he thought. Bunch of wankers who couldn't paint properly, showing off. Normally, given the chance to attend a modern art exhibition, he would rather stay in drinking cocoa and watching a late-night football match between, say, Ghana and Burkina Faso.

'Thanks,' Tom said. 'I'd love to come.'

And he smiled, looking deeply into the green eyes of Phill Janowitz.

'Yes?' said the steely voice from the speaker-grille.

Ella swallowed hard. 'Hello,' she said. 'I'd like to see Mr Ryder, if I may.'

She really wasn't sure about this. Standing here, shivering, looking so out of place and clutching a brown-paper package to her thumping chest.

She looked around the empty, grey playground, then up at the electronically secured door in front of her. The blue paint on it was seared and bubbled. Rubbish was piled up beside it as if nobody could really be bothered to put it in a bin. Beyond the playground wall was a main road. Beyond that, houses, houses, houses as far as the eye could see, stretching down the hill in front of her, across to the left and to the right. She'd watched them from the bus, scrolling past her like a film. They huddled together as if for warmth. Grey and beige as if all colour had been drained from them by the air of Parkfield Estate, they bristled with antennae and satellite dishes. Some of them, she could see, had dead eyes, wooden blankness where windows should be. The air smelt of decay and tar.

The door buzzed. Ella pushed, and it gave. Odours of smoke, damp and sweat hit her as she stepped into semi-darkness.

No going back now, she said, and hugged her little package close to her body.

'Mr Ryder's teaching,' said the secretary, who appeared to be behind bullet-proof glass. 'Would you like to wait?' She gestured to a small area populated with a handful of rickety, foam-filled chairs, and handed Ella a clip-on badge saying 'Visitor'.

Ella waited, becoming increasingly nervous and unsettled. She glanced at her watch every couple of minutes.

When the bell shattered the silence, she felt it in her teeth and sinuses, and almost leapt from her seat.

Those *noises*. She had forgotten. The crashing, the booming of feet descending distant stairs, the whoop and cackle of liberation, the casual profanities spat high above the babble. And the smells: cabbage, festering trainers, paint.

She felt in need of protection. She pictured the suits of armour in the Castle, and thought: my armour is of the twenty-first century variety. Claudia Sträter silk jacket and skirt, Kyrie Eleison suede boots. I should perhaps have gone for something more low-key.

'Hello there,' said a familiar voice, and she jumped. Matt Ryder had appeared beside her, seemingly without making a sound.

'Hello again,' she said, a little flustered, and stood up, smoothing down her skirt. She saw that he looked. Briefly. 'I...hope you don't mind my dropping in,' she said.

'Not at all. But, um, follow me, I need to, like, get to my class?'

He led her up a broad, clattery flight of stairs, passing groups of chattering kids who stared at her or laughed behind their hands or pointed.

'What brings you round here?' Matt asked. 'Slumming it?

Ah, I know.' He lifted a finger and tapped his nose. 'I get it, you're on a mission for *Crimewatch*, yeah? Well, I'm sorry, we don't have any, like, stolen paintings hidden in the bike sheds? Maybe you'd like to rummage through my form's lockers in case they've, y'know, got the odd antique vase stashed away?'

'OK, OK... I deserve all that, and more. I've come to say sorry. Honestly.' She held out the brown paper parcel to him. 'Peace offering,' she said, as they reached the top of the stairs.

He took it. 'Hmmm, reassuringly weighty. What is it?'

'Guidebooks, a History of Cherford Castle DVD and a few interactive CD-ROMs. I...thought your kids might find them useful. For their projects.'

'That's very kind. Let me, um, pay you?'

'Don't be silly. It's a present, like I said. I want to give you something to apologise for getting the wrong end of the stick. It was...completely my fault. I don't want you to think badly of the Trust.'

Matt smiled wryly. 'OK. Your apology and your free resources are, um, accepted?'

She smiled. Relief swamped her.

'But I think,' said Matt, taking her arm gently and steering her towards the double doors, 'that you should come and say hello to the kids while you're here.'

She broke away, held her hands up, feeling panic rising. 'Oh, God. I mean, look, I've got to get back.'

'Really?' Matt grinned, folded his arms. 'Come on, you've got children.' He raised his eyebrows, showing her that it was a guess. 'Haven't you?'

'Yes, a boy and a girl.'

'So, you know what schoolkids are like. They don't bite, yeah?'

'Well.' Every nerve in her body was screaming to get away from here. 'Um...'

'Oh...' Matt grinned. 'Don't tell me, let me guess. You and hubby send yours to a *good* school, I bet. Private, maybe? You wouldn't be seen dead somewhere like this normally? Let me guess... Brookwell?... No, probably somewhere progressive, because you think you're right-on... Millmount. Yeah, Millmount.'

Ella scratched her ear and looked away. 'I *really* should be going. The office—'

'I'm right, aren't I? Our lot are playing yours in the city inter-schools footie.'

'Yes. My son's on the under-14s team.'

'Yeah, ours are, like, looking forward to the chance to hospitalise a few posh kids.' Ella looked up in alarm, and Matt held his hands up. 'Joke?' he offered.

'Not a very good one. Ben had to miss half his games through injury last year.'

'I'm sorry. They're not that bad, really. Are you sure you won't come and say hi?' He gestured towards the classroom door.

'I'm sure. Look, Matt, some other time, OK?'

'I'll phone you, then,' he said, smiling.

'Possibly,' she answered, backing down the corridor now. 'Right now, you can just show me the way out.'

'If you insist.' He pointed. 'Straight back the way you came, Ella.' He paused, amused. 'If that's what you want?'

She smiled, hoisted her handbag on to her shoulder and

straightened her shoulders. Be in control, she told herself. You
are choosing to walk away here.

'Thank you.' She nodded. 'Goodbye.'

She turned on her heel and strode off with a click-click
down the almost-empty corridor towards the stairs, not
looking back.

'Ella.'

She didn't stop, at first, at the sound of his voice. She
slowed, set her jaw, kept walking.

'Hey, Ella!'

She closed her eyes, sighed from between her clenched teeth
and spun round, facing him down fifty feet of grim, mud-
stained, badly lit corridor. '*What?*'

He grinned, folded his arms and leant against the wall. 'I
think you're, um, lots of things. But I don't think you're, like,
a coward?' He winked at her again, just like that time in the
Castle Keep. 'I'll see you back here soon.' And he was gone.

Muttering, she hurried down the stairs, keeping her eyes
straight ahead. Get out, she thought, get out out *out* of here.

The noises had almost settled down, now, all the kids safely
contained in their little boxes for another forty minutes or so.
Her footsteps echoed up the stairwell.

Outside, Ella took a grateful gulp of the city air and headed
off across the car park towards her bus stop. At the school
gate, she turned, looked back once at the shabby glass-and-
concrete building. She let her eyes linger over it, heard her
heartbeat quickening with...fear. It had to be fear.

Out of the corner of her eye, now, she saw the yellow bus
climbing the hill, and, shaking her head, she hurried towards
the stop with her arm outstretched.

CHAPTER FIVE

It's Not The Answer

The eyes of Phill Janowitz haunted his thoughts.

Impishly promising him – what? Something better than what he already had? Or just something a bit different?

So he'd said he would *love* to go to an exhibition of contemporary art. Not like – *love*. He couldn't quite believe that. There had to be a good reason. Normally, he would sit at home and scoff at these idiots with their cardboard-and-string sculptures, their patchwork tents and their eviscerated sharks. So it couldn't be the exciting opportunity to go along and get a sneak preview of the next Brit-Art wunderkind that was making his heart beat faster. It had to be Phill. Which was interesting, because she wasn't the kind of woman he would usually fancy.

But then there were those eyes. Cat's eyes. Behind them lay a life totally unlike his own – a bohemian, restless, reckless existence.

And that voice of hers, too – so damn seductive. It was a teasing, late-night, Irish-coffee, reclining-on-a-leather-couch voice.

It all made him stop and think, and wonder if it was time for an adventure.

'I just can't stop playing with mine,' Tom confessed in the pub. 'Even after all this time. I find myself sitting there in meetings, twirling it.'

'You must get used to it after a while,' Jeff argued. 'I mean, some blokes can just ignore theirs. Just think of it as part of them and leave it alone.'

'I know, I know...but I'm always really conscious of mine. It's all sort of...tight and hard. Mind you, I'm sure it's got bigger these past few years. Much easier to move up and down.'

'You could try just leaving it alone.'

'Yes, but – look how easily it comes off.' Tom held his wedding ring up between thumb and forefinger and looked through it at Jeff.

'Yeah. I see what you mean.'

'I'm a compulsive twiddler,' he said, and spun the ring on the pub table like a coin, stopping it with his fingertip. 'My brother, Andy – he got married in France, you remember? They got a local goldsmith to make them these exclusive rings. He's never taken his off in eight years, as far as I know.'

'Horses for courses, mate. Some people don't even wear them.' Jeff grinned. 'And some of us don't ever want the whole bloody marriage thing ever again.'

'Yes, how's Inez, by the way?'

'Oh, you know. So-so,' said Jeff with a shrug, and he hid behind a gulp from his pint.

'You treat that girl badly, Jeff,' said Tom, frowning. 'And she's so devoted to you, as well.'

'Oh, right, and who are you? Mr Relate, all of a sudden? Look, I'll do a deal – you can start giving me advice when I start moaning to *you*.'

'Just don't have children with her if you're not serious about her, that's all.'

'Christ, no danger there. Inez can't bear children.'

'Oh.' Tom put down his pint, suddenly chastened. 'Jesus. I'm sorry, Jeff, mate. That was really insensitive of me.'

'Was it?'

'Well, yes, when…well…you know. Is it something to do with her tubes?'

'Her *tubes*?' Jeff said, looking perplexed.

'Well, her, um…biology. Whatever you call it.'

Jeff shook his head. 'Thomas, mate – what the *fuck* are you going on about?'

'Sorry.' Tom could feel his face roaring red. 'Digging myself deeper. Just…you know… I thought you might want to talk about it. About Inez being infertile.'

'Infertile?… She's not bloody infertile, you twat!'

'But you…you said she can't have children!'

'I said she can't *bear* children. As in, can't stand the little sods. She only has to be within a hundred yards of one and she starts having palpitations about them being sick on her Gucci trousers.'

'Oh. Right.' Tom laughed. 'I feel a bit silly.'

'Nothing new… So, you fancy this Phill bird, then?' Jeff asked.

'Oh, God, I don't know,' he lied.

'What d'you mean, you don't know? Are you some kind of poof? You always know whether you fancy someone. It's not rocket science, Thomas. OK. Would you shag, given half the chance and all other stuff being equal, et cetera, et cetera...hmm, let's see... Angelina Jolie?'

'Yes, of course. Not half.'

'Right, how about... Roseanne Barr?'

'God, no.'

'There, you see? That isn't hard, is it?' Jeff grinned. 'Multiple choice with only two answers, and only one that can ever be right.'

'Yes, but don't you get an option for Don't Know? Can't you circle a question mark? There must be some women you're not sure about. When they look good in some lights and a bit rough in others.'

'Like who?'

'Well, how about Carol Vorderman?' said Tom, who had already given this matter some thought. 'Seriously. She's, what, seven or eight years older than us? Now, I never showed any sign of fancying her at school – did you, mate? No rushing home suspiciously early to put *Countdown* on, no fevered muttering about having two from the top and one from the bottom. And fair enough, really, because back then, well, she looked like your mum.'

'Bouffant hair,' said Jeff, nodding and wincing. 'Big frilly blouses. Not good.'

'Right. But now – having kids seems to have made her a fox. She's the world's hottest mother. Tight tops, a fit arse and fuck-me leather trousers...worth putting the telly on for at teatime. Or videoing. Only on a good day, though.'

'You know,' Jeff said, 'the saddest thing about this conversation is that I'm friends with someone who admits to videoing *Countdown*.'

'You're right,' said Tom, fumbling for his wallet. 'There's no hope for me.'

He got two more pints and placed them neatly on the beermats, spilling a little of the froth from each as he did so.

'So, you going to shag this Merkin bird, then, or what?'

'Not American, Jeffrey. Canadian. She sounds like Gillian Anderson. Really sexy. Same hair colour too.'

'Oh, my God, she's *ginger*?'

'Auburn, if you please.'

'Natural? Carpets match the curtains?'

'Jeff, if you'd been listening, you'd know I haven't yet got close enough to find out, OK?'

'And are you going to?'

'Maybe,' said Tom, and took a deep, thoughtful drink of his pint. 'Whatever happens, I've got to get it out of my system, or I'll still be chasing skirt when I'm fifty. And that would be so sad.'

There were no rules, Tom reflected. That was the problem. If you wanted to mend a tap-washer or wire a plug and didn't have a clue about it, you could buy a book on the subject. But there was no *Bluffers' Guide To Adultery*.

'Listen,' he said to Jeff, 'I need to ask you something really important, mate. Think about it carefully, because the future of our friendship may depend on this.'

'Fire away.'

'For three points. Which Eighties record label takes its name from a Rolling Stones album?' And he sat back, looking smug.

Jeff frowned, drew a sharp breath, leant back. 'Hmmm, good one. Good one. Was there a Sticky Fingers label...? Possibly not. Black and Blue?'

Tom's mobile rang. 'Keep trying,' he said. 'Yeah, hello, Tom Barclay?'

'*Tom?*' said the voice of Patrick Newlands. *'Just come from the Board. We have some news for you. They've pulled something out of the hat, but it has...implications. It's not the solution I'd wanted, Tom. Not at all.'*

He wondered what on earth Newlands was going on about, and shot an apologetic look at Jeff.

'Look, I think you'd better get back over here, old man. I'll explain then.'

Tom sighed, switched the phone off. 'Sorry, mate, duty calls.'

'Hey, I understand. What have you got, sudden influx of asylum seekers pinching all your hostel places?'

Tom grinned weakly, tapped his nose. 'It's hush-hush,' he said. 'Oh, by the way – Beggar's Banquet?'

Jeff groaned and leant back, slapping his forehead. 'I'll get you back,' he said. 'Don't you worry.'

'Is that risk assessment typed up yet?'

Ella lobbed the question like a hand-grenade into the main admin office. It caused a scattering of secretaries, with the odd guilty glance and awkward shuffle of papers.

'It's coming,' said Tessa – or was it Trisha? Ella got them muddled up.

'It would be coming a lot quicker if people didn't stand around gossiping,' Ella snapped, and stalked back to her office.

She slumped into her desk, still tingling with a strange mixture of anger and elation.

She wondered, for a moment, what Matt Ryder was doing right now. What would constitute an everyday problem for him, and what would be a stressful day? She shivered as she thought of the alien landscape of the Parkfield estate. Shivered, and yet felt intrigued by it. *Why was that?*

Her intercom buzzed.

'Sir Nigel for you,' said Tessa or Trisha.

She sighed. 'Thank you.' She closed her eyes.

'Ella, dear,' said the languid voice of her boss. 'That conference on the fifteenth, I can't make it. Will you go instead?'

'The fifteenth,' she said, trying to locate her diary under the debris on her desk. 'Right.' Fifteenth of what, she thought desperately? Which month was it now? Which day?

'I'll need you to give feedback to the Board on the seventeenth. Obviously not much time to formulate a presentation, but I know I can rely on you... Now, then, the draft of the strategic plan needs a few nips and tucks. I've put it all in an email. Have a look at it, will you?'

'Yes. Yes, OK.'

There was a pause on the other end of the line, and she could imagine Sir Nigel's kindly, pink face wearing a small frown of concern.

'Everything all right, Ella?'

'Yes, fine, thank you, Sir Nigel. Everything's great.'

'Family all well?'

'Yes, they're well. Thank you.'

Family all well. This was what male executives, in their

well-meaning way, said to female employees. She wondered if Sir Nigel would say it to a man. Probably not.

'I keep meaning to say, you and Tom must come over for drinks one Sunday.'

'Yes. Thank you. That would be lovely.'

She closed her eyes, screwed her face up tightly in a silent wince and slumped back in her chair. No, that would be *awful*. All kinds of people sidling up to Tom and asking him what he was *in*, as if he had a job that one could be *in*, and then being all bluff and hearty and impressed when he told them, and secretly thinking 'Poor sod'. He would hate it.

'I'll leave that with you, then, Ella. Bye for now.'

'Yes, Sir Nigel. Thank you.'

She sank back into her chair, sighing deeply as she opened her desk diary.

Well, he didn't blame Newlands. Don't shoot the messenger, Tom thought ruefully. The poor guy had done his best.

'Look, if there's anything I can do...'

Patrick Newlands seemed edgy as he and Tom descended the stairs, heading for the car park. Once again, the lift in the building was out of order.

Tom nodded. 'Thanks,' he said.

In the car park, Patrick Newlands flipped a keyring towards a night-blue BMW, which chirped and flashed its lights three times at him. Tom realised that he was looking at Newlands' car properly for the first time. Sizing it up. Trying to work out how much it had cost, and how expensive it was to run and maintain. He had never done that before.

Tom had always thought of himself and Newlands as equals

– even though Newlands probably earned more, which Tom just put down to his being a few years older. Now, though, it was suddenly clear for the first time that they occupied different worlds.

'Look,' Patrick Newlands said, as he placed his briefcase on the passenger seat. 'You're a survivor, old chap. Don't let it frighten you. If Appletree goes under, well…it's always precarious in this sector, your staff know that. They're talented young people. They'll all go far.'

'Yeah, well. It's not my staff I'm worried about, really.'

He took the letter out of his pocket again, unfolded it and squinted at it in the sunlight. The key phrases were all there, but they didn't seem real. In some ways, he reflected, it was the news he had wanted. Appletree would not fold yet. It would go on. The money, by a very cunning means, had been found.

The letter in Tom's hand gave him official notification of the decision which the Board had, in his absence, reached last week. By unanimous vote, they had decided, as permitted in the charity's constitution (Clause 7, subsection d) to draw down emergency funds by terminating one of the salaried posts in the organisation. The Board's strong recommendation was that the deleted post – which would cease after the statutory one month's notice required, and no more – was to be that of Project Manager. The post currently held by Tom Barclay.

The Board had arrived at this conclusion following a report by the team of consultants who had carried out interviews with all the staff several months ago. The fees paid to the consultants for six days' work had been approximately twice Tom's monthly salary.

'So you might have to have a career swerve. Happens to the best of us, old boy.' Patrick Newlands leant on the car roof, sighed. 'Trust me, Barclay, it won't be the end of the world for you. Your lovely Ella's still raking it in at the old chateau, isn't she? Swallow your pride and let the little lady keep you for a while, till you get something new sorted out.'

'Easier said than done. We've got a bloody enormous mortgage, for one thing.'

Newlands whistled softly. 'Hmm, I can see your point. Upper Ashington, isn't it?… Daylight robbery there. Well, face it, Tom, you could always move somewhere cheaper.'

Sometimes, Tom thought, Patrick Newlands could just be *too* pragmatic. He knew he was just trying to be helpful in his bluff, cut-to-the-chase sort of way, and that was the problem. Tom didn't want clarity right now – he wanted obfuscation. Preferably alcohol-induced obfuscation, with Jeff.

'Move somewhere *cheaper*,' Tom repeated hollowly, as if it had been suggested that he should move to the moon.

An image flashed into his mind of the two-bedroom terrace which he and Ella had first rented together. Horrible brown wallpaper, noisy radiators and a resident mouse. They had thought it was amazing. Before they even put sheets on the wobbly bed, they had fallen on it and had eager, half-clothed sex, christening their new home, laughing and panting their way to joint orgasm. He tried to imagine that happening now. Ella would probably want to stop halfway through, saying, sorry, I've just *got* to dust that shelf. And what about a new bed? And shall we go to B&Q and get some fresh paint for this room?…

The house, though, was just the start of it.

Tom wiped the prickly sweat from his forehead. 'We've...got both our kids at Millmount Hall. It doesn't come cheap.'

Newlands shrugged. 'Well, that's not insurmountable. My daughters thrived at St Mary's, absolutely loved it.'

St Mary's was the outstanding state school in the region – it always got the best results, its partisans adored it and everybody else hated it for its success. The Manchester United of the school league tables. And if you hadn't lived in the cordon-tight catchment for two years, Tom reflected grimly, you might as well forget it.

'Yeah,' Tom said. 'I'll think about it.'

'That's the spirit, Barclay,' said Patrick Newlands with an affable nod. He slid into his car, revved up and was gone.

Tom was suddenly alone in the sun-blasted car park, raising a hand.

It was the first time ever, he realised, that he and Newlands had said goodbye without a firm, gentlemanly handshake.

He wondered if he was going to tell Ella now or put it off until it was absolutely inevitable. He slipped his hand into his jacket pocket. There was a cold, hard coin there. He flipped, smacked the coin down on his wrist, lifted his hand and looked.

He pulled a face.

At home, he gave the coin to Isobel and watched as, wide-eyed, she took it to her room and let it drop with a clink into her varnished pink piggy bank.

'Sounds like there's quite a few in there already,' Ella remarked as she passed the bedroom door, clipping on some earrings.

'She's a little saver,' Tom murmured, smiling fixedly.

He looked up at Ella, did a double-take. She was wearing a leather biker-jacket, with a polka-dot skirt and an armful of silver bangles. Her earrings were sky-blue plastic flowers, and there was something weird and sparkly about her eyes.

'Are you going *out*?' he asked accusingly.

She sighed, put her hands on her hips. 'No, Tom, I dress up like Molly Ringwald just to stay in and watch *Friends* with you. Of course I'm bloody going *out*.'

'Oh. I did wonder. What's with all the bling-bling?' He jabbed a finger at the earrings.

'Get off. It's kitsch chic, of course.'

'Kitsch chic…hmm. *Where* are you going?'

'Tom, I only told you two days ago. It's Eighties Night at the Basement. I'm going with Bex. And some others are coming later – not people you know.'

'Well, don't drink too much,' he said.

'Christ. You sound like my dad. I haven't had my unit allowance yet this week, you know.'

'Your what?'

'My unit allowance. You know, fourteen units of alcohol, as recommended for the healthy woman. I'm about ten in credit, at last count.'

'Um, yes – Ella, I think that's supposed to be a *maximum*, not a requirement. And don't let that Bex get you into trouble.'

'I shall give her your sweet regards,' she murmured, and kissed him on the cheek as her taxi beeped its horn downstairs.

Tom tapped the piggy bank and ruffled Izzy's hair. 'Hold on

to it, Izzy,' he said. 'I'm not sure how many more I'll have for you.'

And later, as he ran a bath for Isobel, he noticed in the mirror that Ella's bright lipstick had left a perfect, pouting imprint on his cheek.

He touched the mark tenderly for a few seconds. Then he sluiced his hand under the cold tap and, with one firm movement, wiped the kiss off.

CHAPTER SIX

Thirties Kicks

'Here, get them down you.'

Ella's best friend Rebecca Lydiard, known to all as Bex, shimmied over in her silver catsuit and slammed two vases of lager-and-lime on to their chrome table.

'Oh, God, do I have to? I thought we were drinking wine.'

The Basement, thumping to the sound of the Human League, was awash with green and purple lights. A motley assortment of thirtysomething Goths, New Romantics and punks jostled with a few ironic wearers of late Eighties pastels and big hats evoking the Stock, Aitken and Waterman era (at least, Ella hoped they were being ironic). All together in a big, sweaty underground melting pot, Ella thought, when they wouldn't have been seen dead with each other two decades ago – she found that funny.

'Darling, we are drinking, full stop. And then we're dancing.' Bex's high-cheekboned, glitter-washed face wore a mischievous grin.

'I'm not dancing in these,' Ella said, lifting a foot to show off a stiletto boot.

'You'll have to take them off, then. Cheers.'

The music was cranked up as 'Don't Leave Me This Way' by the Communards swept in, and the two women leant in slightly so they could hear one another.

'So, how's hubby?' Bex asked, waggling her spindly eyebrows.

Bex had ash-blonde hair, teased up into a tangle of spikes. Her lipstick was always cobalt-blue and she sported one violet crescent earring. As often as she could get away with it, Bex wore outfits that were tight, sluttish and utterly impractical. Ella often thought, admiringly, that she looked like a young Annie Lennox.

'Oh, much the same. Distracted, irritating, lovable.'

'You need a bloody good shag, girl. And I don't mean with *him*.'

Bex had been knocking back the Chardonnay with her TV dinner. So, this was a four-drink topic, Ella realised, the sort which normally didn't happen until the place was heaving and all barriers were gone. Usually, by this stage in their conversation, Bex was blitzed on vodka and Coke (and coke), hanging off Ella's neck and practically spitting in her ear when she laughed; by now, the crossover should be complete, punks doing the lambada and the New Romantics getting down to 'This Corrosion'. But it was only nine-fifteen, and everyone was still fairly restrained.

'Rebecca, love, we have talked about this before. I just don't do that.'

'I bet he has.'

'Oh, don't be fucking ridiculous.'

'Fucking ridiculous? I am *never* ridiculous about fucking.

It's a subject I am fucking serious about, is fucking.' Bex paused, wrinkled her nose. 'Too many fuckings. Sorry. I would try and find another expletive, but there aren't any as good.'

'There's sodding,' Ella offered.

'Yeah, but it sounds too much like laying turf. You can't put the proper feeling into a *sodding*. And don't try and change the subject. When they put "Into The Groove" on, let's go out there and flirt our arses off with every unsuitable bloke we can find.'

'We always do that,' Ella pointed out.

'Yeah, yeah, but this time I mean for *real*. Get a phone number. Or even have a little liaison tonight.'

'It's all right for you. My children are expecting me to come home.'

'Well, just blame me!' exclaimed Bex in frustration. 'For God's sake, you need to get some cock while it's still hot, Ella. You won't be young for ever.'

'Hmm, you should know.'

'You cow. I'm telling you, I'm staying thirty-nine, and if you send me a card with *Life begins* on it, I'll fucking disown you.' Bex sighed, slammed the table with both palms. 'There you go again, subject changed in your favour once more. God, I fall for it all the time. So easily distracted.' She held up a finger. 'Was this song '86 or '87?'

'Tom could tell you. He can tell you the chart position and year of practically any single from the last two decades.'

'God, that's so *sad*.'

'Tell me about it. His mate Jeff's just the same. You remember Jeff?'

'Ooh, I remember *Jeff*. He pinched my arse at your tenth

anniversary party. He's quite cute, actually.'

'They're an equally sad pair of buggers. Do you know they've been banned from doing the pop quiz in their local, because they were always winning?'

'And I bet,' said Bex, waggling a finger, 'he's kept those little tape compilations off the Top 40. All on a shelf somewhere in chronological order?'

'You know my husband pretty well, don't you?' asked Ella with a wry smile.

'Yeah, well.' Bex grinned. 'I'm having an affair with him.'

Ella scowled. 'Don't joke about stuff like that.'

'Who says I'm joking? This is my astral body sitting here in a sad lurex catsuit, distracting you, while the actual me is round at your place, shagging your husband senseless.'

'You're not his type, babe,' said Ella.

'He's said that, has he?'

'Yes, actually.'

Bex shrugged, grinned. 'Well, that means *somebody* is.'

'What?' Ella didn't get it.

'Somebody is, potentially, his type. Look, let me guess how the conversation went. After a couple of bottles of wine one night, snuggled on the sofa watching *Celebrity DIY Disasters*, you start asking him which of your friends he fancies. How about Bex? you say. God, no, he says, I can't stand the mouthy cow. Not my type at all. Am I close?... Yes?... So, if I'm not his type, that means *somebody is*.' Bex took a triumphant gulp of her lager. 'Trust me on this, darling.'

'Why do I always end up believing what you say about men? I mean, I'm married to one, so I should know better than you sometimes.'

Bex laughed, so hard that she almost shot her drink out of her nose. 'Yeah, yeah! Right!'

'Watch that septum.' Ella couldn't resist the little dig.

'I'm sorry, it's just the concept of marriage making you an expert. That's like saying that doing the same desk job for fifteen years makes you the ideal person to give careers advice. Trust me, Ella, I'm a serial slut, I know what I'm talking about. Write it in stone and put it above your bed – *men are all the same.*'

'That's unfair.'

'It's pure biology, my love. The Creator blessed them with a brain and a dick, but only enough blood to run one at a time.'

She should have expected no less than this level of cynicism from Bex, Ella told herself. This was a woman who quite openly said that she didn't believe in love, and that a vibrant sexual encounter every week or so was all she ever needed. Bex had once told Ella that if she had been walking through a forest and encountered a frog who said 'Kiss me and I'll turn into a handsome prince,' she'd have replied, 'Well, frankly, love, I'm more interested in the potential of a talking frog.'

Bex liked to advance the cynical view that most people, especially couples, were out for themselves in life, to get what they could from their time on the planet. Couples stuck together through inertia, or sheer laziness, Bex claimed. What about love? Ella had asked indignantly. Bex had made a dismissive noise. Just a biochemical reaction, babe, she said. Like cocaine. Like most things that make people behave stupidly.

Bex waved over Ella's head. 'There's Jen and Anni looking lost at the bar. I'll go and grab them while you mind the table. Same again?'

Ella tapped her two-thirds-full glass. 'Steady on.'

'Oh, you'll want one.'

Half an hour later, with Jen and Anni now matching Bex shriek for shriek, Ella found herself hauled on to the floor for 'S'Express'. It had never been one of her favourites. As the beats thundered through the floor, she could hear Tom's scathing voice whispering in her ear at an end-of-term bop: 'Bloody manufactured stuff. Music with machines. It'll be dead in two years.' Hmm, one of his less accurate predictions there, she thought.

Bex grabbed her shoulder, pressed hot lips against her ear and shouted, 'That guy *so* wants you, Ell.' She jerked her head towards the far side of the dance floor.

She gave a wan smile. Why should it irritate her, she thought, glancing over to the corner, if her friends wanted to act like teenagers? They couldn't get away with it for much longer, after all.

She was right, though. The man was eyeing her up. And he was gorgeous. In his early thirties, Mediterranean-looking, with close-cropped hair and a slim, muscular body under a tight white T-shirt and black jeans. He began to dance with a certain amount of style, directing his body movements towards her. Catching her eye.

She played along, letting the music throb through her, responding to it more.

His grin flashed ultra-white in the darkness, and he did a little spin on his heel so that he had moved into space, right beside her. She wiggled, tossed her hair. She glanced at him, and looked away at the key moment, closing heavy-lashed eyelids with insouciance. What was it you had to do, according to that book *Flirty & Dirty*? Lower your eyes, count to four, look back again.

She did it. He was still gazing at her.

What am I *doing*? she thought. She fought to the edge of the dance floor, pushed her way into the toilets and staggered to the basins, where she clutched the enamel firmly with both hands and stared at herself in the ultraviolet mist. Toilets everywhere were drenched in it now, she'd noticed, the bluish-purple haze which stopped the junkies finding a vein. Something else she could never have imagined when she was a teenager.

She pushed her fringe back angrily, hating her sweat-slicked face and her puffy eyes. Beside her, two girls were lapping from the taps.

'That's not drinking water,' Ella chided them. 'You'll give yourself stomach ache.'

One of the girls looked up, her white face drenched, her crimson bob plastered to her forehead. She grabbed Ella's arm and swung from it, laughing. She was about eighteen, Ella realised. 'God, do you think you're my mum?' the girl said. 'Chill, darling.' And she pawed Ella's jacket with unnecessary affection. 'Mmmm,' the girl said. 'That's lovely. I love the feel of this. Is that real leather? Oh, wow.'

'If you're doing E, you should get yourself plenty of proper water.' Ella couldn't stop herself saying it, but the girl just floated off, spinning her arms and smiling.

Bex was beside her, arms folded, glowering. 'Hey, you. Are you going to come out and have a good time, for fuck's sake, or are you staying in here to be a social worker?'

'Sorry. It's just that they're so *young*. I mean, you and I know what we're doing, but they could be our daughters.'

'Yeah, well, they're not. Come on, that bloke's looking for you.'

'Hell, I look awful.' She pulled down one reddened eyelid. 'This light doesn't help. God, I look saggy and mumsy. Pay me a compliment.'

'OK. Your eyesight's great.'

'Thanks so much, darling. I knew I could rely on you.'

'Oh, come on, it was a joke. You're fit, fuckable and not yet forty. Get out there and tease his cock off.'

Ella looked at herself in the mirror, tucked her hair behind her ears. Her face didn't look too bad now that she'd cooled off, and, if she was honest, her mouth was just aching to get impish and flirty again.

Well, bugger it, then, she thought as the blood rushed to her cheeks. Let's prove I'm not dead yet.

Bex led her by both hands on to the floor, then let her go, like someone getting a child to swim. Ella shrugged, shook her head, but she was already moving with the beat. The guy was still there, in the little space he'd created for himself. The distance between them narrowed to about six inches. The steaming dance-pit was filling with punters, the volume was rising to wall-shattering levels. Now 'Fade To Grey' came on. At the siren-like swoop of the synths, she pushed up the sleeves of her leather jacket, lifted her hands above her head and let the bangles cascade down her pale arms as he watched. She unleashed a full, dazzling smile in his direction.

OK, so she was doing it. Having a good time. Her sweat-soaked body throbbed and her fingertips tingled.

A few feet away from her, Bex had her back to a pillar, her

tongue down the throat of a man about fifteen years younger than her. His hands were giving her glossy catsuit a detailed exploration. Anni and Jen were skulking in the shadows with two dodgy-looking characters.

The thunderous, pile-driving intro of 'Blue Monday' shook the speakers. Normally, this would have galvanised Ella, had her dancing like a madwoman, imagining herself back at college again, sticky glass of cider in one hand, blagged cigarette in the other, her mind carefree. Now, though, she panicked at the man's proximity, shook her head.

Dry ice started to gush from hidden vents, causing squeals of delight across the club. It tickled Ella's nose as she scurried for the bar.

'Vodka and orange, please,' she said, shrugging off the biker-jacket and slinging it over one shoulder.

'Ice, miss?' asked the barman.

'Yes, not too much, though.'

She felt a hand on her backside. Her friend from the dance floor. 'Let me get this.'

Ella smiled uncertainly. 'It's OK,' she said, 'I've already got it.' She desperately tugged a fiver from her purse and threw it at the young barman.

The man sidled closer to her. 'You're a good dancer,' he said.

'When I want to be,' she said, trying not to make eye contact now.

'We should dance again.'

'I think I've had enough tonight. Would you take your hand off my arse, please?'

He held up both hands, defensively. 'Just being friendly.'

Her drink arrived and she gulped its icy kick. Her plan was to zip back round the dance floor and intercept Jen and Anni, but they had receded into the fog. Three giggling rock-chicks with bottles of Newcastle Brown were blocking her in, and beyond, wild crowds and dazzling green beams of light cut off her escape.

'I've not seen you here before,' he said, closing down the space between them.

Ella tried to back off, but found herself pressed against the bar. 'Yeah, well,' she said, and stared desperately through the pungent fog.

'I thought we might get to know each other,' he said. 'If we, you know, chatted for a while. Who's your favourite band?'

Ella did her best cold smile. 'I don't think so,' she said. She held up her ring finger. 'I'm sorry, but I'm boring and married.'

'I'm not prejudiced.'

'Yes, I'm afraid that isn't the point. I've just come here to have a good time with my friends.' She was forced to lean in to make herself heard, and found this doubly uncomfortable. She wanted to keep her distance, even though every hormone in her was screaming out to place her palm on his chest and take it from there.

He shrugged, smiled again. 'Hey. You don't need your friends to have a good time.'

'Um, well, I think I do.' A gap opened up in the crowd and Ella took her chance while she could. 'Please excuse me.'

'Oh, come on!' His voice pursued her. 'Why the hell were you dancing with me like that? What are you, some kind of fucking prick-tease?'

She stopped dead, clenched her teeth as the fury made her heart thump like 'Blue Monday', and she turned towards him, giving him her best glower.

She knew she wanted to head for the door, now. A booted kick swung it open, and she hurried up the sticky stairs, grateful for the rush of cold air.

He was pursuing her, berating her, so she gave a quick word to the bouncers. One of them instantly blocked the man's path with a firm hand, while the other hailed a taxi for her and ushered her into it with a soft, 'You take care now, love.'

The taxi hurtled through a strange, alien Cherford, past lights and sounds she no longer felt she knew properly. Carrying her home to her sleeping husband and children, as her tensed body finally succumbed, calves and shoulders releasing the lactic acid which would make her ache for hours.

She phoned Bex, who was giggling and incoherent, to apologise for not saying goodbye. Bex didn't seem to mind. She was having a good time. The line went dead halfway through.

Her burdened eyes stayed open, but only just, until she was conveyed to her front door. Inside, she remembered a pint of water before she went upstairs, and managed, shaking with tiredness, to sluice off her make-up and coat her face in moisturiser before ripping off her clothes and crashing into bed.

Tom, oblivious, snored beside her.

PART TWO

Home Front

'Society is one vast conspiracy for carving one into the kind of statue it likes, and then placing it in the most convenient niche it has.'

Randolph Bourne, *Youth and Life*

harrison, baines & black

Independent Strategy Consultants to the Voluntary Sector

Partners: J.V. Harrison, S.R. Baines, W. Black

26, Woodley Mews, Oxford OX2 4RZ

Tel: 01865 567567 Fax: 01865 567568

email: admin@harrisonbainesblack.com

Mr Patrick Newlands

Financial Adviser, The Appletree Project

Westwell Industrial Estate

Cherford

CR12 1FY

2nd July

Dear Mr Newlands

Following our telephone conversation, please find enclosed a full report on the recommendations regarding The Appletree Project. Also attached is a one-page executive summary.

These conclusions will not present the easiest options for your Trustees. However, we believe they are the most realistic.

I would like to take the opportunity to thank you and the staff of the Project for cooperating with **hbb**, and also to express our thanks for using our services. We wish you every success in the future.

Yours sincerely

E. Harrison

Eugene Harrison

Senior Consultant

From: Jeff Aspley <aspleyj@quantum.co.uk>
To: Tom Barclay <tom@appletree.uk.net>
Sent: July 04, 09:16 AM
Subject: pasta vs. curry

hiya tom-tom

further 2 chat about dipping in the cookie jar
- a reality-check.:-)

got your basic types of participant: married man
mm), single woman (sw), married woman (mw) &
single man (sm).

mw & mm: best possible deal all round - you've
got an equal amount to lose so nobody can
blackmail anyone - limited in where u can meet
tho - down 2 seedy hotels & stuff, or lots of
skulking.

mw & sm: fun for him - she's obviously getting
something out of it or she wouldn't be there,
right? - he'll feel a pang of guilt tho, unless
hubby is total arsehole. (why do yanks say
asshole? I mean, that's like a donkey's bum,
innit?)

sw & mm: most dangerous combination. she's
desperate, possibly fixated - not just talking
bunny-boilers: potential for emotional manip. is
huge - watch out.

just me 2p worth as usual
seeya mate
jeff

CHAPTER SEVEN

Interference

'Once upon a time, there was a princess who lived in a beautiful pink and gold castle with her mummy and daddy, the king and queen.

'Because she was a princess, she had everything she could ever want. If she wanted a new dress, she just had to go to the king and say, "Daddy, please may I have a new dress?" and the king would command the royal dressmaker to produce her a lovely new silk dress which sparkled in the sunlight.

'If she wanted a new doll, she just went to the queen and said, "Mummy, please may I have a lovely new doll?" and the queen would command the royal carpenter to make her a lovely, new wooden doll with a shiny face and blonde curls.

'But the problem with the princess was this – she was a very naughty girl.

'She didn't always ask for things in a nice way. Sometimes, she would say "I want a new horse to ride!" or, "Get me some beautiful shoes made of the finest leather!" And sometimes, she would bounce on her bed, so hard that she broke it in two.

And the king and queen would scold her angrily, but the princess just laughed and said, "You can buy me another one!" And sometimes, she would get her toys and throw them against the wall until they broke. And the king and queen would chide her most severely, but the princess just laughed and said, "You can get me all the toys I want!"

'One day, the king and queen decided they had had enough. "If you keep being naughty and breaking things," the king said sternly to his daughter, "you won't have anything new, ever again."

'And the princess just laughed, and said, "You're the ruler of the kingdom – you can get me whatever I want!"

'The king and queen were at the end of their tether, and didn't know what to do. Until one day, news came to the castle that an old, wise woman from the forest had arrived in the village. The king and queen immediately sent for the woman, and asked her counsel. They asked if there was anything they could do to make their daughter do as she was told and make them realise that they meant what they said.

'And the woman nodded, and her old blue eyes glinted, and she stroked her old white chin, and she wore a strange smile on her thin mouth. And she explained that yes, there was a spell she could perform, one which would teach the little princess once and for all. It would teach her that, if she didn't behave and do as she was told, she wouldn't have anything she wanted, ever again.

'The king and queen looked hopefully at one another, and nodded, and asked the wise woman to cast her spell...'

* * *

'But how does it end, Mummy?'

'I'll tell you tomorrow, darling.'

'That's no good. I want to know now.'

'It's called a cliffhanger, precious Bizzy. Oldest trick in the book when it comes to storytelling. If you're good and go to sleep, I'll give you the rest tomorrow.'

Two years ago.

Tom and Jeff are in town. They are on an escalator by the bus station, heading for the taxi rank, when Jeff asks him if he has ever played the Street Girl game.

'What's the Street Girl game?' asks Tom.

They've just been to see an above-average tribute band called Peroxide Blondie, whose singer is Julie from accounts where Jeff works. She is young enough, Tom realises, to have been in nappies when the real Debbie Harry was at the peak of her fame. Still, she ripped her dress during 'Union City Blue', so it was worth the three quid. He has had worse nights out.

'It's really easy,' Jeff explains, lighting a cigarette as they hit street level. 'You have to assume you're still single for this.'

'Still single. Right.' Tom cannot really remember being single.

'Now, before we get to the taxi, you have to point someone out to me – and imagine she's the woman you've chosen to spend the rest of your life with.'

'But what if I don't see anyone?'

'Ah, well, there's the rub, mate,' says Jeff with a grin. 'If you don't manage to pick one, you're destined to die alone and unloved.'

'And if I do pick one?' Tom asks frantically. They are walking up a small alleyway, now. Ahead, he knows it opens up into the soft lights and paved precincts of Canterfield Street.

'Well, once you choose, you can't change your mind. Even if you see one you prefer after that. The elements of skill and chance, you see. The ideal balance.'

Tom shakes his head, exhales. 'That's an awful idea,' he says. 'But fun. I'll give it a go.'

It's weird, watching the women coming towards him, like all life's opportunities in microcosm. Laughing, they clutch the arms of friends or boyfriends, stagger in high heels, swish past in clouds of cheap perfume. They scurry for buses and taxis with arms clasped across their breasts, they stuff their fat, painted faces with chips. Glossy hair ruffles in the wind, navel-rings glint in the sodium lights, silver heels click on pavements.

It is odd, he reflects, how often you think someone looks OK from a distance but you go rapidly off them as they come closer. He fixes on one girl – a supple-looking brunette with firm breasts and extensive legs – and is about to nominate her when he sees the Artex-thick foundation on her face and realises that she's a lot older. He bites his tongue just in time.

'Yes?' says Jeff.

'No,' Tom mutters.

'Should think not. Body off *Baywatch*, face off *Crimewatch*.'

Tom is casting his gaze about. He pivots as they home in on the glossy row of insectoid taxis.

Two young blonde women, arm-in-arm, both wearing

feather boas, stride past them, giggling, micro-skirted, obviously on their way to a club. Tom lifts one finger, shakes his head. 'No.'

'Good move,' Jeff says. 'They're what you call aeroplane blondes.'

'Eh?'

'Black box,' says Jeff.

By the time they get to the taxi rank, Tom still hasn't been able to make a selection. Jeff is tutting, shaking his head and laughing.

'All right, I'll have her after all. That brunette. She was only about forty. Probably got a bit of juice left in her if you squeeze her hard enough.'

'Sorry, mate, game over. Your juice-squeezing days are done. You've just condemned yourself to a lifetime of takeaways, masturbation and ironing your own shirts.'

'Bugger. I want to go again.'

'See how cruel it is?' says Jeff as he flags down a taxi. 'A wife is for life, not just for Christmas.'

'Well, it's difficult,' Tom protests. 'Especially when you only get one shot.'

Jeff claps him on the shoulder as he swings open the taxi door for his friend. 'Too bloody right,' he says. 'That's the *point*.'

The taxi bears them away through the night, and Tom watches blurred shapes of women he will never know passing like ghosts in the translucent neon. Swish. Swish. Swish. Like time peeling back, like day upon day of lost opportunities taunting him with glossy hair and glittering smiles.

* * *

'Haven't we got any *proper* coffee?' Tom asked, holding the red-topped jar gingerly as if it were someone's ashes. 'There's just this homosexual decaff stuff again.'

'If you want something else,' Ella called from the dining room, pulling her shoes on, 'you'll have to buy it.'

'Oh, great. I can't drink brown water. I need a stimulant.'

'Izzy, have you got your piano music packed?' Ella asked, fixing an earring in place as she breezed through the kitchen.

'Yes, Mum... Dad, what's ho-mo-sex-ual?'

Ben got there first. 'Queer and gay,' he said through a mouthful of toast. 'You know, boys who want to snog boys. Like Damian out of 3-Boyz-3,' he added, waving the cover of a magazine at her.

'*Uuuugh!*' Isobel put her hand over her mouth and giggled. 'That's horrible. But funny,' she added as an afterthought.

'Behold,' said Ella, spreading her hands wide in despair, 'we have raised the future readers of the *Daily Mail*. Gotta go.'

'Don't forget that thing tonight,' Tom said. 'The Zeroes Heroes.'

It was important to talk normally, he decided, as if there was nothing wrong. Having breakfast before going to work, as usual. Discussing the evening, as usual.

'Are you sure you want to go to that? Modern *art*! Didn't think it was your thing.'

'Yeah, well, I thought we might give it a whirl. No harm in trying new things, is there?' He wondered if his tone sounded too jaunty, too false.

'OK.' She gave Tom a peck on the cheek. 'Sorry about the decaff. Maybe you could add Pro-Plus to it or something? And soon,' she murmured, 'we must have The Talk with

Bizzy, OK?... Can you wash the pots before you go?'

'Dishes. Isn't Beth coming in today?'

'Tom, we pay the wretched girl the minimum wage to dust and hoover, not wash our pots. She's not our bloody skivvy, for God's sake.'

'Really?'

'Yes, really. You do it, please.' Ella snapped her fingers, held out Izzy's coat. '*Isobel Lucy Grace Barclay*, are you coming with me or not?'

Isobel was spreading a doorstep of toast thickly with peanut butter. 'For God's *sake!*' she mimicked with feeling, and scowled. For a moment, Tom thought she was going to ask what a bloody skivvy was, but she was obviously still dwelling on an earlier part of the conversation. 'What's The Talk?' she asked, scooping up the toast in one hand and her school-bag in the other.

'Something boring,' said Tom. 'Have a good day, darling,' he added, kissing her soft cheek. And he gave the smirking Ben a stern look as Ella and Isobel left the house in a whirlwind. 'Who are you playing today?' he asked Ben.

Tom didn't particularly like football – the old adage about it being designed by gentlemen and played by thugs sprang to mind – but he took an interest for his son's sake.

'Parkfield,' said Ben moodily. 'They're evil. They always go for the nads.'

'Really?' Tom was shocked. 'Don't they get booked?'

'Oh, yeah. They reckon it's worth it to cripple the opposition. That means me, Dad.'

'Oh, well. Now you'll know how it felt for me.'

'What do you mean?'

'When you were a toddler, young man, you used to run into our bedroom at six in the morning and jump on us. You'd invariably whack me right in the balls. Frankly, I'm amazed you ever got a little sister.'

Ben sniggered into his toast.

Tom remembered doing The Talk with Ben – half an hour all told, including a hearty discourse on nocturnal emissions and masturbation – and not being surprised that he half knew most of it anyway, from whispers at school. Given what Ella had said, they were pretty soon going to have to explain it all to a seven-year-old. Well, Ella could do periods. He wasn't going there. He'd just do the bit about not going out with any boys, ever, until she was eighteen, and never wearing a skirt above the knee, and perhaps staying in every night to revise for her exams rather than going to any parties.

But seriously, how far should they go? Marriage – how did they talk up that one?

It didn't always do to be honest. There was that time when Izzy was four, when Mr Squirrel had unaccountably dissolved in the washing machine. He'd had to tell her a tale about Mr Squirrel being very high up in the Teddy Council and being called to do some important work for them in London. Tom was quite pleased with that one. Worthy of a Government spin doctor, he'd thought.

That was a major dad-skill. To promote honesty, but use lying sparingly, strategically, when it protected your children's feelings. But he couldn't be honest with them at the moment.

He stared at the paper as they chewed their toast. Looking at the daily celebrity questionnaire, he found himself wondering who on earth the interviewee was, and why he should have heard of her. One question they always asked was 'Where and when were you happiest?' The celebrette – who, he now recalled, was an actress in a teen soap – perkily replied 'Here and now'. Tom wished he could give that answer.

'Dad?' Ben was waving a hand in front of his face. 'You're miles away.'

'Sorry, Ben. What?'

'I was just asking if we're going to get that widescreen telly. You know, from the catalogue.'

'Oh, possibly.' Tom smiled at his son. 'We're not made of money, you know.'

There he went again. That was another area where they always had to lie. The family finances had been secure for the last five years. Two months ago, Ben would probably have got his TV if he'd cajoled a bit, done some token car-washing. And Izzy, well, she would have got her Zillah Zim house just by hugging his leg and pouting. Now? It wasn't so straightforward now.

Tom tapped the cover of the glossy magazine. 'So,' he said, 'Damian from 3-Boyz-3. The rumours are true, then?'

His eyes, though, were elsewhere.

'This doesn't happen every day,' says Tom. 'Let's enjoy it.'

They could have gone for a couple of other options – supper for just the two of them at a little corner table in L'Oliveraie, or a curry with a dozen or so friends at the Heart Of India. But in the end, Tom wants his children there, so it's a Saturday lunchtime at the Carpenters' Arms. The pub is in the middle of nowhere, but it does fantastic food and actively encourages families. This is just as well, because they have a lively eight-year-old and a warmongering toddler with them.

The dining area is a big, sunken room with mustard-coloured walls. French windows lead on to a terrace and lush gardens. It's busy, mostly with family parties, although there are no other children as young as Isobel.

When they try to strap her into the high chair, she arches her back, makes herself rigid so they can't even force her in. Her screams shake the windows and make the woman at the next table drop her fork in alarm. Meanwhile, young Ben puts his hands over his ears, sticks out his tongue and pulls a melodramatic face.

'Leave her,' Ella says, hauling her daughter up. 'Let's put her in a proper chair.'

Ella's hair is richly dark and almost to her waist; in six months' time she will get a jaw-length bob and have her grey streak tinted for the first time.

Tom has a trim goatee beard. Today, he has made three resolutions: a) to love his children more (as if he could), b) to get a job which is more challenging than his current penpushing role, and c) to get in touch with his sensitive side.

'It's pricier than when we last came,' Ella remarks, unfolding a map-sized menu and widening her eyes at the options.

She glances at the next table. Luckily, the couple, who are in their twenties and obviously still infatuated with one another, are having a very intense conversation. They're holding hands across the table, murmuring in low voices, gazing into one another's eyes.

'Look,' says Tom, 'I'm pushing the boat out. Let's get a bottle of that, to start with.' He points to the most expensive wine on the menu.

'We don't know what we're eating yet. And anyway, who's driving home?'

'Sod it, we'll get a taxi. I'll pick the car up tomorrow.'

'Izzy's seat won't fit in a taxi, Tom.'

'Well, she can sit on my lap. It won't hurt for once in her life, will it?'

'No, until the taxi slams the brakes on and, Isobel-stop-that-at-*once*-please!'

Their toddler, her face innocent but determined, has wrapped herself around the table leg like an eager puppy. Rubbing herself against furniture, or sometimes pressing a soft toy between her legs, is her new hobby. Although Tom and Ella have been assured by a doctor, a health visitor and numerous self-help books that it is perfectly natural and won't do her any harm, they are still horrified when she indulges in these acts of public frottage.

'Izzy, darling, stop that, please,' Tom says, tapping her shoulder lightly.

He remembers the parenting classes with their uncannily mild facilitator, a shiny-faced woman who looked as if she had never mopped up a drop of baby sick in her life. She advised them against using *no* and *stop that* to discipline children. 'It is more effective in the long run,' she suggested in her gentle Scottish voice, 'if you say "Mummy and Daddy would prefer you not to do that," or, "Darling, I'd like it if you'd come and play with this instead." Try it.' Tom pointed out, not unreasonably, that Ben had been about to stick his wet finger into a plug socket last week, and that he'd possibly have got as far as *Daddy would pref—* before his son was electrocuted to death.

'Come on,' he says gently to Isobel, 'sit on my knee and let's choose something to eat.'

Her chubby red face looks up at him, big brown eyes wide and innocent. She stops for a moment, repositions, and then continues pleasuring herself.

Ella, her face roaring red, looks over briefly at the couple next to them, the fork-dropping girl and her boyfriend. 'I'm sorry,' she says. 'She's just showing off.'

The couple smile briefly in their direction, but then return to their hand-holding and their intense, important conversation.

Isobel is puffing and panting, evidently deriving a great deal of comfort from the table leg.

'Isobel,' Ella snaps, trying to prise her off with one hand, 'will you please stop that. *Now*. You're a very, very bad girl.'

'You know what Mrs McCrory would say about that, darling,' Tom remarks from behind his menu. 'We shouldn't label *her* as bad, we should make it clear that it's a bad *act*.'

Ella sighs. 'All right. That's a very bad act, you little sod. *Stop it*.'

It elevates, of course, into a full-scale confrontation, and by the time the food comes – steak for Tom, smoked salmon for Ella, sausage and mash for the children – Tom is physically having to prise Isobel off the table. They've only had a few mouthfuls before a great, ululating wail of protest wells up in the girl's throat and her eyes are streaming with tears. Ben makes a token attempt to eat his, but Isobel won't even pick up a fork.

Ella slams her glass down, slopping quality wine on the tablecloth. 'Jesus. She bloody does it deliberately. Smack her.'

'I am *not* going to smack her.' Tom lifts the screaming

Isobel over one shoulder and bobs her gently up and down, just managing to support her with one hand while eating with the other.

A waitress comes over, anxious to help. Would she like a colouring book and crayons? Isobel contemplates them, throws them to the floor and continues wailing. Tom apologises profusely to the waitress, who smiles in a way which suggests she has seen it all before.

Ella, though, has her head in her hands. 'If you don't smack her, I will,' she says, with a dangerous edge to her voice.

'Darling, we agreed we would only do that when they're actively putting their lives in danger. She's just tired, and hungry, and wanting attention.' Tom chews another forkful of rump steak. 'It's all right,' he says softly, stroking the screaming girl's hair. 'Darling, darling Izzy.'

'It's easy for you to say that, Tom. She only has to wobble her bottom lip and go *Daddy, my Daddy* and you're all over her with hugs and biscuits. Then it's me that gets the bloody full-on, spoilt little minx treatment.'

'Mum said bloody,' Ben points out through a mouthful of sausage, and he waves his fork at Ella. 'Bad word, Mum.'

'Look, I want to try and enjoy this meal,' Tom says, bouncing Isobel on his knee and taking a long gulp of wine. 'Have a bit of sausage, Izzy.'

'No, don' want sossis. Don' *liiiiiike* it.'

On Ella's birthday, she and six girlfriends went out for an all-night party on a riverboat. It was a hedonistic affair: cocktails, a comedian, a live band. There was also a strongly Colombian influence on the night, thanks to Bex, a girl Tom dislikes (he describes her as 'born with a silver straw up her nose'). So perhaps Ella thinks he should be doing something correspondingly laddish today? Tequila shots, a curry, a lap-dancing club? He shudders at the thought. No, a nice family meal was what he wanted, and a nice family meal is what he's going to get.

Ella is having none of it. 'She's being so embarrassing. Let's go.'

'She's just being a toddler. Look around. Nobody's *bothered* except you, Ella.' Tom kisses Izzy's tear-stained cheeks. 'Darling Izzy-bizzy. Little bit of sausage for Daddy?'

'No no don' want sossis. *No don' want sossis*, NO DON' WANT SOSSIS NO NO NO DON' WAAANT IIIIT!'

'Oh, for fuck's sake,' Ella mutters, folding her arms.

Ben gasps. 'Ummmm!' he says, wide-eyed, and puts both hands to his mouth like one of the Three Wise Monkeys. 'Oh, *ummmmm*! Mum, you said a very, very bad word.'

Eventually, the tide turns, as it always must. After a walk around the gardens and a stern but gentle talking-to from Tom, Isobel is calmed, coaxed into her seat. She is bribed with the promise of ice cream into having three small mouthfuls of sausage and mash.

Tom and Ella exchange rueful smiles over a second bottle of wine, and Ella becomes more relaxed about the prospect of getting a taxi home. Eventually, by about half past two, they start having quite a pleasant lunch.

The couple at the next table are paying their bill and leaving.

Tom looks up at them as they put their coats on, and the young man gives him an affable nod as he goes over to the bar to pay.

'Don't ever have kids,' Tom jokes. He ruffles Ben's hair as the boy finishes the last of his chocolate ice cream, then he strokes Isobel's flushed, food-stained cheek. 'They'll only make you broke and give you indigestion.'

The young woman smiles sadly, and Tom realises that her eyes are glistening as she looks down at Isobel.

'Actually,' the woman says, toying nervously with the crucifix at her neck, 'we can't.'

'I'm sorry?' says Tom.

'We've just been told today, at the hospital, that we won't ever be able to have children.' She glances over at the young man, who's hovering by the door, jangling his keys nervously. 'Greg's taken it really badly. We've just been looking at you, saying what a lovely family you are.'

Ella and Tom exchange a brief, guilty glance.

The young woman leans down to stroke Isobel's hair. 'Hello, precious...' She bites her lip, smiles bravely at Tom and Ella. 'You're so amazingly lucky. They're lovely. So *lovely*.'

She bites her lip, and then turns, hurries away without looking back.

The beard's hours are numbered. It is ceremonially shaved the morning after his birthday, when he wakes up, looks at his red-eyed reflection and decides that facial hair is no longer desirable.

Ten minutes later, while sipping a large coffee, he's browsing the job section of Wednesday's *Guardian*. At the bottom of the page (tucked unobtrusively beneath a Disaffected Young People's Counselling Facilitator) he sees that a new homeless charity called Appletree needs a manager. The money is slightly more than he's on now. Almost on a whim, Tom picks up the phone, dials the number, requests an information pack. It's done.

Later that same day, he signs up for a 10-week Men's Group at the local college. It can't do any harm, he thinks, and it'll help his other resolution.

Josephine Tarrant, kneeling on the rough, smoky carpet of the Parkfield School staffroom, had her head between her knees and her arms outstretched.

She felt a light tap between her shoulder blades.

Jo swung her head back to an upright position and the drab, functional walls came into view as her tangle of blonde curls fell back into place. She experimented with breathing normally through her aching lungs. It was almost successful, although she could smell little but smoke.

'Jojo,' said Matt Ryder, who had a pile of folders under his arm and a history textbook in the other hand. 'What are you, like, doing?'

'Exercise,' she said. 'You should try it sometime.' She gave him a hopeful grin.

'Um, right. You know the bell's gone for registration?'

'Yes, Matt, I do know.' She lifted herself up, cautiously, tried swinging her arms. When she was happy that they could move without dropping off, she started unzipping her tracksuit. Matt, she noticed, nonchalantly pretended to be looking out of the window, but still sneaked the odd little sidelong glance. She smiled as she turned away, pulling her trousers off and striding, coolly and comfortably, to her locker in a vest-top, pink briefs and trainers.

'Don't tell me,' he said. 'Forgotten your kit. Gnasher's going to make you take the girls' footie in your knickers?'

Jo giggled, pulling on jeans and a lambswool jumper with a practised wiggle and shimmy. 'Nothing to do with Mrs Nash,' she said, and strode over to stand behind Matt, poking him in the small of the back.

'Ow! That hurt.'

'Good. You pervy fucker. You can look now.'

'Oh, right. Yes, very nice. So what was with all the…' He tried to imitate her bowed-head stance, although it was difficult without dropping all his folders.

'I've been running. Through the estate.'

'What, the drug dealers and their Alsatians finally caught up with you, did they?'

'Ha-bloody-ha. Running for *exercise*, dumbo. Followed by five minutes of deep breathing and psycho-inductive actions.'

'Psychobabbling *what*?' Matt Ryder mocked, holding the door open for her as they both headed out into the corridor. 'You looked like you were getting a rush of blood to the head?'

'That's one aspect of it, yes. Carrot?' She pulled a scrawny, earth-coloured root out of her pocket. 'Go on, it's from my garden. Very good.'

'I'll pass, thanks.'

Jo shrugged, crunched on her carrot. 'Suit yourself. I've been feeling…weird lately. Like something's going to happen. And I just need to feel a bit better in myself.'

'By eating rabbit food and getting dizzy, is that it? Look, I know it's hard arriving in the summer term, but don't let it go to your head.'

She sighed, growled – almost roared – at him in frustration and flapped her arms at her sides. 'Don't you feel it?' she snarled at him. 'The pressure, building up. It feels like something's brewing, Matt, and the school's at the heart of it. There are times I feel I'm being watched from the corner of the estate. Times I feel...like every plane flying overhead could be the one to kill us all. Or every car could be the one with some mad gunman in it.'

'Perfectly normal post-millennial angst, mate. Nothing to worry about. Life, Jo, is about enjoying the bit that comes in between your two bouts of incontinence, y'know?' He winked at her. 'Lighten up. Bring a bit of sunshine into your life. Anyway, I'll see you at break. And eat some proper food!' he called, backing through the swing doors. 'Oh, and Jo?'

'Yes?'

'Nice perspiration, yeah?'

She gave him a joyous one-finger salute, grinned at him and strode off, hoping that he was checking out the tightness of her bottom in the jeans.

Some people, thought Ben, frantically dummying past two Parkfield defenders, would be happy with 1–1 at half-time. Some teams would play conservatively, hang back, glad of the single point.

Millmount didn't play football like that. They couldn't. Mr Powell would give them one hell of a talking-to if he thought they weren't playing to win, especially against a vicious bunch like Parkfield.

And that was why he did it.

As the hulking defender stuck out a foot, skimming the edge

of Ben's ankle just inside the penalty area, Ben smacked to the ground, making sure the mud flew up, roaring in mock pain as he rolled over and over.

He could smell the grass and mud in his nostrils, and he could hear the yells and catcalls from the touchline. He winced in agony, played it for all it was worth. Don't get up. Not yet. Another few seconds. *Hang on to it.* You're inside the area and that big bastard Gary Collins brought you down. Milk it, milk it, because that's what Parkfield would do, that's what they all do.

The referee came running over. Parkfield boys were colliding with Millmount boys, pushing and growling. Somebody spat, and it sizzled into the mud millimetres from Ben's head. Will, the other Millmount forward, clapped his shoulder and helped him up. He was grinning broadly. A second later, Ben saw the referee's arm in the air and knew that Millmount had, in the eighty-seventh minute, been awarded a penalty.

The defender, Collins, came storming forward. 'Oh, *what?* I never touched him! He took a fuckin' dive, the little shit!' He shoved Ben hard on the shoulder. 'You little *bastard!*'

'Whoa!' Ben staggered, but didn't go down. 'You fouled me, mate,' he said, holding his hands up in a pacifying gesture. 'It's a fair and square penalty.'

'Enough!' The referee held a stern finger up at them both. 'Penalty. Take it, please, Millmount.' He nodded to Collins. 'And you – calm down, less of the language, or you're off, all right?'

The ball was in Will's hands, and he was ready to place it on the spot, but still Collins hadn't had enough.

'He's a cheating little *cunt*!' he was yelling. 'And you're a fucking *shit* ref!'

Ben's heart was thumping, because he knew what was coming next. The referee, who was a deputy head from St Mary's and had been quietly containing himself during the last exchange, certainly wasn't going to stand for that. He was beckoning to the Parkfield boy, writing down his name. A second later, the referee held up a rectangle of red.

A roar of delight went up from the Millmount posse, but Ben didn't dare look in their direction. He was only aware of the look of pure, murderous hatred which Gary Collins sent him as he stormed off for his early bath.

Thirty seconds later, as Will put the ball in the back of the Parkfield net to another roar of approval, Ben had cause to wonder what the victory might have cost him.

CHAPTER EIGHT

Fool's Gold

The white room smelt of flowers, Tom decided. White light fuzzed the borders between ceiling, floor and walls, but it seemed pure, natural.

They stood with about fifty other people, nervously clutching brochures. A waitress in black PVC gloves dispensed generous glasses of a flinty Chablis.

'You look great tonight,' Tom said to Ella, smiling and looking into her brown eyes as they sipped their wine.

It wasn't just an idle compliment. She'd pulled out all the stops: hair tousled elegantly on tanned shoulders above a sheer black cocktail dress, lips gleaming with Revlon Chrome, silver earrings shining like mirror-balls, legs in teasingly sheer black stockings, feet in sinuous slingbacks. She was radiant, iridescent, desirable.

'Thank you, darling.' Peering over steel-rimmed glasses at her brochure, she gave him a smile. 'You don't look bad yourself. You ought to bring a suit out of mothballs more often.'

'*The* suit, you mean.' It was the only one he had – black,

Nehru-style, worn with his whiter-than-white collarless shirt and opal cufflinks. He felt good in the suit. It looked important, smart, yet didn't scream 'wage slave'.

The bold colours of the flock – emerald shirts, buttercup dresses, crimson high heels – sang out to the ante-room as if trying to negate its whiteness. Although the room was the size of a school assembly hall, they crowded together in the middle, forming a jittery knot of colour. It was, Tom thought, as if nobody wanted to go too near the edge in case they fell off.

'Maybe this is art,' Ella said, peering over her glasses at the culture-vultures. 'The audience as exhibit... Were the children OK with Debs?' Ella had come straight from a planning meeting, leaving Tom to liaise with the babysitter.

'Fine. I left Izzy asleep and Ben talking Debs through every move of his match. They won 2–1, you know. Bit controversial, I gather.'

'No doubt she was fascinated.'

'Well, when I left, he was trying to explain the offside rule using the cashew nuts.'

'Yes, what *is* the off – no, never mind.' She drained her glass with a flourish. 'Look, things are happening.'

Tom craned his neck, looking hopefully for Phill, but instead a young man in a silver tuxedo had strolled in. Tom recognised the bleached-blond, earringed head which had first greeted him at Centrespace. The young man bowed.

'This had better be worth it,' Ella hissed, *sotto voce*.

The light was sparkling off her best evening bag, the one whose price had made him shudder. It's a little *bag*, he remembered saying, not a flaming luggage set. How can it cost that much? Ella had given him a withering look, saying: Darling, it's Swarovski crystal and it's *Gina*. Who the fuck is Gina? he had asked, baffled. It was an academic conversation. She was always going to buy the damn thing, because she could.

'Just go with the flow,' Tom muttered, and he adjusted his cufflinks nervously as the crowd swept in.

The first room was swathed in ultramarine carpet. Tom heard Ella give a gasp as they entered, something which half a dozen people around her took to be a sign of approval and promptly imitated. In the centre of the carpet was a plinth, on which a domed glass case was mounted. In the case sat a tall, slim vessel like a Continental beer glass, full to the brim with a pale, yellow liquid. It took Tom a second to work out what it was.

This installation was entitled *'of man's first disobedience'*: *tamara day*. And the more Tom stared at it, the more he began to see a kind of crisp logic at play. Of course, peeing and guilt. The glass's contents were pale and still, like an underwater cavern. It was lit well, he had to give them that. Not sure what the blue carpet was all about – dreams of being at sea? Still, at the end of the day it was just a jar of urine. Tom checked the name again. Tamara Day. Hmm.

'Here today,' Ella whispered, unimpressed, 'gone Tamara.'

He nodded, grinned. 'She's taking the piss.'

The next room was dark, and he felt his eyes adjusting. They were in the domain of *'origins'*: *quentin hope-gallagher*. Dance music cued in – William Orbit's version of Barber's 'Adagio'. As they entered, the walls blossomed into a collage of monochrome clips, all playing in reverse. Grey London buses and night-black taxis reversed down a packed Oxford Street, ultra-white neon flashing in the background as crowds walked backwards into the night. A mushroom cloud folded, sucked up its smoke and dwindled. A cricketer, intensely white, scooped up the ball in his whirling hand and jogged backwards from the crease. Foaming waterfalls shot upwards towards jagged rocks. A rotting peach healed itself, filled out, became firm and smooth.

'It's actually not bad,' Ella whispered. A pale, bald young man in front of them turned round and narrowed his eyes, his face lurid with blotches of video-light.

'Yes,' Tom answered, 'it's clever, technically, but it isn't art, is it, love? Just boys with toys. I bet this Quentin has a very small penis.'

The next room housed *'god, save us from the queen': kara keith*. Five punked-up waxworks of the Royal Family stood proudly in a row. The Queen was spiky and green, Charles displayed a tattoo and knuckledusters, Edward had a Mohican and piercings, Andrew sported a ripped Union Jack T-shirt and safety pins. And there, set apart from them all, he saw, was the sainted Diana herself, blonde hair teased into gelled spikes, shapely legs squeezed into tartan Vivienne Westwood bondage trousers. (Di would be middle-aged by now, he realised. She'd probably have found it funny.)

'This,' Ella muttered, 'would have been a puerile joke even in 1977.'

'They wouldn't have had Diana in 1977,' argued Tom. 'But I know what you mean.' He took a swig of wine and wondered where that magic little waitress was when you needed her. He steeled himself for the next exhibit.

Tom's first relieved thought when they walked into *'only human'*: *steve kantobe* was: thank God, *pictures*. The room was pine-floored and light, giving a sense of space, and a dozen blue frames were positioned at intervals around the room. The paintings themselves looked a little abstract, but he was willing to cut some slack here.

Tom peered at the first one. People around were mumbling their approval, so he smiled and tried to join in. The figures on the canvas were stylised, hollow, rendered with just a few reddish-brown strokes.

Tom looked more closely. There was something oddly familiar about the pigment.

'Oh, my *God*,' said Ella in disgust.

'That's very nearly an armful,' Tom tried to joke, but the reference was lost on Ella. Minus another point for Humour in his mental *Top Wife* tally.

She was wrinkling her nose. 'Imagine squeezing out your own blood,' she whispered, 'just to make a painting.'

'Just to make a point,' Tom added.

Two clean-cut young men beside them looked disapproving, pointing their cheekbones at them in a way which suggested they didn't entirely agree.

'Well, sorry, guys,' Tom said. 'I may not know much about art, but I know what I like.'

The other Kantobe works developed the theme with depressing inevitability. There were abstract human forms smeared in glistening brown earwax. There was a grinning pumpkin-visage picked out on an indigo background in a silvery tracing, like slug trails. Tom sensed Ella shudder beside him. 'Truly onanistic,' she said. As they moved around the room, the artist's palette expanded to include faeces, bile and vomit – all his own, Tom supposed, although one didn't like to presume. As they got to the end, he noticed that each frame was hermetically sealed, buzzed quietly to itself and sported a small orange light in the bottom right-hand corner. They were all fridges.

They had kept the most memorable until last, however.

The final room was *'calendar': trish tregarran*. It was lit in harsh, unyielding white and surrounded with mirrors, thus picking out and reflecting the imperfections in every face. Not too many people were examining their reflections, though, as the eye was drawn immediately to the washing line which ran across the room. Thirteen primary-coloured pegs were fixed to the line. On every peg there was a label with a date, each date being about four weeks from the last. From each peg hung a small white oblong, about fifteen centimetres long and curved at the ends. Each of these was stained with a crusty, reddish-brown splodge, all slightly different in texture, hue and size. They stretched away into infinity, endlessly reflecting, and quivered in a gentle current of air.

The party stood there for a few seconds in silence, looking at the neatly pegged array as if they could not quite believe the audacity of the artist. Or perhaps, Tom wondered, the stupidity of the paying public.

'Is this her red period?' Tom asked jauntily. There were a few disapproving tuts from in front of him.

Ella took a deep draught of her wine and breathed out, nodding. 'I'll say one thing for...' She glanced at her brochure. 'For Trish Tregarran, whoever she might be.'

'What's that?' Tom asked.

'She's regular.'

They joined the exodus to the bar. It was painted the same blood-red as the lobby, Tom noticed, and was enhanced by fiery lighting. There was Phill, her hair shining, her curves contained in a little black silk dress. His heart rate increased as she detached herself from a small group and shimmied over.

'Hell-ooo there, Tom. *So* glad you could make it...' She beamed at Ella. 'Hi, Phill Janowitz. Delighted to meet you.'

'Ella Barclay. Likewise. Thank you.' They shook hands. Tom took refuge in his wineglass.

'So,' said Phill, 'do tell me what you thought of our Zeroes Heroes?' She had a glimmer of wickedness in her eye, Tom thought, as if she was daring them to say it was utter crap.

'It was certainly...striking,' said Ella, with her diplomat's smile.

'Uh-huh, uh-huh. That's what we were hoping for.'

'I must admit,' Ella went on, 'I hadn't realised it would be quite so...*visceral.*'

'Oh?' Phill was interested now. 'You found it visceral? I'm so pleased. Some of the artists are here, so I hope you'll get to chat to them.' Tom followed her gaze to a tall, handsome black man in a white suit. 'That's Steve Kantobe, over there. And that's Trish.' Green hair, leather dress, boots. 'And that's Quentin.' Chinless, pale, earnestly nodding at something Trish Tregarran was saying.

Ella said, 'I know art's meant to be blood, sweat, toil and tears, but I didn't realise some people took it so...literally. I'm surprised nobody stuck a few used condoms in there for that extra edge.'

Phill didn't miss a beat. 'Actually, Kantobe's early works

did. He utilised a number of items of what society would term "waste", and put them into a new context by sealing them in perspex. His work likes to play with concepts of preservation, containment, storage. As I'm sure you noticed.'

Ella smiled icily. Tom was wondering if he could, somehow, steer the conversation away from the exhibition. It was a bit difficult, as it was their reason for being there.

A jaunty electronic tune cut across the room, emanating from Ella's handbag. She pulled the mobile out, flipped it open. 'Yes?... Is she?' Ella frowned. 'For how long? Well, tell her we're not far away... Try to get her to go back to bed, Deborah.'

Tom smiled at Phill. 'Babysitter,' he said. 'Next door's daughter.'

'Ah.' Phill nodded, sympathetically. 'How old?'

'Errr...' Tom frowned. 'I think she's about twenty-three. I'm not sure, actually.'

'No. I mean how old are your children?'

'Oh. Sorry.' Tom laughed nervously, and tried not to look at the tautness of the black silk dress across Phill's breasts. 'Ben's thirteen and Izzy's seven.' He cleared his throat. 'Do you, um, have...?'

'Kids? Me?' She laughed that wine-rich laugh again, pushed her hair back. He got a brief scent of something gorgeous and herbal. 'Hell, no. I haven't even found the right guy yet. Don't really want to. I'm something of a...free spirit.' She lifted her eyebrows at him, and sipped her wine.

Holding eye contact.

Tom held too.

And held.

And Phill looked down at his mouth, then back up to his eyes, with just a hint of impishness.

Ella was still hectoring the babysitter. 'Let her get some milk and a biscuit and read a book...or watch something innocuous... Sorry? She's what?... Oh, bloody *hell*. And they were clean on. She's not a baby any more. This shouldn't be happening.' Ella covered up the mouthpiece. 'Izzy's wet the bed.'

'Shall we go back?' Tom asked, suddenly picturing the big, innocent eyes of his daughter.

She's not a baby any more. Did Ella have to be so blunt? She was still *his* baby, his little Bizzy. If she'd had an accident, he wanted to bath her, make her laugh with Mr Sponge and his silly jokes, cuddle her, ask her what was wrong. His shoulders still ached from where she had jumped up and grabbed them earlier in the day. She'd been laughing, wanting him to give her a ride around the house like he used to when she was little. He liked the ache, and didn't want it to go away.

He was counting down the days to being unemployed, and unconditional love was one of the few pleasures that cost nothing.

'You OK?' Phill Janowitz asked.

'Yeah, yeah. Cigarette smoke. Sometimes gets my eyes watering.'

Ella, having concluded the conversation over by one of the pot plants, snapped the phone shut. Sighing, she came back over. 'I'll go back,' she said.

'Are you sure?' he asked. 'Shouldn't we both go?'

'No, no. You stay here and fraternise with the intelligentsia. Can I take the car?'

He lobbed her the keys. 'I've had a few drinks anyway. I'll need to get a cab.'

She nodded, smiled briefly. 'OK. See you later. And don't worry.'

'Hug Bizzy from me. And – Ella?'

She paused at the door 'What?' she asked, irritably.

'Don't be *cross* with her. Find out, you know, if she's upset.'

'Of course I won't be bloody cross with her,' Ella snapped, and was gone.

When Tom drank properly, it was often to forget. Not to forget deep, existential misery, but just the niggling annoyances of the day.

Tonight, he was torn. He knew he wanted to ruffle little Izzy's hair and kiss her soft cheek and murmur to her. But he needed a drink to blot out the impending catastrophe at Appletree. And he wanted to stay in the womblike redness of the bar and watch Phill Janowitz leaning against the wall, the blood-light catching every movement of that dress.

And Ella had offered to go. She had *volunteered*.

So he circulated, socialised. He found himself in a group of art students hanging on Steve Kantobe's every word. Tom asked the man himself a question about artistic sacrifice which was intended as ironic, and one of the students thought she got the sub-text and giggled so hard she snorted her wine up her nose.

The hubbub of the bar became enclosing, friendly. Tom allowed his glass to be refilled a few times and suddenly found that he'd become tremendously witty and erudite.

Time collapsed. Tom had procured his own bottle from the

bar, and was pouring wine for the art students, for Steve Kantobe and the green-haired Trish Tregarran (she was Period Woman, he remembered). He got them all laughing uproariously at some joke he'd read on the Internet about the Pope, Tony Blair and Saddam Hussein jumping out of an aeroplane. At the punchline, he felt something swish at his shoulder, scented camomile up close. He caught a brief, complicit grin from Phill as she shifted her feet, a silken buttock passing dangerously close to his thigh.

Through the vaulted windows, the cityscape darkened. It was picked out in a join-the-dots pattern of orange as the street lamps flicked on.

And then there were just ten or so people left on a crescent of comfortable chairs, breaking open the whisky as, outside, the city revved up for the long night haul. Tom was sprawled in a chair, dangling his glass. Phill Janowitz was perched on the arm of his chair, her smooth buttocks just inches from his hand. Shiny-eyed, she giggled affectedly at every small witticism of his.

Ten became six, and a fragmented discussion about a club ensued. And then the other four were staggering into the night, shouting for a taxi, and Phill called that she would catch them up or meet them later.

Tom narrowed his eyes at the bar. Its lights were off, and a second later the two bow-tied young men who had been serving them started to bring down the noisy metal shutters.

'God, is it chucking-out time already?' he said to Phill, who was laughing and swaying uncertainly in front of him. If he wasn't very much mistaken, she had just swigged a neat dose from the Laphroaig bottle.

'Sure. For *them*,' she said, waving a hand airily. 'I work here, I can stay as long as I like.'

Her gorgeous scent was getting right inside him. Definitely camomile shampoo, and a very subtle perfume – and the easiest one to recognise, the warm, luscious feminine aroma which had no proper name.

There was a hierarchy of the senses, when you met someone. Inevitably sight came first, then sound, and then smell was usually the third. If touch came into it, you knew there was more. And if you got to taste, well, then you were home and dry.

'So,' she said, 'kids, huh? I hope your little girl is OK.'

'She'll be fine,' he said, feeling suddenly guilty that he hadn't phoned to check. 'I'm sure she just wanted her mummy.'

'Mmm. Hey, it must all be worth it. You're a great dad, I'm sure.'

He shrugged. 'I s'pose. I do my best.'

'It must be great having kids,' she said. 'You feel...connected.' She looked up at Tom. 'Don't you? I mean, they keep you in touch with stuff.'

'Oh, yes. Stuff.'

Thanks to Isobel, Tom thought, he knew more than he had ever wanted to know about the lives of Zillah Zim and It-Girl. And thanks to Ben, he could name at least a few Premiership footballers and identify various screaming, goatee-bearded gangs of Americans with guitars.

'This whisky's great,' he said, lifting his glass. 'Well kept.'

'Here, have some more.' She poured him another generous measure. 'So, did you see them born?'

'I'm sorry? What?'

'Your kids. Were you there, you know, in the delivery room? Mopping Ella's fevered brow, and all that?'

'Oh. God... Yeah, yeah, I was there.'

'What was it like?' Phill asked with a smile.

Oh, *please*. Tom's heart sank. How the hell had she got started on *this*? Weren't childbirth stories meant to be kept for women-only conversations? And he didn't even like her saying Ella's name like that. If she had just said 'your wife' it would have been so much better.

'Um. Um... Well, it was...well, it was OK. She got through it fine both times. You know. Not too much swearing.'

'Really? Uh-huh. Did you cut the cord?'

He couldn't quite believe he was having this conversation. 'Oh, Christ, no. Ben was a Caesarean, and with Izzy, well, anything involving sharp implements I always leave to professionals, frankly...and...um, Phill, it was all a long time ago. Do you mind if we talk about something else?'

'Oh, sure, no... Sorry. I just, y'know. Never having been there.'

'Oh. Yes, of course. I'm sorry.' He fingered his glass awkwardly. 'You said you'd catch those people up,' he said, and instantly regretted reminding her.

'Yeah, well. To be honest, two of those guys are assholes. The other two I like, but I can see them any time.' She grinned. 'You, on the other hand, are rare.'

'Medium rare,' he said.

She laughed, offering him the bottle. 'Here.'

Now this was better. Meaningless, flirtatious chat, combined with reckless drinking.

'Cheers.' He drank from it, aware of the sudden intimacy of

the bottleneck, still warm and moist from her mouth. The whisky burned. 'Don't you run to glasses now?' he asked, croaking. 'Terrible, these cutbacks.'

Phill laughed, and her fingers brushed his arm.

The first time she had ever touched him.

He realised, with sudden amusement, what had happened. A sense had skipped the queue. The taste of her mouth, on the glass neck, had got there first, passing touch to finish fourth out of five.

'How much did this bash cost?' Tom asked, pretending to ignore the caress.

'Oh, it cost *loads*, Tom. But it's worth it for the fucking great publicity. You'll see.'

He grinned at her. He liked the way she swore. She rolled the profanity round her mouth, made the word sound rich, chocolatey, rather than spitting it like a grape pip as Ella did. And Phill wasn't about to rattle the swear-box in his face.

'Hey,' she said, nodding at the bustling barmen. 'These guys need to close up. You wanna come see the nerve-centre? I promise you, it's terribly exciting.'

And just a minute later, they were in her small office along the corridor. She didn't touch the light. The room smelt of camomile and coffee. In the dim glow from the corridor, he saw a smart desk, a shiny new computer, a column of window looking out across the shimmering river. The bellow of a pleasure-cruiser boomed beneath Commerce Bridge; he saw the boat down there, a distant block of light slicing through the treacly waters. It glided like a ghost and was gone.

He heard her lock the door. She twirled her keys from one elegant finger, then let them spin off under the desk.

'Jeez,' she said, 'I really shouldn't get this drunk.' She held up the flat of her hand, let it glide towards his face. 'My palms get so hot. Feel.'

He rested his cheek against the flat of her hand. It was comfortingly warm. He turned his head, coolly, and kissed her palm.

Phill closed her eyes, drew a deep breath, and gave a shuddering giggle. 'Mmmm,' she said. 'Nice.'

Smiling, she swished closer to him. She took his left hand, turned the palm towards her face, gave it an equally light kiss. Then, she extended her tongue and licked his middle finger, with almost unbearable gentleness, from tip to base. And then lower, to the centre of his palm. He wasn't sure if it was deliberate, but her nose nuzzled the edge of his wedding ring.

'Hands are underrated, I feel, as erogenous zones,' Phill whispered in his ear, slipping her arms around his neck.

'Mmm. Mouths, on the whole, get a good press,' he said, with his lips centimetres from hers.

'Justifiably, I feel,' murmured Phill, closing in.

Her tongue was eager, probing, almost angry in his mouth, and she opened and closed her lips as if trying to eat him. He had not kissed anyone with such intensity for...how long? He didn't remember. He didn't care.

They broke off, looked at each other searchingly.

She took his face in her hands. '*Shit!*' she said with a grin, then laughed and pulled away from him, swaying. She steadied herself against the wall. 'I *rrrreally* should not get this drunk.'

Tom slid over to her, slipped his arms around her soft waist.

'I don't know,' he said. 'I think it's quite fun.'

He kissed her again, pressing her up against the wall. She was just as eager, probing and responsive this time. She broke off to giggle halfway through, then plunged back in, licking around his tongue with renewed fervour.

They pulled apart again, swaying slightly. Tom felt his hand going to his mouth. An instinct, but he wasn't sure what brought it on – a theatrical gesture of guilt, a desire to feel the place she had just kissed, or a need to wipe away the evidence? Maybe it was all three. His cock betrayed him now; pounding away, limbering up for action, it nuzzled lightly against her.

Beneath them, the city groaned and mumbled, and the lights from a passing boat splashed ripples on the office ceiling.

'Look, I'd…better be getting back,' he muttered, with a sheepish grin. 'See…how Isobel is. You know.'

'Yeah, sure.' Phill held her hands up briefly with a smile. An open, friendly gesture allowing him total freedom. He liked that. 'I'll let you out,' she said.

On the bridge outside, he stopped and breathed the night air, looking out for a few seconds over the shimmering river.

He hated the feeling of an unused erection. That sudden, adolescent rush was wilting, but he still had the thrill of a new taste on his lips, a new face in his mind, and a new intensity to his heartbeat. As he headed unsteadily for Commerce Street to hail a taxi, he felt like an actor in a weirdly edited commercial where you had to guess what the product was going to be.

Whether he liked it or not, the world had shifted slightly today, and nothing was the same any more.

* * *

'This is Janie Jones, and you're listening to the Janie Jones phone-in on Three Counties FM. Yes, folks, tonight it's the one. We're going to be talking about affairs. That's right – affairs. Men who cheat on their wives, women who cheat on their husbands. Even, sometimes, people who have extramarital relationships with the full knowledge – sometimes the full consent – of their partners.

'Later on, I'll be speaking live in the studio to the Reverend Dr Simeon Mackey, the Bishop of Cherford, about what he has called the "moral disintegration" of today's society. Also in the studio I'll have Babs Keel from OneStep, the single parent charity, and she'll be talking about attitudes to marital break-up.

'And, of course, we'll be taking calls from you – that's right, you at home. We want to hear from you in the first hour if you're a mistress or a toy-boy, a kept man or a loose woman, a bit on the side or the third person in a marriage. Phone us after eleven... Ahh, but wait, cuckolded husbands and scorned wives, you'll get your moment – because we want you to speak in the second hour. Has your husband been unfaithful? Has your wife walked out on you? Maybe they had a one-night stand and you've forgiven them. Or, hey, maybe you haven't. Whatever the case – we want to hear your side, after twelve midnight.

'Coming up in five, the news and weather, but right now, let's sneak this one in. A bit of an Eighties oldie tonight, one of my favourites too – it's Black and "Wonderful Life"...'

CHAPTER NINE

Kiss And Make Up

'I can't decide which colour goes best,' said Ella, holding up two silk blouses against herself in front of the mirror. 'What do you think?'

'They're both fine,' said Tom from beneath the bed. He was trying to retrieve the computer disk which had just fallen out of his briefcase. Bugger these laminate floors, he was thinking. If we still had carpets it wouldn't have skidded so far.

'You haven't even *looked*.'

Tom sighed audibly, glanced up for a second. 'They're both the bloody same,' he said. 'Both sort of off-white, aren't they?' He returned to stretching his arm under the bed. The disk was just out of reach...if he could only get his fingertips to it, knock it round at an angle...

'Tom, I know you're colour-challenged. You only have to look at the shirts you choose to inflict on yourself. But even you *must* be able to tell the difference between a soft cream and a crocus white?'

'Yes...naturally, darling... I think about little else.' He tried to get even closer to the floor, wedging his shoulder right under. Almost there...

'I mean, for God's sake, they're not even *similar*.'

'Just like film and videotape,' he said.

'Sorry? What the hell are you on about now?'

Tom managed to get a fingertip to the edge of the disk and spun it round so that he could pull it towards him. Sighing with relief, he eased backwards from under the bed, clutching the disk.

'Film and videotape,' he said, breathless, standing up and dusting his trousers off. 'You can't tell the bloody difference. And that awful filmised effect they used on *Brookside* didn't bother you, either. When I tried to explain it, it was like you spoke a different language.'

Ella sighed. 'I haven't got the faintest idea what you're talking about. Is this some geeky equivalent of the offside rule?'

'It's similar.'

'Anyway, which one?' she asked.

'Sorry?'

Ella held up the two blouses, practically stamping her feet. 'Tell. Me. Which. One.'

'Oh. Um...'

Tom pretended to think. This was some kind of test, he thought. Like that time when she had Bex and Tori round for a red-wine evening and she'd badgered him afterwards to say which one of them he fancied the most. The correct answer, of course – which she helpfully didn't provide as one of his options – was, 'Oh, neither of them compares to you, darling.'

If that was the case, then it was important not to get it

wrong. Especially this morning, when his mouth was still tingling from the sensation of someone new.

'Um...' He pointed to one, then the other, then the first again. 'Look, this really isn't my field. Just wear whichever you prefer, OK?'

Ella was still saying something as he hurried away to the bathroom. Luckily, he managed to block out the actual words, and it just sounded like the teacher's voice from the *Charlie Brown* cartoons, an incoherent mumble of *mwarb-mwarb-mwarb* noises echoing down the landing.

Adultery. Just a word.

OK, it wasn't technically adultery because he hadn't shagged her yet. Or was it? Did even a kiss count? After all, it hadn't just been an affectionate kiss on the cheek or even a gentle and teasing brush of the lips. That was the thing; it had been a full-on, get-your-tongue-down-me, pre-fuck kiss. The only reason they hadn't gone further, if he was honest, was the inconvenience. So there you had it – the intention was there.

Some vague memory of a passage in the Bible came back to him, about a man looking at a woman with lust and committing adultery with her in his heart. Well, he wouldn't go that far – if that were the case, he was unfaithful about twenty-five times a day. But the kind of snog where you were practically devouring her, licking round her tongue, getting down so deep in there you could almost taste her tonsils – not to mention caressing her arse and pulling her close to your rapidly unfurling hard-on – yes, not much question about that.

So why had he done it? Because it was easy and enjoyable?

Because Phill was cool and sexy and funny (and, he suspected, more than a little dirty)? But then so was Ella. He had a wife who made many other men go weak with lust. Why eat out at great expense when he could get fine cooking at home?

It was the novelty. The difference. He always came back to that. A lush, unexplored valley awaited his incursion (unexplored by him, anyway) and he was going to make his way there as soon as he possibly could.

And, if he was honest, it was about this – the chance to have unfettered sex with a woman who wouldn't bore him with the details of the gas bill, or indeed ask him what colour blouse she ought to be wearing that day.

It was irresistible.

How, Ella thought crossly, could anyone think crocus white was the same as soft cream? Sometimes he was just plain *dim*.

She crashed about in the kitchen, inflicting breakfast rage on the fridge, percolator and cereal bowls.

'There was a message for you, Mum,' said Ben as he stuffed textbooks into his school-bag. 'Some teacher from Parkfield?'

Ella felt a momentary, excited shiver, like the one she'd felt when that man eyed her up in the Eighties club. She imagined herself attached to one of those machines which betrayed your heart rate; hers was zooming up, up.

'Er, hell-ooo? Earth calling Mum?' Ben waved a hand in front of her face.

'Right, yes, sorry.' She sipped her pink grapefruit juice. 'What did he want?'

'I don't know,' Ben said with a shrug. 'Something about a talk you promised to do? He just said to call him back.'

'Oh, right.' She kept her tone neutral. 'Yes, I remember.'

Ben wrinkled his nose. 'They call it the Death Zone up there.'

'Why?' asked Isobel, who was buttering toast. 'What does that mean?'

'Means if you go up there, you get slaughtered. Eaten alive. *Deeeeaaath!*' Ben bared his teeth at his sister, who squealed appreciatively. 'Will says they're, like, in-bred scum.'

Ella frowned at him. 'Will should learn that there are people in this city less fortunate than him,' she said, stirring her coffee with enough force to carve a hole in the Denby mug.

'Mum, seriously, they're a bunch of flipping headcases. We've just played them in the city schools league, yeah? They were, like, totally mental?'

I know that, she remembered. She thought of a draughty corridor, Matt Ryder's cheeky grin, the odd feeling she'd had outside the school.

'The ones you beat this week?' Ella asked, trying to sound nonchalant.

She always said to Tom that she would rather their son played a sport that involved less mud and less swearing. Badminton, she thought, seemed nice. Anna Hopworth's two boys were into that. They won cups and things, went on tour in France and always looked so...fresh.

Ben said, '*Yessss...*' And he clenched his fist. 'But they were total thugs. They got three sent off and two of our defenders were almost crippled.' Ben winced. 'Really vicious bastards.'

'*Benedict.*' Ella held up an index finger, tapped the swear-box.

Ben groaned, tutted. He pulled a coin from his pocket and sulkily put it in the slot. It landed with a dull clink.

Isobel had been quiet since her nocturnal incident. By the time Ella got back, Debs the babysitter had put the soiled bedclothes and pyjamas on to wash, which was a blessing. Izzy wouldn't let anyone but Mummy run a bath for her, though, so that still needed to be done, and then she had taken some cajoling to go back to sleep. She kept insisting – and Ella shivered a little to recall it – that there was a man watching her in the room. They had been all round the bedroom, of course, pointing out all the friendly objects in every corner. Ella had dimmed the light a little each time they passed the switch, eventually managing to get Izzy into bed at around eleven o'clock and lying with her until she fell asleep.

A man. She had definitely said *a man*.

The Bizzy had never been a good sleeper. Ben had been a dream baby, sleeping regularly for nine hours a night once he got into a routine. Isobel, however, was a real shock to their softened systems: attention-seeking, demanding more stories, more milk, more cuddles. She shredded their nerves by screaming at ear-splitting volume. 'Ohhh, what's the matter with her?' Ella's mother would sometimes murmur, clucking and tutting as she picked up her granddaughter and rocked her, causing Izzy to shriek even more loudly. And Ella, who could hear the undertone of criticism, would snap back, 'Nothing's the *matter* with her, Mother, she's a baby. Sometimes they just cry. We have to put up with it.'

Isobel would wail in desperation if she was left alone in her room, even when supplied with a cotful of friendly soft toys and a glowing lava lamp. In fact, she had not properly started to sleep at night until she was about five. 'Monsters' were sometimes claimed as the cause, although never with any seriousness. Ella blamed Tom for this, because his way of lulling the toddler to sleep was to take her downstairs, give her some warm milk and watch *Doctor Who* with her. Shortly after one episode – some hammy Gothic hokum involving a disembodied glass brain in a tank – the lava lamp had to be retired. *Bagpuss* was then slipped into the late-night video schedules instead. *The Clangers* had already proved traumatic, as the Soup Dragon sent Izzy whimpering behind a cushion.

And now it was *the man*. When Ella looked in on her sleeping daughter, she glanced quickly up at the wardrobe, creating shapes from shadow in the corner of her eye. It's all that modern art, she told herself. Fucks with your head.

Now, though, Isobel seemed back to her usual, cheeky self.

'Ben said *bar-starrd*,' she pointed out.

'Yes, it's a very rude word, and your brother was very naughty to say it.' Ella paused, but her commitment to openness made her add, 'It means, as I'm sure Benedict knows, someone born outside wedlock.'

Isobel weighed this up, milk dripping from her spoon. 'Where's Wedlock?' she asked eventually.

'North Yorkshire,' said Tom, as he breezed through the kitchen. 'Come on, kids, are you ready yet? I've got a hell of a day ahead.'

Isobel threw her spoon down in the remains of her cereal.

A lone, soggy Shreddie, catapulted to freedom, arced across the table in a perfect parabola, landing between Ella's breasts on her immaculate blouse.

'Oh, dear,' Tom said, snapping his briefcase shut. 'Looks like it's the other one after all.'

Matt Ryder jammed papers into his briefcase as he fought his way downstairs through a waterfall of jabbering, squawking kids. He was trying to thumb the messages on his phone with his spare hand, and was in danger of overbalancing.

'You have,' said the impersonal woman in his phone. 'One. New. Message.'

He sheltered in a classroom doorway, letting the rivers of pupils surge past him.

'Hi, Matt, it's Ella Barclay here. Thanks for the message. I appreciate the reminder, and no, I hadn't forgotten. I'll see you at two-thirty as arranged.'

He had a broad smile on his face as he entered the staff-room. Ella Barclay, with her lustrous hair and dark crinkly eyes, with her bank name and her voice full of money, intrigued him more than any woman had since Jenny had left him high and dry.

He didn't, in general, like it to be known that he hadn't had a proper girlfriend since starting work, and he certainly wasn't going to tell anyone – not even his closest friends – that Jenny had finished with him by texting him. Six bytes, flipped across Europe from (he discovered later) the Piazza San Marco in Venice; the pithy but charmless information *yr dmpd*. Subsequent attempts to involve her in dialogue about the situation had been like knitting fog. She refused to be drawn on exactly why he was *dmpd*, or indeed what he had done to *dsrv* being *dmpd*. As far as he could fathom, he'd just been the victim of her mercurial moods.

'Those damn things,' growled Bill Hollis at his elbow, pouring himself a cup of tea and ignoring everyone else. 'Cause more trouble than they're worth, if you ask me.'

Matt switched on the automatic smile he always used to disarm people. 'Really, Bill?' he said. Matt enjoyed baiting Bill Hollis, and had become used to the permanent expression of disgust on the year head's crinkled face. 'I think they're rather useful, myself.'

'Bloody *Star Trek* gadgets.' Bill Hollis piled three sugars into his tea with unnecessary force. 'Kids are obsessed with them. Ought to chuck all the things in a skip and be done with it.'

'Now, you know Ms Moretti doesn't like us to call them kids, Bill,' said Jo Tarrant, sidling up with mineral water in hand and winking at Matt. 'It's students or young people – isn't that right, Matt?'

Bill Hollis gave a deep, derisive snort. 'They were bloody kids when this place was falling apart under Maggie sodding Thatcher. And they're bloody kids now it's falling apart again. No respect, that's the problem.' Bill slurped from his tea, a noise which made Jo close her eyes and wince. Matt, chewing on a biscuit, struggled to suppress a grin. 'I mean, look,' Hollis said, and gestured out of their first-floor window at the schoolyard bedlam below. 'You can't call 'em students. It's, whaddyuocallit, politically correct claptrap. I mean, just look at 'em. They're no better than animals.'

'Hey, Bill,' said Jo, 'I bet if we brought back National

Service and the birch, things would be different.' She winked at Matt again.

'Too bloody right. Too damn soft, we are. We don't have any power at all. No wonder there's no respect.' Bill slurped again. 'Little shits,' he said. 'I tell you summat,' he went on, and he waggled his teaspoon at Matt and Jo in turn. 'If you can get through the day without 'em killing each other or killing you, it's been a good day all round. You can't hope to bloody *teach* the bastards anything. We're just minding them till those feckless yobbos who like to call themselves parents get back from drinking their bloody Giros. Zoo-keepers, we are. Just bloody zoo-keepers.'

'Quick word, Matt?' said Jo. They sidled over to the window. 'Sorry, mate,' she murmured. 'Didn't want to give hang-and-flog-'em Hollis any more ammo, but I need to talk to you about Gary Collins.'

Matt grimaced. 'Must you? I'm eating.'

'Yeah, I know... Look, you and I know it's only a matter of time before he does something seriously stupid and gets himself excluded. We've thought that for months, now, and yet he always seems to wangle his way out of it.'

'Mmm. So I've noticed. His little team still on the prowl?'

'Yeah, but the stuff they do, it's only hearsay. And as long as he's the star of the footie squad, my department's under pressure to keep him in. They'd be lost without him.' Jo pulled a face. 'Something's not quite right. I dunno what.'

'Keep your finger on it,' Matt said. 'It could just be your *Zeitgeist-angst* again... Anyway, I gather they lost yesterday?'

'Yeah, that's the other thing. Apparently one of the Millmount boys did an Oscar-winning performance in the penalty area and the ref fell for it. That's how they got the extra goal.'

'Oh, you're joking.'

'Nope. Collins went off on one – usual sort of thing – and got a red. Now there's murmurings about him somehow getting back at Millmount.'

'Blimey, Jojo,' Matt said, taking a thoughtful bite of his Rich Tea. 'Class warfare on our very doorstep. Who ever said it was dull here?'

'Well, just thought I'd mention it, seeing as you've been here a bit longer than me and you know your way round the delicate politics of the place. I just seem to keep putting my foot in it... Hey, there's only a couple more weeks of term – maybe it'll get forgotten over the summer.'

'Mmmm,' said Matt. 'Maybe, and maybe not... OK, look, I'll see if I can find time to talk to Moretti about it.'

Coincidentally, Matt was to remember Millmount Hall in another context later on that same day, and would recall Jo's comments in the light of it. However, he would have forgotten that he had promised to speak to the head, and wouldn't make the significant connection in his mind.

'Bye, Bizzy. Be a good girl today.'

'I'm always a good girl, Dad.'

'Then be a better girl. Kiss... OK, bye, Ben. Be a good boy. Manly hugs?'

'Dad! People are *watching*. Hugging is *so* for faggots.'

'But we always have manly hugs. Come on. Bruce Willis hugged his dad in that film the other day. I'd like to see you call *him* a faggot.'

Millmount unsettled Tom today.

Usually, when he dropped them off at the gates, he allowed himself a complacent little smile. Despite the soul-searching they had been through before choosing the place, it always delighted him to see the neo-Gothic splendour of the building, its sturdy clock tower, the big sweeping drive for decanting kids from Range Rovers and Audis. (Or modest Astras, like theirs.) It made him feel snug and smug. It comforted him to watch the boys and girls in blue blazers with shiny satchels, hurrying up the steps, looking as if they actually enjoyed being there. Pupils flaunted their middle-class trappings: brushed hair, Alice bands, good teeth and glowing skin, music cases and instruments. And then the fragments of conversation: '*actually*, Harry,' and 'I don't *think* so, Flora,' and fifteen-year-old girls talking about 'Mummy' and 'Daddy' and the house in France.

All right, he admitted, some of the parents were unbearable – braying hunting-set Tories, or snobs who sneered at Izzy's second-hand blazer. But most of them were just normal, nice people, professionals like him and Ella. (Well, like Ella, anyway.) The thought that his children were being educated in an environment which they had bought – and, to a large extent, controlled – was usually a reassuring one.

Today, though, he gazed longingly after his children as they scurried into the cavernous entrance. He wanted them back. He wanted to hug them both and tell them that nothing was the same any more, tell them that Dad didn't know what was going to happen, ask if they could please forgive him?

'Never quite understood the private school thing with you two,' Jeff had said to them once, a year or two ago, on one of his rare visits to the house. (He'd offered to sit the kids while he and Ella went out to the cinema, Tom remembered – Jeff had spontaneous, random attacks of kindness like that.) 'I mean, come on, I thought you were both Labour voters?'

Ella, zipping her boots up, had paused and looked up at him reprovingly. 'Having a conscience, Jeff, doesn't mean playing Russian roulette with your children's education.'

'No,' Jeff had admitted with a shrug, settling on the sofa with his four-pack of Stella. 'But I thought it meant you didn't think of schools in that way. I mean, if all you bleeding-heart pinkos sent your little darlings to the local comp, like, it'd stand a better chance, wouldn't it?'

Tom smiled ruefully, now, as he remembered how they'd managed to deflect the subject. It hadn't been mentioned again, not even on his own with Jeff.

He swung the car back townwards. Feeling unsettled, he fished for a tape at random, stuck it in the machine. One of his compilations. It slammed into the middle of a Beta Band song on Side A, so he knew it would be Jean-Jacques Goldman next, then Erin Rocha. His tastes were nothing if not wide.

He drew into a multi-storey, parked in a space as far from any other cars as he could, and switched the engine off. The tape cut out.

He flicked his mobile on. It beeped once and sat there, green, glowing and expectant.

It took a couple more minutes of indecision before he made his fingers do the job, did it before his mind and his hammering heart could stop him. Phill's number sat there in front of him and he thumbed the call button.

Three rings.

'Centrespace Arts, Duncan speaking?' The multi-pierced blond man, of course.

'Hi, could I speak to Phill Janowitz, please?'

'Who shall I say is calling?'

'It's Tom Barclay from Appletree.' He was still on the Appletree payroll for three weeks, so it wasn't exactly a lie.

It could so easily have been a terrible mistake, all this. But it made him come alive once more, and it made him feel young and stupid again.

'Hi there,' said the soft Canadian voice in his ear.

And now he was grinning like a schoolboy.

'Hi,' Tom said. 'So how are you?'

'Very bored, actually,' said Phill's seductive voice. 'Sitting here eating a large chocolate muffin and trying to make sense of an Arts Council document.'

'Right, right.' He thought of Phill's mouth around the dark, moist, crumbly form of a chocolate muffin, and was suddenly half crazed with lust. 'Well, that's um…great.'

Pause.

Oh, God, he thought desperately, leaning back in the car seat and closing his eyes. She's not even going to mention it and we're back to square one. Help. Probably embarrassed by the whole thing.

'So, are you calling on official business, Tom?' There was, perhaps, a note of light mockery in her voice now.

'Errr…well…what you might call unofficial business. Or unfinished, perhaps.' He lobbed it in, as an act of desperation.

'Oh, goooood, I was thinking that. I was actually just remembering our little encounter and thinking how nice it was. How about you?'

He had a sudden flash-frame in his mind, of the Rowan erupting into jubilant chaos at that famous lunchtime goal by David Beckham against Argentina. A forest of hands in the air and the glass-shaking roar of a hundred revved-up Englanders.

Calm down, he told himself, grinning broadly.

'Yes, I was thinking how nice it was too.'

'It was a shame we had to stop, just as it was kinda getting interesting.'

Now that was better than Beckham, he thought with a wicked grin. That was bloody well Geoff Hurst and his hat-trick, that was.

'We...did. I'd agree with that.' Pause. 'Although, um, what we did was fine. I mean, not that I'd be happy with just that. Um, I mean, I would be happy with that, if that was all that ever came of it, but... Oh, God. It's like, um, a trailer, isn't it? You know, Forthcoming Attractions. You're sitting there with your popcorn and coke and you think, hmmm, that was good, I might go and see that one.'

He winced silently, scrunching his eyes up. Oh, great, he told himself. I've kissed this woman once and I've just compared her to a night at the fucking *Odeon*.

'Well, yes,' she said, laughing. 'I suppose so.'

'Sorry,' he said, 'I'm wittering, Phill. I can't even think straight, let alone speak properly.'

'Why's that?' He knew her well enough, already, to hear the impish smile in her voice.

'Because I've been thinking about you, I suppose.'

'You English guys. So smooth. So...are you gonna get round here, then, you cute bastard, or do I have to come find you?'

* * *

It was important because Tom's enemies were all young.

Here he was, running a charity, while the newspapers were full of these dreadful success stories. Steve so-and-so, director of Markon Holdings Ltd, about to retire at the age of forty-three with a personal fortune of $20 million. (What exactly were 'holdings', anyway?) Or Simon what's-his-name, dot-com entrepreneur who had ridden the big crash, the country's richest and most eligible bachelor at thirty-five. Business directors, film directors, guitar heroes: there they all were, doing what made them happy and made them rich, women at their beck and call (probably), and all from Tom's generation.

He used to laugh when his mum referred to 'that young woman in the Post Office', as Mrs Maples, the sub-postmistress in their village, was a forty-year-old mother of two. These days, it wasn't funny any more. Forty *was* young. It had to be. But yes, policemen really were getting younger, and so were doctors. Last time he'd had a twinge in his knee, he'd scarcely believed that the brisk girl with the nose-stud who'd examined him was fully qualified.

How had that happened? People ten, even fifteen years behind him were suddenly doing proper, glamorous or exciting jobs. That was a big culture shock. The cool new acts on the cover of the NME were all in their early twenties, and those were the ones who already had a couple of albums out. Tom only knew one person in the music business – a bloke from Shelter who was in a Queen tribute band called The Champions. He was their John Deacon.

Sometimes, late at night, he'd lie awake working out how long it would take him to do something really high-profile and sensible – like, say, get into Parliament. He had an old friend from university days who'd just become leader of a city council. Richard had started in their first year at college: going to Labour Party meetings, treading the streets, fighting for every vote and bouncing back each time they lost. To become an MP, Tom thought, you had to count on years of slogging, leafletting, ridiculous highway committees, gnawing your lip in frustration and hoping that the incumbent Member would drop down dead from a heart attack or be caught in bed with a rent boy. And then, you only got a winnable seat to fight if you said all the right things to the right people.

He'd recently tried to discuss this with Ella.

'Do you realise that, on that basis,' Tom said, 'I couldn't expect to be MP for Cherford North before I'm about...fifty-two? Not much of a career to look forward to, is it?'

'Tony Blair was Prime Minister at forty-three,' Ella pointed out.

'Yes, thank you, darling. I am aware of that.'

Ben looked up from his cereal. 'Michael Owen captained England at twenty-three,' he put in helpfully. 'I've got ten years to beat that.'

'Anyway,' Ella said, 'to be an MP you need political conviction.'

Tom was affronted. 'I vote Labour. I always have done.'

'That's not quite what I meant, love. You need vision. You need to *believe*, not just put a cross in the box beside whoever's the "least odious of the tossers on offer", as you put it.'

'Thanks,' said Tom, aggrieved and hiding behind his paper.

'Oh, come on, you don't even *know* anything about the Government. Who's the Minister of Defence?'

'Oh...him. That bald bloke.'

'Hmmm. Name me *five* key differences between Government and Opposition policy.'

'I don't think there are many now, are there? Look, you're just getting technical to catch me out. It's not fair.'

'Asylum seekers,' said Ben.

'Good one, thank you, Ben.' Ella grinned at her son. 'I wonder if Dad has any offers?'

Tom frowned. 'Well, there's unemployment and all that.'

'Unemployment and all that. Right. So one party wants unemployment and the other doesn't? Is that what you're saying?' Ella's eyes were mocking as she buttered her toast.

'It's all about how much state control you want in your life,' said Ben. 'We've done it in Citizenship.'

That was it, then. Humiliation at the hands of his family just served to clinch it. He was never going to be Prime Minister, or even MP for Cherford North, or even head of the city council. He would never play the guitar on MTV, score a goal at Wembley or write a blockbuster movie script. These things just didn't happen to minor charity managers from Middle England.

Shagging a gorgeous woman, on the other hand, was a goal he now didn't feel was totally beyond him.

Matt knew Ella was nervous.

'Well, on a normal Sunday, Kelly,' Ella was saying to the girl who had asked the last question, 'we average about a thousand visitors. But on a bank holiday, for example, we can expect to double that. They're our busiest time.'

He tried not to smirk as he leant against the back wall of

the classroom and watched her there at the front – tanned skin, black-stockinged legs crossed (mmm, hell-*o*), fixed smile on her face. Yes, exuded confidence, but Matt was used to people who did that. He could always spot someone who was quaking inside.

He didn't know what she was afraid of. She was doing brilliantly – answering their questions, laughing with them, being informative and not patronising. He'd primed them, of course, and this was a top GCSE set, but she had still taken some persuasion.

'Well, yes, there *is* a rumour that it's haunted. I think every stately home in the country has a ghostly legend attached to it. Let's face it, most old buildings do. Even your school's probably got an alleged ghost of some sort hanging round.'

'Yeah, Mr McGuire,' said Stacey Shaw, and everyone laughed.

'Er, well, I wouldn't know about that. But yes, there have been sightings of a figure known as the Grey Lady of Cherford. There are some old steps in the Chapel – do you remember? – which don't actually lead anywhere. The bell-tower was sealed off in the 1920s when it crumbled and became unsafe. But a couple of people – cleaners, working late at night, or staff coming in first thing in the morning – have seen the Grey Lady hovering at the entrance to this staircase, and when they called out to her she turned, pulling her grey cloak tightly around her face. And when they ran up the stairs after her, she'd always completely disappeared.'

A hush had fallen over the classroom. One or two of the girls were giggling uncertainly, but she had the wide-eyed attention of most of them, Matt realised.

'Is that true, miss?' Bradley Thomas asked. 'Or is it just, like, made up for the tourists?' Several people groaned, and someone threw a ball of paper at Bradley. 'Well, it's good for bringing the punters in, innit?' he argued, spreading his hands.

'Good point, good point!' Ella laughed. 'But think about this – even those who've seen the Grey Lady have never seen her face clearly. She always hides it in the hood of her cloak. The rumour is that she's hideously ugly – deformed, maybe from the Plague. The Black Death... When was the big outbreak of the Black Death in this country?'

They looked at each other uncertainly. A few shrugs.

'Eighteen-summink?' someone ventured.

Shit, Matt thought, and covered his eyes. Oh, well, they're only human.

'No, no, earlier than that. Seventeenth century,' said Ella. 'Although there were instances well before that. It wiped out huge swathes of the population, didn't it, Mr Ryder?'

He nodded, tapped his nose. 'In their defence,' he said, 'they're doing a Modern History course. Ask them about the causes of the Second World War and you can't shut them up. Has anyone got another question for Ms Barclay?'

Yes, Matt thought, it was going well. He wished he could hold their attention with just questions, answers and anecdotes for fifty minutes. And she'd seemed pleased by the questions, too: about why some parts of the Castle were older than others, the renovation work, the depth of the Moat and the meanings of the different flags flown on the Keep. She seemed amazed, he thought, that she should be speaking and they should be listening to her. He wondered if she'd expected a room full of baying, spitting animals.

Just before the bell, he called them to order, expressed sincere thanks to Ms Barclay for coming all this way to talk about Cherford Castle and got them all to give her a round of applause. One or two of the brasher boys even clapped above their heads, whooping in a manner he'd thought they reserved for their football teams.

He glanced at Ella, and grinned. She was blushing.

'That wasn't too bad, was it?' he said out in the corridor, as he led her through the lunchhour crowds.

'I quite enjoyed it,' she admitted, and smiled without opening her mouth.

They passed Jo Tarrant at the noticeboard, where she was pinning up some team sheets. 'Coming for lunch?' Matt asked.

'Bit later,' she said, and smiled uncertainly from him to Ella and back again.

Matt introduced them, and enjoyed the slightly stiff handshake the two women gave one another. Prowling cautiously round each other, he thought. He had a sudden mental flash-frame of them having a snarling, spitting cat-fight, slashing at each other with red fingernails and white teeth, rolling on the floor... He had to swallow hard and close his eyes.

'You've been talking to his lot, then?' Jo asked.

'Yes,' she admitted with a grin. 'They learnt quite a bit, I think, didn't they, Matt?... Matt? Are you OK?'

'What? Oh, yeah, fine. Just came over a bit...dizzy for a second.' He cleared his throat. 'It's these lights,' he explained feebly. 'Awful...'

'They seemed like a *nice* class,' said Ella.

As soon as he heard the way she said it, Matt wondered about the inflexion. Jojo's going to bridle, he thought. And he was right.

'You sound surprised,' said Jo, frowning.

'Well, no – I mean...' Ella smiled awkwardly. 'What I mean is, you don't know...until you come...'

'That's the problem with Parkfield,' Jo snapped. 'Everyone comes here with such bloody low expectations. Excuse me.' And she hurried past them, not looking back.

'Don't mind her,' Matt said, embarrassed on Ella's behalf. 'She's just, um, stressed? We're all stressed. Everyone's, like, working a full timetable at the moment?'

'No, don't worry. She's right.' They continued walking down the corridor, and Matt held the door open for her as they reached the exit to the car park. 'So you're short-staffed?' Ella asked.

'Bloody hell, like, just a bit?'

'I thought teachers found places like Parkfield a challenge.'

Not that old chestnut, he thought. 'Don't you believe it. For everyone who thinks like that, there are half a dozen who think, I'm not applying to that shit-hole, I'll be eaten alive.'

Ella smiled. 'And what about you, Matt? Why do you do this job? What makes you get out of bed in the morning?'

'Breakfast radio, usually. It's so bad I have to get up.'

'I was asking a serious question.'

I know you were, he thought. I was trying to avoid answering it. He shrugged, grinned. 'Always something new. A different problem every day, a chance to make things better for kids who don't have individual music lessons or school skiing holidays or ballet or—'

She held up a hand. 'Yes, Matthew, spare me the class-war rhetoric. I'm talking about *you*.'

'I know. Well, every day when I get into the car park and lift my briefcase out and look up at the building, I just remind myself of what I thought when I first saw the advert.'

'Which was?'

'I'm not applying to that shit-hole, I'll be eaten alive.'

She laughed. It was a genuine, joyous, silver sound, and he couldn't remember when he had last heard a woman laugh like that. 'You're funny, Matt.'

'Yeah, well, only when I'm trying not to be, it seems. What I mean is – you soon learn? You learn to distrust hearsay, put aside your, like, prejudices? You learn to walk through a place like this with your eyes and ears open. Right?'

She shrugged, nodded pensively. 'Sure.'

'It's been great meeting you again.'

'And you.'

'We should, umm...'

He didn't know what he'd been going to say, and now he'd done the worst thing possible by leaving it unfinished. *We should, umm.* You prat, Matthew, he told himself, wincing inwardly. Of course we should *umm*. Gosh, why don't we push the boat out and *er* while we're at it? I mean, there's nothing like a bit of *umm*-ing for giving you a taste for a bit of *err*-ing.

'Yes, maybe.'

She offered her hand.

Her grip was cool, light, firm but not overwhelming. He fancied that she let it linger for a little longer than was necessary for professional courtesy. Then they nodded and smiled their goodbyes. As he turned and went back inside the building, he glanced over his shoulder across the car park, just in time to see her doing the same, and pretending not to.

It took him the rest of the afternoon to lose the stupid, adolescent grin from his face.

Tom and Phill pulled apart, breathing hard, staring excitedly at one another in the dimness of Phill's office.

'You definitely wanna do this?' Phill whispered.

'Of course.'

'OK. It's fine for me, but I know it's kinda more...complicated for you.'

'It's not complicated.'

'OK, then.' Phill shrugged, grinned. 'Look, it would be difficult here. Do you, um, know a hotel?'

'A hotel?' Tom was taken aback for a second.

'Yes, honey. You have them in this country?... There is my flat, obviously, but it's out in Hawley. I think we need somewhere a little nearer.'

Yes, he knew lots of hotels. Cherford, like any tourist-trap, had dozens. The city centre was thronged with the timbered and haunted kind, the ringroad was flanked with the chunky, glass-and-concrete variety, while the nearby villages sported inns and B&Bs galore. He couldn't imagine making love to Phill in any of them. Now he came to think of it, he realised he hadn't planned exactly where they were going to go when they reached this stage. Offices, Tom thought ruefully, should have little en suite bedrooms for these moments. Maybe some of them did, but not in the circles he moved in. He really hadn't thought this through at all.

'What sort did you have in mind?' he asked.

She shrugged, grinned as she caressed his chest. 'Hey, you know. Somewhere anonymous, somewhere that does day rates.'

'Day rates?'

'Jeez, Tom, you really are new to this, aren't you?'

'Um, yes, actually. That I happily admit. Phill, what the hell are *day rates*?'

'Honey, it's what you ask for in a hotel when – with discretion and charm and understatement and all that other shit that you English are, y'know, meant to be good at – you let the staff know that you're hiring a room for, say, two hours? For the, uh, purposes of a pleasurable encounter.' Phill frowned, put her hands on her hips and her head on one side. 'Do they teach you guys *anything* in this country, or is it all just rugger-buggery in the showers?'

The English slang sounded oddly cute in her accent, Tom thought. Something flashed through his mind – the Harrington. The large, new hotel he passed on the way out to the motorway. It looked crisp, austere, anonymous.

'OK,' he said. 'I think I know somewhere.'

And so there was a short drive, followed by an uneasy encounter at reception, during which he didn't even meet the eye of the smartly dressed woman who handed him a key-card.

And in the white room, Tom moved forward, caressing the curves contained within Phill's dress, feeling the smoothness of her buttocks, then up to her back as she collided with the bureau. He was pressing her firmly against the edge, now, and he heard something slide to the floor. He buried his face deep in her soft red hair.

She shuddered with delight as he pushed the almost frictionless cotton up her thighs, ruching it, bunching it.

'Yes, yes... Like this...' Phill steered his hand to the moist triangle of silk he found beneath, and together they removed it; he didn't even see it. 'That's good,' she murmured.

Almost on autopilot, he steered his finger into her, applied the usual dexterity, inhaled her pungent arousal. Phill squealed appreciatively. She plunged her tongue into his mouth again, pulled him down towards her as she unfastened his trousers. He realised she had one foot on the floor, the other in the air. He felt her sex nuzzle his aching cock; she was gorgeously and deliciously soaking.

'I – I haven't brought...we didn't...'

'I'm popping the little white pills, honey, OK?'

On the bed, they were angled superbly, and he entered her with ease, enjoying the languid growl she gave. He could see her hair fanned out, strangely bright in the dimness, and now his hands cupped her breasts as he moved inside her. He brushed her nipples with his thumb, and then, when the time was right, tweaked them hard, in tandem with a firm, angry thrust. She growled, swore fervently, licked his tongue as it came down to meet hers. She pulled his ear close to her mouth and whispered: hot, eager, dirty, all the right words.

He rammed into her again and again, loving her receptive tightness, spurred on by her hands inside his shirt, on his back. He felt invigorated, enormous, as if powered by some engine within him; he felt as if he could go on for ever.

Intuitively, he knew from her shudders and her squeals that he could finish, and he buried himself so deep in her that her head was pressed up against the wall. He gushed inside her, growling, then, with a sudden ache of guilt, pulled savagely out of her. She righted herself with skill, cupping a hand between her legs with a giggle.

In the surreal aftermath, the room seemed to shimmer and sway. Exhausted, semi-clothed, they made no attempt to rearrange themselves; complicity decreed no need.

Phill rested her head on his chest and he stroked her hair.

'Are you OK?' she asked, after what could have been ten or even twenty minutes.

He was surprised by the question. 'I'm fine. Are you?'

'Yeah. You just seemed deep in thought.' They turned to face each other, their voices croaky with intimacy.

'Just drained,' he said, with a wicked smile, and turned to nibble her ear. She giggled and tried to retreat under the duvet, but he intercepted her with a hand.

'You're sure that's all?' she murmured.

He shrugged. 'Work hassles,' he said. 'You know charities. Always on the edge.'

'Hmmmm. You can't complain, though, can you? You do OK. Hell,' she said with a grin, 'I only wish I could afford to live in Ashington.'

So do I, he thought.

'Hey, shall I make a cup of tea?' she asked. Tousled and naked, she smiled at him as the water whooshed from the tap. 'It's a rhetorical question, right?' she said. 'English guys always want a cup of tea after sex.'

She's probably right, he thought. The Men's Group would have made something terribly meaningful out of that.

* * *

'What,' says the earnest young man with the red hair and goatee beard, 'can women *teach* us as men? How far do we have to go in our process of re-evaluation, to gain some understanding of the crisis of masculinity from a...feminine viewpoint?'

It's only Tom's third week at the Group, and he is already thinking it's a very bad idea. The fresh camomile tea (with organic shortbread) is pleasant, but it makes him want to go to the toilet after about half an hour. The bare room with its fifteen chairs in a semi-circle just makes him cringe. Why the hell did he decide – *volunteer* – to come to this?

Ella just thinks it's funny. She says she can't imagine meeting a bunch of other women to talk about getting in touch with themselves. She says if she wants to talk about women's issues she gives Bex a call and has a bitching session.

Mark, the red-haired facilitator, is cradling an invisible globe of air in his hands, looking round at each of them in turn. 'Let's start with a bit of a brainstorm!' he says excitedly, and leaps to his feet. With a smart *pop*, he uncaps a marker pen. (Tom, who's sitting nearest to the board, inhales the scent of pear-drops.)

'Actually, Mark,' says Timothy, the bespectacled man next to Tom, 'I think we have to be careful about using that term. It's seen as possibly offensive, to, um, people who've had mental health problems.'

'Mental health *issues*, I feel,' says a pony-tailed man opposite.

'Sure, yeah.' Timothy holds up his hands in acknowledgement. 'Thanks, Nik, I stand corrected. Mental health *issues*.'

Tom looks around. Several people are nodding vigorously, so he decides to join in.

'Sure, sure,' says Facilitator Mark, tapping the pen on his knuckles. 'Um, what, uh, can we have as an alternative? Anyone?'

'I believe the correct suggestion is "think-tank"?' ventures Timothy.

'Yeah, yeah, that's good.' Mark grins broadly. 'Let's have a think-tank, then.'

'Isn't that offensive,' Tom says, 'to people who have swimming issues?' Nobody laughs. 'Sorry, just being facetious,' he mutters.

'Yes,' says Mark with a wan smile. 'Thank you, Tom. Your humour is an important part of these sessions.'

Tom leans back and closes his eyes. It's only five minutes into the session and he is already losing the will to live. Buzzwords, jargon, hot-sounding phrases are tossed across the room and Mark scribbles them all with excited fervour on the flip chart. *Empowerment. Equity. Respect. Tolerance. The Conflict Zone. Emotional Terrorism. Self-actualisation. Maslow's Hierarchy Of Needs.* In one or two places, he marks words with asterisks and links them to other words with wiggly lines or dotted lines. Tom doesn't know what the difference is between a wiggly line and a dotted line, but he imagines it is of huge importance to Mark.

Mark stands back from the flip chart, stroking his beard thoughtfully. 'That's a really, really good overview,' he says, nodding with enthusiasm. 'Some great issues flagged up there... I'm gonna come back to all your ideas in a moment. First, though, I'd like to introduce another element into the equation. I'd like us all to do a little exercise and think about it in the context of all these ideas – all these *think-tank* ideas.' He nods in acknowledgement at Timothy, who smiles smugly.

Mark starts peeling pieces of A4 paper off a pad and passing them round with coloured crayons. 'What I'd like us to do,' says Mark, 'is a little drawing exercise. Now, hey!' He suddenly throws his hands up as if deflecting a glancing blow. 'Some of you may be thinking, gosh, I can't draw! Well, don't worry, because, hello, you're looking at a man who failed his Art O Level, guys. It isn't about how well you can draw, it's about...*envisaging*. I want you to think holistically, think in symbols.'

'Is there any significance to the colours we've been given?' Tom asks, waggling his red crayon.

'Ahhh! Gooood question, Tom. Well, you chose that colour, so is there any significance for *you* in the fact that you took that particular one out of the box?'

Tom frowns. 'It was on top,' he says.

'Aha, on *top*. Well, that's an issue for you to explore, Tom.'

'Thanks, Mark,' says Tom. He decides that's the safest response.

'It's a pleasure, Tom.'

Mark explains that they are each going to draw a representation of 'where they are at' as a man. He reassures them that it can be a picture, a diagram, a symbol, maybe even a combination of all three. He'd like them to try and include some of the key elements and relationships in their lives. Then, after ten minutes, they will talk about what they have produced.

They work in near silence.

Tom sighs. 'Can't believe it's come to this,' he jokes to Timothy. 'No sharp objects allowed.' He waggles his crayon, mimes cutting his throat with it.

'Actually, that is a serious point,' says Timothy, blinking at Tom from behind his glasses. 'Suicide rates among young men are higher than in any other group.'

'Right,' says Tom. You're a bundle of laughs, he thinks. 'I was just making another joke,' he says with a shrug. 'Bit of a lame one, I know.' He takes a gulp of camomile tea to cover his unease, and is aware that his bladder has started pressing early tonight.

After the allotted time, Mark asks them all to hold up their drawings. Tom tries to speak, but doesn't get there in time.

'Now,' Mark says, 'this is where we make our exercise just a little bit challenging, perhaps, dare I say it – a little bit *dangerous*.'

Oh, good, Tom thinks, we're going to set fire to them.

'I'd like you to swap your drawing with your neighbour, and I'm going to ask each of you to interpret – sensitively, of course, guys – what you feel your neighbour's drawing means.'

Dutifully, the men swap pictures.

Mark nods, beaming like an evangelist. 'OK, OK,' he says. 'Tom, can I start with you? What do you read from Timothy's drawing there?'

Bollocks, thinks Tom. Better try and do this seriously.

'Um, well,' he begins, 'Tim has drawn himself as a matchstick man in green crayon, as you can see, and he appears to be being hit by a bolt of lightning. Um… I feel he is trying to represent himself with the traditional, universally recognised symbol of "man", seen on everything from cave walls to modern toilet doors...but with this very simplicity he is almost *undermining* the concept, challenging us to re-contextualise it.'

This psychobabble is so piss-easy, Tom's thinking. Look at the buggers, all nodding as if I am actually talking sense. I'm on a roll now.

'I think what Tim is showing us here is himself as Modern Man, beset by the storms of daily battles and internal strife. The fact that he's given himself this...fairly neutral graphical representation is indicative of his uncertainty about Modern Man's role... I think that represents all of our concerns and insecurities, in a way.'

Tom raises his eyebrows at Timothy, who is open-mouthed with admiration.

'Would that be a fair reading, Tim?' asks Mark.

Timothy seems lost for words. 'Well, yeah,' he says eventually. 'That's just amazing, actually. I mean, I wasn't, perhaps, thinking consciously of all those elements. But Tom has really got to the heart of what I was trying to say, and said it far better than I could have myself. Tom, may I shake your hand?'

He does so. Tom is muted. He knows the rules of the Group – a thank you is routine, but a handshake is reserved for a profound, outstanding contribution.

'Um,' says Tom. Just in time, he recovers to remember the correct response. 'Certainly, Tim, you may.'

'Now, then,' says Mark. 'Timothy, perhaps you have a few words to say about Tom's self-portrait?'

'Well, I'll try,' says Timothy, 'but it seems challenging.'

'We wouldn't be here if we didn't want to be challenged, Timothy. I'm sure we'll all appreciate your best shot. Remember, this a Safe Place.'

'Right, right.' Timothy holds up Tom's paper, which is totally blank. 'Um, Tom,' he gestures towards Tom in the correct way, 'has depicted himself as the blank canvas, the *tabula rasa*, if you like. I feel that this shows he is uncertain of where his potential lies, and which of his many talents he should be putting to good use. Tom is...giving himself to the world, saying, "here I am, world, *draw me*." And I think that is incredibly honest of him, and incredibly brave.'

Mark has been nodding in agreement. 'Would that...be fair, Tom?' he asks, stroking his beard.

'Um,' says Tom. 'If you like. Yes.'

He decides not to elaborate further. It might undermine Timothy – who seems pretty pleased with his analysis – to say that his page is blank because he was still trying to think what to draw when Mark called time. And that, somehow, wouldn't seem fair.

He smiled at the memory as he let his fingers caress Phill's taut, smooth back. The hotel kettle powered up in the background, taking an age as they always did.

He thought about her words – *English guys always want a cup of tea after sex* – and felt a twinge of jealousy.

'So how many English blokes have you slept with?' he asked, realising that he didn't even know how long she had been in the country.

Phill slid off the bed with a languid smile, giving him a good long look at her body as she pulled a towel around her.

'Enough to know you all like tea,' she said, and went to fill the kettle.

'That's not an answer.'

'Oh, Tom. Do you really want a number? Four, five? Does giving a Scottish guy a blow job count as a half? Look, it's not like I'd just *shag* anyone who didn't have two heads.' She grinned, acknowledging her ironic use of the slang again. 'I am pretty fucking choosy, you know.'

'What's in this for you, Phill? I'm a married man.'

'Jeez, you don't hold back on the big questions, do you?' She laughed as the kettle rumbled in the background. 'Look, as long as you wanna have fun, I wanna have fun. I'm not seriously expecting that you'll ever leave your wife. I mean, hell, I know the routine.'

Tom gave her what he hoped was a reassuring smile, and wondered if he knew the routine himself. Probably not, he thought. But he had just had sex and was about to have a cup of tea, and so there was very little point in complaining about the state of affairs. Or even the state of this affair in particular.

'So,' Phill said with a sly grin, 'any special requests?'

'Yeah,' he said. 'Milk, no sugar.'

Ella, in the course of her job, had met several MPs, innumerable chief executives, three minor royals, David Attenborough, a handful of footballers, a former US President, Bono and The Edge, a Booker Prize winner and two Archbishops. They had mostly been present at official tours or charity dinners, and she had charmed them all without so much as a quiver in her Marc Jacobs boots. But – she remembered now, back in her office – she had never felt so nervous as she had today, facing a peeling orange door in a grey corridor, standing beside a quietly smiling Matt Ryder.

She remembered the conversation before he had shown her in.

'I look too...*posh*. They'll make fun of me.'

'You are posh. Don't try to be something you're not.'

'Thanks a bunch. I grew up in a three-bed terrace, if you must know.'

'Oh, bully for you. Was it a council house?'

'No. They owned it.'

'Uh-huh, and did your dad have a car?'

'Of course he did. He needed it for work.'

'Understand this, yeah?' said Matt with a grin. 'Round here, love, if your parents owned their own house and had a car, that makes you posh.'

'Let's not argue the matter,' she said, scowling, adjusting her hair and flexing her arms. 'And don't call me *love*.'

He grinned again. 'Sorry. No offence.'

'None taken. Go on, then.'

She was smiling, now, thinking about it. And about the way he had looked back at her as she left, thinking perhaps that she hadn't seen. Because she had been looking over her shoulder at him, too.

Oh, for Christ's sake, Ella, get a *grip*, she told herself. This boy is over a decade younger than you, and probably has a harem of pneumatic nineteen-year-olds lining up to shag him senseless. He may have been flirting with you, but he probably flirts with *everyone*.

Hang on, she thought – no, maybe not.

I'm thinking about this from a female angle. Too much

projection. Men don't, in general, flirt for anything more than the obvious. Women they don't find sexually attractive might as well be invisible, so if they flirt with you, their intentions are plain: everything means *I'd eventually like to go to bed with you.*

The phone interrupted her thoughts.

'Yes, hello?... No... No, no, it's the other way round, for goodness' sake. Don't you remember? We *talked* about this... Jay, we have talked about this *twice* before.'

A frustrating conversation, after which she slammed the phone down on yet another useless employee. Did they just not *listen*, she thought exasperatedly, or was it just that everyone else in the world needed to be told things three times? She had told the chief steward last week that Elkie Brooks was now closing the Saturday open-air concert and Chris De Burgh was doing Sunday, rather than the other way round, and also that Joanna MacGregor was doing a longer slot – hadn't she? The chief steward had talked about it all as if it had been news to him, and he had adopted a slightly aggrieved tone with her.

She sighed, leant back in her chair and allowed her eyes to wander across the lake, watching the Hordes with her usual dispassion.

What was good for her in life? Her socialising didn't give her that buzz, didn't make her feel alive. She danced and drank while her friends got off with people, and then if anyone showed an interest, she played the marriage card, made her excuses and left. Her children were lovely, but there had been some connection missing, recently; little phrases and references which Tom understood better than her, simply because he spent longer in their company.

So, that meant her job had to be pretty damn fulfilling – right? Wrong, she told herself. This job was prestigious, well-paid, stress-inducing and *meaningless*.

People didn't come here because they were interested in Heritage. They came for a *fun day out*. They came to bring Gran in her wheelchair, to let the kids scare the ducks, to buy them all T-shirts, mugs and ice creams and laugh at each other getting lost in the maze. The mindless bastards. Most of them didn't have a clue who had owned the Castle, or what had happened here over the centuries. They couldn't have told you what its key role was in the English Civil War or what the purpose of Henry VIII's visit had been. On the other hand, they all asked about the episode of *Bad Boy Billy* with that roguish soap actor – what was he called, Terry something? – which had been filmed here last summer, and they all asked about the tickets for Elkie Brooks and Chris De Burgh. And every week someone, usually a man with an earring, made the same fucking tedious old joke about Henry and his wives and having them all in the big bed at once before chopping their bleeding heads off. Hur hur hur.

It was depressing.

And maybe, she realised, with a slow, inward glow – maybe it didn't have to be like this any more.

CHAPTER TEN

Countdown

'You know what terrifies me, Jeff?'

'Several possibilities spring to mind, mate. I mean, basically, you're a big girl's blouse. You're scared shitless of small spiders, odd noises and friendly dogs.'

'Be serious, Jeff.'

'Oh, OK, it's that kind of conversation. Fair enough. Let me guess...the thought that your illicit little shag might come out?'

'No... Well, yes, but it's not that.'

'Errrm...that your best days are behind you? That the colostomy bag and hearing aid are just around the corner?'

'That's closer. Yeah.'

For a change, they weren't in the Rowan. This was lunchtime, a quick pint in a pine-and-chrome tapas bar near the city centre.

On his way there, Tom had strolled down Canterfield Street, a bohemian boulevard packed with wine bars and delis, a golden mile for the ciabatta classes. It was a therapy precinct, a soft landing for those still shell-shocked by their company's decision to relocate north.

The street was always dotted with eager clipboarders and leafletters. Tom was used to smiling as he took a club flyer from an attractive girl, or nodding affably as he accepted a two-drinks-for-one voucher from a young man with a pierced eyebrow. But today, he had consciously noticed something for the first time. The young things in their stretchy tops, handing out their lurid passports to hedonism, now *looked right through him.* He'd reached the bar unencumbered by glossy paper. He went back, just to be sure. He slowed down, hovered by them, zigzagged to take his trajectory close to theirs. They broke eye contact; they changed direction, looking for someone else.

Almost overnight, without realising it, he'd slipped out of the demographic. The message was clear. He was no longer in the box marked 'Mad For Hardcore Clubbing' – he was in the one which said 'Pub Lunches And Soft Rock Compilations'.

'I'm thirty-seven,' said Tom, shaking his head. 'Thirty-bloody-seven. I'll be forty before I even know it.'

'Oh, you'll know it,' said Jeff with a grin. 'Don't you worry.'

'It's going to be terrible. I always really pitied people who dreaded being forty. I felt like saying, *look, it's your age, get over it.* Then when it's you, when it's actually looming, you just think it's far too soon.' Tom shook his head and took a rueful sip of his pint.

'Have you been reading those bloody "Things you should have done" articles again? They're shit, just ignore them.'

'I know. There was one last week where the first thing on the list was "have sex with two women". I thought, great, I can tick that one off. Then I realised it meant *at the same time.*'

Jeff grinned. 'Mid-life crises, they're so easy to map. Get 'em over early, that's what I say. I had mine at twenty-eight.'

'It just...crept up on me, you know?' Tom began.

'Yeah, yeah,' said Jeff, sighing. 'When you got to thirty, it felt as if everybody had a secret game plan except you.'

'Sorry, mate, have I told you this before?'

'Well, kind of. But usually after a few pints, so it's good to hear it with a bit of clarity.' Jeff settled back with his beer. 'Go on.'

'Well, it bears repeating... So we got married young. There was I, thinking I'd done great. After Mum died, and when Dad went off to his new life, it was like I'd reinvented myself. I had a wife, we had a house. It was brilliant. And then, slowly, it was like everyone turned their cards over and showed their hands, and I was there going: *What*? I thought I was playing Happy Families. All the time, everybody else had proper cards and was laughing at me as they raked the money in, because they'd been playing Canasta.'

Jeff nodded. Tom appreciated that with Jeff – he always knew when that was his job, just to listen and not offer an opinion yet.

'I'll never forget the time,' Tom went on, 'when it dawned on me that most of my college friends had jobs where they either had "senior" in the title, or they had staff to boss around, or both. I mean, for fuck's sake, you don't expect someone of thirty-three to be a Senior Accounts Manager. You expect a Senior Accounts Manager to look like your dad.'

He took a ruminative sip of his pint. Two girls were settling at the next table, and his gaze followed them automatically. The curvier of the two was black, with cropped hair and gleaming teeth, her skin burnished and lustrous, her bottom taut beneath a black satin skirt. Her more lissom friend had striplight-blonde hair to her waist and wore a white, clinging shift-dress with matching strappy heels.

Now that's good, Tom thought. Some women make the effort and some don't. It isn't rocket science.

'You've done all right, though, now,' Jeff was saying.

'Mmm, what?'

'Eyes right, mate. You don't stand a chance. I was saying you've done all right. You've got responsibility, staff under you.'

'College leavers, marking time till they can get a proper job. Trust me, Jeff, I talk it up. It's Ella who's got the proper grown-up *career* in our house.'

Jeff laughed. 'What a woman, your Ella. I keep telling you, you're on to a good thing.'

'She always seems to have known what she's *doing* with her life.'

Jeff rubbed his nose. 'I dunno. I had this weird conversation with your missus once, you know. I think it was…yeah, it was your house-warming when you moved into Ashington. She was going on about how guilty she felt, being there, like it was someone else's life and she didn't belong. Bit weird, I thought. Think she was a few sheets to the wind. I tried to joke her out of it.' Jeff shrugged, avoided Tom's eye for a moment. 'And it was just after…well, what happened. You know.'

What happened. It was as good a euphemism as any. Tom moved on, rescued Jeff.

'Ella says these things from time to time,' he said. 'She doesn't mean it. She's always been in control... There was the teaching first, and granted, she left that, but when she went into tourism, she never looked back. We decided between us – she was more ambitious, so her career came first. In turn, I got to do the school run and be Superdad. That's how it worked in theory, anyway.'

The world was full of Superdads, so keen to wear their credentials on their sleeves that it hurt. *Yeah, I bath Theo and Oliver every night, and I get up and give them their breakfast before work. And I usually cook three or four nights a week. Proper cooking, I mean. Then on Sundays I take them to the park for a kick-about while Lydia has a lie-in, bless her.*

'They've always loved Ella, her work people,' said Jeff.

'They have. And she had a *path*. Assistant in Library Heritage, then Coordinator at the City Tourist Office at thirty. And then she got made Visitor Manager at Cherford Castle four years later... God knows where she gets all her energy from.'

'Maybe she lives off stress. Some people do.'

'Ella never suffers from stress,' said Tom moodily. 'She's just a carrier.'

'Oh, very good. Been saving that one up, have you?'

'Seriously, she loves the high-powered stuff. She ought to have been in business in the Eighties. She could be a bloody Chief Exec before she hits the menopause.'

Ella was working, Tom remembered, the very first time he had set eyes on her – working on an essay in the incongruous surroundings of the college bar. Leaning on one hand, rich black hair falling over her eyes. He'd put a song on the jukebox. He couldn't forget that evening, really, because it was the night when—

'Sorry, what?' He realised Jeff was saying something to him.

'I said, does it matter? If she wants to be a fucking workaholic, let her. You sit back and spend more time with the kids. I mean, if that's what makes her happy...'

'That's the thing,' said Tom, and he took a long, deep gulp of his pint before putting it down on the table with a hefty thump. 'I'm not sure she *is* happy. Not sure at all.'

Jeff nodded, shrugged. 'Up to you to find that out, mate,' he said. 'So what about this Phill bird? Where does she fit into it all for you? Just one more box to tick before you finally sign up for Saga?'

'Jeff... Look, promise not to take the piss when I tell you this.'

'Me, take the piss? I never have... Well, all right, except when you actually *bought* Charlotte Church's techno record.' He shrugged. 'OK, OK. I'll be serious. Scout's honour.' Jeff held three fingers to his head. He looked like a man miming Russian roulette with a triple-barrelled pistol.

'Well,' Tom said, sighing, 'unless you count a drunken fumble with Anita Barrington after the sixth-form disco – when, technically, I didn't actually, um, manage anything – then I've been making love to the same woman all my life. Ella's been the only one. Up until now.'

'Pasta,' said Jeff, nodding, tapping his nose. 'I remember.'

'So you can't really blame me for...you know...wondering. How it, um, compares.'

Jeff gave a wry smile. 'And the spicy version is...not that much different?'

'It's too soon to say, really,' Tom admitted, and got to his feet. 'Won't be a minute.'

In the Gents, he washed his hands with unnecessary force, then glowered at himself in the mirror, squinting at first one side of his face, then the other, looking for new wrinkles. 'Thirty-bloody-seven,' he muttered. 'Jesus.'

He looked around for a hand-drier, spotted the white box on the wall and put his hands under it. He waited, still with one eye on the mirror and turning his face this way and that.

The drier didn't seem to be working. Irritably, he thumped it. Nothing.

A man came out of one of the cubicles, gave his hands a peremptory rinse. Then he leant past Tom with a brief ''Scuse me, mate,' and pulled a paper towel from the dispenser under which Tom had been holding his wet palms for the last thirty seconds.

Good God, he thought. That clinches it. I'm having senior moments now.

Back in the bar, he drained his pint. 'Another?'

Jeff glanced at his watch. 'Shit. I'd love to say yes, mate, but I'd better be getting back before they think I've been abducted.'

'I understand. The world of washing-machine components falls apart without you.'

'Well, kind of. Anyway, what's with these lunchtime pints all of a sudden?' Jeff asked as he pulled his jacket on. 'You never used to have time to fart during the day, let alone get away from the place. Your homeless looking after themselves these days, are they?'

'Pretty much,' said Tom.

He didn't elaborate, and Jeff didn't ask any more. That was the good thing about friends. They knew when to stop asking questions.

Unlike wives.

'How's work?' Ella asked. Her hair was wrapped in a towel and she was rubbing her face with a blue pulp. Tom vaguely knew it was made of wheatgerm and sea kelp, or something equally unlikely.

'Oh, fine,' he said, pretending to sort out a stack of magazines beside the bed. 'You know.'

'They seem to be keeping you there a lot.'

'Yeah, well, homeless people don't stop being homeless when we leave the office, love. It kind of goes with the territory.' Moral high ground, he thought. Nice one.

'Did you get anywhere with that art project?' she asked suddenly, blinking behind her death-mask of gunk.

'Sorry?'

Tom was used, these days, to not getting what Ella was talking about. Sometimes, her words just skimmed past him like curling stones on frictionless ice.

'Well, weren't you going to get the A-level group to paint a mural, or something? At that dreadful gallery thing we had to go to. I thought we only had to endure that evening of frightful so-called *art* so you could hob-nob and get a bit of funding.'

'Um, yes...yes, actually, I will be working on that. Problem is,' Tom said, getting reckless, 'a lot of it might be, you know, out-of-hours support. So I'll be down there quite a bit for, um, a few weeks.'

'I don't know,' said Ella with a sigh, leaning in to her mirror. 'Fucking Phill what's-her-face.'

Tom went hot and cold, and suddenly wanted the bed to disappear through the floor, taking him with it. 'Sorry? What did you say?'

'Oh, I can't remember her bloody surname.' She waved a hand. 'That fucking *arty* woman. She's making you do all her work for her, she is. I mean, I know she's a good contact and all that, but, really, Tom, don't let people use you for free overtime.'

'Oh,' he said. 'I see.'

'You're too good to these people. Cut yourself some slack. I can't do it in my job, so one of us might as well.'

'I'll try,' he said, still feeling his heart settling back to its normal level. He started leafing through *Empire*, being exaggeratedly casual.

'Is it Jacobson?' Ella asked. She sounded as if she didn't really care.

'Er, um... Sorry?' His heart began to thump again.

'That woman at the art gallery.'

'Er, something like that.'

'No... Jacowitz?' Ella stared into space, narrowing her eyes. 'No... Hang on, don't tell me, I remember...Janowitz, that was it. She's quite nice, I suppose.'

'Er, yes,' said Tom. 'I suppose so, yes. If you like, you know...arty types.'

'She's all right. Just doing her job,' said Ella. 'Up her own arse a bit, though, isn't she?'

'A bit.'

'Oh, well, you meet all sorts of vegetarian weirdos in your

job. You don't have to like them, though, do you? Just work with them.'

'Well, yeah. I can be diplomatic.'

'Hmmm. I'm going to call Mum before I go to bed, OK?'

'OK.'

Ella, her skin fresh and taut, cradled the phone under her chin while washing the mugs. This was a pre-emptive strike – what she wanted was an early night, so she'd got her call in first.

'No, everything's fine, Mum. I just fancied a chat.'

'Oh, I see. I thought you might be ringing with some news or something.' Maggie MacBride's tone was, as usual, slightly accusing. Ella never rang for chats, and Maggie knew it.

'News?'

'Well, I sent you those brochures the other day. You must've had time to look at them.'

Brochures. What brochures? Ella's mind raced. What did she – oh, of course. Glossy adverts for new homes near where her mother lived. She'd ripped open the envelope while mopping up a cascade of Shreddies and milk, chiding Isobel and shouting to Ben to iron his own bloody shirt. Also in the envelope had been a photocopied article from the *Daily Mail* ascribing most of the country's ills to immigration and the pill, with various key phrases – similar to her mother's favourite expressions – highlighted in yellow. They'd all gone in the bin, sluiced with sodden Shreddies.

'Mother, we're not moving.' She slid the mugs into the cupboard with excessive force. 'We work in Cherford, our friends are here, the children go to school here.'

'Well, I don't know,' her mother was saying. 'There's some

folk as would be a little more grateful... I did ring earlier, but I got that answerphone thing-gy.'

Quickly skip on, Ella told herself, and with any luck we should avoid the guilt trip. 'So, how are things with you?'

'Oh, you know, much the same... Were you out somewhere nice, then?'

Ella hated this, and inside she was seething. Maggie MacBride would have been horrified at the idea of her daughter being slumped on the sofa, half an eye on *Midsomer Murders*, too tired (for which Maggie would read too lazy) to have picked up the phone.

'Can't remember. So, did you find that dress you were looking for at Debenhams?'

'I did, yes, but what a palaver. It was the right colour, but would you believe it, they didn't have my size... I suppose you were out with chums from work, maybe?'

Only in conversations with her mother did Ella have 'chums'.

'Maybe. It's not important, Mum... Perhaps you'll find the right size in another branch. It's terrible trying to find the right thing in shops, these days. I do shopping by catalogue. You should try it.'

Ella decided not to mention that her catalogues were actually designers' websites. Her mother found affluence rather vulgar.

'Well, catalogues might be more convenient. I suppose they have quite a wide range... So is that where you were, then?'

'Um, probably, I often am... Stuff usually arrives the day after you phone your order through. It's brilliant.' She crossed her fingers. The word was carefully chosen in the hope of ending the verbal tennis.

'*Brilliant*. Yes, they all say that on the telly, now, don't they?... Ella, I can't think why you want to make such a big secret out of things. I mean, I'd not have a problem saying where I'd been, if the hat was on the other foot.'

'Mother, it is not a big secret. I just think that I shouldn't have to account for my whereabouts every single time I don't answer the telephone.' She took a deep breath, lowered her voice an octave. 'So, um, this dress. What was the colour like?'

'Not quite right, either. Said burgundy, but it didn't look like any burgundy I've ever seen, I can tell you... I don't know, when I had a young family I never went out drinking. It just wasn't done.'

She always used the same phrase, turning every innocent visit to a pub or bar into something disreputable. *Going out drinking* painted a picture of tattooed men playing darts and sinking sugary gallons of Old Wifeslapper before rolling home, propelled by belches, to slump in front of some late-night football on Sky.

'Pubs are very different, now, Mum. They're not spit-and-sawdust places where blokes go to pick fights, like the *Lion* used to be.' The house where she grew up had been a hundred yards from the rowdy local – she remembered her dad slipping away there whenever he could. 'You can even take children to some of them.'

'Yes, and I don't hold with *that*, either. Goodness, children in pubs. You'll be telling me they do baby food and high chairs next.'

'Well, they do. You know they do. We used to go out for

family pub lunches all the time when Izzy was little.' It was astonishing, how her mother forgot things from one conversation to the next.

'Well, I suppose everything's different now,' Maggie went on, 'what with you being sent out to work and all that, so that they can go to that posh school. And you know your father would never have held with *that*. He was a proper Labour man. Nothing wrong with a good Secondary Modern, he'd have said. Well, I'm only taking an interest, love. I've said my piece. I know it's a voluble subject.'

Ella wondered, for a second, what her late father would have made of spin doctors and focus groups, and suppressed a shudder. She tried to rally. 'Mum, I'm not *sent* out—'

'You'd think after all these years he'd be supporting his family. Never mind, I suppose I'm not "with-it". I don't know about all these things. He's still doing that voluntary work, isn't he?'

Ella had to grit her teeth. There it was again. Her mother was like a computer which didn't save updates, meaning you always had to start from scratch.

'For the umpteenth time, Mum – Tom works in the voluntary *sector*. That's completely different. He helps to make things a lot better for people who have very tough lives.'

Eventually, she managed to finish the conversation. She was, as ever, polite but firm, leaving the question of their next 'popping down' reassuringly open-ended.

'Well, I don't know,' her mother said. Ella could hear the tightness of the lips. 'I sometimes like to know what I'm doing. Not be kept, what's-it...hanging in libido.'

* * *

She slipped into bed beside Tom, without saying a word. She wasn't sure if he was awake. He murmured to acknowledge her, although he didn't turn round. She lay on her back under the heavy quilt, hands behind her head, feeling her eyes sting in the darkness and her fingers aching as her head crushed them to numbness.

I am a mother, she thought, and I have made it my life's ambition not to be like mine. And what, in the process, have I become?

'When did you first get a real sense of the future?' she murmured.

Tom didn't answer.

'I know when it was for me,' she said. 'When we had Ben. It was suddenly, wow, there's more than just *us*. Things matter beyond just you and me. If – God forbid – we were ever to split up, it would have repercussions for ever, not just in our own little enclosed lives for a few months or whatever. Suddenly, we were responsible. What we bought, what we ate, where we lived and the jobs we did, it was all trickling down, all impacting on this strong, inquisitive little person.' She glanced over towards her husband. 'Tom?'

'Mmm-hmm. Yeah.'

'That was the defining decision. No going back after that. We love them both so much and yet, God, they shape your life, you feel so much is...*expected*.' She stopped, closed her aching eyes for a second or two. 'We were so young.' She exhaled deeply.

There was silence from the other side of the bed, but no deep breathing.

'And Izzy. We should have known more about what we were doing by then, but of course someone changed the rules.

Moved the bloody goalposts. So we had to get all those brand new books... God, do you remember searching the Internet to find a "My Toddler Won't Stop Whingeing" support group?... And that phase of almost *hating* any of our friends who didn't have children because they couldn't possibly know anything about life, couldn't have any worries? Or because they could go out on a Saturday and we couldn't?'

'Mmmhhgh.'

'I'm looking forward to seeing how many plums we get this year. It was a good idea, that, wasn't it? Planting it that same day. I still can't believe we both knew we were going to go into that garden centre. It was like telepathy.'

'Mrrrrrrgghh.'

'We're so lucky, Tom... It's weird, but I always remember that woman in the Carpenters' Arms. You remember? We were worried about the kids upsetting them, and it turned out they couldn't have children, so they just thought ours were heartbreakingly wonderful. I mean, hell, we ought to think like that more often. We're lucky. Bloody lucky. And some people...they just *aren't*.'

There was silence for a moment. Ella thought she could hear the babble of late-night radio from Ben's room. He always had it on low, under the covers, thinking nobody would hear. He liked to listen to the problem phone-ins. She imagined he was waiting to hear something about sex.

'I did something really special today, Tom. Really... I don't know, almost... I can't find the words. I had a glimpse of a different life.'

He didn't answer. She ploughed on, hopefully.

'Because, you see, everyone at the Trust thinks I'm

wonderful, and I can't tell them, can I? Can't tell them how bloody awful I find it all. Smiling at those ignorant people, sucking up to funders just because they're giving us a few thousand to run a Family Heritage Day or mend a bloody tapestry. Nobody knows how much I hate it. If I died tomorrow, I can't face the thought of that being all I've *done* with my life.'

Her husband, she realised, was snoring contentedly, oblivious to her.

'I'll sort it out my way, then,' she said. 'If that's OK.' And she turned over, away from him, and closed her eyes.

That picture hovered in her mind: Ella and Izzy on the beach with their spades crossed like swords, laughing so brightly that you could almost hear the sound singing from the photograph. It was from that holiday on the eastern coastlands, that strangely detached, alien place at the edge of the world. The first time Izzy had ever held a kite.

'Come on, darling! Run with it! *Run!*'

The place is the wind-blown expanse of a Norfolk beach, and Isobel's little hand is wrapped round the guide-handle of a kite. Ella, squatting behind her and running backwards, holds her own hand in place with the lightest of touches.

Isobel, running faster and faster, squeals with laughter.

The kite is just flimsy plastic, from the seafront shop; it features some children's TV characters whose names she cannot even remember. Their faces, with their leering banana-mouths, are framed in a jagged, lurid V. The kite slaps and flaps in the currents like some predatory plastic bird, wheeling around the humans below.

It catches Ella by surprise how the taut cord jerks itself alive, spooling off the handle in swift, whiplash movements, tugging at their hands.

'Whoa, whoa! It's OK!' Ella laughs.

Wet sand churns beneath her feet as she struggles to keep her balance. Isobel shrieks. On the edge of the water, Tom and Ben have stood up from their buckets of shells and Tom is waving, shouting something.

Ella doesn't see the dog until it's too late. The cannonball of fur and teeth knocks into her, sends her sprawling on the sand, flat on her back. She tries to call out, and for a moment she cannot. Then, she sits upright, feels the hot breath rushing back into her. The dog, its owner somewhere distant, has pounded past and is cutting up the water's edge with its powerful paws. A second later, she hears Isobel's wail and knows what has happened. Ella looks up, and she sees the kite going up, up into the sky, the handle dangling from the flex, now as high as a house, as an office block. The kite has gone.

They muster on the dunes, and Isobel is inconsolable. Her tiny face is like a squashed plum drenched in juice, wringing out the tears in an unending flow, her screams and wails echoing across the beach. Even Ben, his sandcastle forgotten, just wants to comfort his sister, alternately flinging his arms around her neck and bringing her pretty seashells which she dashes to the ground in anger.

'OK,' says Tom, narrowing his eyes, 'this isn't going to work.' He casts his gaze up and down, and espies the outcrop of beach half a mile or so further up, where all the shops and cafés are clustered. He mouths 'ice cream' at Ella, and she shrugs in agreement.

They trudge to the crowded beach, Tom carrying the screaming Isobel on his shoulders; her chubby little legs are making his neck and back ache, so he's relieved to put her down.

They set up the deckchairs in a space, and Tom says, 'Right. Who wants an ice cream?'

Ben jumps up and down with an exuberant, 'Me, me, me!' and Izzy rubs the tears away from her eyes and gives a hesitant smile. Tom, checking he's got enough in his wallet, strides off towards the shop; behind him, the children run in circles around Ella as she struggles with one of the deckchairs. Isobel says she wants an orange lolly, not an ice cream. Ella, exasperated, tells her to run after Daddy. She shouts to Tom, calls that Izzy is coming with him and he waves in response.

Ella is now turning out the bag, looking desperately for the suncream. She finds it, and squeezes out too much, a gloopy ball of the stuff in her hand. 'Come here, Ben,' she says imperiously, and she starts rubbing it into his bare shoulders. He cackles, shaking and twisting. 'Keep still!' Ella rebukes him, then laughs. 'OK, you're done.'

After five minutes, Ella has deckchairs, papers and towels in place and Ben has already made a start on another impressive sand-sculpture. She looks over her shoulder, scanning the promenade for Tom and Isobel. No sign of them yet. 'Can you see them?' she asks Ben.

The boy looks up from his engineering project, narrows his eyes. 'There,' he says, and points.

Tom, grinning broadly, flip-flops over with two melting vanilla ice creams in each hand. 'Get them while they're cold!' he says.

'Didn't Izzy tell you she wanted an orange lolly?' Ella asks, taking two of the cones from him and passing one to Ben. She reaches for her purse. 'Do you need more money?'

'No.' Tom frowns, straightens up. 'What, she… Where is Izzy?'

A chill pierces Ella, and the summer's day is like something from another world. The jabbering and squealing and splashing suddenly sound alien and terrifying. The sea and the blood roar in her ears like a football crowd.

'She came after you.'

'No, she didn't.'

'She caught you up,' Ella says angrily.

The two remaining cones drop, drop as Tom lets them go, unheeded; they smack and form rivulets on the brown sand. Ben, too, knows there is something wrong.

'Isobel?' Ella yells, straightening up. '*Isobel!*' she shouts towards the dunes.

'Izzy?' Tom whirls around towards the sea, bellows that way. 'Izzy!' Other families are turning, looking interestedly to see what's happening.

'You and Ben head down the beach,' Ella says, 'I'll take the dunes and the promenade. Ben, you stay with Dad, understand?'

The boy, his face alert and keen, nods.

Ella scrambles up the sand to the powdery, tufty dunes, slithers down small gullies, climbs up little twisting sandy paths. Her daughter. *Her daughter.* There is no other thought in her mind.

At the top of the dunes, she stands in the salty wind, hands on hips, scanning the distant grass and the car park. No. Not there.

She scrambles back down to the promenade, hurrying past carefree families and old and young couples. She stops one or two of them, gives a hasty, breathless description, cuts it short each time when they shake their heads apologetically.

Ella has reached the shops and cafés now. Surely she is somewhere around here? A four-year-old girl cannot wander around unnoticed for long, and she knew she was following Tom – didn't she?

She runs into each trinket shop and ice cream parlour and restaurant, shouting her daughter's name, oblivious to the stares from people. She runs back into the middle of the promenade, makes a funnel of her hands and bellows her daughter's name.

'*Is – oooo – beeeeeellll!*'

Two of the young life-savers on duty, a man and a girl, have spotted her. Commendably, they have sized up the situation without needing to be told.

'What does she look like?' the girl asks, and Ella tells her gratefully. A second later, the girl is rapping out the description on a two-way radio while the boy has climbed the ladder to his look-out seat, armed with binoculars.

'I have to find her,' Ella says breathlessly. There is a rushing in her ears, and the salty air is making her feel sick. The sun seems to be getting brighter, hotter, angrier. 'She's my little girl. She's my only little girl. She lost her kite. And then we got her an ice cream, but she wanted an orange lolly and we can't even give her that. Please, we have to find her.'

Please God, please please please.

'Don't worry,' says the girl. 'She can't have gone far. This is a very safe beach.'

'Yes, but you don't know, do you? People...people...' Ella stuffs her fist in her mouth, bites it hard, hears herself making an agonised, keening noise.

The girl lifeguard puts a hand on Ella's arm. 'Come on, love. We'll find her. We'll find her.'

The sun is like a hole punched in hot sheet metal, letting in floods of furnace-hot light, filling Ella's eyes and ears. She feels her legs give way beneath her. Hot tarmac smacks her calves and she manages to put her hands out just in time.

She hears a concerned voice mention a glass of water, and realises her eyes are burning with tears.

At home in Ashington, now, she lay in the dark and felt the fear again.

She had to get up. She crept to Isobel's bedroom and caressed the sleeping girl's soft cheek, sat on her bed and watched the rise and fall of the bedclothes as her daughter breathed. It was a daily miracle, Ella sometimes thought, that they were all here, all happy, all healthy, fed and clothed.

The four of them. A quadrilateral. A closed unit.

It was Tom and Ben who had found her that day. She had been happily pouring water into sand-troughs with two bigger girls on another part of the beach. Tom hadn't known, he told Ella, whether to shout in rage or cry in hysterical relief. Izzy didn't even know she was meant to be somewhere else.

When they got back to their abandoned towels and deckchairs, everything was as it had been left – except that her purse, which she'd dropped, was no longer there.

When they started looking around, a middle-aged man in baggy shorts hurried over, waving the purse, and handed it to Ella. 'I saw you drop it,' he said, 'when you ran off. I didn't want anyone to pinch it. I shouted after you, but you didn't hear.'

He was, Ella recalls with a smile, probably bewildered by the strength of their gratitude, demurring when Tom offered him a drink for his kindness.

Ella, hugging Isobel tightly in her Sleeping Beauty beach-towel, had forgotten the purse completely and would not have cared if she'd lost it for ever.

They lie side by side in that Norfolk guest house, unable to sleep after the trauma of the beach.

The window is open to the night, and the sea forms a soft backwash to their conversation. They hold hands, look at one another, smiling, and nod.

'I think we should,' says Tom.

'I think we should, too,' says Ella. 'Why not? We're still young.'

Her mouth closes eagerly over his, and she giggles with delight as his hand steals to her hot, steaming loins, his flat palm caressing her already-soaking openness. A second later, her hand finds a fierce, proud rigidity and pulls it eagerly in, unprotected. He rams home with an angry delight, making her gasp and squeal.

'God, that's good,' she breathes. 'Fuck me. *Fuck me.*'

It is as if the pain and the relief has somehow found a new home; a home in desire. It wants to manifest itself as warmth, as passion.

For those who have so nearly experienced loss, risks take their place in the background. Love wants a form; it wants a new day and a new dawn.

It wants a new purpose.

It wants creation.

CHAPTER ELEVEN

Family Fortunes

Tom, leaning against the minimalist chrome table in Phill's flat, had finished lying to his wife and was about to lie to his children. It was a necessary evil.

As he dialled the number, he smiled, thinking about his last conversation with Jeff.

'Now, your French,' said Jeff, 'have got it so *sussed*. You've got to admire your French.'

Tom had forgotten it was Bastille Day. The Rowan's landlady, Sandrine, was half-French, and in the week of 14th July each year the pub would adopt a Gallic theme. Imported beers were brought in, Sandrine tuned the satellite to some Parisian football and a French flag was proudly draped behind the bar.

'I admire Sandrine,' said Tom. 'Well, I like her tits, if that counts.' He nodded at the buxom landlady, who gave him a mock scowl in return.

'I mean your Frenchmen,' said Jeff, sipping his frothy Alsace lager. 'Bit of lechery is encouraged over there. It flows in the old veins like a nice glass of Bordeaux. They're not so bloody scared of giving offence as we are. You eye up a Frenchwoman's tits or squeeze her arse and she'll take it as a compliment. Which it is.'

Tom wasn't sure. 'I don't know. I think some of them would be offended if you squeezed their arse.'

'Oh, yeah, maybe a few hatchet-faced Parisian feminazis would. But, let's face it, who'd want to screw them anyway? Problem we've got, Tom-boy, is that, in our country, our fucking generation's been expected to take on *all* the political correctness. I mean, what the hell is there left for the boys growing up?' Jeff shook his head and took a weary sip of lager. 'You know, I sometimes wish I'd been working in the Seventies,' he said.

Tom didn't see it. 'What, so you could have a bad moustache and wear flares? Go home to a packet Vesta curry and three TV channels?'

'Yeah, yeah, but the totty, mate, the *totty*. Birds weren't afraid to *be* birds back then. Women used to get their arses pinched and their tits felt up in the office and nobody thought anything of it. It was just, you know, what went on? Kind of a mutual understanding. Then along came the bloody feminists with their dungarees and their bad haircuts and things were never the same again. These days, you so much as glance at a fit bird's jugs and she'll have you up for bloody harassment. Jesus, they get you in court for making polite conversation. But not your French. They, you know, they understand the *power* of flirting.'

He lifted his glass at Sandrine and winked at her, and she half-heartedly showed him the finger in return. Tom smirked.

'And,' Jeff went on, undeterred, 'what about the way they deal with all this mistress stuff? I mean, it's almost acceptable over there. Look at their politicians. They're all at it.'

'Jeff, aren't we meant to be challenging these stereotypes now that we're all Europeans?'

'Oh, fuck off with your PC *Guardian*-reading bollocks, you. I'm serious, mate. They even have an expression for it. *Le cinq-à-sept* – five till seven.'

'What's that?'

'It's the gap between the time when the guy leaves the office and the time when Madame thinks he leaves. Two hours spent having a bit of *haw-haw-haw*, two hours undisturbed *avec la petite* bit on the side. You get it?'

Tom pulled a face. 'Well, yes, except if you get delayed by the photocopier jamming... Or by someone asking you a bloody stupid question which you absolutely *must* answer that day, and which then involves looking something up in an archive file. And then, say she lives across town – half an hour if you bomb it – and you get there absolutely knackered, and more in need of a cup of tea and a little sit down than a hot shag... She starts to undo your tie, and you feel all sweaty and flustered, so you go and have a quick freshen-up, by which time it's ten past six, and she's lost interest anyway.'

'Tom, mate, I think you're taking this a little too seriously.'

'And the traffic's getting heavy on the motorway,' Tom went on, 'so you really ought to head off, because if you don't help bath the kids and put them to bed you'll be in for a bollocking. So you give her a little kiss, and then a more passionate one, and you say you really have to go, even though she's trying to yank you back in the room. But no, you have to get home. So you head off, hot and sweaty again and sexually frustrated. Next thing you know she's there on your front lawn, drunk, pelting your house with rocks and screaming the whole thing to the street.' Tom winced and shook his head. 'Not good.'

'Bloody hell,' said Jeff. 'Look on the bright side, why don't you?'

'I'm just being realistic, Jeff.'

'Listen, John Thomas, if you're in France, you get to have a wife and a mistress and nobody thinks any the worse of you.' He clapped Tom on the shoulder. 'You, my son, get to have your curry and your pasta and to eat them both.'

'But the maths doesn't quite work, does it?' asked Tom with a frown.

'How d'you mean?'

'Well, if all these blokes have wives *and* mistresses, then where do all the extra women come from? There can't be enough to go round. And they won't all look like Isabelle Adjani, either. Some of them are going to be right old dogs.'

Jeff shrugged. 'Yeah, yeah. You may have a point.'

'Some of the mistresses,' Tom suggested, 'are going to be other blokes' wives.'

'Which kind of makes you wonder...' Jeff could see where this was going.

'If your Madame is doing it too. And then, of course, you have to ask yourself what it is that makes her such a desirable commodity in the eyes of this other bloke. Is he seeing all the good things that you've forgotten about?'

'Maybe he's more forgiving?' Jeff suggested.

'Or maybe it's just that he always gets her at her best –

squeezed into the little black dress, with a flirty neck-scarf and wearing her nicest perfume and lippy. He never has to see her in old pants, or when she's got a face-pack on, or taking the bins out in a tatty T-shirt.' Tom lifted his glass with a knowing nod. 'What do you think of that?'

'Nice. Makes sense. But you still don't believe it actually happens?'

Tom shrugged. 'I think if it were that easy, it would have been adopted by the rest of the European Union. You know, after having run in France on a sort of...pilot basis.'

'Common Mistress Policy,' agreed Jeff. 'Anyway, it's all academic for me. I'm never getting married again. As somebody said once – why buy the cow when you can milk it through the fence?'

'You know, Jeff, I can see why you're such a hit with women.'

'It's a gift.' He waggled his glass at Tom. 'Bloody hell, it's strong stuff, this. We should ask her to import it more often. Another?'

'Go on, then. For England.'

'While I'm up there, I'll ask Sandrine if she fancies being my mistress. Liberty, equality and a bit of how's-your-papa.' Jeff winked. 'Well, a man can dream.'

'Izzy wants to talk to you,' Ella told him. 'Hold on.'

Tom had to do this. He knew that Phill, who was leaning idly against the door in her red silk dressing gown and painting her nails, accepted that. He still wanted to get it over with as quickly as possible.

Izzy's voice was there in his ear. 'I'm off to bed, Daddy.'

'Night-night, Bizzy. I'm really sorry I can't be there, precious. I'll make it up to you.'

She was wearing her pink teddy pyjamas, she said, and she brushed her teeth down the phone at him to prove she was doing it. The soft sound tickled his ear. He told her she was a good girl, and that he loved her. The receiver resonated with a kiss from her.

Ella came back on. She sounded full-on, upbeat, artificial, he thought – like when she came home drunk and exuberant from one of her girly evenings with Bex and co. She said that Ben obviously loved him too but couldn't come and tell him in person because he was on level six of HyperCritters and was about to get his highest score ever.

Tom said that was fine. He said to tell Ben to zap a baddie for him.

'Are you OK?' he asked her.

'Of course I am.' Her answer came back quickly. 'I'm absolutely, totally fine. I'm brilliant. Brilliant tonight. Why do you always ask me if I'm all right when you know I'm all right?'

This was very strange. It didn't sound like her. He wondered if she was trying to be funny. 'Ella,' he said, 'you're gabbling.'

'Oh, go off to your boring meeting. Look, when you get back, we need to have a talk. There's something I need to tell you. I think you'll be pleased.'

He felt only mildly troubled as he thumbed the phone off.

Out of the corner of his eye, he glimpsed a red-robe cascade. He saw Phill wiggle as she stepped from the shimmering pool of silk.

'Everything OK?' she murmured, slipping cool, naked arms around his waist.

'Yes…yes, I think so.'

It was weird, having sex with someone new after all this time. The basic moves were the same, but the minor, practical differences unnerved him. Ella had a mole just there; Phill didn't. Ella liked this to be licked first before that was stroked; Phill liked the opposite. Ella squealed in agonised delight if her earlobes were nibbled; Phill found that uncomfortable, but moaned wildly if her fingers were sucked.

Other things were even more awkward. Ella liked his wedding ring to be part of foreplay, and he had become quite adept with it. She always shuddered in pleasure when he brushed its hardness across her nipples. If she was on top then, close to orgasm, she would pull his hand savagely to her, make him slip his ring-finger between them. Then she would give a squeal and a writhe of pleasure as she pressed her engorged clitoris against the little gold band. Phill, on the other hand, didn't pay the ring that much attention, and so he wondered whether he ought to remove it while making love to her. It was an awkward point of etiquette. If he did so, it was a move which had certain overtones – and yet, if he didn't, it was there, hard and metallic, solid against her liquidity. Again, he doubted whether any self-help books would have much to say on the subject.

'You only think so?' Phill pouted and frowned. 'Ella doesn't suspect anything, does she?'

'No, no…absolutely not.'

There's something I need to tell you. I think you'll be pleased. He couldn't imagine what it could be.

He turned, looked Phill's naked body up and down and gave her a reassuring smile. 'You're so lovely.'

'Good. And where are you, by the way?'

'I'm at a City Council strategy meeting for the allocation of funding to preventative initiatives, if you must know. It's likely to go on for...quite some time.'

'Gosh, how very dull,' said Phill. 'Tell you what – let's fuck instead.' And her warm, eager arms slipped around his neck.

Today's decision was done and dusted. And now...shadows.

Her parents used to say – often – that everyone recalled exactly what they were doing on that day in 1963 when President Kennedy was shot. She used to get fed up with the way people went on about something that had happened before she was born. And then, half a lifetime later, her own age got the tragedy it craved. It had since been superseded by global angst, by toppled towers. But back in that weird summer, Isobel was born into a world gone mad.

The last Sunday in August. She gazes down between her bloodstained thighs and touches the fragile little hand in wonderment.

Last time was not like this. She didn't bring Ben into the world with pushing, squealing and roaring; she let the professionals take care of it, all the while thinking of Macduff, 'from his mother's womb/ Untimely ripp'd.' *Ripped.* The only word possible. Shakespeare got it so right.

But Isobel, she's not untimely. She's right on time. She's squeezed out in the traditional way, because Ella has insisted. In a pethidine haze. In. Screams. Of. Pain.

The blood isn't such a problem, but the *shit*, that's a shock. They told her she'd crap herself in front of everyone, but she doesn't quite believe it until she does. She still finds it incredible that such a loss of dignity routinely happens to thousands of women worldwide and that it doesn't make the national news. And nobody *tells* you.

But the surge of joy kicks through Ella like an injection, and that old-but-new feeling, for which she has no words, grips her as she lifts the child in her arms. It glistens with fluid and is astonishingly light. She watches its eyes trying to focus, its tongue, lizard-like, darting in and out. And then, Ella sinks back with relief on the pillow, holding her warm, moist daughter close and feeling that furious, *fighting* heartbeat thump against her own. Oh, God, she thinks, oh *God*, and she feels the sense of warmth that the word brings, properly now, for the first time in years. My daughter. My daughter. *My daughter*. She closes her eyes and murmurs a brief, well-known incantation. She thinks she does so quietly, but Tom will tell her afterwards that her Hail Mary echoed down the corridor.

When she becomes properly aware of the TV in the corner of the room – the solemn BBC tones, the stilted images – she recalls what she was told, in her delirium, what she thought she might even have dreamt. So, it is true, then, this crazy story. How bizarre. How sad.

'I'm telling you one thing now,' she hears herself saying to Tom and the midwife, and her own voice echoes in her head, far off. 'No *way* am I calling her Diana.'

Dreamlike, time passes.

A nurse, smiling sadly, wheels the phone over to her. With

a guzzling, nibbling Isobel attached to her breast (*hurt!*) and a receiver clamped to her ear, she calls her parents. She is irked to get their answerphone.

'Mum? Hi, it's me. Everything's great, I'm – *ow!* – we've had a girl! A beautiful, gorgeous little girl called Isobel. Born on her due date, seven pounds six. Looking forward to seeing you. Bye.'

Who else? Tom's dad lives in Australia now – he moved there two years after Mrs Barclay died, and has a great new life with his new, lissom slip of a wife. He and Tom communicate, mostly by email, but they're not close. They'll probably mail him some pictures.

She dials another number. 'Claire?'

Her old friend sounds as if she has a cold. 'Oh. Yeah. Hi, Ella.'

'Hey, I'm just ringing to tell you I've had the baby! She arrived on time, the little angel.' Pause to allow reaction, but there is none. 'Born at midday on her due date – thirty-first of August. Isn't that great?'

'Oh...right.' Another lengthy pause. 'Um. Yeah, sorry. Congratulations.'

'You don't sound very happy,' says Ella suspiciously.

'Happy?' There is a sudden silence, as if with realisation. 'Oh. My. *God.* If you were in labour, you...you won't have seen the news, will you?'

'Well, yes – yes, actually I have. Poor woman, I know. Terrible...' She leaves what she thinks is a respectful pause, then launches again. 'I've had another *baby*, Claire, a girl, a beautiful little baby girl! Ben's got a little sister. He's been in, he adores her, you should see him looking at her...'

'Oh. Right.'

'We've called her Isobel Lucy Grace. She weighs seven pounds and six ounces. That's a bit lighter than Ben was. And, you know, I'm sure she's smiling at me? Like she's really wise and knowing about something. God, I'd forgotten how it felt. It was so totally different from last time. You know, Ben was a Caesarean. Bloody cakewalk in comparison to this little one, I can tell you. It's just...amazing. And I've had no sleep, and I'm totally a mess, you know, down there. But I feel great, just...*incredible*! So when can you come and see her?'

'Um... Ella... I'm...not sure. Look, don't get me wrong, I'm really pleased for you...'

'Yeah, you sound it! Hey, lighten up! I'm meant to be the one who gets the post-natals.'

Claire is still speaking. '...off work right now. I...don't think you realise quite how upset everybody is. They showed her coffin. Her *coffin*!'

'I'm sorry, what? Whose coffin?'

'Princess Diana.'

'Jesus, are we still talking about *her*?'

'I just feel, like, totally devastated. I think I might get the train down to London, go and put some flowers at Kensington Palace like other people are doing.'

'Oh, right. Great. How about sending *me* some flowers? I may not have copped it in a car crash, but I have got a busted cervix and an exploded arse.' She laughs. Claire doesn't.

'Ella, I can't believe you're being so self-centred at a time like this.'

'I'm sorry. Oh, good God, no, why am I apologising? You never even *met* the silly bitch!' Several of the women who are huddled around the TV turn and glower at Ella, as if she has made the worst possible *faux pas*. 'Well, she didn't!' she snaps at them. 'God, Claire,' she goes on, 'don't waste money on train tickets and flowers. If you want to do something useful, give twenty quid to one of her charities. That landmines thing, or the AIDS one. Or just buy me a jumbo pack of nappies. But don't mooch around being a maudlin cow. I don't think I can stand it.'

'You're so callous, Ella,' says Claire, and hangs up.

She tries other friends. In their varied ways, all of them make muted sounds of congratulation, before venturing nervously to ask if she has, um, seen the, err, *news*, and does she *know*...?

She starts to feel guilty. It is as if all happiness is banned.

When they let her home, she puts Radio 1 on for the first time in years, deciding that she needs a burst of cheap music and childish inanity. The station is playing a slow and dreary Radiohead song, which sounds just like every other slow and dreary Radiohead song. Thom Yorke and Isobel join together in an incoherent yell. When the dirge finally yawns its way to an end, the DJ says, '*We're letting the music do the talking here this morning. We've been struck by the unspeakable news just as much as you all have. Believe me, we're all sitting round reading the papers in disbelief, and—*'

Ella switches off in disgust. She flicks the TV channels while feeding Isobel, to try and see if anyone is being sensible.

She gawps in horror at the pasty people in Kensington, all wailing and gnashing their teeth in a most bizarrely un-British manner, and giving up their offerings of five-quid bunches of carnations. She mentally estimates the number of bouquets, and tries to work out how much a charity would get if they all made a donation instead. She rings Tom, who's had to go into work for a couple of hours, and tells him. He feels the same way. 'I know. All these people weeping on national TV for a woman they never met. Has the entire country had an irony bypass, for fuck's sake?'

Of course, it's sad. Two boys have lost their mother. But there are tragedies every day in which healthy women die and leave their children motherless. And we're hearing about this one to the exclusion of *everything* else? So the Middle East is having a little break, is it, and the boys in Northern Ireland have stopped for tea? New Labour government getting along just fine? Oh yes, and Mother Teresa – where are the wailing crowds in the streets for *her*? And – my God – they even cancelled *EastEnders*! That would normally cause riots, but obviously the soap-guzzlers have higher priorities right now. After all, they have a real-life episode, the greatest story arc ever. All unfolding live.

The giant, stupid, useless rubbish tip of flowers sits there in the London heat, turning to mulch under layers of sweaty plastic. Isobel, with her deep eyes and her puckering, ever-hungry mouth, doesn't seem impressed.

Ella wants to climb on the roof with a megaphone and shout to the world, 'I've got a *baby*! So shut *up* about Princess fucking Diana!'

It is the perfect, defining moment for her; a time which crystallises her attitude to what is important and what is not.

She does not, in truth, much care if there is war in the Middle East or famine in Africa, and if there are people sleeping on the streets of Cherford within spitting distance of the Castle. At least, she cares in the way that everybody thinks they ought to care, and she puts money in collection tins like a good guilty citizen, buys the *Big Issue* from the most persistent vendor on Castle Street. She knows wars, famines and homelessness are wrong and unjust, but she will not scream and shout about these things. She will not fight. She will not kill.

But for Ben and Isobel – to protect them and to love them and to keep them safe from harm – she will always scream and shout.

It is terrifying how much she loves them.

For them, she will fight.

For them, she could kill.

It was dark when Tom finally drew up in the driveway, but he wasn't surprised to see the house blazing with light.

He unfolded the letter once more. He didn't know why he was still carrying it around; it wasn't as if Ella was going to ask for proof.

The worst thing had been the ringing round, the trawl through his book of supposed contacts. Everyone had been apologetic, wary. 'You know what things are like at the moment, Tom.' Word had got around that he was disposable, and nobody in the most precarious of sectors wanted to be associated with a failure.

The tingle of satisfaction in his loins hardly made up for it. Anybody could get sex, after all. Success, that was the true challenge.

He'd bought a *Guardian* and a local paper on the way back

from Phill's, but the job sections were useless. Plenty there if he was a trained Conflict Resolution Facilitator for victims of abuse in Dudley (did being made to live in Dudley itself count as abuse?) or fancied being an aptly named Joint Commissioning Officer for Substance Misuse Awareness. But nothing for him.

He sat in the car, leafing with incredulity through the paltry selection of local jobs. There was nothing.

He flung the paper aside and made his way into the house, feeling like a naughty schoolboy.

'Hi!' said Ella. She raised a glass at him from the kitchen table.

'Hi, darling. Desperate for a piss, with you in a mo.'

He could still taste Phill on his lips. Only after a swift gargle in the bathroom did he feel able to slip down to the kitchen and plant a kiss on the back of his wife's neck. He saw, with a mixture of relief and concern, that the bottle of wine on the table was almost finished. It was a 2000 Château Margaux, he noted ruefully – not exactly cheap.

How the hell was he going to tell her?

He sat opposite her, and she looked up at him. Her lipstick was smudged, her face was drawn but her eyes seemed oddly shiny, elated. He wondered if she had been taking drugs.

'Ella? You OK?'

'I'm gooooooood.' She waggled the glass at him. 'Not in a fit state to operate heavy machinery...but *happy*. D'you know what? Happier than I've been for a while.'

'Oh. Good. Ella, listen, there's something we have to talk about.'

'D'you know what?' she said suddenly, not appearing to

have heard him. She grabbed his shirt and pulled him gently towards her. 'I know you'll understand. You will. Been saying I should do it forrages. Ages.'

'What?' Tom's vague feeling of concern was solidifying into something else, a sense that he had more to be worried about than his wife being rather drunk. 'What are you on about?'

She released him, sat back and spread her hands, laughing. 'You'll never believe it. Well, you will, I dunno. God, who'd believe it? I'll have to find endless bloody...*coffee mornings* to go to.' She tried to stifle her giggles, but they came exploding out from behind her hand.

'Coffee mornings?' Tom asked, wondering if he should know what she meant.

'Or maybe,' she said, seeming to become serious and thoughtful, 'maybe I could shake tins for charity on street corners. Or stuff envelopes. Good works, that's what women like me do, isn't it? Heading for Menopause City on a creaky old bus called Christian Charity.' She laughed again, and a tear trickled down her face. 'Oh, God, Tom, it's such a fucking relief after all this time. You were *so* right, you know?'

'I was? Um, that's good.'

He had to hang on to that. There was still the vague notion at the back of his mind that the drunkenness was just an act, and that she was about to sit bolt upright, fix him with a diamond-hard stare and say that she knew perfectly well who he'd just been with and what he'd been doing.

But no. One look at her eyes, that was enough. Not to mention the depleted bottle and the vineyard smell of her breath.

She giggled, taking his face between her palms. 'Tom. I've fucking *done* it at last. I went in and told Sir Nigel he could stick the bloody job. I said I was fed up to the back teeth with it and that I wanted out as soon as I possibly could.'

It seemed, for a moment, that the room had chosen to lurch like the deck of a ship. Tom's skin prickled with pins of cold and heat. The inside of his mouth had suddenly become parched.

Ella laughed, grabbed her glass and took another deep gulp of Margaux. '*Yes!*' she said, and fixed him with a triumphant look. 'Oh, come on, don't look like that. We always said we could manage. I mean, yeah, I might get a little part-time job, if it gets tight with the fees. But hey, that's hardly going to stress me out like bloody Cherford Castle.'

'You...you...' Tom gave a nervous laugh. 'Ella, come on. You're joking. You don't just go in and see someone like Sir Nigel and tell him you want out.'

She shrugged, giggled.

'I mean, he told you to sleep on it, surely?'

She waved a hand. 'Pffffft. Yeah, he made noises. Asked if it was the money, tried to fucking bribe me with a bonus. I mean, God, what would we do with *that*?'

'So he tried to persuade you to stay.' Tom was trying to keep the panic out of his voice. 'And you...'

'Told him he was an irritating, pompous twat!' Ella said with a grin.

Tom sat back, breaking into a cold sweat. 'Good grief,' he said eventually.

'I *know*! I mean, you're always saying he pushes me around too much, dumps stuff on me. It's about time I spoke my mind. So I wrote the bloody resignation letter there and then.'

'Oh, Christ, you didn't?'

'Well, yeah, I have to say I did hesitate. A bit. Just once.'

'You did?'

Tom clutched at the straw. Yes, thank God. She had written it, but she hadn't printed it off yet. Or she had it in the envelope, ready to put on Sir Nigel's desk in the morning. Or she'd given it to his secretary, and it would be retrievable if he pumped Ella full of black coffee and drove her into the office right now to grab it off Sir Nigel's in-tray. Please, *please*.

'Yeah, I did. Tried to ring your mobile, but it was switched off.'

'You didn't try the office?'

'Yeah. Got your voicemail.'

'Oh.'

'Don't worry, I wouldn't have let you talk me out of it.'

Well, I think this time you would, he said to himself.

'No, so I just went ahead and wrote it there and then,' she told him proudly. 'Put it in the internal mail, and it was gone an hour later.'

'Oh,' said Tom. He was concentrating on a small knot in the wood of the kitchen cupboard just above Ella's head. 'Oh,' he said again.

'And the best thing is, I won't have to go in after this week. They'll do two months' pay in lieu of notice. They're so bloody scared of people buggering off to rival attractions with the insider secrets.' Ella grinned. 'So, I've finally done it, darling. What do you think of that?'

'I'm lost for words,' he said. 'I really am.'

Somewhere down in the heart of the city, a police siren wailed.

He thought, for one ridiculous moment, that they were coming for him.

CHAPTER TWELVE

Crash

At the age of three, Isobel is going through a stage of maintaining staunchly that Baby Jesus lives under her bath.

Every night, as the soapy water flows out, she leans right down to the plughole and calls 'Night-night, Baby Jesus!' as if it were the most natural thing in the world. She waves a chubby arm at the whirlpool and giggles.

Ella even takes to joining in with her, until Tom puts his head round the bathroom door and says crossly, 'Don't encourage her.'

'Why not?'

'Because it's silly.'

'Tom, she's three. Being silly is in the person spec.'

Tom ignores her, and comes and squats down next to his daughter. 'Izzy,' he says, 'you know Baby Jesus isn't a real person, don't you?'

Isobel scowls. 'You don't say *dat*. Baby Jesus *is* a person. Baby Jesus lives in my *baaaaath*.'

'Bath.' Instinctively, Ella repeats it with the short 'a' instead. 'There, see? You can't argue with faith.'

'I don't want you filling their heads with religious claptrap.'

'I've told you before, Tom, I'm not religious. I don't like the word.' Ella scowls. 'I prefer to say I know God.'

'You never compromise, that's your problem.'

'Oh, now that's not true. I took the metal fish off the back of the car, didn't I?'

'Yes. Only because you don't want people expecting you to be nice when you're behind the wheel, you said... Anyway, we've talked about this often enough. You don't believe half of it yourself.'

She shrugged, pouted as she towelled Izzy dry. 'Maybe I do, maybe I don't.'

'Well, you'd better stop eating shellfish, then. And you should go and sit outside the house when you're on the rag. It's all there in Leviticus.'

'It's easy to mock the detail, Tom. Doesn't mean the basic stuff isn't sound.'

'Look, the sentiments, the philosophy – yeah, fine. And yeah, sure, someone called Jesus, or something like it, was around in first-century Palestine, got a lot of people interested in him and put the wind up the Romans. Little doubt about that, historically.'

'Oh, you're so gracious.'

'But you don't think he *literally* turned water into wine, do you? And made two fish and five rolls turn into an open-air picnic for five thousand people? So JC's some kind of early cross between Jamie Oliver and Paul Daniels. *You'll like thith, not a lot, but it'th pukka.*'

'Oh, ha ha. This is all very cheap, Tom.'

'And as for the Enormous Assumption, let's not even go there.'

'Oh, please do. It's a long time since you did a bit of Catholic-bashing. I almost come to expect it every couple of months or so.'

'Izzy,' says Tom, kissing her wet hair, 'Baby Jesus is just a person in a story. Like Cinderella, or Snow White. Or Father Chr—'

Ella's finger jabs into the air. 'Whoa, don't you *dare*.'

'All right, all right.' Tom sighs and straightens up. 'Look, I don't mind her reading Bible stories, but I don't want her learning a load of Creationist propaganda as if it's all absolute truth. We can't go teaching her about miracles and all that guff. We might as well tell her there are leprechauns at the bottom of the garden.'

'There might be,' says Ella, 'for all you know.' She folds her arms and scowls at her husband. 'Have you forgotten what it's like to be a child, Tom? Sometimes people need to believe in miracles.' She throws him Izzy's toothbrush. 'Anyway, your turn. Make sure she reaches the back ones.'

'Come on, Izzy,' Tom says, leading her by the hand to the washbasin. 'Let's brush properly. Then you and Mummy can say goodnight to Jesus and the Tooth Fairy.'

On the pavement outside the estate agent's office, Ella drew a deep breath. It had seemed so much easier then. Right now, they could really do with a miracle.

'Hello,' she said to the perky receptionist. 'Ella Barclay. I have an appointment.'

While she waited, she took the piece of paper out of her

handbag for the fifteenth time and looked down the small column of figures which she had hammered into the Excel spreadsheet. She knew they were right. She had stayed up till three in the morning with water and coffee, using a laptop which they would soon have to sell.

She looked around at everything, now, with a dealer's eye. That pine-framed mirror, that designer armchair, her clothes, Ben's PlayStation.

Last night, after Tom had gone to bed, Ella had looked round the kitchen in despair, taking in all the useless stuff they had spent money on. Terracotta tiles, granite worktops, Caltagirone pottery from Sicily. She picked up the pestle and mortar – designer perfection in aluminium and jatoba wood – and glowered at it, wondering what on earth had possessed them to buy such a beautiful but useless object. It had cost about the same as a week's food bill. She hefted it for a second before hurling it against the kitchen wall, where it made a large, satisfying dent in the plaster.

Today, she had locked the car by the old city walls, and then stood and stared at it for a full minute, looking at the gleaming bodywork properly for the first time. The car. Shit, they were going to have to sell the car. She would have to travel by *bus* alongside sweaty teenagers and shouting mums and cackling pensioners.

'Mrs Barclay?'

A pale young man emerged, shook her hand limply but too eagerly, then offered her a seat in an enclosed section.

Ella smiled, crossed her legs, sized the young man up. Too tall for his grey suit, gangling. His hollow cheeks made him look half starved, while his blond pudding-bowl hair looked as if his mum had cut it for him.

'I understand you're looking for some advice, Mrs Barclay?' said the young man, folding long fingers together on the desk, trying to look as if he owned it all.

Ella smiled indulgently. 'I just need to make the buying process as painless as possible,' she said, unfolding her piece of paper and handing it to him. 'It's all on here. What I want, what I've got, all in black and white. It's got to be a cash deal. I can't – that is, I don't want a mortgage.'

The young man nodded, smiling. He had a gleam in his eye, and the look of a hungry whippet handed a juicy bone.

He ran his eye down the page, making the odd 'hmm' noise. Ella watched, crossing her legs once, resting her chin on one elegant finger.

The spare cash didn't come to very much at all. It ought to be enough, though, surely? It was a few years since they'd been in the market for houses, but she was sure she recalled some decent property going for the sum she had in mind.

'Rrrrright!' said the estate agent, and he actually rubbed his hands together as he swung round to his computer. Ella almost laughed out loud. 'Let's see what's out there,' he said, cracking his knuckles. Ella winced. He tapped a few keys and sat back to wait. 'This,' he waved the paper approvingly at Ella, 'is *very* comprehensive. Very good indeed. I wish all our clients came with such a...realistic assessment of their needs.'

She would berate herself later for not having heard the alarm bells at the word 'realistic'.

'You think so?' she said, feeling brighter by the second.

'Oh, yes, absolutely. We can certainly work much better

when we have a definite budget. Could I just ask, are you...buying for yourself, Mrs Barclay?'

'Well, for myself and my family.' She suddenly felt a raw, angry urge to explain, to justify herself. 'My husband is...freelance. His...contracts tend to be irregular.'

'Oh, yes.' The young man was tapping at his keyboard again, and didn't sound in the least surprised. 'We have a lot of people in that position, you know.'

'We...well, we feel a bit stale in Thorpedale Avenue. Fancy moving on, you know.' Ella felt her face burning red, and imagined a neon sign saying LIAR above her head.

'Just one or two things,' said the estate agent, tapping a pencil against his teeth. He made eye contact with her. 'Absolutely set on three bedrooms?'

'Well, yes. That should be easy enough, shouldn't it? I mean, the children can't really share.'

'All right. It helps define our options.' He clicked his mouse. 'We do have one or two interesting things in up-and-coming areas.'

This was sounding better by the minute. *Up-and-coming.* She pictured bohemian Birchwoods, the busy little suburb where Bex lived. It had a bank, a traditional butcher's shop and a French bakery, while trendy cafés were springing up beside the musty second-hand bookshops. The primary school, built of sturdy stone, sported a big playing field and solid gates, outside which cheerfully chattering mothers waited every day at three-thirty, hands in the pockets of moufflon coats or fake-fur jackets, lounging against the doors of small, unshowy Fiestas or Micras. It wasn't Ashington, but it would do nicely.

He was flicking through a selection of properties on his screen. 'There's one here...no garage, though. Do you need a garage?'

They had already decided to lose the car. A garage, Ella had said firmly, would be an unnecessary luxury. 'No,' she admitted, shrugging.

'Might suit you, then. A nice apartment, good access to public transport—'

'Sorry,' said Ella, interrupting him, 'what did you say?'

'Good access to public transport.'

'No, before that. You said *apartment*.'

'Um, yes, I did.'

'I thought I made it clear I was after a house.'

The young man blinked, twice. Very slowly. 'Oh,' he said. There was a long silence. He cleared his throat and went, if such a thing were possible, a shade paler. 'Um,' he said. 'I thought, you see, with your, um...budget...You see, the market is incredibly...'

Ella fixed a cold, unblinking gaze on him, one which she had perfected in the last few years of her professional life. 'I. Want. A. *House.*'

He cleared his throat again. 'I'll have a look,' he offered, frantically punching keys.

There followed a couple of embarrassing minutes of key-tapping, sighing and shrugging. Ella, increasingly concerned, shifted position in her seat.

'Look,' she said, 'if you can't find anything, just say so.'

'Are you...tied to the postcodes you've got down here, Mrs Barclay?' he asked her somewhat desperately. 'It's just that they are the most popular areas of the city. Property in these districts is likely to go for, ah, well in excess of…' He waved the piece of paper awkwardly.

'Of my budget,' Ella completed.

'Yes.'

'Look, don't you have anything in, say, Birchwoods? For God's sake, we'll even go out as far as Great Lynton if we have to.'

'Mrs Barclay,' he said, turning to face her again, and spreading his palms awkwardly, 'you've just named two of our most sought-after areas. The location, you see, with the new bus links…and the reputable schools, of course. The market's incredibly competitive in those areas right now.' He shrugged, half smiled apologetically.

'Oh, don't give me that,' Ella snapped.

'I'm sorry?' He actually shrank back in his swivel-chair.

'You talk about "the market" as if it were the weather,' she said. 'Something you've got no control over. You don't fool me. A market is something you design, and you people are totally complicit in creating it.'

He smiled nervously. 'We respond to demand.'

'Oh, *bullshit*. It's your job to *create* demand. Look, everybody knows about the classic stuff you guys do. Describing a house as "in a quiet location" because it's miles from the nearest dirt-track. Or calling it "convenient for local shops" because it's on top of a bloody petrol station. People aren't stupid, you know. They do go along and see these things with their own eyes.'

For a moment, Ella was aware of how she might seem – a little unhinged, perhaps, unnerving and hectoring, the sort of person her previous self would have been embarrassed for. But the insight lasted only a second. She was warming to her theme.

'And then there's the tricks you *think* nobody knows about. Just one example. Phantom bidders? Getting people to ask their friends to put offers in, just to bump a house way up above its asking price and get everybody to play poker?'

'Mrs Barclay, you're not suggesting—'

'Damn right I'm not suggesting, I'm bloody telling you it's true. And then there's those cosy little deals with the council, where they restrict access to the plans for the sewage works or the asylum centre down the road until you've sold the last of your desirable executive homes... Oh, yes, these things aren't state secrets, much as you'd like to believe they are.'

'Mrs Barclay,' the young man said nervously, 'it's a competitive market. I think some of your ideas are a little fanciful.'

Ella folded her arms in satisfaction. 'I got drunk with an estate agent once,' she said. 'At a party. We swapped tricks of the trade. It's all from the horse's mouth.' She leant forward. 'So, be straight with me and I'll be straight with you. I want to know what I can get to match *this* set of criteria,' and she stabbed at her printout, 'and *this* budget.'

The estate agent shrugged. He leant back in his chair. 'Nothing,' he admitted.

'*Nothing*?' she echoed. She wanted to add the line from *King Lear*, 'Nothing will come of nothing', but knew it would be wasted on him. Estate agents' knowledge of the Bard, she thought, probably extended as far as knowing the most outrageous prices they could get away with in Stratford-upon-Avon.

'I'm sorry, Mrs Barclay, but you're asking the impossible. You'd need at least twice that for a three-bedroom house in the areas you're looking in. Even most of the apartments would eat your budget up.'

Ella held his gaze for a full five seconds, not wavering even when he raised his eyebrows in an impudent, smug, *What do you expect me to do about it?* kind of way.

'Now, on the other side of the city, of course,' he said, tapping a few more keys and pointing to what came up, 'it's a different story. Very reasonable prices, a lot of market stability, strongly established residential areas.'

'In-bred, you mean. And the prices are *reasonable*, as you put it, because the areas are shit. Will you please stop trying to dress this stuff up for me?'

'Lots of fantastic investments in former local authority housing, Mrs Barclay. It's a great time to seize that opportunity.'

Ella ran the wording through her mental translator, and flared her nostrils as if at a bad smell. 'You mean ex-council houses,' she said, hardly able to believe the suggestion.

'Well, we don't...use that particular terminology as such, but...'

'But, at the end of the day, you are still trying to get me to spend a large sum of my own, hard-earned money on a fucking council house.' She stood up, smoothing her skirt. 'I'll not waste any more of your time.'

'Have you considered rented accommodation at all?' he asked, with an air of desperation.

She gave him a withering look. Then she folded her arms, waiting expectantly.

He frowned in puzzlement. She snapped her fingers – making him jump – and pointed to the printout, which he was still holding. He handed it back to her without a murmur.

'You know where we are, if you change your mind!' he called after her.

'You can't just put "anyfink",' said the bored girl behind the counter.

Tom had switched to autopilot. He had the continual feeling that this whole thing was happening to someone else. Especially now, sitting in a temporary building on a muddy wasteland beyond the ringroad.

This place – he had discovered after walking through the mud on planks – was currently the home of the Employment Service. The mobile office was a scabby mushroom-grey, and the space within was bleached bone-white by argon lights. It stank of smoke and sweat and the cabbage-stench of uneasy bowels. The windows were stained almost opaque, like those of old railway carriages.

A building with the soul sucked out of it. No wonder the people here, sitting on their plastic chairs awaiting their turn, looked as if they had abandoned all hope.

When Tom's number came up and he took his seat, his heart sank at the sight of the painted creature behind the desk. She had a ring through each nostril and a multi-coloured braid in her hair, and looked as if she had just left school. And now she was telling him what he could and couldn't say on his benefit application form.

'I'm sorry?' he asked. 'Where can't I put that?'

'There,' said the girl, sighing as she pointed out the relevant section. 'Under "other employment considered". You can't just put "anyfink". You gotta be pacific.'

'I'm sorry, I have to what?'

'You gotta be pacific.'

'I have to be specific?' Tom asked cautiously.

'That's what I said.'

'Rrrright. Look, level with me here. I'm supposed to be filling in this form to maximise my chances of finding employment, right?' The girl nodded dumbly. 'So the more wide-ranging a brief I can give you, the more useful it is, surely?'

The girl shrugged, looking past him out of the window. 'You gotta put sumfink pacific,' she said again, twirling her pen.

'Oh, God, give it here,' said Tom with a sigh. He pulled the form towards him, crossed out 'anything' in the box and wrote 'astronaut'. He pushed the form back to her. 'Is that all right?'

The girl didn't seem bothered. She flipped through another couple of pages, nodding (and, Tom noticed, moving her lips). 'You gotta put Saturday down an' all,' she said, pointing to the box where Tom had filled in the hours he would be willing to work (9–6, Monday–Friday).

'Why?' he said. 'I don't want to work on Saturdays. I want time with my children.'

The girl sighed. 'If you don't put you're available for work on a Saturday, we carn give you no benefit for a Saturday,' she said.

'So if I put that, somebody could ring me up at six o'clock one Saturday morning?'

'Well, we tries to give people adequate notice of job offers what comes in.'

Tom ignored her. 'They could say, "Get your arse down here and stack these boxes. You said you'd work Saturdays, so jump to it, mate, or we stop your benefit." Couldn't they?'

The girl stared blankly at him. 'I am only trying to assist you in yer search for employment, Mister Barclay.'

'All right. Give it to me.' Tom snatched the form, made the necessary addition and thrust it back at her. 'Is that OK? Can I go now?'

Another five minutes crawled by, as the girl leafed through the form, ticking boxes, making laborious notes and tucking bits of paper into plastic wallets.

'Now, Mister Barclay, have you understood the work plan what we've agreed?'

'We haven't agreed anything. You've told me which hoops I need to jump through and I've jumped.' He saw her eyes glaze over again and hastily added, 'But yes, if it makes you happy, I can say I've understood it. Christ, I have got a degree, you know. This is hardly rocket science.'

'In addition,' the girl said, 'you might wanna approach some companies specktively, like. Y'know, write to them with a CV, ask about vacancies what they got, and that.'

'That's amazing,' said Tom, folding his arms and widening his eyes. 'You know, I never would have thought of doing that. I expect that's why you're an Employment Adviser and I'm on the dole.'

'Good luck with yer job search, Mister Barclay.'

'Oh, your concern touches me profoundly,' he assured her.

'Sorree?'

'Never mind,' he said, and left as quickly as he could, tucking the sheaf of documents away in his pocket.

'Any *what?*' Bex's voice crackled in Ella's ear.

'Houses. Going cheap round your way.'

'Darling, did you say going *cheap?* Did you actually use that word in my presence?'

'Look, I was just wondering if you could keep an ear open, Bex, love. In case any of your neighbours want a quick sale. You know I've always liked Birchwoods.'

'No, you fucking haven't. You've always gone on about how down-at-heel it is.'

'I've never called it down-at-heel!'

'Oh, no. I tried to persuade you to move here, if you recall, but you weren't keen. You said the children's playground was crap because it didn't have a slide. And then, hun, you didn't like the Co-op because there were some "yobs", as you put it, hanging round outside, yeah? Even though they were perfectly harmless kids.'

Ella winced, holding the phone away from her ear for a second. 'Well, I may have—'

'And *then* you didn't like how you can see the gasometer from some houses. And you went right off the primary school because you saw a kid – *one* kid, Ella – spitting. I mean, I ask you. You couldn't have more of a fucking downer on the place if you were on Mogadon, love.' Bex paused for breath. 'Anyway, what's this all about? Hubby pissed off, has he? Gone to shack up with some floozie?'

'No, he has *not*. Bex, I'm not going into it right now. We're just...exploring some options to free up some capital, that's all.'

'I see.' Bex kept her tone level. 'Well, I can lend you a tenner if you like.'

'That's very kind of you.'

'I've probably snorted through it, but I don't suppose you'll mind.' There was a pause, and Bex audibly shifted gear, her tone becoming more moderated, more concerned. 'Ella-babe, seriously, is everything...all right?'

'It's just fine,' she said. 'Really.'

'OK. Listen, we're good mates, aren't we?'

'Course we are.'

'So you would let me know if you were in any kind of trouble, wouldn't you, honey?'

'Yes. Of course. Look, Bex, I've really got to go...just keep an ear open about houses, all right?'

'All right. And listen – if he does take off with a pneumatic blonde, then you know there's a soft shoulder and plenty of drink and drugs at my place, darling. If you need me, I'll give Nick the heave-ho for the evening and you can come round and chill out with me.'

'I'll bear it in mind.' Pause. 'Nick? Isn't that the guy you met at—'

'At the Eighties night, yes.'

'The one with—'

'The one with the long tongue, yes. Happy now?'

'Not as happy as you. Cradle-snatching witch.'

'You're just *jealous*, Ella-bella.'

'Too fucking right I am.'

* * *

And after that, she had another call to make.

'Hello, Mum.'

'Oh, hello, love. Well, this is a surprise.'

'No, it's *not*,' said Ella crossly. 'I'm your daughter.'

'Goodness me, sounds like you got out of bed on the wrong side this morning. Don't take offence, love. I just didn't think you rang me on the, what's-it-called, spur of the cuff... Let me just turn this down, I can't find the remote control... Oh, the blessed thing, it won't work unless I give it a good bash. Just a minute.' There was the sound of a remote being thumped, and the blare of Channel 4 News abated slightly in the background. 'Sorry about that, love. I was just watching the news. It's that immigrant chap reading it again. He does it quite well, you know, pronounces his words properly, not like some of them who can barely string a sentence together in decent English.'

Ella, closing her eyes almost in pain, tried to think herself into her mother's mindset for a minute. 'Please, Mother, Krishnan Guru-Murthy isn't an *immigrant*.'

'Well, yes, but he's a...coloured, isn't he? Is that what you have to call them? I don't know, so many things you can't say nowadays. I know you're not allowed to call them nig-nogs or darkies any more, I realise that. All that political correctness. But I didn't realise you couldn't even say immigrant.'

'Mum, you've missed the point.'

'I think all these people who want a – what's it called, multi-racialist society – they should go and sort out some of their Third World countries first and leave ours alone. Oh, and these *gays*! Aren't there so *many* of them on the television? It seems like everywhere you look there's another one. And those women, those lesbians, what do *they* do? They look so awful, and this lot who call themselves feminists, they're not very *feminine*, are they?... I mean, yes, we had them, nancy-boys, that's what people used to call them, of course. Don't get me wrong. I didn't spend the Sixties living under a stone, you know. Everybody knew about that Ruby Scotwell's youngest, Graham. He was a bit funny that way, as they used to say.'

'We're moving.'

'But I mean it was all, well, kept in its place. Private was properly private. They didn't all go on the telly and boast about it. These days people go on those, thing-gies, chat shows. At lunchtime, while you're eating. Talking about their *partners* and what they do and how the Church should let them get *married*, for heaven's sake. They even have bishops who are that way inclined. I mean, how can they? We all know about Sodom and Gomorrah. I'm sure you wouldn't want Isobel watching that filth and picking up all kinds of ideas.'

'I said we're moving.'

This time, her mother's stream of consciousness was brought to a satisfying halt.

'You what, love?' The upbeat of excitement, of hope, was quite unmistakable.

'We're both...going in new directions. I've left my job at the Castle and Tom...well, his contract's in a consultation period.'

'I knew it. What's happened, have they given him the chop?'

'No, they...look, it's complicated.'

Her mother's tone became more excited. 'Ella, love, you'd never believe it, but Jennifer Gray's sister – you remember

Nicky, works at the hairdresser's? – well, she's just put their house on the market. They're moving all the way to *Beckton Road*, would you believe? She'll be three *miles* from her mum, so I don't know how she'll cope. Anyway, it's just around the corner, a lovely semi. Bramwell Close, off the High Street. I'll get you a brochure tomorrow afternoon. Well, you could move in here until you got settled, of course. Oh, Ella, love, it was just meant to work out. You're coming home, love. You're coming home!'

'We're staying in Cherford,' said Ella, who had kept her teeth clenched throughout her mother's speech.

Very.

Long.

Pause.

'I see,' said Maggie.

'Look, Mum, we can't move cities as well. It would just be too much.'

'Well, if that's how you feel. If Nicky's house isn't good enough for you, that's no skin off my teeth. Have you never seen it? It's got a lovely garden, and she keeps it so *clean*. Of course, she's been at home since Jayden and Kelly-Anne were born. Well, I'm very disappointed in you, love, it seems like the ideal opportunity and you're just going to quandary it as usual. It's up to you, of course. What does his dad think about it?'

'I've no idea. Tom's not spoken to him in years.'

'I see. I suppose not. Well, I know family's never been as important to him.'

'Tom's dad runs a farm on the other side of the world, Mum, so I don't imagine he really thinks much about us at all. If you want to ring him and have a gossip, feel free.'

'There's no need for sarcasm, Ella love. It isn't big or clever. Well, I suppose you'll be letting me know where you're moving to, then? Oh, they do say the market's a bit slow at the moment, don't they? That nice young lady on that house programme. Now, she always *dresses* so well, don't you think? It's nice to see a young woman on the telly looking after herself. Some of them look so...well, so much like scarecrows, what with their hair chopped and all over the place.'

Any minute now – Angela Rippon, thought Ella grimly.

'People used to have standards. They had to dress properly for being on the telly. Think about that lovely Angela Rippon on the news, she was always so smart... What was I saying? Well, I'll tell Nicola you're moving and she'll probably want to send you a brochure anyway. It's a lovely house. Such a shame you don't want it. There's a downstairs toilet *and* a conservatory, and you could walk to the school. I saw Mrs Carr the other day, you know? She still teaches there. Remembered you very well. So glad to hear about all your successes. You must pop in and see her when you're next home.'

'Yes, Mum,' said Ella, who had closed her eyes about five seconds into the monologue. She didn't even bother challenging the 'home' for once. 'I'll see you soon.'

She switched the phone off, and the beep sounded lonely in the darkness.

In some ways, she had to concede, Maggie was right – it would be easier to leave Cherford, to move, to have help on tap and everything cheaper. But one of Ella's greatest fears was that of incurring the approval of her mother.

* * *

Bathed in the dim light, they held hands across the kitchen table.

'We'll get through this,' said Ella firmly. 'It's not going to last for ever. But we know what we have to do.'

Terrible, angry days had passed since they had fully realised the bitter irony of their new position. Tom had retreated into himself, spending hours out walking. Ella, though, felt galvanised, as if the sharp knife in her ribs had piqued her. She was like an animal roused; she glowed with passion. She was Doing Something About It All.

'Yes, but...*sell* everything?' Tom whispered, horrified. 'Are you sure that's the answer?'

She pulled a face. 'Christ, Tom, I wish I knew what the answer was. But right now, the bottom line is that we need cash. We're two mortgage payments away from total bloody bankruptcy.'

'Weren't the bank any help?'

'Oh, a great help.' She gave a contemptuous snort.

When we had money, she thought bitterly, they used to bombard us with stuff. Borrow this! Please, take out this loan now! And we'd always say, no thanks, we're doing fine. So, now I give them a call and ask them about loans, because we need the money. And they won't lend us any because – guess what? – we're not in a good enough financial position. I tell them that's sort of the point. But no, we haven't got any immediate way of paying it back, so they're not prepared to lend their loyal customers a single penny. Ironic doesn't even cover it.

'Look,' Tom said, 'surely we're going to make a profit on this place?'

'Not much of one, Tom. We've not had it long enough – and prices aren't rocketing the way they were last year. I checked it out. In this end of Cherford it's like in the best bits of London and Manchester and Leeds – the prices have flatlined.'

Tom slumped back in his chair. 'Jesus,' he said. 'I was hoping the house would be our bloody pension.'

'Yeah, well, afraid not. We might have to rent somewhere for a bit while we look around. That won't be too hard, judging by what the estate agent had to say.'

Tom stared at her in horror. '*Rent* somewhere?' he repeated.

The hollow, aching tone in his voice irritated her. He made it sound as if she had just suggested selling the children into slavery. 'Yes, Tom, rent. It's not the end of the world.'

She imagined herself going back to the gaunt young estate agent, tail between her legs, asking for information on rented accommodation. It wasn't a pleasant thought, but it was one she had to face up to.

Tom shook his head, folded his arms, would not look at her.

'There's one other thing,' she said. 'Millmount. We'll take them out.' She was surprised how easily it came to her; it was almost a relief to say it.

He looked up. 'And send them *where*?' he asked.

She felt herself becoming angry now. Was he just being deliberately obtuse? 'To a local *comprehensive*, Tom. Heard of those? Something we pay our bloody taxes for and have never used? Look, we both had a state education, for God's sake. It didn't do us any harm.'

'Well, we both got lucky, didn't we?'

'Tom, the bottom line is this. School fees are a luxury,

they're for middle-class people with disposable income. We no longer have any. Darling, trust me, I've done the sums. Yes, we've got money in the savings, but we're going to need it, OK?'

'Can't we...get them scholarships or something?' he threw out desperately.

'Oh, yeah, for both of them, before next term. Get *real*, Tom.'

They're gifted children, she told herself. Imaginative, bright, applied. They can't go wrong. They would have gone to grammar school, if such things existed any more.

She had been tempted, *so* tempted to go against nature and to vote Conservative last time on this issue alone, but stronger forces had pushed her pencil down a box. Ancient loyalty, perhaps. And an abiding memory of all those marches against the bouffant bogeywoman: No Nukes, No American Airbases, No Clause 28.

She had spent the Eighties looking for something to be Pro enough to march for, rather than Anti. She hadn't found it.

'Look,' she said, 'St Mary's may have places, or Meadowcrofts. They both get good results. We can only ask.'

He sat at the kitchen table, staring at the same knot of wood, for a long time after Ella had gone up to bed.

It was a good table. It was made of iroko wood, sometimes called African teak, prepared to perfection in a little country workshop they knew. Chairs to match. They hadn't even discussed whether it was worth paying the sum quoted, because they both wanted a fantastic kitchen table and they both thought it was worth a decent price.

Tom thought about Phill's welcoming body and her eager

tongue, and allowed himself a little smile. At least he still had that. It had been worth persevering, for she was the ideal lover – giving and receptive, salacious and uninhibited.

He hadn't quite squared in his own mind how he was going to find time for her now with all this other stuff going on, or how – or even if – he was going to tell her the truth about what was happening.

He heard something pattering on the tiled floor.

Looking up, he saw Isobel in her Zillah Zim pyjamas, hugging a striped toy (christened Deborah Zebra, Tom remembered) and standing in the kitchen doorway. Her curls were tangled and her eyes were droopy and crunchy with sleep. She looked puzzled.

He was disturbed that thoughts of his mistress should be interrupted by his daughter, and was then swamped with horrible guilt for thinking like that.

'Bizzy, what are you doing up?' he said softly. Isobel trotted, barefoot, over to Tom, her warm little body nestling into his arm for a cuddle.

'What's the matter?' Isobel asked groggily. 'What were you and Mummy talking about?'

He wasn't really prepared for this moment.

'It's exciting, Bizzy,' Tom said. 'We're going to be moving house. Isn't that great? Going to live somewhere new.'

'Oh, wow! Rosie's just moved house,' said Izzy excitedly, perking up. 'She's got her own playroom up in the attic. And her sister's got a pool table in the basement.'

'Well, isn't that nice? Maybe Rosie will let you go round and play in her playroom. That'd be good, wouldn't it?'

Isobel nodded, silently. She had Deborah Zebra's ear in her

mouth with her thumb, just like when she was a toddler.

'Daddy, why's Mummy so *cross* all the time?' Isobel asked.

'Is she? Darling, you mustn't say that. Mummy's just worried, that's all.' Tom touched his daughter's soft cheek with the edge of his fingers. 'We're...well, we're both a little bit worried at the moment, if we're truthful.'

'What about?'

'Well...' Tom hesitated. Honesty, he reminded himself. Always honesty. It had been the cause of problems in the past, but he'd had to do enough lying recently, what with the whole Phill situation. 'Your mum and I are going to be...well, we won't have as much money coming in for a while. It might mean we have to do without some of the things that we've had. Luxuries, you know.'

'What are luxuries?'

'Treats, darling. Special things.' He hugged her even more tightly. 'But we're not going to let you and Ben starve.' He kissed her forehead. 'Now, Izzy, please don't worry. I want you to go back to bed. Will you do that for Daddy?'

She kissed him, and turned, and he heard her footsteps. They pattered back across the stripped-pine floor of the hall, and then they were soft and barely audible on the warm carpet of the stairs.

He sat there, brooding, taking sips from a scalding glass of whisky. At any moment, he knew, he could let go and this terrible, new world, this anti-life, would crash into horrible focus.

The night was hot and still, the air unyielding. He threw the back door open and, oblivious to the clouds of midges, took his drink out on the springy lawn.

He already felt like an intruder in his own garden. For the first time, it seemed incredible that they owned this many *square metres* of grass, this much masonry, all these flowers and trees and a shed. It was bizarre. It already seemed to belong to someone else.

He walked out as far as the plum tree in the centre of the garden. Tom smiled sadly. He lifted one of the branches in his hand and caressed the leaves, as delicately as he had stroked Isobel's cheek just now.

He closed his eyes for a minute, standing in the darkness and remembering, hearing only the distant hum of the city and the murmur, somewhere, of water.

And then he had the sudden sense that he was not alone.

The air shifted around him. There were footsteps on the grass. Tom, not daring to open his eyes, felt gripped, through the heat, by a shiver of fear.

'Daddy?' said a soft voice.

It chilled him, physically jolted him. He swung round, gasping, his heart thudding away like some alien machine in his chest.

Isobel was standing next to him on the lawn, looking up at him.

Relief drenched him.

'Jesus, Izzy,' he said, 'don't creep up on me like that.'

'Sorry, Daddy.' She didn't move.

'I thought you'd gone to bed?' he said. And then he saw what she was carrying in her hands.

'I want you to have it,' she said, her eyes big and bold, loving and genuine. 'So that you have more money. That's all.'

'Thank you,' said Tom. He realised he was shaking.

Isobel hefted the big, polished pink piggy bank and put it carefully on the grass in front of him. Pregnant with coinage, it clunked and chinked.

It sat there, a smooth, round gift, glossy and almost orange in the pale moonlight. He realised then that it was simultaneously the saddest and the most beautiful thing he had ever seen.

And then he had no control any more, and the world was dissolving into a salty fog, and Isobel's face blurred in front of his eyes like a badly focused photograph.

PART THREE

Location, Location, Location

'Ils se connaissaient trop pour avoir ces ébahissements
de possession qui en centuplent la joie. Elle était aussi
dégoûtée de lui qu'il était fatigué d'elle. Emma retrouvait
dans l'adultère toutes les platitudes du mariage.'

Gustave Flaubert, *Madame Bovary*

From: Tom Barclay <tom@appletree.uk.net>
To: Andy Barclay <andybee@bravemail.com>
Sent: July 28, 15:45 PM
Subject: a bit more news

Handy Andy!

This address won't be valid much longer. I'm
changing jobs - quite an exciting time for us. I'll
let you know my new address as soon as I can.

In fact, Ella has jacked in her job at Cherford
Castle too. Can you believe it?! Yeah, it wasn't
really fulfilling her any more and she has lots
of ideas for brave new ventures, so we both
agreed it was for the best.

We've also given some thought to the school thing
and decided that Ben and Izzy are getting a bit
stifled in that academic hothouse. They need a
bit of room to run about, some rough and tumble,
bit more of an ethnic mix. So we're looking at
moving them into a state school.

Glad yours are doing well. It sounds as if they're
going to grow up bilingual. Your wine collection
sounds terrific - when do you find time to drink it
all? Sainte-Odile seems like a great place to live.
We want to come and visit you, but may need a few
months to settle into the new routine.

Oh, while I remember - I know it's a few months off
yet, but we're probably not going to make a big
deal out of Christmas this year. It just gets more
and more commercialised and so we want to try and
have a low-key one (just small presents, etc.).
Hope this is OK with you. All best - speak soon.

T.

28 Thorpedale Avenue
Upper Ashington
Nr. Cherford
CR7 2FG

Sir Nigel Henderson, Chief Executive
Cherford Castle Heritage Trust
Eboracum Way
Cherford
CR1 6CD

29th July

Dear Sir Nigel

I am writing to inform you that, with regret, I wish to tender my resignation as Senior Visitor and Events Manager at Cherford Castle Heritage Trust.

I have had a very pleasant and productive time in the role over the past few years, but I feel it is now the right time to move on. I would like to thank you for all your support and encouragement, and to wish the Trust every success in the future.

Yours, with very best wishes

Ella

Ella Barclay

Chapter Thirteen

The End Of The World As We Know It

'Apples,' Ella said. 'You've heard of apples? Round, green, crunchy things. Fell on Newton's head when he discovered gravity.' She paused. 'You're not telling me you don't have any apples?'

Friday lunchtime.

Outside Priceworth on the rain-swept precinct, Ella drew a deep breath and adjusted her sunglasses.

She hoped her combination of jeans (stonewashed) and an Agnès B shirt (lime-green, last year's) didn't make her stand out. She had never seen such a profusion of football tops, tattoos and paunchy stomachs. And the men were even worse.

She had tried shopping in the town centre, but M&S, formerly such a calming temple, just made her miserable. She had been standing there with an organic butternut squash in her hand. It was firm, weighty. Problem was, if she got all her vegetables from this counter, it would blow her budget for the week. It was no good; choices were now a luxury. Shop at

Priceworth, bitch, the butternut squash seemed to sneer. Don't get above yourself.

She wondered if the string-bag with wooden handles – a masterpiece of rustic chic which she had picked up in a little village near Avignon – was a bad idea. Everybody else had things in carrier bags slung over pushchairs or dangling from yellowing fingers, and the last thing she wanted was to draw attention.

She chucked the bag into a bin by the newsagent's. She wouldn't be needing it here.

Priceworth stood at the heart of the Parkfield Estate on a circular island of tarmac known as the Hub, which also housed the bank, the medical centre and the school. The streets radiated out from it. Someone in a planning office a long way from here had obviously thought this would be a good idea, that it would provide a sense of community. What it actually provided was a rat-run for boy-racers to slice up the tarmac at night, tyres screeching like banshees, the smell of burning rubber mingling with the odours of dogshit and decay. There had been talk of installing bollards, but it obviously wasn't high up on the city councillors' To Do list. Nothing in Parkfield ever was.

Inside, Priceworth was stark and stone-floored, lit like an operating theatre. One-brand choices of white bread, yoghurt, tinned foods, fizzy drinks and beers were stacked on pallets in a take-it-or-leave-it way reminiscent of the old Eastern Bloc. Welcome to the Le Corbusier supermarket, thought Ella grimly – the machine for shopping in.

She walked the aisles, a ghost with ultrabright skin and cola-dark hair, gliding like the other Parkfielders from one purchase to another. A plinky piano version of a Boyzone song played on the tannoy.

This wasn't *shopping* in the sense that Ella understood the word. For her, shopping involved a day punishing the plastic with Bex and Tori, driven by a pathological need to accessorise. It was trying-on, giggling and cappuccinos, it was Harvey Nicks, Karen Millen and Axis – it was *fun*.

As for groceries, she and Tom had bought them on the Internet for several years – partly because it was more convenient, but mainly because Ella turned her nose up at standing in a queue with other people's screaming, snotty children.

But that was then.

Snobbery was a luxury.

She filled her basket with the bland items. She couldn't find apples anywhere. After five minutes of literally fruitless exploration of the aisles, she asked the sullen, pudding-faced girl who was stacking the bread. She was met with a bemused expression. Ella tried sarcasm, but it didn't work. Finally, the girl got off her stool, crossed the aisle and reached down a tin of Priceworth's Finest Apple Filling. The label showed a bowl of verdant gunk being swamped in bright yellow custard.

'We got this,' she said sullenly.

Ella tutted. 'That's not an apple,' she said indignantly. 'That's a tin of stewed fruit and monosodium glutamate.'

The girl stared at her, blinked, pointed at the label. 'Apple,' she said.

'No, dear. It's almost, but not entirely, unlike apple. I'm after Granny Smiths, or Cox's Orange Pippin.'

The girl looked Ella up and down as if she had wandered in

from another planet. 'It's what we got,' she said, and returned to her stacking duties.

So that was it, then, she thought in silent horror. She shoved the anonymous packages into her carrier bag at the checkout as the barcoder chirped.

From now on, it was tins and packets all the way. (Beep. Beep.) Anything non-essential, anything frivolous, now seemed like a laughable indulgence. (Beep. Beep.) Focaccia bread, bruschetta, sun-dried tomato panini? No way. You'll get Mother's Shame, and like it. (Beep.) Organic yoghurt, fair-trade coffee, fresh pasta? Get out of here. (Beep.) Flowers, new clothes? You're having a laugh. (Beep.) Classic FM and *The Archers* now seemed like transmissions from Mars. Izzy's ballet and piano classes, Ben's judo and guitar lessons. (Beep.) A good school, the hope of university for her children. A new laminate floor, a gravel drive. A car. A house. A home. Marriage. Morality. Choices. Security. Love. (Beep. Beep. Beep.)

There were no more options.

(Beep.)

It's what we got.

(Beep.)

This was Parkfield. This was her life.

(Beeeeeep-bip.)

'Twennysix forty, love.'

Monday morning. Ben Barclay stood at the gates of Hell.

He'd marched Isobel into the playground of the primary school next door and walked her over to the least threatening-looking group of small girls. 'Year Four?' he asked. They nodded dumbly. 'This is my sister,' he said, looking each of them in the eye, trying to look adult and stern. 'Look after her.'

And now he stood in the alleyway, blinking the rain out of his eyes, held grimly on to the rucksack on his shoulder and tried to ignore the loose, angry sensation in his bowels. He narrowed his eyes, set his chin firmly.

It was just a question of attitude. Just a matter of fitting in.

He was going to be *acting*.

On either side of him, kids streamed in, either jostling one another or kicking the puddles up into each other's faces, swearing, shoving, bouncing off the walls of the alleyway like pinballs. Most of them ignored him, although some gave him curious looks. They could spot a newcomer round here.

In the short walk to the back gate, Ben had already pulled his top button loose and splashed in as many puddles as he could find. His hair, prison-buzzcut by the cornershop barber, was too short to tousle.

He'd bought some chewing gum from Mr Aziz at the top of the hill. It was a weird kind of newsagent's, not like any he'd ever seen before. A concrete hexagon, bounded on five sides by blue steel plates, stuck all on its own at the top of a hill. Only the grille-covered door on the sixth side betrayed that it was a shop at all. He would have taken it for some lookout post from a long-forgotten war. As he went in, Ben had tried not to look at the scarlet swastika which someone had daubed on the door.

He wondered if he was able to fade into the background. As an afterthought, hurrying through the gate, he picked at a loose thread on the elbow of his jumper, pulling and pulling, until he had quite a decent-sized hole by the time he reached the building.

'Come on, come on!' A burly, sour-faced teacher with a bushy moustache stood on the steps, ushering kids in with what seemed like unnecessary enthusiasm. 'Get yourselves in! We're not having you late on the first day!'

A second after he reached the top step, Ben felt himself yanked backwards, and the teacher's face was centimetres from his. Ben recoiled from the stench of tobacco and bad dental hygiene.

'You, young man. Name.'

Ben deliberately didn't look him in the eye. He knew the routine. He'd watched loads of *Grange Hill*, after all; it couldn't be too difficult.

'Ben Barclay,' he said, looking insolently away and continuing to chew.

'And?' came the outraged response.

Ben shrugged. 'Is it a problem?' he asked.

'*You*, young man, are the problem. Number one, you address me as Mr Hollis or Sir. Number two, you smarten up your appearance *and* your attitude.'

Ben shrugged. 'If you like,' he said, and allowed himself a little pretend grin at a private joke.

A group of tall, bullet-headed boys had gathered just inside the lobby, and were watching with interest, their ties askew and their demeanour contemptuous.

Mr Hollis withdrew a centimetre, hissing like a kettle. 'And number three,' he added through clenched teeth, 'you damn well stop that *chewing* this instant and put it in the bin. *There*.' He pointed.

Maybe he'd pushed things far enough for now, thought Ben.

'Yes, sir,' he said resignedly. He spat the gum into his hand, deposited it in the rubbish bin and wiped his hand on his trouser leg.

'I'm watching you, Barclay,' said Mr Hollis, a bony index finger extended so that one yellow nail was almost in Ben's eye.

There was a sudden shout of 'Wanker!' from outside. Fortunately for Ben, two of the Year Ten boys shuffling on the steps had chosen that moment to turn a playful shove into something more heavy-handed, and Mr Hollis was elbowing his way through to break up a fight.

As Ben hurried through the crowds to his classroom, he knew the knot of tall boys against the wall was watching him closely.

He caught a brief glimpse of the heavy-browed eyes of Gary Collins burning into him; and then he was borne along by the torrent of pupils, out of Collins's line of vision.

Monday afternoon. In his car, Matt Ryder turned the wipers up to full power to wash the torrents of rain aside.

'Sorry,' he said to Jo, who was in the passenger seat. 'Get going in a minute.'

Jo smiled, pushing her wet hair out of her eyes. 'No problem.' She snuggled down in the seat of the shiny blue MG and giggled. 'So, this was the treat you gave yourself over the summer. I dunno, you heads of department with your money to throw around.'

'I didn't, like, have a holiday or anything. Saved up. And it wasn't brand new. A mate of mine refurbished it. What do you think?'

'Well, it's a car. But as cars go, I expect it's very nice.' She grinned.

'So, how's your new form?' Matt asked.

'Oh, I've got them taped,' she said. 'Usual troublemakers I can spot a mile off. Yeah, gonna be a fun year. I just hope the fucking weather gets better, though. I don't fancy taking Year Ten netball in this.'

'Ooh, I could watch you and the girls all getting wet from my nice dry classroom, yeah? Grandstand view, I've got.'

'Shut it, pervy.' She slapped his hand.

Out in the car park, kids scurried through the rain, zipping parka hoods tight around their faces or simply pulling feeble, thin jackets over their heads. Matt had a twinge of guilt, but reasoned that he could hardly take everyone home. In any case, they all lived no more than a few streets away. That was the thing about Parkfield.

'Hey, you'll never guess,' said Jo, 'who I saw up here the other day.'

'I don't bloody know, do I? The Pope? Michael Jackson?'

'Keep guessing,' she said with a sly grin.

'Errm...a policeman?'

'Now you're just being silly.'

'Sorry, Jojo. You're right.' Matt grinned. 'Go on, then. Tell me.'

'That snobby woman. Your friend from Cherford Castle.'

Matt frowned, briefly confused as he tried to match pieces from one jigsaw with gaps in another. 'Ella? What do you mean?'

Jo leant back, smiled smugly. 'Aaah, well, I can tell you're interested. This has got to be worth at least a pint or two, I'd say.'

'Jojo, I'll buy you as many pints as you want, complete with pork scratchings, prawn cocktail crisps or any other snack of your choice? I may, like, even promise to have a drunken grope of your arse at the end of the evening. But just tell me what you're talking about, OK?'

Jo sighed, smiled as she turned towards him. 'I *saw* her, all right? You know my kitchen looks out over the Greenway?' Matt nodded. 'I saw her, struggling along with two moaning kids in tow. She looked a bit bedraggled. But it was raining. She kept stopping to yell at the little girl, because she was dawdling. In the end, she went and grabbed her wrist and practically dragged the poor kid up the path.'

'On the Greenway?' Matt frowned, confused.

'Yup. Looked like she'd just been to the shops. She was in a foul mood.'

'You're *sure* it was her?'

'Matt, trust me. It was her.'

'So they could have been visiting someone?' All right, Matt told himself, it was unlikely, but then the alternative was even more so.

'Yeah, well, I wondered about that. So, being the curious type...' Jo grinned.

'You followed them? Jojo, you're shameless.'

She shrugged. 'Well, why not? It's not as if they know me. And do you know where they went? All the way up Greenway Crescent, right, to the top of the estate. I couldn't quite believe it. She turned and looked back at one point, like she was frightened of being seen, so I had to pull my hood up and pretend to be on the phone. I don't think she really noticed me.'

'And then what?' Matt asked.

'And then, Matthew, she only took them in the gates of bloody Renaissance Towers, didn't she? In through the front entrance. I followed them as far as the lobby, and I checked out the lift – it had gone up to Ten.'

'Renaissance Towers?' Matt looked at her in incomprehension. 'I thought it had been condemned?'

'I'm telling you, Matt, she bloody *lives* there.'

'No, no, no… Doesn't add up, mate. She and her husband live in some nice little Stepford Wives enclave, out Ashington way? Kids are at Millmount. Costs flaming thousands.' He grinned. 'Maybe that's it. The school fees have cracked them and they've had to sell the house.'

'Or maybe she's split up from hubby,' Jo offered, wickedly.

'It's a possibility.'

'One which you'd be quite keen on, I'm sure.'

'Oh, shut up, Jo.'

'Why? I've seen you, trailing behind the old bitch with your tongue hanging out. One sniff of her knickers and you'd be on your knees – whoa! What the *fuck*?!'

Matt had slammed his foot on the brake. They'd only been doing about twenty miles an hour, but the MG still swerved a little before stopping beside the kerb. Luckily, the rain-lashed street was deserted.

'Barclay,' he said.

Jo relaxed her whitened knuckles. 'Jesus,' she said, shaking her head. 'Those brakes don't feel good, Matt. Get your mate to check them out... What are you on about now?'

'Her name. That's why I remembered it – Barclay, like the bank. Voice full of money? Like Daisy in *The Great Gatsby*, yeah? Have you read it?'

'Can't say I have. PE teachers don't read, remember, we're illiterate.'

'Seen the film? Robert Redford? No?... Well, the book won't take you long. It's really short. Brilliant, but short.' He turned to her, eyes alight. 'It's all about, like, the American Dream, yeah? This guy runs these parties to impress this woman, and they're all, like, a hollow sham? He doesn't really have this great life or know all these people at all? And at the end, when he gets shot—'

'Oh, cheers, I'm really gonna read it now, aren't I?'

'When he dies, nobody comes to his funeral, yeah, because nobody really knew him?' Matt gave a low whistle.

'Is there a point to all this?'

Matt grinned briefly at her, as the car pulled off again. 'I've only just realised. There's this new kid, Ben Barclay, in Year Nine, yeah? Old Hollis was talking about him at break, saying he's a bit of a shit-stirrer. Jesus, it would be too much of a bloody coincidence, wouldn't it?'

'Too much,' Jo agreed. She shook her head, smiling and wondering. 'Wow, I wonder why they're slumming it, then.'

Matt wondered why, too. Jo, he knew, wasn't really interested, but he was. There was a suspicion in his mind – and once he'd confirmed it, there was something he needed to do.

* * *

Tuesday afternoon.

The bus rocked Ella back and forth as it hauled itself, with a creak of metal and a grind of gears, up the hill to Parkfield.

It had to feel different, now, of course. She had done the journey before, but this time she had to make a mental adjustment. She was using the return half of her ticket.

The bus stank of smoke, sweat and petrol. It seemed to hit a bump every few metres, and was packed full. People swayed in the aisle, juddered in their seats. Everywhere, plastic bags bulged, the familiar names – Boots, Argos, Woolworth – stretched into demented shapes by their contents.

People were chatting and laughing, and some were reading the local paper. They all seemed remarkably unperturbed, she thought, to be clattering in a metal death-trap towards the foulest, most dismal part of Cherford.

That first day, back in the summer holidays – they hadn't quite been able to believe it.

'They can't mean *here*.'

Tom says it with the conviction of a desperate man. He turns to Ella, across the roof of the taxi. She can't read his eyes because his sunglasses mask them, but she knows they are crumpled, defeated.

In front of them, they see gates which sit gaping open, wires ripped from the lock mechanism. A chain-link fence runs round the perimeter, savaged as if by giant fangs. Beyond the gates, a vast, empty car park stretches away, the tarmac scarred and pitted like old paint, leading to revolving doors and the austere building itself – twenty floors of tinted glass set in an ugly, custard-coloured frame.

'This is the address,' says Ella, her stomach churning.
'Renaissance Towers.'

The metal gates, Ella notices, are emblazoned with 'PAKI'S
FUCK OFF OR YOUR DEAD' in green spray-paint. For a
moment Ella isn't sure which offends her more, the racism or
the slapdash grammar.

Just inside the gates are two twisted shapes of molten black
plastic, each about the height of a child. It takes Ella a second
or two to realise they were once litter bins, and that nobody
has bothered to clear up the effects of some local youths'
experiments with firebombs. Items she does not want to
investigate too closely are pulped into the rugged tarmac,
deformed by weeks of rain-soaking and sun-bleaching.

'It's just like the Stack,' Ben says in horror, as he hauls a
suitcase from the taxi.

'It is *not* like the Stack,' Ella snaps, rounding on him
angrily. 'It's a complex of private accommodation, not a
council block. And quite remarkably priced, too.'

'Yeah, well,' Ben mutters darkly. 'They have to bribe people
to live in this fucking dump, don't they?'

'Benedict, I don't expect to have to tell you about your
language again. Save it for the guttersnipes you'll meet at
school.'

'Renaissance Towers,' Tom says emptily, holding the
brochure up to the sunlight and comparing it with the grimy,
battered building in front of them. 'It doesn't look like this in
the pictures.'

'*I want Blue Rabbit!*' wails Isobel.

She has been standing there silently, contemplating the
grim, featureless world around them as if she cannot quite

believe what has happened. She looks up at Tom, eyes limpid, clutching her small, battered Angelina Ballerina suitcase. 'Dad, I want Blue Rabbit and I want to go *home*.'

'Good God,' Ella mutters, leaning against the gates and folding her arms. 'After three years of leaving the stuffed creature in cruel isolation in the attic, she suddenly wants it back. Is the child regressing?'

Tom squats down and strokes Isobel's cheek. 'Darling, I'm afraid we can't go home, not to our old house. We don't live there any more. Blue Rabbit will come with all the rest of the things when the removal men bring them, OK? We just haven't got everything with us for now.'

Ella grits her teeth. So, this is to be the tone for their crisis. Despite everything she's done for them, the tough decisions she's made to keep them all *alive*, they're all just going to moan and she'll constantly have to defend herself. And Tom, despite his infernal stupidity, is going to play Mr Nice Guy again and get away with it.

'Look,' she says, 'with any luck, it isn't going to be for long. Now, pick up your bloody luggage and let's get inside.' She grabs a suitcase, totters a few paces ahead of everyone and realises that nobody is following. 'Well, come *on*!... Oh, for God's sake, Isobel, stop blubbing. You're not a baby any more.'

And now, Ella felt invisible on the bus.

She buried her head in her magazine. It seemed the best way of remaining anonymous, and this was the only indulgence she had allowed herself in the last few weeks.

As the bus creaked and wheezed its way past the

boarded-up shell of the library, Ella started to read.

'Amanda, 32, is the director of a Web-based firm offering its clients tailor-made graphic prints on silk. She is married to Jonathan, 37, an investment banker, and they live in Crouch End. Amanda personally designed the retro-minimalist chic of their six-bedroom Victorian house, giving the interior a vibrantly contemporary feel while maintaining its traditional integrity. Amanda and Jonathan entertain every week, usually trying out Thai or Lebanese recipes from an exclusive online newsletter which Amanda subscribes to. They are both vegetarian and strongly believe in a healthy lifestyle. Three times a week, after dropping their children Cassian (9) and Hera (7) off at their local prep school, Amanda visits the renowned gym and fitness centre, Camomile, for a two-hour workout. In her spare time—'

Ella did not want to know what the fuck Amanda did in her spare time, as she already hated the woman's guts. Is this bitch *real?* she wondered idly to herself. And if she is, can I go round and put in her retro-minimalist windows and shove her smug, elegant head into her stainless-steel wok?

She knew why she hated her, of course. Because once, not long ago, she would have wanted to be exactly like her.

When she got off the bus, one other woman followed her, trailing three children – two shaven-headed boys with ear-studs and a slim girl of about six with brown skin and lustrous brown eyes. Ella wondered why they weren't in school.

'All right, love,' said the woman to Ella, with a nod. She had the rough-edged voice of a pantomime villainess.

'Er, yes. Fine.'

All right? What were you supposed to say? She had hardly

spoken to her neighbours in Thorpedale Avenue – she wasn't even sure of their names. And she'd certainly never been addressed by any strangers. You just didn't do that in Ashington. Holding on grimly to her shopping, she fell into step with the woman.

Ella had a lot of bags, and yet she'd hardly bought anything. It was so frustrating, having to do everything by hand. Before, on the Internet, she always got the giant economy packs of stuff like washing powder, coffee and cornflakes. Now, she was limited to what could be carried – which inevitably meant the smallest packets of everything, a disaster in budgeting terms. Ella had decided that they ought to be called False Economy Packs.

'You all right with all that, love?'

'Yes, fine. Thank you.'

The woman was lean and sinewy, and looked to Ella as if she could easily take care of herself. Her lined face was the colour of raw lasagne, while her frizzy, split-ended red hair had the rough texture of fibreglass. Ella guessed that she had seen about forty summers (and quite a few harsh winters).

She offered Ella a cigarette.

Ella smiled reluctantly. 'Sorry. I gave up a while ago.'

'Good for you,' said the woman, lighting up. 'Only pleasure I get, me, *Ryan, get off the fuckin' road, now*!' Ella jumped. The woman had suddenly barked at her younger boy, darting forward and yanking him by the hood of his jacket. A battered car zoomed past with a screech of tyres, missing the boy by a fraction.

Ryan grinned, looking up at Ella in the hope of finding an

audience. She glowered down at him sternly, and he looked abashed for a second.

'Blimey,' said the woman, 'wish he did that for me. They're hooligans, the pair of 'em. I blame them teachers. They don't learn 'em nothing.'

'Er, well, I wouldn't say that.'

The woman looked Ella up and down. 'I'm Dee,' she said. 'You're new,' she added. It was a statement of fact, just like the giving of her name.

'Yes. I'm Ella. Wow, you, um...seem to have your hands full, er, Dee...'

They reached the scabby, gashed gateway to Renaissance Towers, and Dee, like Ella, slowed down. Ella realised now, with a slight lifting of her spirits, that she was talking to one of her fellow occupants.

'Always the way, innit?' said Dee with a crooked grin, cigarette waggling in her mouth. 'You up on Six?' she asked as they crossed the car park.

'Ten,' said Ella. 'Actually.'

'*Ten?* Fuck, didn' think they even let dogs up there. No offence. You got any electric yet? Gas?'

'Yes to the first, no to the second. I somehow get the impression we're not a priority.'

'Well, no,' said Dee cautiously. 'Watch it, love,' she added.

'What?'

'*Watch it!*'

Dee grabbed her lapel with bony fingers and yanked her to one side. Ella was opening her mouth to protest when she felt the air rush beside her, saw a flash of white, then heard something like a huge fist slamming into the ground. A second later, a rusty, battered washing machine was teetering on the ground a few feet away, right where she had been standing.

The round smoked-glass door, ripped from its hinges, hurtled through the air like a demented satellite before hitting the tarmac and disintegrating with a loud explosion of glass.

Ella jumped back, shrieking and covering her face. The rest of the washing machine rocked for a second as if uncertain whether to fall over, then its four sides fell outwards like the doors of a circus clown's car, baring its innards.

Dee strode out from the cover of the entrance and glowered up, giving a one-fingered gesture to the floors above. 'Yeah, nice one, love!' she bellowed. 'Make it your fuckin' stereo nex' time, then we won't have to put up with your fuckin' crap music all hours of the day.' She tutted, shook her head. 'Stupid bitch up on Five,' she said for the benefit of Ella, who was still clutching the door-frame for support and feeling rather weak at the knees.

The two boys bellowed with laughter, jumping up and down and sticking two fingers up at the unseen occupant of the flat on Floor Five. One of them grabbed a nearby piece of wood and set about the washing machine's carapace with a zealous vandalism.

'Does that...happen often?' Ella asked nervously, risking a brief glance skywards.

Maybe this was normal. Perhaps Parkfield was cursed with its own version of the Egyptian plagues, and a shower of dilapidated kitchen appliances was due to descend from the heavens at any moment.

Dee shrugged. 'Nah,' she said. 'Normally it's just stuff. Y'know, rubbish an' shit.'

'What sort of...rubbish and shit?' Ella demanded, aghast.

'Well, usually jus' black bin bags an' that. Nappies. Yeah, lot of nappies. I mean, there's supposed to be chutes, but they're fucked. Fact, I reckon they took 'em out 'cos kids was chuckin' firebombs down.' Dee shrugged again. She aimed a kick at the eviscerated washing machine, which clanged like a broken bell. 'You can't blame folk, really, can ya? Costs a fuckin' fortune to get this kind of shit taken away.'

'So they...throw it out of the *windows*?' Ella said. She heard herself saying the words as if in a dream or some enhanced form of reality. Which bloody century was this?

Dee shrugged, made a little 'Phht' noise, as if the hazard of dodging high-velocity white goods on one's way to the bus stop was just one of those little things you had to live with. 'Like I says, what else can they do?' She motioned to Ella to go first as they entered the pungent lobby. 'Where you from?' she asked, with just a hint of suspicion in her voice.

'It's...a long story,' said Ella with a tired smile. She glanced fearfully up the stairwell in case a turbo-driven 1970s chintz sofa was about to come thundering down into the lobby, but it all seemed suspiciously quiet.

'That's all right. I'm used to long stories. I were married to the biggest fuckin' bore on the estate for six fuckin' years. Yours buggered off too, has he?'

'Well, actually—'

Dee held a hand up. 'Yeah, I know. Long story,' she rasped. 'Save it, love, I'll make you a cuppa. C'mon. We're only just here, on One. 'Scuse me a minute.' She kicked the outer door open again, stormed out on to the steps and bellowed at her older boy, who was busy pelting the smashed washing machine with stones. 'Ryan, get in *now* or I will knock your fuckin' block off! I *mean* it, Ryan!'

Ella frowned. She looked back into the lobby at the other two children, who were shoving one another into the dry fountain, then back out towards the surly Ryan, who turned to spit on the car park before trudging towards the steps.

'I thought...' she said. 'Um, I thought Ryan was...the other one?'

Dee looked her up and down for a second. 'They both are,' she said, her hard and lined face not changing its expression.

'Oh. Right.'

'I liked the name.' She cuffed the older Ryan around the ear as he slouched inside, trailing mud from his unlaced trainers.

'But what do – I mean, what if—' Ella wasn't quite sure how to phrase her question in a way that didn't sound stupid. Surely it was obvious? Dee must have been asked before. She swallowed hard, tried to remind herself that her old rules no longer applied. 'What if you shout one of them,' she said, 'and the other comes?'

'Don't happen usually. They know which one I mean.'

'OK, what if you want one to lay the table and the other to, I don't know, take the rubbish out? What do you do then?'

Dee looked at Ella with a sad, pitying frown as if she thought her to be slightly mentally defective.

'I use their surnames,' she said, pulling out the key to her flat. 'Milk'n'sugar, love?'

* * *

'Mum?'

'Yes, Izzy, darling?'

'You never finished that story.'

'Which story is that, my love?'

'The one about the princess who kept asking for stuff.'

'Um...the princess who did what?'

'Kept asking the king and queen to get her things. *You* know. The one where she was always saying "I want" and if she wanted a new dress she'd just get the royal dressmaker to make her one, and if she wanted new toys the royal toymaker would make her one, and all that.'

'Oh. That one.'

'Yes, that one. Did you get it out of a book?'

'Um...no, I think I made it up.'

'Well, can you tell me what happened at the end? What the wise woman said they had to do?'

'Welllll...'

'Oh, go on.'

'Aren't you a bit old for fairytales now?'

'Oh, Mum, you're just trying to get out of it.'

'Yes, I am. Oh, all right then. What the wise woman said was that she'd cast a spell, and that the little girl would only get what she wanted if she asked nicely and said "Please". But if she was horrible and said "I want" or "get me this and that", then she'd get exactly the opposite of whatever she'd asked for.'

'That sounds good. Go on.'

'Well, one day, the little girl was running round the palace playing hide-and-seek with the courtiers.'

'With what?'

'The courtiers. You know, the people in the palace who, sort of, attend the king and queen and the princess.'

'OK. Go on.'

'Well, she started to get fed up that she always knew where to find them, and said it was too easy. "We haven't got enough space here!" she moaned to her father, the king. "It's such a poky old palace. I want a nice, new, lovely palace with hundreds of floors and hundreds of turrets, so I can play and discover a new room every day. And I want it full of toys and games and dresses and…"'

'And?'

'Well, she didn't get any further.'

'Why didn't she get any further?'

'Because there was a blinding flash of light, and a thunderclap, and all of a sudden she and her mummy and daddy weren't in a palace any more. They were in a nasty, run-down little hovel with rats running around and slime dripping off the walls and cockroaches in the corners. They had to sleep on wooden beds and dress in rags, and every day they had to go out and work in the fields for a pittance of pay from the local lord.'

'Right.'

'OK? Happy now?'

'No, no, *wait* a minute, Mum.'

'What?'

'Well, that's not the end, is it?'

'Why isn't it?'

'Well, it can't be. Fairytales all have happy endings. They always end with "they all lived happily ever after", or something.'

'Not this one.'

'Oh.'

'Goodnight, darling.'

'Mum?'

'Yes, love?'

'You're right. I am too old for fairytales.'

'I see.'

'Hope you don't mind.'

'No, Bizzy, I don't mind.'

'Goodnight, Mum.'

'Goodnight, Bizzy.'

CHAPTER FOURTEEN

I'm Not Scared

Saturday afternoon.

Ella and Ben were peeling potatoes in the sink. Isobel, slumped on an old armchair, watched black-and-white television with Deborah Zebra.

'You know that bit in *The Wizard Of Oz*,' said Ben, peeling potatoes with Ella at the sink, 'where, um, what's-her-name arrives and her house lands?'

'*And don't forget – to make that really special, memorable impression on your buyer, you have to de-personalise and de-clutter.*'

'What's-her-name is Dorothy,' said Ella. 'I'm quite relieved you didn't remember. Don't ask me why.'

He didn't. 'Well, the whole thing goes into colour, doesn't it?'

'Glorious Technicolor,' said Ella, scraping peelings into the bin. 'That's what I believe it's known as.'

'*Magnolia may say Boredomville to you, but it's by far the best, neutral colour to paint the walls when you're going to sell. Remember, don't get emotionally involved with the décor*

– you're going to be leaving this house, after all.'

'Well,' said Ben thoughtfully, 'this is like that, only in reverse, isn't it? We've gone into black-and-white.'

'Ben, darling, you are frighteningly post-modern. Pass me that big one.'

'Accessorise meaningfully. The fresh white roses Tina has put in this minimalist terracotta vase are just right for this spacious, light dining room. Maybe I'm being presumptuous, but I think she's going to have the buyers queuing round the block.'

'Isobel, why are you watching that rubbish?' Ella called over her shoulder.

Her daughter didn't answer, and instead turned up the volume.

As she scraped, Ella had to admit Ben's observation was clever. Looking out of the kitchen window on to grey skies, on to acres of tower block, cloned houses and waste ground, she realised just what he had meant.

She thought about those begging-bags from charities which used to come through their door all the time in Ashington. To be asked for charity was to be at a certain level in society. Ashington people, after all, lived in homes where one might accessorise, where one thought nothing of putting fresh white roses in a minimalist terracotta vase before popping to the Esporta gym. Parkfield did not give to charity, except through the thousands of lottery tickets sold on the estate. Parkfield gobbled huge chunks of regeneration money and yet remained, year on year, exactly the same.

Nobody was ever going to change the shape of Cherford, Ella knew, despite the city council's extravagant claims to be 'striving towards excellence'. And nobody would ever iron out the disparities in the city, because too many influential people liked things just the way they were.

'So, are you all right?' she asked. 'I mean...the school and everything?'

He wasn't looking at her, she noticed. Hardly did, these days. Teenage years about to kick in, so it was what she could expect.

'It's not bad,' he said. 'It's got a cool sports hall. And loads of laptops.'

I suppose, Ella thought, that isn't really what I meant, but if that's how he chooses to describe it, then fine. Of course it has a cool sports hall and loads of laptops. She'd read about it in the paper. The Government was pouring funding into Parkfield, because that was always the swift, easy answer to a problem – throw money at it. But the sports hall was a bonfire-in-waiting, just like their geography block had been last year. As for the computers, they might as well have had big red price tags attached to them, giving helpful indications of how much they would buy in cigarettes, CDs and drugs.

Ella still could not quite believe that her son and daughter were inmates of Parkfield. She protested to God that she had tried everything. She really had. Was this the best He could do for her?

The blessed St Mary's, as she had expected, had been full. A letter from Father Michael had done no good. It was even turning away families in the affluent catchment, including some who already had brothers and sisters there. Meadowcrofts seemed promising initially, but when Ella had made clear that she was talking about this term, the secretary made a strange, choking noise and then started laughing nervously. The tolerable Sir Walter Scott High and its corresponding primary would have involved two bus journeys, into the city and out the other side. She had pictured them doing this at seven-thirty on a dark, steely winter morning and had physically shivered.

And so it went on – until she had come, by a circuitous but inevitable route, back to Parkfield. Yes, no problem, they had said, plenty of places, junior and secondary. Delighted to take your children. You'll find the uniform is very reasonably priced.

She looked at her son, now: tall, rangy, scraping the potatoes with big hands, his once-floppy hair shorn to an army crop.

'Have you...made any friends?' she ventured.

He shrugged, still not looking at her. 'Some. They're all right.'

At least he spoke to her. Isobel didn't.

Somehow, they had got through her birthday, the three of them. Luckily, Ella's mother had sent the present she was always going to send – a boxed set of *Harry Potter* books – which had cheered her up, at least for a little while, and had helped to distract from the fact that Isobel had no Zillah Zim Magic House and no party.

But since Izzy had started at Parkfield Primary, she had hardly communicated, sitting vacantly in front of the television until she was told it was time to go to bed.

Ella had been to see the deputy head, Miss Thompson, a woman with spiky blonde hair who looked about twenty-three and gave undue emphasis to her words.

'There's really *nothing* to *worry* about, Mrs Barclay,' she had said, smiling at Ella in a way usually reserved for the mentally subnormal. 'It always *takes time* for children to *settle* into a new school. And Isobel's work *has* been very *good*.'

Ella knew she had to do something. But there were a thousand and one things she needed to do first. She needed to keep them all alive. She didn't dare think about the approach of the darker nights. Parkfield under ice and snow was not somewhere her mind wanted to go right now. And anyway, Isobel seemed frightened of her own mother these days. Tom had always been better at communicating with the girl.

Tom.

She closed her eyes for three seconds, as if in pain, and then, as if switching herself back into normal mode, resumed her peeling and chopping. Ben hadn't noticed.

'Anyway,' said Ella, 'here's a funny thing. For years, I didn't realise that about *The Wizard Of Oz* going into colour. First half-dozen times I saw it was on Grandma's telly – and if you remember, she's only ever had a black-and-white.'

'Door, Mum,' said Ben, sliding chopped potatoes into a saucepan.

Every time someone knocked at the door in Renaissance Towers, the sound reverberated through the lobby and stairwell outside. This particular knock was firm, insistent.

'Put the telly off, Izzy,' she snapped, wiping her hands on her skirt.

'Why?'

'You *know* why.'

Ella clenched her teeth and went into the narrow hallway. She undid the lock, pulled the chained door a few inches open, peered round.

'Is this Fort Knox, or can I come in?' Matt Ryder asked.

He was dressed casually, as usual: black jeans, denim jacket, white T-shirt. For some reason, he had a battered khaki satchel slung over his shoulder.

'You!' She felt a mixture of elation, astonishment and guilt. 'Shit, I thought you were the TV licence people.' She blushed. 'If I'd known...'

'Yeah, yeah, you'd have baked a cake. I thought I'd pop round and see if you wanted to borrow a cup of sugar.' He grinned. 'You could have chosen your building a bit better. If you knew half the things they hadn't done, like...'

'Don't tell me,' she said wearily, holding up damp, starchy palms. 'I know enough.'

'Can't believe they're still building these places, like? You know that all the studies prove that high-rise living destroys rather than conserves social interaction and responsibility?'

'Thanks,' said Ella. 'That's really what I need to hear right now. Matt, what are you *doing* here?'

'And there's meant to be a swimming pool? I hate to think what kind of a state that's in. And as for the lifts...' Matt whistled and tutted.

Ella scowled. 'Don't talk about the lifts.'

In her first few days in Renaissance Towers, Ella had not been able to work out why the lifts arrived and left of their own accord. Out on the landing there would first be the soft 'ping' which announced a lift's presence, and the glow of the arrow-shaped light, and then the rumble as the doors slid open. Followed by silence. Nobody emerged on to the dusty landing, no human shape was framed in the block of light within. A few seconds later, the doors would rumble shut again and the asthmatic lift would creak and groan as the cables hauled it up towards the heights of Twenty, or deep into the uncharted basement.

Perhaps ghosts were riding the floors, Ella thought, wraiths idling away the years by flitting between the dark levels. But no. She shouldn't believe in ghosts, or rather, she ought to reject them. Evil spirits. Cast them out. Ella didn't dare think about how long it was since she'd been to Confession, although she comforted herself with the thought that she had at least shown her face in the Cathedral of the Blessed Virgin once this year.

When she mentioned the problem to Dee, the woman gave a throaty chuckle and looked at Ella somewhat pityingly. 'Kids, innit? Pushing them knobs random, like,' she said. 'Kids?' Ella replied. 'But there aren't any kids in the building. Apart from mine and yours.' Dee winced and chuckled. 'Not official, no. But there are. You wouldn't believe the stuff what they get up to.'

Somehow, Ella thought, Dee's prosaic explanation was more disturbing than her theory about the bored phantoms. Whatever the truth, she would always walk up and down ten flights of stairs rather than take one of the sinister contraptions. But no, she told herself now, there were no ghosts. No ghosts of any kind, thank you very much. No spectres of the past, no spirits of Christmas Yet To Come, no phantoms of the mind. *No shadows.* Here in Renaissance, here in Parkfield, you lived in the present. You lived in the here and now or you were dead.

'How long did it take to get your gas on line?' Matt was asking. 'Three days? Four?'

'Five,' said Ella with a tired, wry smile. 'Do you want to know how I managed with no cooker? Cooking gammon steaks on the steam iron, heating tins of mushroom soup in the kettle... Oh, I'm nothing if not inventive.' She pulled a face. 'And I do a lot of praying. Only that doesn't seem to be working. God might move in mysterious ways, but he doesn't have to deal with estate agents.'

Matt shook his head. 'This was the last place I expected to find you, Ella. If you don't mind my asking – what the hell is going on?'

She glanced at her watch, then back at the clock in the kitchen. 'Do you know a good pub round here?'

He shrugged, grinned. 'Sure... But what about your kids?'

'I know someone downstairs. They can go and smash the place up with her hellish brood.' Ella grabbed her coat. 'Ben! Izzy! Come on!'

Phill Janowitz held up a photograph, the fifteenth in as many minutes, and tilted her head as she waited for Tom's reaction.

'What about this one?' she said.

Tom wrinkled his nose. 'Um,' he said. 'I'm...not sure. I don't think it has that...*urgency* you're looking for.'

Phill sighed. 'You're right,' she said. 'It has a charming simplicity, but I don't think it quite gets there.'

The photograph showed a white canvas covered with rows of thickly painted crimson rings. Tom thought it looked rather like the potato-prints Isobel used to produce during Messy Time at nursery. Wisely, he didn't say so.

Like all the others, the picture was a potential piece for the ground-breaking and exciting new exhibition at Centrespace.

Entitled *Wotz Da Crack?* (the title a triumph of chutzpah over naivety) it was to be 'an artistic exploration of all aspects of drug culture; the sound of the streets, the vibe of the tribe, trips in 2-D and 3-D – and maybe more.' Phill had hired a copywriter for the publicity material, she confided to Tom, and she was beginning to doubt her decision. He assured her that the blurb was exactly right.

The artists were all current addicts, recovering addicts, former addicts, victims of addiction in the family, or drug counsellors.

(At Appletree, Tom had sometimes thought it was lucky there were so many drug addicts, otherwise lots of drug counsellors would be out of a job. 'Perfect symbiosis,' he'd pointed out to Ella. 'I sometimes wonder if the counsellors secretly go out pushing heroin at night to keep themselves in gainful employment... You know there's a needle exchange on the floor below us? What the fuck's that about, then? Oh, yes, you're a druggie, here, have a nice clean needle on us. Now go away and take more drugs, there's a good boy.' She had given him the tolerant smile she always reserved for his rants. 'You know, darling,' she said, 'thanks to you, I understand what "cold as charity" means.')

Judging by the selection, there seemed to be quite a lot of aspiring artists among the drug counsellors of Cherford. It was clearly either a job which stimulated a great deal of deep, refined artistic productivity, or one that people were especially desperate to get out of.

'Did any of those other exhibits actually sell?' Tom asked. 'The Zero Tolerances or whatever they called themselves.'

'Zeroes Heroes, Thomas. Don't mock.' Phill smiled. 'Yes,

actually. A renowned collector bought up all of the Steve Kantobe installation.'

'Blimey. He'll need a lot of power points for all those fridges.'

'I think he probably has a few, honey. And we had three serious bids for the Trish Tregarran. It finally went to a solicitor in Hampstead.'

'You're kidding. Someone *bought* Period Woman?'

'Well, Trish is the leading light of Zeroes Heroes. She's rumoured to be up for the Turner Prize.'

'Hmm. Why does that not surprise me? Now, Turner, he painted proper pictures. He'd be spinning in his grave at all these tossers with their soiled beds and pickled sharks.'

'Tom, honey, you're a Stuckist.'

'Not really. It just never ceases to amaze me, the things people would rather have than money.'

'Can't buy you love,' she said enigmatically. 'OK, this one?' She held up another photo. 'A sculpture, this time.'

It was, Tom thought, something that could only be called a sculpture if you were feeling very generous indeed. *Blue Peter*'s Valerie Singleton would have been deeply embarrassed by it: a higgledy-piggledy array of toilet rolls, wire coathangers and ping-pong balls, all sprayed with silver paint.

'What's it called?' he asked. 'Not *Here's One I Made Earlier*, is it?'

'Ummm...' Phill flipped through her notes, pushing her hair back with a clank of bangles. 'Here we are... *Magnificent Isolation*.'

'It speaks to me,' he said. 'Put it in.'

If people are prepared to pay good money to view junk, he

thought, I want to have a laugh about it.

He closed his eyes and tried not to think about his family.

A terrible darkness—

No.

Reclining on Phill's bed, sipping his tea, he thanked his lucky stars that he was not being required to do anything more strenuous this afternoon. Nominally, he was staying in a B&B, but nights with Phill were becoming increasingly regular. She hadn't asked too many questions about his changed circumstances and she seemed glad to have him around. His story about remote-working on his laptop didn't seem to perturb her, either. He just plugged his mobile into the machine over breakfast, looked busy, and then detached it with a sense of relief when Phill left for work.

'Try this one,' said Phill, handing him the next picture.

Tom frowned. He squinted, trying to see if there was anything more to it. 'It's a Rich Tea biscuit,' he said eventually. 'With a bite taken out of it.'

'I think it has a kind of crisp, vital sensibility. Look at how clean the bite is, offset against the stark whiteness of the surface.'

'Yes,' he said, thinking he'd better not start saying what he really thought of all this crap or Phill might chuck him out. Seeing worth in the worthless was her job, and he didn't feel it was his place to question it. 'Well, it's obviously a comment on the sterility of rave culture. What's it called? Can I guess? Something like...um... *Fragment of the Self*? Or how about *Illusion of Escape*?'

Phill consulted her notes. 'It's called *Biscuit*,' she admitted.

'Beautifully *faux naif*. Put it in.'

'You're not taking this seriously, are you, Tom?' she reprimanded him with a smile, as she put the photo on top of the pile on her bed.

'Darling, I consider it an honour and a privilege to be helping you select such a ground-breaking, challenging body of work. You never know, one of these people might be the new Tracey Emin.'

'It's OK. You don't have to pretend.' Phill sighed, folded her notes up and tossed them aside. 'Tom, I've been patient with you, and I'm not gonna pressure you. Believe me, I am delighted to have a little company. And someone to make me cups of tea. But, well, I'm kinda thinking...what is the deal here?'

'The deal?'

So now she was doing it. Now she was asking the questions.

'Look, you haven't walked out on your wife and kids for good, or you'd have told me straight away. I don't think I'd want someone to do that for me anyway.'

A terrible darkness descends when—

No. Not yet.

'But you're obviously not...there,' she went on. 'And they think you're somewhere else. I don't know what your cover story is, and I don't want to know. But...give me some idea, in the next coupla days, of what the score is here? OK?'

'The score,' he said levelly. 'Right.'

He wasn't quite sure what she was talking about. Did she now want more than sex from him, or what? Why did women never come out and say what they actually *meant*? They always had to leave this complicated system of clues and make you work it out for yourself.

Then Phill leant over, put her hands on his face and pulled him close for a warm, wet, and lingering kiss.

'And I just felt like doing that,' she said with a smile.

He returned her smile.

And closed his eyes.

A terrible darkness descends in his soul when he turns his back and walks away.

But no, he has not even turned his back. That would be a statement; it would be communication, of sorts.

No, he has slipped out like the proverbial thief in the night – but a thief who, rather than escaping with a haul of plunder, is leaving as much as he could behind.

This is switch-off. This is closedown.

Tom Barclay, this is your life.

It ends, he is thinking. Somehow, it ends.

Rain slicks the paths of Parkfield. The air tastes damp. Droplets dance like incandescent jumping-beans in the sodium glow. He gazes into the soft orange light of the street lamp as he waits for the bus. Is it meant to mimic the hue of sunset, to give a comforting glow? It is far from comforting. It reminds him of how spectral the night is, how lonely a road is that needs these things. It is a desperate, sad human attempt to drop a gobbet of light into a pool of darkness, and it always fails dismally.

The bus arrives, doors swishing open, a portal to another block of stark, icy light. Inside, fishy-pale and unfriendly faces watch him haul his two bags on board. He feels their eyes on him as he fumbles for his change, feels his face flushing – with fear, anxiety, guilt – as he slumps into a seat and watches the twinkling city approach.

The darkness of leaving.

He closes his eyes as bitter, hateful tears sting them. Ella's wrath he can cope with, that's easy. She is an adult, and she is predictable enough. But the children. He cannot think about the children, because if he thinks about them he will need to go back.

He needs some comfort here.

No, he cannot go home.

He doesn't think he can ever go home.

He thumbs his mobile, entering a pre-programmed number. He is relieved to hear her soft, welcoming voice at the other end.

'Phill, I've… I've made a bit of a mess of things this end. Can I come and stay with you for a while?'

Ella is a mother early, by the standards of her fellow graduates – most of them remain fans of clubs, bars, drugs and bed-hopping well into their twenties. They find it hilarious, the way their friend settles down so quickly into mumsiness. Girls who are still into vodka-and-Red-Bull and Ecstasy pull faces at tales of sterilisers and breast-pumps, colic and fungal infections. Friends who like to party can't grasp that being up all night is no longer a *good* thing. Inevitably, she loses touch with a lot of her university crowd. They make her feel old.

But the Parkfield women make her feel younger.

Here, the mums of teenagers like Ben are not yet thirty. And at the school gates, once the initial suspicion has worn off, these women assume her to be their peer, and marvel when she tells them her age. Their faces speak of anguish, bitterness, teenage lust gone sour and a life which has never got better. Ella – thanks to years of cleansing, toning and moisturising, or a good diet, or perhaps just the lingering sheen of affluence – doesn't look much older than most of them. In fact, she's sure she looks younger than some.

These women wear their skin like carapaces, brandish their cigarettes like weapons. Pocked faces, lank hair and excessive fake-gold earrings are much in evidence, as are grubby cagoules over puce jumpsuits which scream '1989 Janet Frazer Catalogue' to Ella.

But they are survivors.

She has never before given them any thought, and yet, here they are, less than five miles from her old front door, now her neighbours and comrades. What dismays her most of all – and makes her feel guilty – is how these women, despite a lifetime of struggle, all seem to be coping well with the demands of motherhood (with or without the support of a man). She wants them to be feckless, immature, lazy and sluttish. Surely maternal efficiency is her prerogative? For if they are good mothers, what is there left for Ella to be?

She starts to know names. There's mouthy Donna, thin-lipped and permanently smoking, her streaked hair pulled back so tightly it seems to stretch her face. Donna's kohled eyes, caked make-up, highlights and gold jewellery sit oddly with her tracksuit bottoms and trainers.

'Don't fuckin' stand there on that grass,' is the first thing Donna says to her at the school gates. The very first thing, before anything like 'Hi', or 'Pleased to meet you'. Ella blinks and asks, 'Why?' And Donna looks her up and down, obviously wondering what the wind has blown in here. 'Dogs always shit there,' she says, as if it were obvious.

There is Leanne, spilling from a pair of shiny trousers and an orange crop-top. She peers from a blubbery face, her irises like raisins buried in a ball of dough. Her slack breasts swing low; they are udders cling-wrapped in Lycra, sometimes with a guzzling baby attached. Her navel-ring glints between rolls of fat, like a treasure lost at sea, bobbing on the waves. When she smiles – which is rare – she shows a black gap on the top row of her teeth.

'Her fella come round one fuckin'…afternoon and knocked 'em out,' Donna tells Ella, clearly relishing the tale. 'Whacked her up against the fuckin'…wall, he did.'

Ella turns pale. 'You're joking. I hope he went to prison?'

'Oh, yeah. Been in an' out so fuckin'…much they might as well give him his own fuckin'…key. But he's done two year now. Be out before long. Be out on fuckin'…parole, won't he?'

Ella is fascinated by Donna's rhythms of speech. It's not her limited vocabulary, not just the way the swear-words are thrown in as adjectives, even pauses for thought. It is the deadpan way the horrific is conveyed as everyday. Domestic violence is clearly as expected as shopping, swearing or smoking.

Then there's Chantelle, sunken and haggard, her blood-red hair pinned up in clips, her body hidden behind baggy pullovers and stretchy, rubbed leggings. Her eyes look dead, and she hardly ever speaks. Chantelle is twenty-one. Ella feels her own eyes almost popping out when Donna tells her.

Twenty-one? Surely not. Someone must have got their dates mixed up. But apparently not. And her daughter, Mariah ('rhymes with pariah', Ella said in her head) is six, only a little younger than Izzy.

Twenty-one, with a daughter of six. So she had her at fifteen, probably had sex at fourteen. The thought bounces in Ella's mind.

She thinks of herself at fifteen: remote, industrious, adorned with spots and specs, disdainful of her short-skirted peers, studious. About as likely to have sex as Mother Teresa. And then she looks at Chantelle's achingly sad face and thinks of herself at twenty-one. She summons an image, something representative. Drinking, laughing, pushing her hair back in the basement of an indie club somewhere deep in London. Jumping up and down to 'Reward' by The Teardrop Explodes, her body vibrant and supple and ready for anything... Pulling Tom to her as he fights his way back from the bar with the wobbling plastic pint glasses clasped in his hands... And tonguing his mouth deeply, passionately, lovingly, as Helen and Jess shout ribald comments from the other side of the dance floor.

She used to long for him, then. She used to *ache* for him. For him to be gone at the bar for ten minutes was almost physically painful.

And now? Now he's gone. Just gone. She doesn't know how far he is from her, nor does she know when she will see him again. And the sensation she feels almost doesn't have a name, because it is so new to her.

It is nothingness.

* * *

The pub was called The Shakey. Outside, a chalked sign depicted the Bard holding up a flagon of ale and declaring, 'Friends, Romans, Countrymen, come and try my beers.' Matt noticed that it made Ella wince, which amused him. 'I expect,' she muttered, 'that's as close as Parkfield gets to culture.'

Inside it was treacle-dark, smoke-fogged. Its wood and leather fittings dripped with condensed sweat. The air fizzed with testosterone, bubbled with harsh male voices. Ella was nervous and kept her head down, Matt noticed, but he knew most of the clientele only had eyes for the football on the huge TV screen.

'Big game for City today,' Matt explained. 'Perhaps not the best time to come?' He thought he'd better not point out the obvious – that the drinkers were all people who hadn't been able to get tickets for the match. In the case of at least half of them, this was because they were banned from City's ground.

'There's no space!' she mouthed.

'Let's go up there.' Holding two pints, he motioned to Ella to go upstairs. He let her go first, so that he could admire the tightness of her skirt on her smooth backside. They battled their way through the crowds to a secluded area near the back of the pub.

'Here all right?' he asked, sitting down opposite her and dumping his satchel on the table. It was hard, Matt thought, to keep his eyes on her face when those perky breasts were saying hello to him, but he was going to have to for now. 'Don't be afraid,' he added with a teasing grin.

'Oh, I'm not, Matt. Not with you here to protect me.'

'Uh-huh. Sarcasm doesn't, like, become you, Ella.' He hoped it had been sarcasm.

'What's in there?' she asked, pointing to his satchel.

'I'll show you later... So, come on, then. I'm waiting.'

'Tell me what you know about Renaissance Towers first. I want the truth, not the bullshit from the little git at the estate agent's office.'

Matt shrugged. 'Not much to tell, is there? You must have read it in the papers. Turn of the millennium, everybody supposed to be going all futuristic and urban, Cherford City Council decides that *city living* is the big new thing. Great. Loads of affordable apartments for bright young pros. City on the up, looks good for business investment.'

'I remember,' she said. 'They built loads of them down by the river as well.' She took a sip of her beer, and pulled a face.

He grinned, knowing she would find it over-sweet and watery. 'It gets better the more you drink. Honest... Yeah, well, urban apartments were, like, the biggest white elephant of the decade, yeah? They weren't affordable after all, and people would rather get a cute two-bed terrace in Carringworth for the same price?'

'And people don't stay urban venturers for ever. They soon grow out of it when they want families.'

'That's it. Change is inevitable, except from vending machines.'

'Spare me the stand-up comedy, Matt, I'm not in the mood.'

'Sorry. So they just couldn't, like, sell them? On paper, it looked great – cheap sites five minutes from town, ready-made client base – but anyone who's lived in Cherford a couple of years could tell you it was, you know, never going to work? So, within two years, council's started having to let them? Oh, yeah, they were pretty bloody embarrassed about that.' Matt gave a rueful smile.

'And meanwhile,' said Ella, 'Renaissance Towers slips back into the Dark Ages. I get the picture.'

'Nobody cares about them any more. They're a liability. No wonder they were so keen to let you have one.' Matt took a long drink from his pint, and pulled a face as he set it back down on the table. 'Which brings me,' he said, 'to my original question?'

'You mean, how did I end up in a place where the birds fly upside down because there's nothing worth shitting on?'

'I wouldn't put it quite like that. But go on.'

'Well, it's actually horribly simple.'

Quietly, without embellishment or self-pity, she gave him a brief overview of the last couple of months. He realised she had to be leaving out some of the dull details, the workaday admin, but she told him what seemed like all the rest: the desperation of adding up the figures for the first time in years and realising with horror how little they came to; the stress and agony of putting the house on the market; the pain of walking round the empty rooms one last time.

Matt shook his head. 'But how did it get so bad, so quickly for you? I mean, surely you had contingency funds to fall back on? Savings?'

'It's like they say in those awful adverts,' she said, caressing her pint thoughtfully. 'You know, for loans and stuff. "Shares can go down as well as up. Your home is at risk if you do not keep up repayments." All that crap. It sounds different after it's happened.' She sighed, drank deeply from her glass. 'We would have done. If we hadn't used them for a conservatory, school skiing trips, topping up the fees... You name it. If only we'd known.'

'Didn't you get any profit from the sale of the house?'

'Not enough. We hadn't been there long. At that end of the market, you know...' She shrugged, pulled a face. 'Things hit a ceiling. We only just avoided negative equity. Rather than get another bloody mortgage, I decided it was best to rent a place for a while. That's when the smarmy estate agent guy talked me into a flat in Renaissance.' She held up her hands. 'I know, I know. I should have asked more questions. But it was that or leave the area, and I needed to get my kids into a school *somewhere*.'

Matt nodded. He was beginning to understand. 'Why not stay with friends?' he asked. 'You have got friends...right?'

She gave him a tight, that's-not-funny smile. 'I don't want to foist myself and two kids and a lifetime's baggage on anyone right now.'

After what he felt was a decent pause, he asked, 'And...your husband?'

'My husband. Ah, yes. My husband, who'd known his job was going to be scrapped for several weeks and had done bugger-all about it, seems to have decided that he doesn't want to be a part of this nightmare any more. Oh, he came to look at the place, and spent a day in stupefied, how-did-it-come-to-this silence, before slipping quietly away.'

'He's left you?' Matt tried to keep his question casual, but his heart was thumping with teenage excitement.

'I don't think it's as straightforward as that, Matt. Tom can't handle anything big, anything stressful. It's why he's never been that career-minded. No, he likes to coast along with the minimum effort. As soon as it gets tough, he retreats to the cave.'

He shrugged. 'A lot of guys need to do that. We usually come out of the cave with, you know, a few useful ideas?'

'Matt, this is a little more serious than just going to the shed for a sulk. He left me a note telling me not to worry, saying he needed to get his head in order. Said he's gone to stay with *a friend* and I shouldn't try to contact him.'

'Aren't you mad at him?'

'Absolutely flaming furious, lovey, for about three days solid. Then I realised it was just making the children even more upset, and we had the imminent prospect of the new term coming up and my not wanting a visit from the truancy officer.'

'They'd have taken a while to get round to you, to be honest,' Matt admitted with a wry grin.

'Well, still… I had to get all that done as well as the bloody piles of other paperwork this business entails. Believe me, I've had plenty to keep my mind occupied.' She drew breath sharply, leant back with her hands behind her head and smiled at him. 'I just hope Tom has, too.'

'So where is he?' Matt asked, risking a brief glimpse down as Ella moved, her top tautening across her chest.

'Well, he's not with any of his usual mates. If I'm brutally honest with myself – and that is my new aim, after all – I don't know. It did cross my mind that he'd gone to hole up with some little slut for a week or two.'

'Are you serious?' She didn't seem that bothered, he thought.

'Well, I know Tom. You do tend to notice when your husband starts eyeing up other women. And I don't mean some pneumatic babe on *Top Of The Pops*, I mean real-life women with real-life flaws. Attainable women. People he could, if he put on his most charming smile and his nicest suit, actually talk his way into bed with.'

'But would he?' Matt asked, not breaking eye contact as he sipped his drink.

'Oh, God, yeah. I mean, it wouldn't *mean* anything. I always knew he'd do it one day, and that he'd come back once he'd got it out of his system. Women have to be madly in love to have an affair, Matt, but blokes just have to be in lust. And Tom, although he doesn't realise it, has half the women he knows fancying him rotten, including many of my friends.'

'Really?' Bastard, thought Matt.

'Oh, yes. And he could just meet some poor desperate bitch who wants to liven up her social life as much as he does, and *bang*. If you'll pardon the expression.'

'This is just speculation, though, isn't it?'

'Informed speculation. Working late, when he'd never needed to before. A sudden desire to socialise with his colleagues, when he always told me he couldn't stand the bloody sight of them.' She sighed. 'But no. I think…I think it's far more complicated than that.'

'Right.' Matt Ryder cursed silently. It sounded as if Tom was not entirely out of the picture, which made things rather more difficult from his point of view.

'I'm sorry,' Ella said. 'I didn't bring you out here to moan about my husband. And there's something I need to know from you, anyway.'

'Which is?'

'Well, I mean, why the hell do *you* live round the corner

from Parkfield? I mean, OK, it's not on the estate, but it's pretty damn close.'

He shrugged, smiled. He had wondered if this was going to come up. 'Why not?'

'*Why not?* You're a head of department, so I'd guess – no, I'd *know* what you earn. There are loads of nice little places you could buy, and well out of spitting distance of the bloody Parkfield dump.'

'Yes,' he said, 'there are. And what kind of message would that send out?'

'I'm sorry, I don't get you.'

'I'm a mentor for the challenged kids as well, Ella. They don't want someone who disappears at the end of the day, they want someone who's *part* of their community, yeah? They see me down the chippy or the pool hall, like a normal person. It gives them a sense of connection – *and* it helps me to know what they get up to, yeah?'

She folded her arms and tutted. 'Good God. You're not a bloody youth worker, Matt. You're a teacher. Build yourself some distance.'

'Well, that's where you're wrong.' He felt his eyes stinging with passion. 'I *am* a youth worker, and a social worker, and a policeman, and a surrogate parent. I'm a supplier of free stationery and free advice. I'm a guide, role model and all the other stuff we're expected to be these days.' He pointed down to the bar. 'The bloke who runs this place gives me loads of useful information, believe me. He'd never do that if I lived somewhere *nice*.'

He realised he was breathing deeply and was slightly dry-mouthed, so he took a deep gulp of his pint. She was looking at him in amusement, he realised. Oh, shit, he thought, I hope I've not overplayed the worthiness card. Bloody shot myself in the foot.

'Do you own your house?' she asked, with a little flicker of her eyebrows. 'Makes you posh, that, doesn't it?'

He made sure to take a deep breath before answering her. Careful on the hobby-horse, Matthew, don't fall off. 'The LEA owns it, believe it or not. Couple of years ago, they bought up some cheap housing to persuade teachers to come to "difficult" schools, places where it was hard to get people. Jo Tarrant does the same thing. A lot of her principles are the same as mine. Kindred spirit, if you like.'

'Yes, I see. And also, you fancy the pert little tits off Miss Tarrant and want to impress her with your right-on credentials. I see where you're coming from.'

He wasn't sure how to play that low ball. She was right, obviously, but if he ever got his way with Jojo it would be a light-hearted thing, a friendly shag, a comfort fuck. It was nothing compared to the great, angry stirring he felt when he thought about the woman sitting opposite him.

'Ella!' he said, pretending to be shocked, and spread his hands with a smile. 'You must think I'm incredibly shallow.'

'No, I just think you're a man, Matt. It's biological.'

'Oh, right. Thanks.' He decided to move off the subject. 'Anyway, you're a socialist, aren't you? Well, then, here's your chance to walk the talk.'

'I'm rapidly coming round to the view that only the rich can afford to be socialists. The rest of us just have to look after ourselves.'

'Oh, you *poor* thing. So bloody impoverished you can only

afford a black-and-white telly and a two-bedroom flat. You know some people dream of that?'

'Rrrright. You've brought me out to tell me how lucky I am. Spare me.'

'No, but…you seem to be doing OK here,' he suggested.

'Matt, I am delivering a very good impression of a woman doing OK. I buy my food in shops where they've never heard of apples while my children hang around with tartrazine-fuelled yobbos. People either sell crack in my stairwell or piss down it, then break the entryphone when they've forgotten their keys. The man who seems to occupy the whole of Eleven plays gangsta rap at all hours of the day and night, and my neighbours think nothing of lobbing the TV out of the window when it goes on the blink. And I don't dare open my mouth for fear that someone will smack me for being a stuck-up cow. I am really, really not doing OK.' She shuddered, lifted her pint. 'God, I need this.'

The bar below them erupted into tumultuous noise, hands held aloft. For a moment it was as if they were applauding Ella's outburst; in fact, the final whistle had just blessed Cherford City with a victory.

'Good old City,' said Matt with a smile, raising his glass to the supporters.

She smiled, gripped her glass firmly and downed the rest of her pint. 'Good old City,' she said. 'Whoever the hell they were playing. So, my round?'

He tried to seem nonchalant. 'Will your kids be OK?'

'I imagine so. I've given up. One afternoon eating E-numbers and watching cable with Shaznay-Marie and the Ryans is not going to kill them. And don't say "whatever",

Matt, it's so...*slacker*. What'll you have?'

'Another pint of the same, Mrs Barclay. Very kind of you.'

Darwinism in action, he thought in wonderment. This creature was adapting to its new environment with remarkable alacrity.

A purple whirlwind zipped across the widescreen, accompanied by a zany sound effect. It smacked into a wall, turning into a 2-D cat before folding, dazed, on to the ground.

Isobel, Shaznay-Marie and the Ryans screamed with laughter. Ben, on the other hand, tutted. He threw down the computer magazine he was reading and leapt up from his chair, kicking a bottle of blue fizzy-pop over on to Dee's tobacco-stained carpet.

'Ben! That's naughty!' Isobel protested.

'I don't bloody care,' he snarled, snatching up his coat as he swept out into the hallway.

Dee's raucous laughter echoed from the smoke-fogged kitchen. Deep in a ribald phone call, she didn't even see him go.

He slammed the flaking door behind him, turned up his collar, and only now felt a tumult in the pit of his stomach as he wondered where he was going to go.

He'd wanted the City match on, but had been outvoted by the kids and their bloody Cartoon Channel. Too many channels for little kids, there were.

He wondered how Dee, living on benefits, was able to get Sky. His mother had always made noises about not being able to afford it, even when they were living in Ashington. Ben suspected it was less about the cost and more about his mother thinking satellite TV was common.

Steely clouds swept across the sky. Dogs barked, deep within the estate. He trudged across the wasteland of the car park, a lone figure with his hands deep in his pockets, shivering in the autumn wind, wreathed in a blizzard of leaves and crisp wrappers and bus tickets.

He kept his eyes ahead as one grey street after another scrolled past him. Washing billowed out at him from overgrown gardens, dogs growled and scratched at gates. He was lost, now, deep in the Parkfield maze. He slipped between the crumbling bollards at the end of a close, found himself in a tight alleyway flanked with steel fences. Graffiti sneered its scratchy messages, informing the world that City ruled, Tonya loved Liam, Natasha was a slapper, Lee was a fucking queer and the world was going to end on Tuesday.

Ben blinked, stopped, looked again at this last inscription. It looked fresh, dripping its carmine warning. THE WORLD ENDS ON TUESDAY. Which Tuesday did they mean? Was it a Tuesday that had been and gone already, or did it refer to the one just three days away?

The clouds raced faster in the sky. The wind cut through his coat, numbed his lips and teeth, and something made his fingertips tingle.

He looked up.

They were waiting for him at the end of the alleyway.

Gaz Collins, his mate Shaun and one other thick-jawed type Ben didn't recognise. They formed an unbreachable cordon, blocking his way. All with arms folded. All chewing.

He slowed and stopped. Despite his racing heart and his slack bowels, he spread his hands wide, slipped into his most neutral Cherford accent. 'Lads,' he said. 'All right.' He nodded at each of them in turn. They kept chewing, and didn't move.

'I'll be seeing you,' said Ben, and turned on his heel, a swift 180-degree spin.

At the other end of the alleyway, where he had come in from the close, the gap between the bollards was blocked by two more shapes – a wiry, weaselly type in a baseball cap and a chunkier one with six earrings.

Ben grinned nervously. 'Nice one,' he said. 'Good tactics.'

Gary Collins's group advanced slowly, so that they were only a couple of metres from him. 'Good tactics?' said Collins. 'Yeah, right. A bit like a dive in a game, Barclay?' He stepped forward, gave Ben a shove which slammed him against cold steel. 'Innit – Bennyboy?'

'Bent-boy,' said the weaselly henchman, and there was a general snigger.

'Yeah,' said Collins, and gave Ben another shove. 'Benny the bender-boy. Backs to the wall when he's around. Fucking posh queer wanker.'

'I'm not gay,' Ben snapped, and anger warmed his cheeks. 'Don't you dare call me queer, Collins.'

Ben suddenly found the ground disappearing from beneath his feet, and his world shrinking to several centimetres wide. Collins had lifted him by the collar, slammed him against the steel fencing, and his nicotine-yellowed teeth bared in a leer. He gathered a gobbet of saliva and spat it straight into Ben's face.

Ben flinched at the unpleasant impact, but turned back to look Collins in the eye again. 'Is that the best you can do,

Gaz? Gobbing on me? You think you're a bully? You should come to Millmount sometime. People there got threatened by experts.'

Collins dropped him.

Ben staggered, but didn't fall, and relaxed a little as the bigger boy took a couple of steps back, seemed to take a half-turn away from him.

Ben rubbed his aching neck, kept his eyes and voice level.

'Nice one, Collins,' he said. 'I always thought you were all mouth.'

The low punch seemed to come from nowhere, slamming him into the fence and bringing the cracked tarmac up to meet him. For a few seconds, Ben could not breathe properly, could only feel heat and fire in his lungs and stomach. Redness crept in at the edge of his vision. He had no idea how much time went past.

Collins's face was up against his ear. 'That was for your dive, Benny-boy,' he said. 'You won't try that again.'

'Course he won't,' said one of the others. 'He ain't there no more, is he? He's a Parkfielder now.'

'He fucking ain't a Parkfielder.' The voice was harsh, steely with anger – the weaselly one, Ben guessed. 'He'll never be. Posh little wanker. What the fuck's he doing up here?'

Ben was hauled to his feet, and realised that the pain in his stomach was already abating.

'I don't know,' said Collins thoughtfully, and lit a cigarette.

Shaun, the biggest sidekick, made to move forward. 'Come on, Gaz, we're wasting time. Let's do the little fucker over and get out of here.'

'No.' Collins, with surprisingly quiet authority, put out an arm, and Shaun took a step backwards. Collins took a deep drag on his cigarette, stepped forward and blew the smoke into Ben's face. It stung his eyes and throat, but he was determined not to cough. 'No,' Collins said again. 'Sure, we could beat his posh little face in. But he'd take it. He's no weed, this one. And anyway, he's been brought up proper, ain't he? He'd run to Ryder or Moretti. He'd tell 'em straight like a good little boy, and then who'd be in shit?' Collins rounded on Weasel-face, then on Shaun, gave them both a hard shove. 'Who'd be in shit? Yeah?'

Collins, Ben noticed, looked round each of his gang in turn – meeting the gaze of them all and getting a respectful nod from each.

One thing was beyond doubt. Whatever his intentions, whatever his plans, Collins had power. He had respect from this little rag-tag bunch. And Ben knew that could be a weakness as much as a strength.

'Gaz,' Ben said. 'Look, I know I was stupid. I know I lost you the game. But I'm not at Millmount any more. Like your mate said, I'm a Parkfielder now. I'm on your side, Gaz. And I know you're the one to talk to. You're the man, Gaz. It's what everyone says.'

He was so glad his mother could not hear him right now.

Weasel-face laughed derisively, and one of the chunky types shook his head and spat on the ground, but Shaun and the other one looked uncertain. They looked to Collins for guidance.

Collins narrowed his eyes. 'Listen to me, Barclay. I know when people are bullshitting me, all right?'

Ben spread his hands. 'Straight up, mate. No bullshit, I promise you.'

Gary Collins stared levelly at Ben for five seconds, and then his ugly, taut face broke into a yellow grin.

'In that case,' he said, 'we got a little job for you.'

The landlord had decreed an early Happy Hour if City won that afternoon, so Matt wasn't surprised to see Ella balancing four pints and two packets of crisps on a tray.

'Sorry I was so long,' she said as she set the drinks down. 'Hell, I hope the kids are behaving.'

'Your children are sweet,' he said. 'They're bound to settle in, you know. What are their names again?'

'Ben and Isobel. Ben's short for Benedict and Isobel's long for Izzy.'

'Nice names. I'd keep the Benedict bit quiet, though.'

'Don't worry, I will.' Ella shuddered. 'I don't know what possessed us... And if Tom had got his way, you know, Izzy would have been Candida. He was thinking of the keyboard player from Pulp. But I said there was no way any daughter of mine was being named after a yeast infection.'

Matt chuckled. 'You know,' he said, 'I often think about our very first conversation, in the Castle.'

'Yes. Actually, I try not to.'

'I thought you were such a stuck-up bitch,' he said with a grin.

'Careful, Matthew, political correctness, if you please... But yes, I rather got the feeling that you did.'

'I remember being surprised to find out you'd been a teacher.'

'Yes, I remember that too,' she said. 'Cheers.'

'Cheers.' They clinked and sipped.

'You know, you're right,' Ella told him. 'It does taste better the more you drink of it... As I recall, you accused me of only ever having taught well-to-do young ladies. You didn't have a very high opinion of me, Mr Ryder.'

'Well, then,' Matt murmured, 'you may have something to prove.'

She frowned. 'What?'

'Ever think of coming back into the fold?'

She laughed. She kept laughing, until it was obvious he wasn't joining in with her. She turned pale. 'Oh, my *God*. You're serious.'

'You see, I look across the table and I see an intelligent, talented woman with a natural sense of communication, yeah? And you need a job, perhaps just a part-time one for now. And the job needs you.' He spread his hands, leant back and smiled.

She looked at him levelly for five seconds, without moving a muscle. He thought she was perhaps trying to stare him out, but reasoned that she was probably just stunned. Gobsmacked, as some people said. (Not Ella, though, he wouldn't have thought.) Then, she spent a few seconds opening her mouth and shutting it again as if uncertain how to begin answering him.

'It can't be that easy. You don't just walk into it.'

'Have you any idea how difficult it is to get part-time staff? And in a school whose mere name sends people scuttling behind the sofa? Ella, believe me, Ms Moretti would, like, bite your bloody hand off if you walked into her office tomorrow. She'd think you'd, like, been sent by the gods.' He shrugged. 'Or God. Whichever you prefer?'

'Matt, don't be silly.'

'I assure you, I'm not being silly.'

'It's years since I was in teaching. I'll have forgotten everything. I don't have a clue about the new National Curriculum.'

He unzipped his khaki satchel, pulled out two cardboard wallet-folders and a spiral-bound book and thumped them down.

The rickety table shook.

'Easily fixed,' said Matt with a cruelly knowing grin.

She sat there staring at the pile of paper – looking at it, he thought, as if it were a dead otter or something.

'I mean, there'd be the formality of an interview, obviously? And the induction's a piece of piss. They just show you where they keep the Valium, tell you not to hit anybody and then stroll off, sniggering.'

'Matt—'

'And a police check, although on past form it'll be some time next year before it comes back with all your juicy details, and by then it's too late.'

'Matt, hang on—'

'Look, Liz Moretti has to be seen to, like, jump through the hoops? But the governors basically don't give a shit, as long as the kids aren't burning the place down and nobody's actually shooting up *during* lessons.'

He was enjoying this, because he knew she wouldn't be able to resist it. Not Ella Barclay. He knew her well enough by now.

'What was your unmarried name?' he asked.

'MacBride.'

'Yeah...yeah, that should do.' Matt took a sip of his pint, and realised he needed to explain. 'You'll have to use it. So Ben doesn't get picked on... Teachers' kids tend to be the first with their heads shoved down the bog,' he added apologetically.

'Believe me, Matt, if anyone tries to put Ben's head in the toilet, he'll give as good as he gets... What about the kids I did the talk for? They'd recognise me.'

'They might. But they've got short memories. And I doubt any of them will recall your name.' He grinned. 'So you'll do it, then?' he asked, feeling his eyes prickling. 'Come on, it'll be a laugh!'

Around them, the post-match celebrations had faded to a low babble as the pub geared up for the evening stint.

'Matt, you have got to be *kidding*,' she said eventually.

Matt sighed, spread his hands, sighed. 'OK, you're right. I'm kidding.' He started to pull the pile of papers away from her. 'You couldn't handle Parkfield, anyway. They'd, like, eat you alive? No, you're not up to it.'

Slam.

Her hand, coming down on the folders, was millimetres from his. Firmly clamping the pile down on to the table, not budging. Her knuckles white.

'Now, wait a bloody minute,' she said, and her eyes were almost glowing.

Matt smiled. 'That's better,' he said, and released his hand so that she could pull the folders across the table to her.

Ella sighed, opened the top folder and skimmed the page with perfunctory interest.

'Looks like I'm not in Kansas any more,' she murmured.

'What?'

She looked up, smiled briefly. 'It's all right. Just…something my son said.'

'Oh. Right.'

Matt watched her scanning the pages, and took a deep, comforting drink from his pint. It was going to be all right, he thought gleefully as he watched her face slowly betraying more and more interest.

It seemed it was going to work.

CHAPTER FIFTEEN

Night Waves

Ben knew things were going to be different. But he didn't yet know what he was going to do about it.

Yes, the school was a shit-hole, despite what he'd said to his mum. He could see that. Computers, new paint and anti-bullying policies wouldn't change that.

Collins had told him, proudly, that they never chucked people out. *Exclusion*, they called it. No, Ms Moretti didn't like exclusions. They didn't look good. Made people even less keen on the place, didn't they? So he could do whatever the fuck he liked and they'd never chuck him out. And Collins had laughed, long and hard.

This wasn't really what Ben had wanted to hear. He was rather hoping to get excluded as soon as possible. That was partly why he'd gone along with the stupidity of Collins and his brain-dead mates.

Of course, his mum didn't suspect anything.

Or maybe she did. Either way, she didn't ask.

Even Gary Collins had a mum, he knew that. Maybe she loved him. Or maybe she didn't give a shit. Whatever, it had the same effect. He could get away with murder.

No dad, of course. Stupid even to ask. People like Collins didn't have dads.

But then neither did Ben, any more.

No dad.

At least, not one who was there, one who was around, one who wanted to see him and to know what he was doing.

It struck him in the middle of the night, like an oncoming juggernaut. It kept him awake until the pale light seeped in through the filmy curtains of his bedroom at about six o'clock.

The thought preyed on his mind as he emerged for breakfast.

'I don't know why Daddy's gone,' Isobel said in a quiet, miserable voice, over a bowl of Shreddies. She wasn't eating them; she was just picking them up on the spoon, then placing them back in the milk to get more soggy.

'Nor do I,' said Ben. 'I don't think he's abandoned us, Bizzy. Dads don't do that. I wouldn't, if I was a dad.' *I hope*, he said in his head.

'But why did he go away like that? Why isn't Mum *talking* about him?'

Ben bit his lip. He could hear the shower hissing down the hallway, so he knew their mum couldn't hear them for the moment. 'It probably upsets her too much,' he said, looking at his sister kindly. 'Think how upset you were when you thought you'd lost Blue Rabbit, yeah? Mum feels like that, only worse. I expect.'

'Do you think they're getting divorced?' Isobel asked, not looking up from her saturated cereal.

Ben shrugged. 'Dunno.'

In truth, Ben didn't understand what his father had done. But he had this odd idea that it would become clear, in time.

Divorce – yes, he knew all about that. It wasn't weird, it wasn't unusual. Loads of people at Millmount had parents who were divorced. His best friend Will, for one.

Will's mum and dad had split up five years ago. They didn't even speak any more. Will had told Ben once – with some degree of pride – that his parents only communicated through lawyers.

As for the practical arrangements, it went like this. Will's father parked the Range Rover at the end of his mum's drive in Cherford every Saturday morning and beeped the horn. The car had tinted windows, so Will's mum never even had to see his dad. Ben reckoned that this was deliberate. Will sauntered out, rucksack on his shoulder, waved to his mother, got in the car and drove away. At teatime on Sunday, the Range Rover drew up from the other direction and deposited Will. His dad waited until he got in the front door and then drove off. It was always the same. It seemed to work for them.

Ben knew this because he'd seen it; he'd been invited to Will's dad's house a couple of times, so he knew how it worked. It was a nice house, too – an old place out at Great Lynton, on the edge of the hills. Loads of space for Will and Ben to run around, climb fences, smack sticks into hedges and puddles and build hides out of bales of straw nicked from the nearby farm. They loved it.

He couldn't do any of that at home in Ashington. If you so much as kicked a ball in the street, someone would tap on a window and tell you to stop.

Will's dad was loud, friendly and funny and seemed to have loads of money. He called Ben 'Benito' and always punched him playfully on the arm. He drove fast, smoked a lot and cooked them big English breakfasts. He seemed to have a different girlfriend staying every few weeks, and they were always curvy and glamorous; some of them even liked the boys and played football and PlayStation games with them. Ben usually found his eyes drawn to their breasts, and then he had to look away when he felt himself blushing.

So Will hadn't done that badly out of his parents' divorce. He had two houses, and got the chance to get away from his mum, who was pale, snappy and miserable, and had grey hair like someone's grandma.

Ben would never say it, but he wasn't surprised Will's dad had got fed up with her. She didn't seem an awful lot of fun.

'I wish Daddy would come back,' Isobel said.

'He's probably just had to go away for a bit,' Ben said, finishing his toast. 'I expect he'll be back.'

'Marie Tomlinson's mum and dad got divorced,' said Isobel, 'and she got a new dad. She says she likes him better than her old one.'

'Best not say that to Mum,' Ben suggested. He pointed to her Shreddies. 'Are you gonna eat those?'

Izzy shook her head, and pushed the bowl towards her brother.

He grabbed a spoon and dived in gratefully. Meals seemed smaller these days, and he liked to get anything extra while he could.

* * *

'Thing is, Janie, I dunno what me girlfriend's gonna say.'

'Well, Dean, let me put it this way. How would you feel if you found out your girlfriend had slept with another man?'

'Wot? Well, I'd be... I'd be bleedin' furious.'

Tom had lost count of the number of times he'd listened to the cool, professional voice of Janie Jones late at night. He knew she was in her mid-forties, a quite glamorous brunette if her website photo was anything to go by, and something of a coup for the station. She was undeniably a Voice. She was classy, husky and brisk: Mariella Frostrup, Nigella and Elizabeth Hurley all rolled into one. She loved controversy – her show had debated everything from gay priests to working mothers – and she would give short shrift to prejudice and half-baked theories.

Part of the reason Tom listened to Janie was for reassurance. When he had felt submerged by the children, by work or the complexities of his marriage, all he had to do was spend a couple of hours with Janie's misfits bouncing round his headphones and he would feel better. No matter how pissed off he got, things were never as bad as they were for these characters: the bulimic self-mutilator who was contemplating suicide; the 'weekend dad' whose alcoholic wife was now cutting back his access to once every two months and was poisoning the children's minds with lies about him; the closet-lesbian teacher with a crush on one of her sixth-formers. These were transmissions from another world, and Tom devoured them as eagerly as a soap opera.

Janie dealt with them all firmly but fairly, and if she couldn't resolve their dilemmas, she knew who could. She kept a stack of cards on the desk in front of her, as she regularly informed listeners. Rape Crisis, Relate, Alcoholics

Anonymous, DrugAlert, Citizens' Advice, the Samaritans – the names zipped through the ether like soothing mantras. Tom had come to love the sound of all these places he'd never need. And the more parlous the caller's situation, the more he looked forward to hearing how the call developed.

She was a mother to the lost, the lonely, the drunken and the remorseful. Janie ventured into territory others wouldn't touch. She wasn't just there to play devil's advocate and keep the viewing figures healthy – she genuinely felt herself to be performing a service, to have a responsibility to the lost souls of the night. Where presenters of similar shows would hold back, refer to other agencies rather than get directly involved, Janie was hands-on.

'*Exactly. And what if it was your brother she'd slept with?*'

'*I ain't got no brother.*'

'*Go with me on this one, Deano, it requires a little imagination. If you had a brother, and your girlfriend had slept with him, then you wouldn't be very happy, would you? You'd feel betrayed by them both, wouldn't you?*'

Deano conceded that he would, perhaps. Building on this, Janie Jones tried her best to get some synapse action going between his ears. It sounded to Tom like an uphill struggle. He was relieved when Janie Jones decided to cut the young man off before the news and go with two minutes of Atomic Kitten instead.

His tired mind wandered. Janie's phone-in sounded cavernous and distant.

'I don't *want* to deceive Ella,' he'd said to Jeff, in one of their final drinking sessions before Tom had told his friend he'd be 'going away' for a bit.

'Oh, sure,' Jeff said with a knowing grin.

'No, really. I don't.' He was being perfectly serious about this. 'If there was some way of shagging Phill without having to lie to Ella, then, bloody hell, I'd do it. Nobody asks to be put in a situation where you have to lie. It's just that you get...questions.' Tom sighed, folded his arms. 'It's not the affair that's the problem, Jeff. It's all the additional shit you have to build up around it to make it work. It isn't what you want.'

'Comes with the territory,' Jeff had pointed out philosophically.

'But it shouldn't, should it? I mean, you're just forced into more and more deception against your will, when really all you want is a quiet life. To be left to get on with it.'

It was a real drain on the imagination. There were only so many times he could have late meetings, or go out with people Ella didn't know – old friends back in town had been an excuse, as had colleagues organising a quiz night. The latter were always sports or retro-TV based, so that she wouldn't suddenly be keen to come along. One time, he had even texted her, asking her if she could help out by looking up the name of the Danish goalkeeper in the Euro '92 championships. She'd texted the answer back, which gave him a little twinge of guilt.

It isn't what you want.

He didn't know what he wanted. He knew, though, that this wasn't it.

Phill was at an opening in York tonight and wouldn't be back till the small hours, so it was back to the claustrophobic guest house for Tom.

He lay on his back in his anonymous room, staring at the stain the shape of Australia on the ceiling and trying to picture his wife and children's faces, while listening to the ramblings of some drunken loser who felt the only place he could turn to was a late-night phone-in. Christ, imagine being that sad.

No – this definitely wasn't it.

Yesterday he had almost had a panic attack in Phill's bathroom because he had forgotten what colour Isobel's eyes were.

He had looked into them so many times when kissing her goodnight, but he'd just suddenly had a complete blank. He had to run from the shower, grab his jacket, pull the photograph of his children out and stare at it intently under the light to remind himself that his daughter's eyes were a rich, chocolatey shade of brown. Just like her mother's.

Yes, just like her mother's.

He had to remind himself, sometimes, that he had started seeing Ella just because she was so different from everybody else.

She stood out from the crowd of women with their swept-back Catherine Oxenberg chic and their *Clothes Show* cheekbones. They all looked sleek and slick, as if shot on videotape, neon-lit. You half expected an electronic effect to wipe across the screen when they walked in, bleaching them into white-faced, red-lipped dolls.

Ella was so different. She wasn't trendy or packaged. She favoured dark jumpers, knee-length skirts, sensible shoes. There were really obvious bands and singers she had never heard of, and just about everything she read was published before 1900: Austen, the Brontës, Hardy. Tom lent her

The Catcher in the Rye and she pronounced it 'very modern'. Her hair was often clipped up, but usually fell rather endearingly across her eyes. The way she spoke was precise, polished, as if she were trying to sound more posh than she actually was. Oh yes, and she could never remember jokes and had to have somebody else reconstruct the punchline for her.

And he had forgotten all that, he thought as his eyelids closed.

He had forgotten why he had fallen in love with her.

Love. What an odd word.

He couldn't remember when he had last used...

Daylight.

They emerge together on to the flat roof beside the hospital ward. They are both shaking.

Neither of them is sure who is holding who. They are one, a shuddering mass of grief. The city is blurred beneath them. He grips the handrail, and she holds tightly on to him. Down there, horns beep, lights flash, people cross the road.

People can die crossing the road.

He watches. Five, six, seven people cross the road.

Nobody dies.

'Tom.'

That can't be right. All those people have crossed the road and nobody has died. All those people driving their cars insanely fast and nobody has died. All those aeroplanes screaming overhead, every day they land safely, oh yes, brilliant landing, well done, give the man a fucking round of applause for not killing anyone and not crashing into Canary fucking Wharf, give the man a beer.

'Tom. Please.'

'What?'

She is a fuzzy outline, just black hair and a white face, like Ava Gardner in an old film with bad reception.

'I need to get away from here. Look.'

He looks. There is a big red bus at waist-height. A space-hopper is slouched against the wall. Little dumper-trucks and pedal-cars all over the place.

He realises where they are. The roof-garden is a fenced-off play area, scattered all over with the happy debris of children.

'Somewhere else, Tom. Anywhere but here.'

Inside, still clutching one another, they lurch down a stingingly bright white corridor. Everything smells of disinfectant. Ella is still unsteady, but she is insisting she has to go. The blue bag hangs limply from Tom's hand.

Through more corridors, past bustling doctors and nurses and porters. And then, on the other side of a set of glass doors, Isobel and Ben are waiting with Maggie.

'I can't,' says Ella. 'I can't tell them.'

'We have to.'

'How?'

'Just the truth. Just the truth.'

And the doors blossom open as they stagger through, and the children, who already know, of course, run to embrace them. Ella's mother, who rarely does hugging, moves forward, uncertain.

The blue bag drops from Tom's hand and lies forgotten on the floor, spilling leaflets, creams, tiny nappies and a small, pink sleepsuit.

*   *   *

'Lots of love, folks, that's all for tonight. I'm off home for a nice cup of hot chocolate and a Hob-nob, which is my little treat at 3 a.m., as those of you who are regular listeners will know. Oh, yes, I can be a 3 a.m. girl too, you know. Sometimes, if I'm really lucky, the cat's awake too and she curls up on my lap and we find an old black-and-white film on a cable channel to snooze off to. Yes, I like simple pleasures.

'So, hey, this is Janie Jones signing off and wishing you all well out there in the Three Counties. Take care of yourselves, take care of each other – and if anything's on your mind, see how it looks in the morning.

'Now here's a special something to take us up to the news: it's Black and "Wonderful Life". Goodnight, all.'

CHAPTER SIXTEEN

No Memory

The scissors gleamed like a weapon in the dim light of the bathroom.

Staring at herself, hollow-eyed and unsteady – she'd had a couple of shots of whisky to get herself this far – Ella pulled at a handful of strands and peered critically at herself. The grey filigree had become more pronounced, the texture of the hair more brittle. Kevin at Clara's salon in Ashington, wonderful Kevin with his lovely gentle hands, was heartbroken when she said she wouldn't be coming any more.

Ella scowled. Four weeks of home servicing and sun-bleaching, she thought, and I look like a bloody scarecrow.

She pulled down her eyelids, peered at her face.

She saw the years in her eyes, imagining a crash-zoom on her face: her eye, her iris, her pupil, the black hole of the universe eating up Time and Space as she was carried back through the vortex, clutching at fragments of memories. *Let me look deep inside you and see your soul.* People used to say it so often, in clubs and parties, it became almost the only pulling-line of the drugged-up. Zoom back out. The darkness fringed with brown iris, with lash, pulling back and her face was there again.

The striplight was merciless. Without her daily treatment of wheatgerm scrub, extract-of-caviar toner and cucumber-and-vanilla moisturiser, her skin was dying. The defences she put up against the world were falling apart and the real Ella was emerging: reddened marks around her eyes, pale and lifeless lips, flaccid hair.

She tugged the hair hard, pulled it taut so that her scalp hurt, and then, no more than a couple of centimetres out, she made the first incision.

The sky is an off-tuned, dirty grey as the young man in the ragged pullover and jeans hurries, head down, across the college quadrangle. He glances up for a moment at the trees against the sky; they are bent and black, stooping like mendicant monks. He shivers, scurries on.

The bar has been recently refitted and gleams with Eighties style – chrome, black ash and coloured spotlights. It smells of sweetly chemical disinfectant, buoyed on aromatic clouds of coffee. It's almost empty, though. There's a slender, dark-haired girl at the corner table, drinking coffee and making notes with a book open in front of her. Two physicists in Marillion T-shirts are playing cards over pints of cider. They look up, hopeful that he might join them, but he gives them a wide berth.

Tom, as he fishes for his wallet and nods at the barman, glances over his shoulder again at the girl. Blimey, he thinks. Doing essays in the college bar – how uncool is *that*?

'Where is everyone, Stan?' he asks.

The barman, a laconic type, shrugs. 'Maybe they've all got work to do, Mr Barclay,' he says, and flashes his wonky yellow teeth at Tom. 'Not like you, I expect.'

'Leave it out, Stan, I've done all mine for the week.'

While he's waiting for his Guinness to pour, Tom puts a coin in the jukebox. Almost at random, he's chosen Echo and the Bunnymen, 'The Game'. He watches the girl's irritation as the music crashes out. Stan finishes off his pint with a foam-shamrock from the tap. Tom nods his thanks and strolls across to browse at the newspaper rack.

The girl looks up, irritated, tucking her hair behind one ear, as Tom comes over. He grins at her, sizes her up. Tousled black hair, a wide mouth, little John Lennon glasses, big hoop earrings. Nicely spherical breasts, contained in a sensible black pullover adorned with a discreet CND badge. He glimpses an equally sensible red skirt, just high enough above the knee to be interesting, and long, shapely legs ending in flat shoes.

'Sorry, did you not want that on?' he says with a grin.

'Don't mind about me,' she says, without looking up.

'Oh, I won't, then.' Tom unfolds a paper and skims the headlines. 'God, you can easily forget what's going on in the world, stuck in this place, can't you?' he adds. He sits down opposite her, keeping his pint steady.

'Yes,' says the girl. 'Perhaps I'd quite like to.' She looks up, briefly. Her eyes are a rich brown, bright and mocking.

'It's seminal, this is. Did really well for them in the States.' Drumming the beat on the table, he starts singing along.

'Um, excuse me?' The girl looks up briefly, spreads her hands, continues writing. 'I am kind of busy here.'

'Oh, I *am* sorry,' he says, narrowing his eyes over his glass. 'I don't suppose you've heard of the library? The drinks aren't as good, but it does have certain advantages as a place to work. It's probably something to do with all the books. Oh, and the fact that you can be quiet there. In fact, I do hear it's positively encouraged.'

'Excuse me,' says the girl, putting her pen down with an exasperated sigh, 'did I *ask* you to come and talk to me?'

'Nobody says you have to work in here. In fact, I'm pretty sure it's very, very square indeed.'

The wind is gathering momentum outside, and the leaves, sticks and other debris from the quad are starting to rattle the glass of the bar's floor-to-ceiling windows. Stan the barman looks up nervously from his black-and-white TV. It's sizzling with static, and as Tom glances over at him, the portable aerial falls off and clatters to the floor.

'*Square?* Oh, I see!' she's saying to him, leaning back, folding her arms. 'And you're Mr Cool, are you?'

He can't quite place her accent. It's something northern, steely, but washed through with an almost Celtic breeze. Her hair is wild, tangling in gorgeous chaos on her black woollen pullover. In fact, she's moulting – odd stray hairs have fallen on to her papers and her skirt. She tilts her head on one side, biting into a half-smile as she looks his old pullover and jeans up and down.

He leans his head too. He reads the name on her folder.

'Oh, so *you're* Ella MacBride,' he says in realisation.

She glowers at him. 'What's that supposed to mean?'

'Nothing, nothing at all.' Tom carves a shape in the head of his Guinness, sucks his finger thoughtfully. 'Just that you're the one all the guys doing English seem to talk about. Girl most likely to get a First... Holes up in the library every afternoon, they say. Only ever listens to Shostakovich and Sinatra, they say. Now there's a weird combination I'd like to talk about.'

'Some other time, perhaps.'

Ignoring the comment, he grabs the book from under her nose. 'Aaaaah. *The Return of the Native*. Always found Hardy a little heavy-going, but hey, this is one of his best.'

'Right, thank you, I'll be sure to include that in my essay. Could I please have it back now?'

'Yeah. Sure.'

He slides the book back across to her, his eyes looking past her, out of the big windows at the wind whipping up in the quad.

'So, um, CND?' he says. 'Cool. I always thought I might join. Go on a few marches and so on.' He frowns. 'I haven't got round to it yet.'

She looks up, gives him a withering look and returns to her work.

He gives her a smile. Drumming his fingers on the table, still, he takes a sip of his Guinness.

'That's my name, too,' he offers.

She sighs, slams her pen down. 'What?'

'My name,' he says, pointing to the book.

'Your name's Hardy?'

'No, Thomas.' He nods affably to her. 'Tom Barclay. Politics and economics, drinking, table football and rare vinyl.'

She doesn't pick up the baton. There is an embarrassed silence as Ella, pretending he is not there, continues to take notes.

Out in the quad, there's nobody to be seen. Leaves are being gathered up and scattered as if by the flailing fists of giants. The trees are screaming with the weight of the wind.

Now, Ella MacBride follows his gaze. 'Mary, Mother of God,' she says. 'That's one heck of a breezy day out there.'

Tom remembers being in the TV room. '*Earlier,*' Michael Fish said, smiling to the camera, '*a woman apparently called the BBC and said there's going to be a hurricane. Well, don't worry, there isn't...*'

Ella MacBride is gathering up her books and notes and cramming them into her bag. She gulps back the last of her coffee. 'I think I'm gonna get back to my room,' she says.

'No, don't.'

Tom doesn't realise it yet, but he has placed a hand on her slender arm, lightly tugging at the black woollen jumper.

She widens her eyes at him. 'Excuse *me?*'

'Fantastic character, Eustacia Vye,' he says, gazing into her eyes. 'Drawn with such depth and dark, supernatural beauty, don't you think? Remember how we first see her...standing on top of that hill. Part of Nature, and yet still human...'

She stops, clutches her folder to her breasts, and grins slowly, nodding, her head on one side. 'So you really do like it,' she says.

Tom shrugs, smiles. 'Yeah, well.' He lifts his drink for a sip.

She nods over at the speakers, where the closing bars of 'The Game' are ringing out of the jukebox. 'Echo and the Bunnymen aren't bad, either,' she says.

Tom pauses, the Guinness halfway to his lips. 'Blimey,' he says.

'Yeah, well, come on. Don't believe everything you hear.' She perches herself on the table beside him. 'I may have a lot of Sinatra and Shostakovich, but it's hardly all I listen to.'

'So choose something else,' he says, and flips her a coin.

She catches it in one hand, not breaking eye contact. 'OK, mister.' She gives him a half-smile, sashays over to the jukebox and, almost without looking, makes her selection.

A swaggering guitar intro starts up and he recognises it instantly: 'What Difference Does It Make' by The Smiths. Tom nods in approval, eyebrows and pint both raised.

However, the song gets no further than the opening bars before the jukebox screeches to a halt. At the same time, the lights in the bar flicker and go out, and Tom hears Ella gasp.

Somewhere on the other side of the bar, one of the Marillion physicists swears. There is a crash as a drink is knocked over.

'Don't panic!' Stan shouts from somewhere behind the bar, and Tom sees a torch-beam flicking on, waving about. It dazzles Tom for a second. 'I've got some candles back here somewhere,' says Stan, and disappears behind the bar, taking his torch with him. 'And a lamp!'

Tom and his new friend, Ella MacBride, sit down gingerly, side by side at the big table.

'I don't think you'd better go back, now,' Tom ventures. 'It's always safest to stay where you are in a power cut.'

She shivers. The wind is rattling the whole building. It is as if the earth itself has become angry, shaking these insignificant creatures who stand on it. Putting them in their place.

'I don't know,' she says. 'I think I'd rather be in my room.'

An orange flash suddenly bathes them, and they look up,

startled. Stan is grinning, arms spread wide, looking alarmingly like some demonic DJ behind the roadworker's lamp which is spraying its disco light across the rattling bar.

'And there we have it, ladies and gents!' says Stan, throwing a bar-towel over his shoulder and leaning in customary manner. 'We are still open for business, come rain, shine or hurricane. It'll have to be hand-pulled only, though,' he adds with a shrug. 'Still, Mr Barclay won't mind that. He likes a bit of hand-pulled.'

And Stan winks at Tom, who feels his face roaring with a blush.

'Um, yes. Right. Would you like a drink?' he asks Ella.

She pulls a face, looks out through the picture-window at the blackened sky and the bending trees. She shrugs. Grins.

'OK,' she says. 'Pint of mild, if it'll stop you being such a pain in the neck.'

As they drink their pints in the corner, others start to fill the bar: bedraggled, shivering souls, attracted by the light, perhaps driven from the chilly library or their shuddering rooms. Tom wonders about the fabric of the college. It loses a few tiles every year, that's normal; people who default on their rent have been known to end up on the roof helping to fix them back on. Or maybe this is one of those myths the finalists like to tell them.

He sees Ella MacBride looking at him over the top of her pint, wondering what he's thinking about. He finds himself smiling at her, deciding he rather likes her Little Miss Clever glasses and her tight lambswool pullover covered in stray hairs. He decides that she is, in fact, extremely sexy.

Tom's mother reminds him on the phone – with monotonous regularity – that he's there to work hard and get a top-class degree, and that 'all that other stuff' can wait its turn. Tom knows what she means, because he's of the exact opposite opinion. He's here for the beer, the parties and the girls. He would rather leave with a Lower Second and a healthy shag-rate than take a First and still be celibate. People out there have jobs doing bugger-all, don't they, earning thousands? A successful career, that'll be easy. Ugly, charmless blokes can have successful careers. Sex, on the other hand, is a true challenge.

'I was meant to be meeting some friends,' says Ella MacBride nervously, glancing at her watch.

'And instead you ran into me. Bummer.'

She grins shyly. 'Yeah. Looks like I'm stopping,' she says, waving her half-empty glass at him.

He frowns. 'Sorry? Stopping what?'

Does she mean she's sticking to half a pint? Doesn't want to drink any more?

She looks at him as if he's stupid. 'Stopping. Oh, God, don't tell me that's something else people allegedly don't say.' She spreads her hands. 'Stopping here. In the bar.'

'Oh…you mean *staying*,' he says, relieved.

'Yeah, whatever. God, they told me to expect a bit of elitism, but nobody ever said I'd need subtitles.'

'Hey, Stan, OK if I put this on?' shouts a tall, wild-haired second-year, brandishing a battery-operated ghetto blaster. The barman gives him a thumbs-up, and a second later the makeshift jukebox kicks into action with Van Morrison's 'Brown-Eyed Girl'.

Tom notices that Ella is laughing, singing along between sips of her beer.

'I like a woman who drinks pints,' he says, leaning across the table so she can hear him properly.

'What?' She's laughing, cupping her ear.

'I said I like – *fucking hell!*'

Tom doesn't know how he's managed to move so fast, or what instinct makes him grab Ella MacBride's hand and yank her down on the floor.

The large, heavy roof-slate which splits open the bar window, sending their drinks smashing to the floor, would almost certainly have cracked her skull if she hadn't moved.

The table pivots through ninety degrees and slams to the floor, flush with the broken window like a barricade.

Her face is pale. She's shivering.

The slate ends its journey against the far wall, shattering into a dozen grey shards. Behind them, it's bedlam – screams, shouts, the music still playing. Under them, glass and beer slopping everywhere. Wind rips in, grabbing anything loose – ashtrays, beer-mats, newspapers and books – and dashing them against the walls. A blizzard of leaves blows through the bar.

She's close to him, her hair falling on his face, and their heads touch the underside of the bar table as another volley of branches splinters the window open in several more places.

'Jesus,' says Ella, and crosses herself. 'It's bloody Armageddon.'

He watches her wide red mouth move as she speaks, and then he takes her face in both hands and kisses her.

* * *

'Hey, Mr Daydream.'

He looked up, alarmed.

Phill was there, her face glowing and scrubbed beneath a towel, her body soft and curvy in a bathrobe. She was deliciously sweet-smelling; apple shampoo and shower gel.

'Um, hi,' he said.

He realised he'd almost drifted off.

He remembered now: Phill had been taking a post-sex shower in the en suite, and the splashing of the water had lulled him like soft breakers on a beach.

'You were smiling. I wondered what you were thinking about.'

'I was thinking about your gorgeous body,' he said, and slipped an arm round her waist to pull her in for a kiss.

The lie didn't bother him unduly, as it was just one of many, these days. It really did get easier.

He'd never imagined that he'd have to lie to Phill as well as to Ella, but he had decided that you simply couldn't give women – *any* women – honest answers to all the questions they wanted to ask. That was just inviting trouble.

All the same, it was supremely ironic that his mistress had almost caught him thinking about his wife.

'Tom?' she murmured, caressing his chest.

'Mmm?'

'Who's Charlotte?'

He went cold. He grabbed her hand and pushed her away, sitting suddenly bolt upright. 'What do you mean?'

'Hey, hey, hey!' Phill laughed, stroking his back. 'Jeez, don't over-react. You've just...said the name in your sleep since you've been here. That's all.'

'How often?' he asked her sharply.

She shrugged. 'Um... A couple of times. That's all.' Phill leant forward, touched him again. 'So who is she?'

'It's my business.'

'OK, OK. Tom, chill out. I'm not jealous. I'm not checking up on you. I just thought it might be an old girlfriend or something.' She grinned, shrugged. 'Someone you'd looked up on Friends Reunited,' she added, trying to lighten the mood.

'Sorry,' he said. 'I'm sorry.'

He lay down again, turned away from her and closed his eyes. 'Look, I'm...really tired. Do you mind if we just sleep?'

Phill thought about this for five long seconds, pouted and shrugged. 'OK,' she said, and lay down, not sleeping, beside him in the darkness.

The distance between them was no more than the span of a hand, but it might as well have been the expanse of a city.

'Hello, and welcome to Don't Make Me Over, the show where we take your partner and give them the look you've always wanted them to have. I'm Chrissie Kaminsky, and in the next half-hour we'll be seeing just what a difference one day's shopping and pampering can make to Col and Luce from Milton Keynes – and what they think of each other at the end of it!'

Pampering, Ella thought grimly – what a word. It meant manicures and hot waxing and eyebrow-plucking and aromatherapy. It took as its starting point the idea that Woman was basically fat, hairy, sweaty and undesirable and that she required a week in a health farm to make her ravaged body acceptable to her nauseated husband.

She ran a hand through her hair. It still stuck up in awkward places – Kevin would have a fit if he saw it, she thought with a wry grin – and it made her feel colder and lighter, more exposed. Her reflection didn't catch her out, but she couldn't get used to the spiky, boyish shadow she cast on the pavements of Parkfield.

'First of all, I'm going to get Col to show me how Luce normally presents herself to the world, and how he'd like his new, improved Fantasy Luce to look!'

The iron hissed on her trouser suit as the television chattered away in the corner. Selling the widescreen TV and the video-DVD from the Ashington house had been an easy decision, but she had bought this second-hand portable to prevent outright mutiny from Ben and Isobel. It wasn't tuned in properly and the four channels she could pick up were only visible through a swirl of dots, but it was better than nothing.

She hadn't bought a licence, but then she didn't imagine anyone else on Parkfield bothered with one. Detector vans were empty, according to Dee. Visiting unregistered addresses was how they really found you out, and these days even the police treated Parkfield as a no-go zone.

'So, Col,' said the unfeasibly bubbly voice of Chrissie Kaminsky from the TV, *'you and Luce have been together for…two years?'*

'That's right, Chrissie.' Col, a roguish type in a faded denim shirt, nodded and grinned.

'And – well, let's take a look at the sort of thing Luce normally wears, shall we?'

Split-screen pictures bounced into place of an attractive but dowdy girl, dressed in a variety of sensible tops and slacks.

Ella winced as she finished off the sharp crease in her trousers. Yes, she could see what they meant. Mind you, the guy was hardly Mr Fashionable either – she hoped they would also be doing it the other way round. A second later, she shook her head in despair that she was actually taking an interest in this rubbish.

Col, it turned out, thought Luce had a 'great body' which she always 'hid away too much', and he'd always fancied the idea of seeing her in 'something more feminine'. Under pressure from Chrissie Kaminsky, Col was coaxed into naming the film stars and pop singers he fancied, and then they brought in a computer with a fancy graphics package and got him to design his ideal outfit for his beloved. It consisted of a tight vest-top, a skimpy suede skirt and matching boots, accessorised with chunky bangles and hippy pendants. A twenty-year-old's club gear, Ella thought grimly as she ran the iron over her jacket – right, she knew where *he* was coming from. She couldn't see a nudging-thirty Miss Debenhams going for *that* without a fight. But off they went, printouts in hand, taking Luce on a surprise shopping spree.

It was all too tedious. She flicked the TV off and went into the bedroom to get changed.

Ella buttoned up the jacket she hadn't worn for several weeks, smoothed the skirt and swivelled in front of the mirror. 'You'll do,' she told herself.

She had never tried to change anything about Tom. Perhaps that was where she'd gone wrong? Bex's old joke hadn't applied to her (the one about the bride walking into church and thinking about the aisle, the altar and the hymns, saying to herself: 'Aisle Altar Hymn, Aisle Altar Hymn...').

But maybe if she'd tried to shave off a few of his rough edges, give him a bit more of a kick up the backside occasionally... She shook her head. These things were stupid to think about.

She double-locked the door to her flat. The lift buttons had been melted again, so she made her way unsteadily down the stinking staircase.

Crashing, wailing R'n'B music echoed from a door on Three, making her wince. There was noise in abundance on Parkfield – perhaps because it was the only thing the poor could afford in quantity.

She didn't know any mothers who still enjoyed loud music. She'd found a Curve CD while clearing out the house and was astonished to realise it was hers, not Tom's – she hadn't heard it for years. While men could cheerfully keep their Rage Against The Machine albums well into fatherhood and beyond, women lost the appetite for high-decibel pleasure once they'd been subjected to screaming babies.

On Two, a couple of teenage girls – pale, with dreadlocks, sports tops, trainers and giant earrings – were lounging against the wall, smoking. They looked Ella up and down with undisguised hostility, their gazes boring silently into her back as she descended.

Down on One, Dee was in her doorway, gossiping on her phone. She gave Ella a wave as she crossed the lobby. Ella could see through the acrid fog into the hall, where one of the Ryans was running up and down with a cheap toy gun.

'All right, love,' she said, covering the receiver and looking Ella up and down in mock admiration. 'Ooooh, look at yer. Off to see the Queen, are we?'

'No,' Ella replied with just a hint of irritation. 'I've got a job interview, actually.'

'Blimey. I'd keep that one quiet, love. Make sure you get cash in hand, like, or they'll stop your benefits.'

Ella stopped and gave Dee a withering look which, predictably, bounced right off her. 'Dee, if I get the job, I won't be wanting to claim benefits.'

Dee took a long, thoughtful drag on her cigarette. 'S'pose you're right,' she said eventually, nodding through a haze of smoke.

'Thanks for the other day,' Ella added, feeling guilty now. 'For looking after the kids.'

'No problem, love. Sure you'd do the same for me.' She gave Ella a big yellow grin, and Ella was able to manage a feeble smile in response as she sidled towards the door.

'Yes,' she said unconvincingly. 'Yes, I'm sure I would.'

'Good luck with it,' Dee called after her.

Ella waved in response. She pushed open the lobby exit and – after the usual glance skywards to check for fast-descending consumer waste – she hurried across the car park to the bus stop.

Monday lunchtime.

'Ben,' said Elizabeth Moretti, head teacher of Parkfield, clasping her hands together and peering over her green, wire-framed glasses. 'I had thought better of you. Much better.'

Ben folded his arms and glowered.

He felt uncomfortable, angry. The one thing he didn't feel was remorseful. He'd not done anything wrong. He had to survive in this shit-hole, didn't he? And now, he was sitting here in Moretti's office in the lunch hour, and she was obviously waiting for an apology. Well, she wasn't going to get one.

The squeals and shouts of the playground floated up to him. Cold autumn sunlight picked out the dancing dust and the grubbiness of the windows.

'You can't prove anything,' he said sullenly.

He didn't look up at her, but he could see the wiry, short-haired, middle-aged woman pacing up and down in front of him. He noticed she was squashing a stress-ball in her bony, blotched fingers. They look old fingers, he thought. She must be ancient. You wouldn't know it from her face – all smooth and stretched, almost polished-looking, like a newly waxed car or an apple.

'Ben, please. Don't be foolish. CCTV covers every centimetre of the school perimeter, even outside school hours. I think we have ample evidence on which to get you, at the very least, a suspension.'

Ben looked up for the first time.

'You know, I had thought a boy like you to be quite a catch for this school. Bright, motivated, strong sportsman...' Ms Moretti leant back, sighed, removed her glasses and twirled them thoughtfully. 'I'd hoped you might be a calming influence on some of the more...disreputable elements in Year Nine. Obviously they got to you before I did.' She leant forward again. 'You may think that chucking a few stones at the assembly hall is no big deal. Well, I'm afraid it is. Fourteen windows were broken, Ben. *Fourteen.*'

He said nothing.

'Criminal damage, Ben, is a *very* serious offence. Are you

going to tell me why you did it?' She smiled on one side of her face, cutting three firm creases into her polished face.

Ben shrugged, he looked to one side of Ms Moretti and smirked, because he thought it would probably annoy her.

'That's not an answer, Ben.'

He looked up, his eyes prickling with anger. 'OK. Here's an answer. Because I'm not supposed to be here, in this bloody place. And, let's face it, Ms Moretti, who's going to notice a few more broken windows in this dump?'

There was a long, dangerous silence, during which Ms Moretti got up, strode thoughtfully around her desk and came to sit on the front edge, her long legs crossed, her glasses still swinging from her thumb and forefinger.

'You know,' she said, 'I have had people – adults, I'm talking about – absolutely pilloried for ignorant, prejudiced comments like that about my school. I've written to the papers about them. I've even got near to making slander charges stick with some of them, I can tell you. So it doesn't bother me in the slightest to hear it from a snobby little public schoolboy like you, Mr Barclay.'

'I'm not snobby,' said Ben indignantly.

'*I haven't finished.*' Ms Moretti's face was knowing, almost mocking now, which scared him more than her severity. 'I not only have the evidence for a suspension, I have enough to refer this matter to the police. Fortunately, as the head teacher of this school, I am able to use my discretion.'

Ben frowned.

'I'm under no illusions, Ben, about who the troublemakers are in this school. I can tell the difference between them and those who simply go along for the ride because they have nothing better to do, or because they are too scared, or too stupid, or – like you, I think – because of a misguided sense of adventure.'

She went over to the safe in the corner of her office, turned the dial. After a series of barely audible clicks, it swung open. From within it, Ms Moretti pulled out a videotape.

'The CCTV footage of your little misdemeanour,' she said. 'I haven't shown it to anybody yet.'

Suddenly, she had lobbed it across the room, and he caught it, a pure reflex action. He sat there staring at it.

'Go ahead,' she said. 'Unspool it. Smash it. Throw it in the bin.'

This, for Ben, was bizarre adult behaviour. He wondered if being head of Parkfield had finally sent old Moretti barmy. Tipped her right over the edge.

'Why?' he asked, bewildered.

'Can't do it?' she asked. 'Well, you've missed your chance, now.' And she sailed past him, plucking the tape out of his hands.

He leapt up, trying to grab it. 'No. Hang on.'

'Aaaaah!' Ms Moretti rounded on him, her apple-face glowing with triumph. 'So it does bother you. Excellent. I had hoped as much.' She slipped the tape into a padded envelope, sealed it up and replaced it in the safe. Ben stared longingly at it as she slammed the door shut and gave the dial a twist.

'As I was saying. I know the difference between you and, say – Gary Collins.'

Ben looked up in alarm.

'Oh, don't worry. He doesn't know you're here. Yet. Although I'd have a good cover story ready, if I were you, because he's going to ask you a few questions.'

'Why don't you haul Collins in here?' Ben asked indignantly.

Ms Moretti sighed. 'It isn't that simple, Ben. Your friend Collins isn't a mindless thug, he has a particularly...calculated way of going about things. As I'm sure you've noticed. Catching him doing something we can pin on him is a job and a half.'

'Plus his family practically runs Parkfield,' said Ben. 'So if you get on the wrong side of him, you might wake up to find your sports hall barbecued. Miss.'

Ms Moretti leant down so that her face was level with Ben's. Her breath smelt of smoke and peppermints. 'That may or may not be true, Benedict. But now you're here. Which makes things so much easier.'

'How do you mean?' he asked, wrinkling his nose.

Ms Moretti strode over to the window and lit a cigarette. If Ben was shocked, he didn't let it show.

'Ever seen *Reservoir Dogs*, Ben?' she asked, exhaling out of the window.

'Course I haven't,' he said, too quickly. 'It's an 18.'

'Oh, come on, Ben. You're a clever boy, nice background, but a bit of a tough edge to you. I'm sure you'll want to impress a few girls in three or four years' time with your working knowledge of Quentin Tarantino. You're not telling me you don't have a friend with an older brother who's got the DVD, or something like that?'

Ben shrugged. 'OK, so I might have seen...bits of it.'

He wasn't going to admit to being impressed with her powers of deduction. He supposed it was a head's job to know this kind of thing, but it was a bit disturbing for them actually to display it.

'Excellent. That makes my job a lot easier.' Ms Moretti swung round from the window, and she was framed in light, wreathed in smoke, wearing a strange, hard smile. 'Ben,' she said. 'You're going to be my very own Mr Orange.'

Ben felt himself turning pale.

'Although I would hope,' Ms Moretti added, allowing herself a grim smile, 'that nobody's actually going to have to get their ear cut off.'

CHAPTER SEVENTEEN

Since Yesterday

The lift doors close. They rumble like thunder, and the internal lights bathe Ella in a carmine flood. She blinks, wondering why her eyes feel so crisped, crunchy, in need of a good splash of water.

The lift seems to rock and sway alarmingly as it descends into the bowels of the earth, and she thinks it's getting hotter, too.

Mu-mmy

She reaches up to loosen the collar of her blouse, and realises that she is actually wearing nothing but a baggy, sweat-soaked Duran Duran T-shirt. 'Hungry Like The Wolf' crackles over a rickety speaker in the top corner of the lift.

The doors growl open, and Ella emerges, walking in leaden slo-mo through a tunnel of smoke, its thick greyness punched here and there by hot, red spotlights.

Muuuuuuu-mmmmmmmy

'Hello?' she calls. 'Hello?'

A tall, dark figure drops down in front of her, neatly landing with both feet on the ground. As she watches, it crash-zooms towards her, does a kung-fu flip and ends up right in front of her. It's Keanu Reeves from *The Matrix*, she notices without much surprise. He caresses her breasts, making her feel amazingly turned on.

'Don't worry about the kids,' he says. 'Any trouble, just call on me.'

He suddenly flips round so that he's behind her, twirling his guns with an elegant swish.

'Don't stop, Keanu. I was quite enjoying that. What am I doing here, anyway?'

'Oh, the usual stuff. Panic, terror, groundless fear. It's judgement, Ella.'

She spins round to face him, and he lifts his sunglasses to reveal the tired, accusatory face of her husband. He looks as if he hasn't shaved for a week.

'Tom!'

'Oh, you remembered my name, then.'

'That's not fair, Tom. You're the one who's shagging some tart somewhere.'

'Ah, now, you don't know that. That's interesting. Very interesting. Maybe that's your subconscious making a link? I'd have a think about that one later if I were you.'

He leans forward, his eyes bright and piercing as he looks into hers. Somehow, her damp Duran Duran T-shirt has become a sweat-drenched power-suit complete with prickly stockings and wobbly high heels. She is itching, and starts scratching at her arms, legs and buttocks.

'And what the *fuck* have you done with your hair?' Tom adds. 'You look like a bloody lesbian.'

A cloister bell chimes somewhere in the dark depths – sonorous, magnificent.

Muuuuuummm-yyyyyyy!

'Time for registration,' says Tom with a grin, and flips the sunglasses back down over his eyes again. 'Sure you can cope? You may seem like an organiser, Ella, but I know you're a stresser. Those kids are going to have you for breakfast. Talking of which...' He reaches into an invisible cavity and pulls out two covered plates. 'Breakfast?'

She lifts the lid. Crisp, blood-red bacon, perfect oval fried eggs and plump mushrooms, all ranged neatly beside three golden triangles of toast.

'God,' she says, 'I could murder that.'

'What about *my* breakfast, Mummy?' Someone is tugging at the hem of her skirt, desperately brandishing a box of Cheerios. 'I can't get this open! I can't get the bloody thing open!'

'Swear-box, Izzy,' says Ella automatically.

'Fuck the swear-box! I want my bloody breakfast!'

With an enraged scream, the little girl rips her teeth into the cardboard and a shower of Cheerios erupts, forming a vortex around Ella and Tom.

Bam. Bam. Bam.

Three times, Tom strikes the ground with a wooden staff. It is enough time for Ella to realise that the little girl tugging at the hem of her nightdress

is

not

Isobel...

'Come on, Ella! Time to get going!'

He's laughing, his teeth bright in the darkness.

Bam. Bam. Bam.

'But I can't!' she screams, lifting up a wheelbarrow full of all the folders which they have given her. 'I've got all this to read! And I don't bloody understand it!'

Bam bam bam
Bambambambambambambam—

'Mother of God!'

Ella turned over with a sudden jolt.

For a second, she had to concentrate to remember where she was.

Her heart was thumping under her T-shirt, she realised, and her cropped hair was heavy with perspiration. She checked the clock. Nine forty-seven. Was that in the evening? Dark outside, so it had to be.

Bam bam bam bam bam!

She realised she had been ripped out of her vivid dream by somebody hammering on the none-too-sturdy door of the flat.

Her heart skipped like a damaged CD and her bowels loosened.

Instinct made her check on both the children. They were there, asleep. Ben was sprawled across his top bunk with an open computer magazine dangling from one hand. Isobel was back-to-front as usual on hers, snoring heavily beside a chewed Blue Rabbit and the impassive Deborah Zebra.

Mummy.

That's my name.

'All right, all right, for God's sake.'

Ella made a detour to the kitchen. She checked that she knew where the knives were, and only then did she go to the hall.

She unlocked the door, peered across the taut chain.

'I come bearing gifts,' said a familiar, female voice.

Ella blinked.

It was Bex.

Trim and stylish in an urchin cap, denim shirt and leather trousers, she was holding up a ciabatta loaf in one hand and a bottle of red wine in the other.

'Let me in, you bitch,' she added, 'or I swear I'll fucking camp out here on these pissy stairs.'

It took five seconds for Ella to recover from the surprise of seeing her friend, after which she unchained the door, flung it wide open and embraced a startled Bex with an enormous hug.

'Jesus,' Bex muttered from somewhere in Ella's shoulder. 'If I'd known I was gonna get this kind of reception, babe, I'd have tracked you down earlier.'

'Come in,' Ella said gratefully. 'Please.'

Bex took a step back and looked in amazement at Ella's hair. 'Bloody hell. The dykey look works for me, love, but I'm not sure about you.' She put down a bulging John Lewis carrier bag in the hall, and gave Ella another hug.

Ella shrugged, gave a weary smile. 'I wanted something I could manage easily,' she said.

The next few minutes were dominated by Bex's stream-of-consciousness chatter about how she had found out where Ella was living (something to do with having a friend at the Post Office who dealt with the forwarded mail) and her subsequent attempts to actually find the place.

Bex paused to look around, wrinkling her nose slightly as if taking in the inauspicious surroundings for the first time. Ella didn't blame her. There were clothes drying on the radiators, a stack of pizza boxes on the kitchen worktop, coats and books and games piled on every available surface. The kitchen had no wallpaper – just bare, scabbed plaster.

'Yes, I know,' Ella said wearily from the sofa. 'It's not the bloody Ritz. I wanted spartan minimalism, and I got half the deal... You know all those fucking Sunday supplement homes with people in their ice-cool designer lounges? Nothing in them but a couple of Panton chairs and a wooden fruit bowl with two glass pebbles in?'

'I worship them, darling,' says Bex.

'Yeah, well, people don't bloody *live* like that, you know. I mean, where do minimalists do their washing?'

'I dunno,' said Bex, lighting a cigarette thoughtfully. 'Where do minimalists do their washing? Oh, sorry. I thought it was a joke.'

'I don't have much time for jokes these days, Bex,' said Ella bitterly. 'Humour's an indulgence. Humour costs money.'

'Rrright... Ell, I wasn't dissing the pad, believe me, although I realise this ain't your usual taste in interiors, babe. Hey, where are the kids?'

'They're in bed, Bex,' said Ella wearily. 'It's ten o'clock at night.'

'Oh, right. Course. Um, got a corkscrew?'

'Ha, well, that's one thing nobody could take off me. Second drawer down.'

Bex found it. She extracted the cork from the bottle she had brought, grinned and held it up for inspection. 'Nice bit of Fitou?'

'That'll do me,' said Ella.

'Oh, and the great middle-class con,' Bex added, 'ciabatta bread.'

'Lovely. Almost like being at home... What do you mean, the great middle-class con?'

'Well – got any glasses?'

'You'll have to use mugs.'

'Bloody hell, Ella. This is like being a student again.'

'Um, yes. Only without the brilliant social life, freely available sex and promise of great things to come.'

Bex poured them each a generous mugful of red wine. 'No, the thing about ciabatta bread,' she said, 'is that people buy it, right, thinking it's some fantastic medieval Italian recipe, yeah, 'cos it looks all rustic and homemade and that. Whereas actually, it was dreamt up by some marketing bloke in the early Eighties. But nobody seems to mind. It's like they've bought into the invented history of it.' Bex paused, looked around. 'Bread knife?' she asked hopefully.

'No. Just break it in half.'

Bex plonked herself down opposite Ella and they clinked mugs. 'Cheers, you old tart,' said Bex. 'So come on, I want to know how you got yourself into this bollocks of a mess. Christ, last thing I knew you were on the phone wanting to buy a house near me. I knew something was up then. You'd never be that desperate. What are you *doing*?'

'I've got myself a new job,' said Ella. 'One that actually means something, for once.'

'Jesus,' said Bex. 'And I take it that you've traded a fuck-off salary for more of a fuck-you salary? What job? Where?'

'Well,' Ella said, swinging herself into an upright sitting position and holding her mug in two hands. 'It's like this.'

* * *

Elizabeth Moretti opens another door.

'And here,' she says, 'is the IT suite. As you can see, we're fully Internet-linked and we have all the latest software packages. There's a full library of CD-ROMs which we encourage everyone to use.'

Fully Internet-linked. Ella wrinkles her nose. Is this a boast, she wonders? It's a bit like saying, 'As you can see, we're on the phone.'

There are two Year Ten boys in the corner of the room, downloading a picture which looks, from the half which is visible, like a bare-breasted woman in some sort of leather harness. Ella does a double take. Ms Moretti gives a small, tight squeak of indignation, stalks over to the computer and reboots it.

'You two can see me in my office at lunchtime,' she tells the two sniggering boys. 'Get out.'

They hoist bags on shoulders and swagger towards the door, not showing a trace of shame. Ella feels their eyes looking her up and down, and for a second she has the uncomfortable feeling of being mentally undressed by two hormonal teenagers. Her face blazing red, she looks away.

Ms Moretti clears her throat and closes the door after the pair. 'Sorry about that,' she says. 'We do have security blocks on the Web, of course, but they're not infallible.'

Ella flicks a smile back on. 'Well, what is?' she asks.

Her afternoon, so far, hardly counts as a whirlwind of activity. There's an astonishingly brief, undetailed interview with Ms Moretti, two deputies and the Year Nine head, a lugubrious type called Hollis who watches her as a dog might eye up a bowl of Pedigree Chum.

Then comes the whistle-stop tour, during which she catches Matt Ryder's eye in the corridor. He gives her a wink of encouragement, which she volleys with a cool flicker of her eyebrows.

'So,' says Ms Moretti, hands clasped behind her back, 'as you can see, we are a challenging and developing learning environment, offering a multiplicity of opportunities for students and striving towards excellence at all times.'

'Yes,' says Ella, 'I believe that's what it says in your prospectus.'

This is all most unnerving. Her last teaching interview – which admittedly was fifteen years ago – was a day-long stumble through one tripwire after another. The four fresh-faced candidates had first been forced to interview each other, were given a grilling by each and every member of the panel, then sat a succession of aptitude tests before being let loose, without warning, in a classroom full of bright and exuberant twelve-year-old girls. After individual sessions, Ella was discreetly steered aside to be told she had the job while the others were gently given the news. And the Cherford Castle process had been even worse: two days of psychometric testing, role-plays and group-exercise hell in which she had barely known what she was doing.

Today – well, it's just a spelling test by comparison. She's the only candidate for the job. She has gained the distinct impression that nothing will get her turned away short of a string of paedophile convictions.

Now and then she will remember some of the things Matt told her to mention – policy on special needs, links with the community – but Liz Moretti just recites bored, textbook answers, as if giving out such information is terribly beneath her.

'Your GCSE results will be a real challenge, if I may say so,' Ella ventures. 'Thirteen per cent last year, wasn't it? What's the current policy for getting them up?'

Liz Moretti looks at Ella as if she has asked her how the school intends to meet the challenges of little green men from Mars. 'Forgive me for asking, Ms MacBride, but I take it you don't really know the area?'

Ella bristles. 'Actually, I live in Parkfield,' she says, scratching her nose.

She is amazed at how it sounds. It's the first time she has uttered the words out loud, and she is astonished that, far from feeling the despair she expects, saying it actually gives her a ridiculous sense of pride. She stands up straight and looks Ms Moretti in the eye.

'Oh.' The headmistress blinks and almost recoils, but seems to recover her blank, beatific smile just in time. 'Then you'll know, Ms MacBride, the kind of problems we have to deal with here. I think that, in the circumstances, thirteen per cent was an excellent result for the previous academic year.'

'Right,' says Ella uncertainly.

'Any more questions?'

'Do you have many children from ethnic minorities?'

Ella knows the answer already. Parkfield is not one of England's multicultural estates. A more solid, white-bread, narrow-eyed place would be hard to find. The only Asian she's ever seen around here is Mr Aziz from the shop, and he puts up with the kind of intimidation which would drive lesser mortals to violence.

Ms Moretti smiles indulgently. 'We don't have that problem here,' she says.

Without hearing that brazen answer, Ella probably wouldn't dare put her last question. 'Do you have children yourself?' she asks.

Ms Moretti looks a little uncomfortable. She pulls her jacket tight as if protecting herself from such insolence. 'Yes,' she says. 'Two girls. Twins.'

'And do they come here?'

Ella enjoys the odd, rattling choke which comes from Ms Moretti's throat. She hears her swallowing hard as she tries to recover herself. 'Aaah, no. They don't. Anyway we're...not in this catchment area.'

'Oh, right. I just thought, you know, as it's obviously so excellent you might send them here.'

'My girls are at Millmount,' says Liz Moretti. 'It seemed...more appropriate for them.' She folds her hands together and puts her head on one side, as if weighing up Ella's response.

'Of course,' says Ella.

Millmount. Jesus, maybe she recognises me. Her mind races as she tries to remember if she's ever seen Liz Moretti at a Parents' Evening, garden party or concert.

Liz Moretti claps her hands, evidently keen to move on from the subject. 'Well,' she says, and blinks. 'Everything seems to be in order. Can you start as soon as possible?'

Ella feels the world shift slightly, and realises that she is holding on to one of the computers for support. Maybe this is some sort of test, she thinks. Or maybe we really are in joke-land, an alternative universe where you swan up with a dusty degree, a fifteen-year-old teaching certificate and a slice of attitude, and someone offers you a job starting on Monday.

'I can start whenever you like,' she hears an echoing voice saying.

It is her own voice. For a minute, she has the odd delusion that it is a message broadcast on the school loudspeaker system. She imagines the Parkfield kids stopping mid-chew, mid-swagger, mid-spit, to look up and hear the words, to pause for a second before bursting into ragged, spiky, threatening laughter.

She realises that Ms Moretti is shaking her hand and speaking.

'If you don't mind my saying so, Ms MacBride, your call did take me aback slightly. We've not had anyone approaching us to do part-time work for a couple of years now.' She beams. 'I'd given up hope of ever filling the spare English post.'

'Oh, well,' says Ella faintly. 'You should always have hope.' She sighed, took a deep breath. 'It's what gets us through the day,' she adds.

'She just offered it to you?' said Bex. 'There and then?'

Ella grinned over her mug of wine. 'You'd better believe it. I just walked out of the place in a state of shock.' She leant back in the chair. 'It was weird, actually.'

Well, she thinks, that could have been a lot worse.

Ella smooths down her skirt, lifts her head (it still feels strangely light) to look up and down the grubby glass-and-stone cliff of the school.

Surely that's not it? It can't be that easy?

Something makes her look over to her left, where the playground turns into the tarmac driveway, then joins the road. In front of the boxy little council houses, a man is standing, waiting for a bus.

Her heart skips a beat as she makes out the shape of a dark, untidily spiky haircut, a casual suede jacket, jeans. Even the jaunty way he is leaning looks familiar.

'Tom.'

She has mouthed the name so quietly that she almost doesn't hear it herself.

She turns on one smart heel, marching away from her new place of work (still can't quite believe that), towards the road. Reality bounces up and down in front of her as she walks, and she imagines a hand-held camera recording it all. Like on *The Bill*. Videotape, not film. She knows that. She knows that thanks to him.

Her heels click on the pavement. Closer and closer. He is still lounging against the bus shelter.

She is going to walk over to him and tell him that she has worked out the difference between Ashington and Parkfield. It isn't that Ashington is in colour and Parkfield is in black-and-white, despite what Ben says. It's that Ashington is shot on lush 35mm film and Parkfield is shot on cheap Outside Broadcast videotape.

Maybe if she tells him that, then they can start a conversation.

They can talk about themselves. About the children.

They can decide what they are going to do.

The bus shelter is only a few metres away, and there is a bus approaching now. She sees him stick his hand out, sees the flash of the indicator, a spark in the grey air, as the bus slows and pulls over.

'Tom!' she calls. Then, louder, picking up her pace, her heels going clicketyclicketyclickety. 'Tom!'

He doesn't respond. The doors of the bus swish open.

She half runs, half staggers to the edge of the pavement and grabs his suede-clad shoulder, spins him round.

The face of a stranger looks back at her.

The man raises his eyebrows at her, smiles uncertainly.

He doesn't even look like Tom. He is about forty-five, with scrappy eyebrows above a lined forehead, and thin, pale lips.

'You OK, love?'

She holds up her hands, backs away. 'Sorry. So sorry. Mistook you for…for someone else.'

The man smiles, winks. 'No problem, love. You take care, now.'

He gets on the bus, pays his fare. Ella realises the driver is waiting for her, having assumed her haste was caused by the need to catch the bus. She shakes her head, waves him on.

As the bus swishes and judders away in a cloud of exhaust fumes, she sinks on to the seat in the shelter. Her teeth are clamped firmly together. She looks up and down the deserted street, then stands up, clenches one fist and slams it hard against the glass. It reverberates satisfyingly, and makes her hand ache.

'Shit,' she says softly to herself. 'Shit, shit, *shit*.'

Bex poured her mug full to the brim and leant forward, sucking up the surplus wine so that it was less unwieldy.

'You're amazing, Ell,' she says. 'Blimey. Parkfield Comp… Those who can, teach, eh? Jesus, you'd never get me doing it.

And if I'm honest I never thought I'd see *you* doing it again.'

'The world is full of people who have underestimated me, Rebecca. They are about to find that I'm not just going to lie down and accept my lot.' She plucked a cigarette from Bex's packet, lit it and leant back, inhaling gratefully.

'Bloody hell. Things that bad, are they?'

'What?'

'You, smoking again. I can't fucking believe it. After all the shit you've given me these past few years.'

'Oh, chill out, love. People change.' Ella dragged the beautiful badness from the little white cylinder, loving the familiar taste as it coated her mouth, adoring the glow, exhaling gratefully.

Bex sat up straight and clutched the edge of the table, then looked wildly around the kitchen. 'Oh, no. This isn't some religious thing, is it? Going all Churchy La Femme on me? You've not decided that God's called you to give up your house to the poor and, I dunno, come and work at the crappiest school in the city to Do Good?'

'Relax, darling. I'm a Catholic, not a social worker.'

'Just checking... So where is he, then? Your man?'

'My man has gone AWOL,' said Ella through gritted teeth. 'I'm rather hoping he's going to put in an appearance any day now, because, whatever happens, there are some issues to do with the children which need resolving.'

'Well, yeah. Too bloody right.' Bex leant back in her seat and looked at her friend with a new expression, a mixture of respect and incomprehension. 'Do you...want him to come back?' she asked.

Ella gave a hollow laugh. 'After he's abandoned me, you

mean, and now that I'm doing perfectly well without him?' She sighed, leant forward, the cigarette dangling perilously from her fingertips. 'Of course I bloody do.'

'Why?' Bex was outraged. 'I mean, surely he's... Jesus, Ella, don't be a fucking doormat.'

'I am not a doormat,' Ella snapped. 'Believe me, if Thomas Barclay enters my line of sight again, he is going to get the biggest bollocking any man's ever had in the history of bollockings. But he's the father of my children, Bex. Whatever he's done – whatever he's doing right now – he still loves them, and they adore him. I know that. Why the fuck would I want to disrupt their lives even more? I've no desire to be a single mum.' She shuddered. 'Believe me, I've seen them. There are other ways.'

'Yeah, well.' Bex didn't seem convinced. She slumped back in her chair and took a long gulp of wine. 'It's up to you.'

'Yes, it is. And I thank you for your concern, darling.'

'So...what's it *like*?' Bex asked. 'Teaching at Parkfield?'

Ella smiled. She dragged deeply on the cigarette until the tip glowed with demonic fire. Puckering her lips to a perfect O, she blew a neat jet across the table.

'Oh, it's just wonderful,' she said. 'I don't know why I didn't do it before.'

'Really?' Bex wrinkled her nose.

'Well, what do you think?' Ella inhaled again. 'Look, some of them are total shits, I'm not denying that. On my first day, this hulking six-foot thug from Year Eleven spat chewing gum down the stairwell and it landed right by my feet. So I called him down – which was hard enough, what with everybody else surging up the stairs the other way – and I told him to pick it up. And do you know what he said?'

'What?'

'He said, "Fuck off, bitch, I ain't picking it up".'

'You're joking, honey.'

'No. Then he said it again, just in case I hadn't heard the first time. And then he walked off.'

'So...what did you do?'

'Well, I couldn't drag him back by his ear, much as I'd have liked to. You can't touch them, you see. You can use "reasonable force" to break up fights, whatever that means, but otherwise you can't lay a finger on them. So I just put him down for a detention. I shouldn't imagine he'll turn up.'

'And what about teaching the little buggers? You're not going to tell me you've got them all convinced Shakespeare is cool? Are you Cherford's answer to Michelle Pfeiffer in *Dangerous Minds*?'

'No, Bex, I'm not. Don't take the piss.'

'Darling, look at this face. Look. Am I mocking? I'm full of admiration, babe. I couldn't do it. Not for twice the money.'

'At the end of the day, you have to stop being a stand-up comic and get them to work. And most of them aren't bothered.'

'Surely you can play the education-gets-you-out-of-here card?' Bex asked.

'Been there, done that. Too many of them have seen brothers and sisters leave school with nothing, go on the social and have a nice life. Booze and fags aplenty, Sky Sports, off to Benidorm every summer. Why should they bother to work? They just shrug. They look me in the eye and tell me they're not doing it.'

Bex winced, leaning back in her chair. 'Jesus. They let them get away with that?'

'I've no idea. I do my bit, make it clear they're not speaking to me like that. I mean, part of me thinks they're just trying it on. They're just...'

An expression of her mother's floats into her mind: 'cocking a snook'. One of her favourites, it covered any activity which was not in line with *Daily Mail* teachings: wearing mini-skirts, living in sin, being a vegetarian, taking drugs, dyeing your hair purple. People did all of these things and more to 'cock a snook' at the moral panickers of the nation. Ella was quite smug that she had done all of them, without yet being struck by a life-shattering thunderbolt.

Not until recently, anyway.

'But the staff are cool?' Bex asked.

'Well, you do get people like Hollis, the old fart, who's convinced that the kids are beyond redemption. He's the kind who still says stuff to kids like "Are you deaf as well as stupid?" in a class where there is a girl with a hearing problem... No, he thinks the best you can do is get by without clouting one of them.'

'That's a bit cynical.'

'Maybe. I think poor Bill's just been to too many vacuous talks about "raising standards" and "fostering a culture of excellence". Nobody ever talks about fostering a culture of mediocrity, but that's what you're going to get. We can't all be bloody *excellent*, can we? It's a fucking joke.' Ella thought she had better change the subject. 'Are you still seeing that bloke? That accountant from the Eighties night?'

'Nick? Yeah, I am, actually.' Bex caught her friend's eye and grinned. 'Yeah, yeah, so he's young. Look, he's legal, isn't he? Has been for seven years.'

'He's not quite an accountant, then, is he? Still training.'

'Yes, babe, but he's a master of the double entry. Anyway, what's the totty like on your staff?'

Ella smiled. 'Oh...passable,' she said, and tried to keep her smile Sphinx-like, inscrutable. She wondered why she bothered, though. Nothing got past Bex, ever.

Bex raised her eyebrows, put her head on one side and gave her a knowing look.

And Ella knew, then, that she wasn't going to get away with it that easily.

'OK,' she said. 'We had this night out last Friday...'

'And congratulations to Ella,' shouts Matt, his pint held high, 'on surviving a month at Parkfield!'

There's a round of applause, followed by appreciative stamping and thumping which shakes the upper floor of the Freemasons' Arms.

Ella, who is downing her third half of bitter, holds her glass aloft in triumph. By scouring the charity shops, she's got herself some leggings, a black off-the-shoulder top, a distressed denim jacket. Her tousled, bed-head hair is streaked with home-made highlights. Her nose is pierced and sports a tiny stud, a dewdrop of fake gold (a mate of Dee's did it for her one afternoon, for free – hurt like hell, but she enjoys the look). Her eyes are blackened and her lips reddened.

When she looks into the mirror, she sees a vampish, slutty stranger. And she likes it. Her old look belongs to someone else. In her bedroom, she gazes at a photo of her and Tom from just three months ago and it is a picture of a stranger – someone who lives in a detached house, owns a Gaggia espresso machine and shops at Waitrose.

'Let's see if she makes it to two!' Jo calls from the next table, where she has her feet up among a pile of empty glasses. The two other young women teachers on either side of her snigger into their wine.

'What, you think I might not?' Ella growls, moving forward and grabbing the table for support.

Jo laughs, waves a hand in a 'don't-take-it-seriously' way. Ella tries to focus on Jo and wonders why the room is tilting like the deck of a ship.

She shrugs, turns back to Matt. 'My round,' she hears herself say, her voice slurring a little. 'Come with me.' And she slips an arm around his waist to guide him along her eccentric path through the tables, staggering once with a giggle and hiccup, knocking a drink over and apologising profusely, hanging on to someone's table and having to be pulled away by Matt.

At the bar, she lights a cigarette with shaking hands.

'Jesus,' she mutters. 'That girl is chippy.'

Matt steadies the lighter for her and lets his hand stroke her knuckles. She notices, of course, and can't be bothered to make him stop. 'Aw, Jojo's all right. She's just, you know…'

'Sus…picious of me?' says Ella calmly. She tilts her head back, relishing the lavish, carcinogenic jet she blows into the air. 'She's got every right to be.' She stifles a hiccup. 'I br…breeze in, this posh cow slumming it on the estate, sending her two well-scrubbed children to the comp for PC points and pl…playing at being a teacher.' She stifles another hiccup. 'That's how she sees me.'

She can't understand why she's simultaneously garrulous and stumbling over her words. She's having to hang on to the bar for support. She reminds herself she has had three halves. *Three halves.*

'Hey, she doesn't know you yet? She hasn't taken the time to. You've only been here a month, on three days a week.'

'She doesn't...like me,' Ella says dismissively. She looks his young face up and down, grins and strokes his ragged chin. 'Hey, d'you ever shave? You must do, to keep that...designer stubble. I'm sorry, they probably don't call it that now. I'm a ch...child of the Eighties. Have you noticed?'

'A good vintage,' says Matt, with a smile. He nods briefly to the barman. 'Same again?' he says, pointing meaningfully at their glasses. Then he meets her gaze again and holds it.

'Yeah, well. They bred us hard back then.' She drags deeply on her cigarette, looks him up and down again with a mixture of lust, affection and wariness. 'God, you were still in nappies when I was doing my O levels. That is so damn scary.'

He is watching her mouth when she speaks. She wonders if he realises how sexy that is. Watching her mouth, unashamedly looking right down the wet barrel. He must be thinking about what it would be like to kiss her. Or more.

His face is so fucking...*blurred.*

She hasn't felt this drunk for ages. On her fourth half.

She keeps telling herself two pints is all she's had.

Something not quite...

'So that's exciting, is it, like? Reminding me what a callow youth I am?'

She laughs, and the laugh becomes a throaty cough for a moment. 'Jesus... No, I mean...' She laughs again, looks away, then sees he is still peering impudently at her over his beer glass. 'Oh, all right, then. Yes.'

'Come outside,' he says.

'Matt...'

'I mean it, come outside. Come and look at the city lights.'

'What about that lot?' She gestures up to the balcony.

'They're too pissed to care. Come on.'

Outside, it's warm, unusually muggy for an autumn night. The city lights are like glowing dust far beneath them. Ella is unsteady as her feet crunch on the pub's gravel forecourt. Three motorbikes zoom into view, each carrying two youths with no crash helmets. Ella looks nervously away.

The motorbike does a spin on the forecourt, showering gravel in their direction. Matt shouts at them, but the oldest of the riders sticks two fingers up in delight. He bellows something not entirely good-natured before zooming off in a cloud of pungent smoke. The raw engine noise makes Ella's ears ring.

'Bastards,' Ella mutters, then giggles, clutching Matt for support. 'Go on, give me the PC lecture. "Oh, they're not bad kids. We just need to understand them." Maybe I'm just too bloody old.'

'You're not,' he says, moving round to face her.

She giggles again, and shimmies to him, effortless in her new, feline form. She slips her arms around his young neck.

So drunk, she thinks desperately.

The brick wall is cool through her thin jacket and leggings, and she does not resist as he inclines his head, opens his mouth, lets his lips explore hers. She finds it amusing that he's so eager with his tongue, remembering that he's not much more than a schoolboy himself. His hands are exploring her breasts now. A tingling, surging power-cable switches on between her nipples and her loins and she reaches for a hardness she knows she will find, caresses it eagerly through his jeans. Their kisses become great, devouring slurps. His dextrous hand has tweaked her bra strap open, and she is seized with an urge to jiggle it free, to let the cumbersome piece of underwear fall to the ground for ever. *God, just like a horny little teenage slapper*, she thinks.

She pulls away from him in sudden alarm, holding his face in her hands. 'Jesus, Matt, we can't do this here.'

And so here is his bed, in his bedroom, in his house. She has no idea of what it looks like or even where it is, particularly, and somehow she has a bottle of whisky in her hand. A light rain has started to caress the windows; autumn's natural state is returning.

She is naked, only dimly aware of where her clothes have fallen. (A kitchen? Wood effect lino?) She crouches down over him, her hair ragged in front of her eyes. She feels drunk and inflamed, confused and yet set on her purpose.

There is no sound but their breathing and the rain, no taste or scent but those of their two bodies in their own world, familiar yet new, exciting and terrifying. She licks his left toe, then slides her mouth up his body, alternating the drizzle of her tongue with the touch of her lips. She kisses across his shin and thigh, allowing only the lightest breath on his genitals before continuing across his stomach and chest and up to his eager mouth, where she gives just a flick of her hot tongue before pulling back, kneeling up.

She straddles him, strokes her wetness against his erection, nuzzling the length of it without allowing him in. She presses a hard nipple into his mouth for a second or two, then gropes for the whisky bottle, finds it. She swallows the first mouthful, but not the second. Instead, she surprises him with a 40 per cent proof kiss, shooting the fiery liquid into his mouth. He gulps it willingly, shudders with pleasure, then pulls her close, eager to kiss her breasts. His tongue travels gently south; she shivers with pleasure as he licks the curve of her belly, toys with her navel. She moves softly up the bed, opens her legs to let him tease there. His tongue is gentle at first on her labia, but then he is inside, drinking her, licking her raw, steaming wetness with animal greed, sending spasms of pleasure shooting through her.

He is devouring her like a moist, fresh fruit. She grabs his hair, pushing him further in, squealing, grunting, giggling. She wants to make it clear that she loves this and needs more of it. She hears herself swearing deliciously. She is moaning at him to lick her, to drink her, to eat her cunt.

After a minute or two of this unbearable delight, he stops, pulls back, takes her face gently in his hands. They are kneeling up, facing each other, acknowledging that they are ready.

He wraps his arms tightly around her so that she feels the full warmth of his skin against hers. She slides her tongue into his mouth once more, tasting herself on him. Encouraged by the whisky burning in her, she pushes him gently on to the bed. She lifts herself up very slightly and envelops him.

His sturdy, angry young cock fills her perfectly, and she feels herself shuddering with delight. Now she grabs his wrists, pinning him to the bed, and begins to move with him.

He is more than ready for her, but something unspoken passes between them, an acknowledgement of rhythm and pace, so that they laugh together at the beauty of it. He reaches for her with his tongue, licking, sucking and biting her whenever she nuzzles close enough, and she keeps him pinned down. But a hand snakes free; his finger slips somehow between their bodies and gave her clitoris the lightest of caresses, and *now*—

She is on fire, drenched in sweat, and does not care, for she can feel, taste, almost *see* the bright lines of fire between her nipples and her loins—

He spurs her on, harsh and tender, teeth in her shoulder and sharp nails in her buttocks. He is unbearably, gorgeously swollen inside her. She is only dimly aware of her own squeals and yelps, of the breathless, harsh obscenities from her lewd mouth. He gives a thrust which almost lifts her off the bed; she grinds herself against him, and her orgasm crashes through her just a few moments later. Sight and memory dim, she loses every sense of where she is, then her head lolls down and she sees his face and hears her own desperate, exhausted gasping.

And then it is over, and they are two weakening bodies, wracked by great sobbing breaths and soaked in their cooling sweat.

She hears the rain hurling itself against the bedroom window.

She thinks of her children in their beds and suddenly wants to cry.

'You lucky cow,' said Bex admiringly.

'You think so?'

'Well, duh! He sounds a bit of all right.'

'Possibly,' she said.

And she told Bex the second half, the part of the story which was still leaving her wondering, leaving her not quite so sure.

Lying in the dark, on her back, beside Matt. They do not touch.

'Thank you,' she says.

'My pleasure.'

She has drunk two pints of water in the bathroom and feels better, but the slightest tingle of a headache is starting now behind her eyes.

'It's weird. You're only the fourth man I've ever slept with.'

There is a pause while he digests this information, possibly analyses it. He may well be dividing by a number of years and working out an average.

'Fourth?' he says eventually. 'Well, I am…like…honoured?'

'The first was shit. Squelchy and horrid. This guy called Paul at uni, just got me stoned and used me, basically.' Her voice is croaky, trembly as it always is when she has been satisfied. 'I mean, hell, I *wanted* it, but yuk, I'd never have gone for him if I had my wits about me. He was a creep. I hate guys like that. I'm sure you do too.'

'I see.' There is silence in the muggy room. 'Second?' ventures Matt.

'Second was Tom.'

'… Oh… Right.'

'He was…so nice to me. I always thought that if I met a man who was nice to me *and* good in bed, I'd marry him. And so I did. Fresh out of college with a cheap engagement ring on my finger, and happy as could be.'

Something hung in the air, unspoken.

'You don't have to, like, tell me who the other one was?' Matt ventured.

'Oh, God, he wasn't important. Some guy on a conference, years ago, just after I'd started at the Castle. He was nice enough, we were both away from home, both knew we could get away with it. You know how it is. Bottle of wine, late night, seemed like a good idea... I felt such a bloody cheap little tart afterwards that I swore I'd never do it again.'

'And here you are.'

'Yeah, well. Never say never, I suppose.'

'Not that I...um...think you're cheap or anything.'

'That's very reassuring to know, Matt.'

There is another brief silence.

'Tom doesn't know, then?' Matt asked. 'About this guy at the conference?'

'No.' Pause. 'I never gave him any reason to think anything of the sort had happened. And it was ages ago. I mean, he'd have said something by now, if he did.'

'Maybe Tom's not, like, the sort to...say stuff?'

'Can we just leave it, Matt? I wish I'd not mentioned it now. Exhuming my bloody sexual history like Andie MacDowell in *Four Weddings and a Funeral*. Only mine doesn't take anything like as long.'

'It's quality, Ella, not quantity.'

'Yes, funnily enough, I wasn't actually *bemoaning* my lack of conquests. I know it's a strange idea for a man to get his head around, but we don't keep notches on the bedpost.'

'I know, I know... I'm, um, sorry?'

'I'm actually pretty comfortable with the idea of being able to count my lovers on one hand, thanks very much.'

'OK, I said I'm sorry.'

'I'm going to go,' she says.

Matt lifts himself up on his elbows, sees that she is pulling her discarded leggings and bra back on, shuffling her gauzy top back over her pert breasts. 'Do you have to?'

'I don't think it's a good idea for us to have breakfast together, Matt. Too much like being an old married couple.' She gives him a sad smile and hoists her handbag on to her shoulder. 'Sleep well.'

'I will.'

'I'll let myself out.'

'OK then. Take care walking home.'

(Beat.)

'Do you want me to call you a taxi, Ella?'

'Nah. They don't come up to Parkfield after midnight, anyway, do they?'

'I think that's one of the myths, yeah?'

'Well, anyway, I'll be fine.'

(Beat.)

She half turns back towards him.

'Is there any reason why you think I wouldn't be fine, Matt?'

'N...no, None at all.'

'I mean, I've only drunk less than two pints. Cheap date, that makes me.'

'Um. Well.'

She smiles. Coldly. She nods and pulls her jacket on, and hovers at the bedroom door for a second.

'Goodnight, Matt.'

'Goodnight, sexy.' He lifts himself on one elbow. 'Hey, maybe we can do this again.'

'I don't think so,' she says.

And she turns and leaves.

Chapter Eighteen

What Difference Does It Make?

'There,' said Gaz Collins. 'That one over there.'

Ben, leaning against the bin with one foot up behind him, peered casually over his sunglasses. 'Him?' he asked, eyeing the plump, dishevelled Year Eight boy who was sitting on the low playground wall, eating his sandwiches on his own. 'Fatboy Fat?'

'Yeah. Fucking dickhead. Do him.'

'Too easy,' said Ben, laughing, shaking his head.

It wasn't that difficult to keep in with Collins, Ben had found. He had a certain shrewdness, perhaps, but he wasn't that bright. He could be kept happy by a succession of feeble (and often homophobic) jokes. 'What's a gay postman do with the letters?' Ben asked. 'Takes them round your back passage.' It was too easy. He made them up on the walk to school. (The only one which hadn't worked was the one about the Russian spy with three balls called Yehudi Nikabollokoff, which Will had told him months ago. He'd had to explain it about four times to Collins and his even thicker mates.)

Being in with Collins was more about the way you walked,

spoke and chewed than what you actually did. It was about wearing your school tie with the thin end out and your top button undone, about keeping your hair short and wearing trainers in contravention of school rules. It was about sitting at the back in class, about not doing your homework and not giving a shit when you got a detention.

Then all you had to do was a bit of low-level thuggery and intimidation, and the rest was just casual bravado.

'It's not for you to say what's fucking hard or easy, Barclay.' Collins thumped Ben's arm, possibly with more force than he intended. 'You go. Get the wanker's money, now.'

'All right. If you insist.'

Ben strolled casually over to the boy. It was a distance of about ten metres.

The victim had already seen him coming, and was frantically packing away his sandwiches. He'd already hoisted his bag on his shoulder and was about to make a break for it when Ben pushed him lightly in the chest, forcing him to step back.

In a very low, earnest voice, Ben said:

'Listen to me. I only have about twenty seconds. You do exactly as I say and you won't get hurt, understand?'

The boy nodded frantically.

'Give me your money. You'll get it back. And when I move my elbow, go down like I've hit you really hard in the stomach.'

'What?' The boy was terrified and confused.

'Look, do you want to live, Fatboy? Do as I bloody well say.'

Fatboy scrabbled in his pockets, pulling out a handful of

change and sending sweet wrappers and bus tickets flying. He handed the money to Ben as fast as he could.

'Good,' said Ben. 'Go down now.' And he swung his elbow back and stopped it a centimetre short of the fat boy's solar plexus.

Fatboy stared at him in astonishment for a moment, and Ben wondered if he had blown this. He was not going to get another chance.

Then the boy fell to his knees. He gave a very convincing yelp, and Ben smiled in satisfaction. He turned on his heel, head held high, and strolled back over to Gaz Collins. The money was fiery and sweaty in his palm, and he upturned it for Gaz.

'Not a bad haul,' said Ben, trying to sound dispassionate.

Ben's stomach was almost permanently churning these days.

The arrangement with Moretti was a simple one. Now he had, through a few minor acts of bullying, vandalism and extortion, been accepted into the Collins fold, his job was to accumulate evidence from within.

He was to do nothing to divert the course of Collins's and his henchmen's actions, but was himself to refrain wherever possible from actively taking part.

It was his job to ensure that Collins and his team carried on as normal, and preferably away from the prominent CCTV cameras around the school – because these were mostly dummies. The real cameras, Moretti had informed him, were all concealed. She wasn't at liberty to tell him where they actually were – only she and the governors actually knew, and this information could not fall into the wrong hands.

Ben's reward, too, was simple. When enough evidence had been accumulated to damn Collins and his hangers-on and to present a case for exclusion, Ben himself would have immunity from prosecution. He'd be the only one allowed to stay on at Parkfield, or – and here Moretti had dangled a juicy peach of a proposition – perhaps another school in the authority, a good distance away.

The hardest thing, of course, was keeping it all from his mother.

'Yeah, not bad,' said Collins, counting the coins out into his own pocket before handing one back to Ben. 'Why'd you hit him?' he asked.

Ben shrugged. 'He was being a mouthy little git,' he said casually. He grinned up at Gaz. 'Besides, I quite enjoyed it.'

Collins sniggered and gave Ben a slap on the back of the head. 'You twat,' he said affectionately, as they made their way inside.

Ella had to do it. Especially now.

She got off the double-decker from Parkfield in the centre of town, head in a scarf and eyes masked with mirror-shades.

She hurried across Castle Street, hearing the familiar catcalls of *Big Issue* sellers by the old city walls. She knew their cries well: 'Biiiiigishoo, Biiiiigishoo, 'Elp The 'Omeless!' and 'One to go then I can go, Big Iiii-shoo!'. Toddler Izzy picked that refrain up once, and walked round the house singing '*Wonder*-go, den *I'd* a go! *Wonder*-go, den *I'd* a go!'

A memory from another world, she thought grimly.

She hopped on to the Cityrunner minibus on the other side of the street. She knew she only had a short space of time to do this, even with Bex looking after the kids. Bex was a great girl, Ella reflected, but not one of nature's childminders.

The Castle flashed by, a golden palace in the sunset, and Ella gave it a brief, wistful look. But no. She wasn't here for that. The Cityrunner headed out on the ringroad, then joined an old, familiar B-road. The city centre dropped out of sight behind her. They whizzed past the pristine Edwardian terraces and shining lawns of Westgrove Park, zoomed through Upper Westgrove with its chunkier, stone-built semis. The shops and restaurants thinned out, and the streets became broader and leafier.

After ten minutes, Ella rang the bell and alighted.

She was alone in the grey evening, with the sun setting over the green expanse of Ashington Park on her right and the stylish, modern residences of Thorpedale Avenue on her left. At the end of the road, she could still see the immaculate playground where they used to take the children, with its chunky, geometric equipment, its connecting tunnels and its sturdy swings. Four-person families clad in Gap would gather there on a Sunday afternoon – partly to let the children run around, but mostly to flaunt their undecayed nuclear status.

Golden beeches lined the avenue, and the postbox on the corner gleamed such a vivid red that it could have been painted yesterday.

There was an aroma of chestnuts and jasmine.

She remembered.

Standing on the pebbles of a beach, they are watching Ben splash in the water when Ella silently hands Tom a small, slim package.

'Another present,' she says, laughing, the wind blowing her hair in her eyes, 'from me, this time.'

And Tom, puzzling over what he thinks is a pen wrapped in silver paper, opens the present with a puzzled half-smile. He pulls out the flat, white tube and stares open-mouthed at the new blue line in its window; a painting in miniature, a hormone-smear which signals the beginning of the most powerful, inexplicable process on Earth once more.

'No,' he says, cautiously smiling. 'No!... Really?'

'Really,' she says, and they embrace softly, watching their son splash at the water's edge, hardly daring to hope that this is it.

The last time they will come to a beach and have only one child to watch.

And the blue line leads through time to the day Princess Diana dies, to another beginning, to the first beautiful, angry, hungry screams of a new person called Isobel Lucy Grace.

Ella shivered. She put her head down as she made her way to the corner, right by the street sign which she used to see every day. Almost every morning she had marvelled that her family actually lived at such a desirable address.

Again, she asked herself why she was here.

Maybe, she thought, her encounter with Matt had caused a shift, a breakthrough in her mind. She had *done* something now, in her new life; she had made a statement, and each statement took her further away from her previous self. She had to go back, had to check what she had left behind. But perhaps she also needed to remind herself where she belonged.

She didn't have long to wait.

After about ten minutes, a smart, gleaming Aston Martin slid into Thorpedale Avenue and turned, almost silently, into the drive of Number 28. The crunch of the wheels on the gravel was a sound which Ella knew almost as well as the cries of her own children. She had stood in the doorway, four years earlier, giving sharp instructions to two burly, tattooed men with a lorry as they unloaded the stuff on to the drive. (She saw herself there now: hair flowing, eyes brighter, maybe wearing that shot-silk dress from Quipu, the one she'd just given away.)

Ella kept in the cover of the privet hedges as she saw a young man get out of the car and cheerfully swing a briefcase from the back. Henry Morrison-Clarke, she remembered, had given the best offer on the house from the start. Nobody else had ever really been in the running. She had shown him and his heavily pregnant wife, Sally, around personally – the only ones she'd not left to the estate agent.

There was Sally at the door, blonde hair loose, wearing a baggy cotton shirt and black leggings. On her right shoulder she was carrying a tiny, sturdy, sleeping person in pink. Ella felt a deep and nameless softness as she saw Sally nuzzle the baby girl's ear. How old could she be? Only a few weeks at most. Ella watched, dry-mouthed, as Henry embraced his family. They laughed together, a shared joke about something Henry had brought home in a brown paper bag. Then the smart, white uPVC door (installed two years ago by a cheerful Geordie called Ron) swung to, sealing them inside.

Ella wiped the mist from her eyes and slipped quietly across the road.

The pathway between Thorpedale Avenue and Spring Close was well kept as usual, and she didn't see anybody else on her way. Round the back of the garden to Number 28, she found the gate in the high fence, checked that the Yale lock was still there, fumbled in her pocket for the key she had kept and slipped it in. The key turned. The gate opened without a squeak. Ella smiled. Henry was obviously keeping it well oiled.

She didn't even need to think once she was in the garden, for she knew the trees and shrubs would give her extensive cover.

She had chosen dusk for the best of reasons. On many spring and autumn evenings, on walks to the pub or the late shop, she had found herself outside in that half-hour gap where people had switched on the lights but had not yet drawn the blinds or curtains. Their miniature domestic dramas would be broadcast to the passers-by: little mute soap operas, one screen per household, just a glimpse as you passed.

She had judged the time right. Henry and Sally had put the uplighters on in the big lounge at the back, and Henry was bouncing his little girl on his knee now.

They hadn't decorated much, she noticed, peering through the shrubbery. The terracotta walls were still there (she and Tom had chosen the paint one freezing December day, and then they'd all gone for hot chocolate and chestnuts round the brazier in the town square). The stripped-pine floor was still in place (nailed down on a March afternoon by Tom and his brother, amid a lot of sweating and swearing, with a rugby international on the television – yes, it had to have been France and England, because Gabrielle, Andy's wife, had been there too, shouting '*Allez, allez!*' at the screen and cackling in delight when England missed a drop-goal).

Shadows deepened, enveloping her in evening chill.

Darkness crept across the roofs and gardens. Lights flicked off downstairs, and on upstairs.

Behind the frosted glass of the bathroom window, Ella knew what would be happening. The child was being bathed in the contemporary, lozenge-shaped bathtub which she and Tom had selected from an online store. She would be about to be fed and put to sleep (if they were lucky), probably in the third bedroom just along from the main one, the beech-floored room which had been Isobel's.

She wondered what they had done with Ben's second-floor den. Maybe it was an office. She vaguely recalled something about Sally wanting to set up a design company from home.

This was ridiculous, she told herself. What the hell was she *doing*?

The lounge blazed with light again and Henry came back in, looking for something. Ella realised that her boldness had made her stretch her head quite high above the bushes. She bobbed it back down, lay almost flat on the damp grass and listened to her own ragged breath and angry heartbeat. Praying.

She risked a glance through the leaves and saw Henry still bustling round in the lounge. He was on the phone, she realised.

Her hand came into contact with something small, smooth and round lying on the grass. At first she was startled, then she realised what it was.

A few of the plums were lying there – Henry and Sally had obviously not been as diligent about picking them up as she always was. Ella lifted the beautiful, reddish-purple fruit to her lips and bit hard. Her incisors sheared off a fleshy chunk, and its sharp juice filled her mouth with an almost sexual pleasure.

These were *hers*. She closed her eyes tightly and took another big, savage bite. She ran her tongue round the roughness of the stone, felt its hardness with her teeth, then spat it into her hand and, almost without thinking, slipped it into a pocket. *Mine.*

They were the fruits of a renewed Earth. The small tree was a symbol of an ongoing life after one which had been lost. The ghost. Driving back from that little church, they had passed the garden centre and, without either of them needing to say a word, they had known what they were going to do.

She shut her eyes.

She can see the trowel in little Izzy's small hands, the soil sticking like chocolate cake on her fingers, and she can hear her laughter as the tiny tree is lowered into the earth. 'That's not a *tree*, Mummy! Trees are *big*!' And she and Tom hug their little girl tightly, on this very patch of the planet.

Where is Ben? Watching, she presumes, from a short distance away.

Right here, the earth is opened, scoured out (as she was). They hope to receive, in time, something new. Fruit is a birth from a death, a life from a life departed. And they hear the laughter of a child as the world turns, as the shadows lengthen, as days and nights sweep on in their endless, terrible beauty.

* * *

In the garden, Ella looked up. It was much darker now, and Henry and Sally had closed the blinds downstairs. There were three plum stones in her pocket, her fingers were stained purple and her teeth felt coarse.

We can't go teaching them to believe in miracles and all that guff.

So Tom had said to her a few years ago, back when Izzy thought Baby Jesus lived in her bath. But why not? The creation of life was a miracle. The setting and the rising of the sun, the spinning of the earth on its tilted axis, the ebb and flow of the tides under the gentle tug of the moon...what was that, if not miraculous?

The tree-planting was a place, she decided, a standing stone, one which they had passed on the way and could now see beside them, casting its lean shadow across the path.

Up ahead, there was something new. Her children were there, perhaps about to ford a river or cross a rickety bridge.

She needed to be there.

To fight. To kill.

She couldn't let anything happen to them.

Silently, Ella slipped out of the garden and shut the gate behind her without looking back. Sodium lights were melting into appearance along the street. Head down, she was absorbed by the night.

'Tom, where do you see this relationship going?'

It made him stop in his tracks, Phill's question. The force acted upon his ice cream and dislodged the little yellow scoop from its cone. It hit the ground and lay there like a dying jellyfish, reaching out tentacles of bright yellow across the path.

High on the city ramparts, Tom stared at the melting blob of ice cream. Something about it stirred a memory, made his heart skip in concern. He wasn't sure why.

Shadows, said a voice in his head.

He shivered, came back to the matter in hand. He looked up at Phill, who was standing in front of him in her long coat and scarf, eyebrows raised, her own ice cream held delicately.

There it was, then. The curve-ball women threw when you were least expecting it. Just when you were comfy, just when you were snug, just when you'd got used to the new taste and scent and feel of her and you were silently congratulating yourself for having pulled it off, she asks you where you are *going*. And the problem with a question like that is, you can never give the right answer. Because the right answer, for you, is not the one she wants to hear. Your right answer is one that stops her deciding it's all too much hassle and running away. For some reason, she wants to start bringing emotions into the equation, and you don't need that. You don't need that at all. You want to keep it easy, simple, sexual.

Christ, what did you do? Had he ever talked this one over with Jeff? He didn't think so. They had filled a whole lunchtime recently deciding which *Doctor Who* girl was the most shaggable (top three: Romana, Leela and Rose). Almost an entire evening had been given over to the semantics of insults, with both of them concerned that there was no proper way of describing a dislikeable woman – with annoying blokes, one had a whole range to choose from (tosser, wanker, dickhead, arsehole, prick) but you couldn't really call women any of those and the alternative terms on offer (silly bitch, silly cow) all sounded too misogynistic. They had once spent an hour debating which was the best Tears For Fears album, *Songs From The Big Chair* (Jeff) or *The Seeds Of Love* (Tom). But they had never really talked about what you said when a woman asked you where a relationship was going. Wasn't it just like a car, Tom reasoned? As long as you kept it polished and serviced, did it actually have to be *going* anywhere to be worth having?

He looked up at Phill, feeling like a gormless child.

She raised her eyebrows at him again – quizzical, challenging, slightly impatient. 'You've lost it,' she said.

'Sorry?'

Phill nodded down at the pavement. 'Your ice cream.'

'Oh. Yes. Never mind.' He grinned. 'If that happens when you're three, it's a major tragedy. When you're thirty-seven you can be a bit more stoical.'

'Have a bite of mine,' she said, offering it.

'No, that's fine. Really.'

'The question still stands, Tom. A few weeks ago I asked you what the score was, and I'm still wondering, if I'm honest.'

'Um,' he said.

After a few more seconds' thought, he felt he was able to expand a little on his initial answer.

'Um, well,' he said.

It wasn't much of an improvement, granted, but it was a start.

They sat on a bench, high on the city wall, looking out over the murmuring city on this sunny September day. Behind them on the grass embankment, a council lawnmower buzzed. The aroma of new-mown grass wafted over, mingling with the petrol and pear-drop smells of industry.

'OK,' she said after a minute or two's silence. 'Try this one. How would you *describe* our relationship?'

What was this? Was she letting him off the hook, bowling him an easier one just to lull him into a false sense of security?... Describe their relationship. Yeah, OK. He could give it in terms she'd want to hear, not in a pint-in-the-Rowan-with-Jeff sort of way. He'd once been to Men's Group, after all. He could do sensitive.

'Well, we have a mutual sense of...fun,' Tom ventured, looking at her hopefully. 'We...enjoy one another's company. We have a...nice time.'

Phill laughed, and gently placed a hand on his arm. 'Tom, you're so funny.'

'I am?' He was confused.

'Shall I have a go?' she asked, raising her eyebrows in that impudent way which had first made him lust after her all those weeks ago.

'OK.'

'We fuck.'

'Sorry?'

Phill shrugged, smiled. 'That's it, isn't it? *We fuck.* I mean, hell, it's great when we do it. Don't get me wrong, whatever the hell you call that technique of yours, it damn well works. But that's all it is.'

'Our relationship's more than that,' Tom protested.

He had a sudden, horrible sense of dislocation, of powerlessness. He realised, with a thud of his heart and an icy shift of his stomach, what it reminded him of. Driving a car when the steering had gone. It had only ever happened to him once, and he'd not been going that fast, and he'd been able to stop safely and call the AA. This was just the same. Except he didn't know if he was going to be able to stop, and he felt the whole thing slipping out of his control.

And there was no AA. Not for this.

The worst thing was, he had known this was coming. She had mentioned coffee. Pre-intimacy, coffee was a welcome euphemism, an invitation to the innermost sanctum. But when the woman you were already having sex with suggested 'a coffee and a walk' because she needed to 'talk about something', you could be pretty sure that it wasn't good news. He wondered if the manufacturers of coffee had ever thought about the changing semiotic values of their drink. In this case, he knew it meant that she either a) was pregnant, b) had a life-threatening illness or c) was dumping him.

His preferred option of the three, given the choice, was the life-threatening illness. What kind of person did that make him?

'I mean,' Phill was saying, 'we don't have a relationship, really. We're so *nice* to each other all the time.'

'You want me to be horrible?'

'No, Tom, that's not the point. What I'm saying is, we've not got…hell, I suppose we've not got comfortable enough to do that.'

'It seems I can't say the right thing today.'

'Yeah, I know, honey. And maybe that's part of it. I don't want you to be obsessed with saying the *right thing*. When I have a long-term relationship – whether or not the guy is married, and, believe it or not, that's not the main issue here – I want someone who's not afraid to screw up occasionally.

You know, not afraid to fight with me and then make up. And fight again, and make up again. That's how you move on, you know? Start wearing stuff on the surface. And I know that's not gonna happen with you, so... I guess... I can't do this any more.'

He was silent. He didn't look at her.

'I also know you think modern art is a pile of crap,' she said with a sideways grin. 'However well you try to hide it. That's not a problem, on its own. But there's other stuff. We both know there's other stuff.'

He didn't dare speak, because he didn't want to give this an acknowledgement.

'I just think,' Phill went on, 'that's it's kind of unfair on you to keep this thing going.'

'No. No, really, it's not unfair.' He was almost gabbling, looking at her in desperation. 'I'm quite happy with things, honestly.'

Phill sighed, closed her eyes, two green-painted shutters coming down. 'Well, I thought you might be. And again, that's what I'm worried about. You shouldn't be. You oughta be pissed off with me now and then. It's healthy. Tom, what are we *giving* each other, apart from some admittedly rather gorgeous sex?'

Tom pondered this for a minute, wondering if it was another trick question. 'Stimulating conversation?' he hazarded.

Phill laughed, shaking her head, her eyes crinkling. She half glanced at him and chuckled again. 'Tom, we've had a great time together. But, hey, things have come to a point where...' She sighed. 'People move on.'

'But we're just getting to know each other.'

'Tom, Tom, Tom... You guys don't need emotional involvement, but you have to remember we're different. When you say "I need a shag" – great word, I love it, I'm gonna try and import it home, believe me – when you say that, it's kinda like, I dunno, it's like when you say, "I need a beer". It's just pouring something in somewhere to fulfil a need. And for...a while, it's not...*unpleasant* to be wanted like that. To be needed. But then...' Phill sighed, broke off. 'I'm not explaining this very well.'

'I thought we were having fun.'

'Hell, yeah. I like my fun as much as the next girl, Tom, but I'm thirty-four, y'know? One of these days, I'd like to get involved with a guy who doesn't have baggage. Maybe even have kids before it's too late... I guess I just need to grow up, and if I'm gonna do that, I need to cut some ties.'

'You do?' He knew his face showed his desperation, but it was too late to hide it. 'Do you have to do it straight away?'

'Tom...' She took his arm, rested her head on his shoulder. 'Please don't make this harder. This little adventure is over, finito, kaput. OK? I need to give you back to your wife and children. You have bridges to mend.'

He pulled away from her, angrily, and strode over to the observation point, breathing heavily, leaning on the rail. 'So what's this? Sudden attack of the moral high ground? The *mistress* gets a fucking conscience because it's not convenient any more?'

'Well, Tom, I'm glad if you're going to be a shit about this. It'll just make the whole thing a hell of a lot easier.'

He gripped the rail, shook in silent fury, didn't turn to look at her. He felt his hands growing slick on the metal.

'OK,' she said, shrugging, walking over to him, 'I take that back. I am nothing if not scrupulously fair, honey.' She leant back on the rail and looked him up and down. 'You're not a shit. You're a nice guy who occasionally says shitty things. But it *is* time to put an end to this.'

She held up a key, dangled it in front of him.

'What's this now?'

'I'm sorry. My turn to be a shit. I've put all your stuff in a locker at the station. I thought it was best if you didn't come back to my apartment again.'

She dangled the key in front of his face. He didn't take it.

'Come on, we're both sensible people, and I knew I wouldn't come home to any slashed dresses in the closet or cress in the carpet. But I thought this would be easier on us both.' She shuddered. 'One guy I finished with had a truckload of manure delivered to me. It didn't faze me. Compared with the crap I'd already taken from him, it was nothing.'

He had to smile. He looked at her for the first time in five minutes.

'It's...cautious of you,' he said.

'I'm always cautious, honey. Perhaps too cautious.' Phill sighed deeply, shook her head and gazed out over Cherford. 'Hell, what do I say now? Thank you for your small kindnesses, Tom. Thank you for the little boxes of Belgian chocolates. And for this.' She flapped the white cashmere scarf she wore. 'It's really lovely. And thank you for some good times. I'll remember you with...fondness.'

He took the key meekly. 'So that's it?'

'Uh-huh. Look, there should be violins. But hey. This isn't the movies.'

'Indeed.' He shook his head, tried not to show how much the rest of him was shaking. 'Well, aren't we adults?'

'Guess that's why they call it adultery,' said Phill. She leant up and gave him a peck on the cheek, and the unbearably gorgeous scent of her camomile shampoo taunted him. 'Hey, have a great life, Tom.'

'You too,' he said.

Phill nodded, turned on her heel and walked a few paces away. She stopped, and for a second he thought she was going to look back over her shoulder. But she didn't.

She kept walking away, walking away along the city wall, then he saw her descend the steps to the bustling pavement, where she was swallowed up by the lunchtime crowds.

'What happens to Lady Macbeth?' asked Ella, prowling the aisles, twirling her board-marker in one hand and her paperback Shakespeare in the other. 'What happens to her as a character – as a *person* – over the course of the play?'

There was some shifting, some sighing, shuffling of feet. She had this Year Nine class under her thumb, now, she thought; they didn't speak when she was speaking and, mostly, they sat up straight and paid attention. But most of them did nothing more than warm the seats and steam up the windows. Getting an answer out of them, getting an independent thought, was like teasing pus from a blind boil.

'Well?' Ella swept round in a full circle, crouching slightly, ready to pounce. She jabbed her pen down on the nearest desk. 'Kiely Morris. You tell me.'

Kiely sighed, rolled her eyes. She appeared unable to keep her head supported without it propped on her hand, and she was scribbling casual doodles in the back of her exercise book. 'Dunno, miss.'

'*Dunno, miss*. Fabulous. Well, I can forgive you for not remembering, Kiely, as we did only discuss it twenty-four hours ago in our last lesson. I know you've had lots to occupy your brain with since then, but can't you just find a little space for Shakespeare's character development?' Ella whipped the book out from under Kiely's elbow, jolting the girl off-balance. 'Let's see...oh, a 3-Boyz-3 fan?' She raised her eyebrows at the scribblings. 'God, *no*, not Damien. He's the gay one. And anyway, that looks nothing like him.' Ella tossed the book back at Kiely. 'Tippex it out.'

Derisive laughter echoed through the room, and a red-faced Kiely sank down in her chair, glowering at Ms MacBride with undisguised venom.

'Perhaps someone else can enlighten us?' She raised her eyebrows. 'Come on, look, what about when she tells her husband "screw your courage to the sticking-place"? What do you think that's all about?'

'She wants him to be brave, miss,' said Laraine Kirk, a girl in the front row. 'Like, not be a wuss.'

'Right! Excellent, Laraine. We'll not fail, she says. *We'll not fail*. So is Macbeth, as Laraine so elegantly puts it, a wuss?' Ella slid to the board like a dancer on a talc-strewn floor and scrawled 'WUSS?' in the column under Macbeth's name. 'Think on, though, to when they have to kill King Duncan. Who does that?'

Murmurs of, 'He does, miss,' and, 'Macbeth does, miss.'

'Right! And why can't she do it?' Ella held her index finger up, swivelled back and forth on one heel in a way that always got a shiver, an anticipation, a certain tension. 'Why can't she do it? Who remembers?'

'He looks like her dad,' said a voice from the back of the classroom.

'Yes! Who was that?'

A lazy hand lifted itself from the very back row. Gary Collins.

'Gary, yes!' She jabbed a finger at him and touched her nose like Una Stubbs playing *Give Us A Clue*. 'He resembled her father, she says. Do you think that's a genuine reason? Or is she just giving an excuse not to do it?'

Gary Collins shrugged. He didn't care. He'd already made what he thought was enough effort for one lesson, Ella realised with a sinking heart.

'Well, what do you think?' she tried, with a theatrical shrug.

Collins snorted. 'I'd fucking kill my dad,' he said.

Some laughter rippled through the room, but it had a nervous edge. Many of the pupils were silent, abashed.

'OK.' Ella moved quickly on. 'The point I'm making, right, is that Lady Macbeth seems, at first, to be the one in control. She's got her husband where she wants him, yeah? But as things go on, well... You know what happens. Macbeth becomes more... What? Remember some of the words we used?'

'Ruthless.'

'Ambitious.'

'Yup. Yup.' She scrawled them up, underneath WUSS. 'So...let's have a think about what brings about that change…and why, shall we?' She caught the movement out of the corner of her eye. 'Gary, where are you going?'

Collins had kicked the door open, with a force that made a sliver of paint fly off and sent the girls in the front row cowering in their seats. 'Like you care,' he threw at her as he left, hoisting his bag high on his shoulder.

Pupils at Parkfield, primary or secondary, all finished at half past three – it was one of the moves to soften the sometimes harsh transition between Year Six and Year Seven. At the school gates, as all the children streamed home, Ben stood like a rock, impassive, waiting.

Isobel appeared at his side, as she usually did on days when their mother was working. 'Come on,' she said impatiently, tugging at her brother's arm.

'Wait a minute, Bizzy.' Ben narrowed his eyes, scanning the jabbering, noisy crowd. 'There's something I have to do first.'

'Ben, come *on*. Mum said not to wait around after school. We're supposed to get home as quick as we can.'

'I said there's something I need to do,' Ben repeated.

He spotted the pupil he was looking for – a lumpen, bespectacled specimen trudging home with his head down. Fatboy Fat.

Ben moved swiftly to intercept him. Fatboy, recognising Ben, turned a shade paler and backed away, trying to dodge back into the playground.

'No, no, it's OK.' Ben, looking furtively around, took Fatboy's arm. 'Wait there,' he said, steering him away from the main body of the crowd.

He hurried back to the gates, then grabbed the sleeve of the first Year Seven he recognised, a sturdy boy in a reversed baseball cap. 'Tomlinson,' he said. 'Job for you.'

'Oh come off it, Barclay, I'm goin' to the shops.'

'No, you're not. You're walking my little sister to her door.' He swivelled Tomlinson around and pointed at Isobel, who was standing there with a face like thunder, arms folded, pouting and scowling. 'And if anything happens to her,' he added, twisting Tomlinson's ear, 'I'm getting Collins to smash your face into the bogs, got it?'

Tomlinson, his face scrunched up in pain, looked up at Ben, realised he wasn't joking, then looked back at Isobel. 'All right,' he croaked.

'Good man.' Ben let him go. He flipped Tomlinson's baseball cap off his head, cuffed his reddened ear and put the cap back on the right way round. Then he hurried back over to the quaking Fatboy, who hadn't dared move an inch.

Ben walked the boy around the corner to the shops, and only stopped when they were in the shelter of the abandoned bookie's shop beside Priceworth. He shoved him up against the graffiti-covered boards in the window.

'Right. Listen,' Ben began.

'I ain't got no more money.' Fatboy's voice was trembling.

'No, no, don't worry.' Ben fished a handful of coins out of his own pocket, grabbed the boy's hand, opened his doughy palm and pushed the money into it. 'How much did I take off you yesterday?' he asked.

Fatboy, dumbfounded, looked down at the handful of coins he was clutching. 'About that,' he said nervously.

'I think it was a bit more than that.' Ben pressed another couple of coins into Fatboy's hand. 'Go on. Take it.'

Fatboy stared down at the money. He reached out, tried to offer it to Ben.

'No, no, *take* it, you prick. Christ, do I have to spell it out? I – am – giving – you – it – *back*. You're really going to have to get some assertiveness classes.'

Slowly, hesitantly, as if expecting to be thumped at every moment, the boy closed his hand over the money.

'Now scarper,' said Ben. 'And you don't tell anyone about this. Right?'

'Rrright,' said Fatboy nervously, and flinched.

Ben could tell he didn't believe this was all there was going to be. He was expecting another trick, some new bully's twist. Ben sighed. It was obvious that he was, at least partly, going to have to do what was expected of him.

He grabbed Fatboy by the tie and pulled him up so that their faces were level. 'Repeat it after me. You're not going to tell anyone about this.'

'*I-ain't-gonna-tell-nobody-about-this.*'

Ben wondered whether to take issue with the grammar, but decided that the spirit of the meaning was there. You didn't quibble over double negatives when you were trying to intimidate someone.

'OK. Now get lost.'

Ben let go of Fatboy's tie. He clapped him on the shoulders and tapped his cheek, just lightly enough for it not to be a slap. His mother, had she been watching, would have recognised the influence of Eric Morecambe.

Fatboy backed off, half walking and half sidling. He was looking at the money clutched in his palm, then up at Ben, then back down at the money again. He shuffled away.

After a few seconds, he broke into a run.

Ben sighed. This was proving more complicated than he'd expected. And he seemed, thanks to Collins, to have gained a reputation he really didn't want.

He hoisted his bag on his shoulder and headed home to Renaissance Towers.

Ella slouched down the steps from the staffroom, her heavy bag on her shoulder and a stack of folders tucked under her arm.

'Heard the news?' growled Bill Hollis, thumping down the stairs behind her.

'No, what?'

'One of the little sods has had a go at Ryder's car. Scratched the door, they have.'

'Really?' Ella felt a twinge. Matt took great care of that car, she knew.

'I reckon it was one of Collins's lot,' Hollis went on, narrowing his eyes. 'Bastards, the lot of them.'

'That's a bit harsh, Bill. Everyone has some redeeming features. He sometimes does try, you know.'

'Who?'

'Gary Collins.'

'Only thing he tries is my bloody patience, the lout. I hear he went AWOL again this afternoon.'

'Yeah.' Ella sighed, hugged her folders. 'Well, I gather he was intercepted. At least it's not just my lessons he walks out of.'

'Oh, God, no. It's a bloody miracle if the little shit turns up at all. Quite frankly, it'd be better for everyone if he didn't.'

Ella narrowed her eyes. 'I think he's got problems, Bill. Home life. You know.'

'Lazy excuse, Ella, me love. Half the kids here come from broken homes. My dad ran out on me when I was nine, but I didn't turn into a flaming little hooligan. Wouldn't have dared. My mum kept us all on a tight rein.' Hollis tapped his nose. 'All starts at home, you know. Fruit doesn't fall far from the tree.'

'Let's not go into it now, Bill.'

'Some days I'd gladly hang the little buggers,' said Bill Hollis, almost cheerfully. 'See you tomorrow.'

'Bye, Bill.'

Ella emerged into the car park. She could see Matt and Jo leaning in concern over the front door of Matt's blue MG.

'Had a problem?' Ella asked, strolling nonchalantly up. She swivelled on one heel and did not meet Matt's gaze.

'Vandalism,' Jo sighed. She folded her arms. 'So what's new?'

'Nothing a bit of touching-up won't fix,' Matt murmured, straightening up.

'Mmm, I know the feeling,' said Jo lightly.

'Maybe you shouldn't bring the car in again,' Ella suggested. 'I walk. It's quite a refreshing way to start the day.'

'Thanks,' he said curtly. 'I'll bear that in mind.'

They were still not looking at one another.

Jo, frowning, looked from Matt to Ella and back to Matt again. 'Don't be rude to Ella, Matt. She's only trying to make a helpful suggestion.' She smiled at Ella, a smile with an evident lack of warmth and sincerity. 'I think that's an excellent idea, Ella. We could all do with a little more exercise.

Especially when we've been a bit poorly.' She tipped her head on one side. 'Are you feeling OK, Ella?'

'Yes. Any reason why I shouldn't be?'

'You seemed a bit worse for wear out at the pub the other night. That's all. I was worried about you. I was gonna see about sharing a taxi with you, actually, but...well, you disappeared. Somebody told me young Matthew here kindly saw you home.'

There was an awkward silence. Matt rubbed his ear and gazed into the middle distance.

'I'm fine,' said Ella, and gave Jo a firm, quelling smile. 'I can handle my drink perfectly well, thank you, Jo.'

'It's, um...only a surface scratch,' Matt ventured, rubbing the back of his neck.

Both women ignored him.

'I never said you couldn't handle your drink, Ell. I was just saying you looked a few sheets to the wind on three *halves* of Cherford City Brown.' Jo shot a meaningful look at Matt.

'Should be fine with a bit of metallic paint,' Matt added hopefully.

'I had a headache that evening, actually,' said Ella, copying Jo's arms-folded pose, 'which was why I was drinking halves. Too much late-night marking. But then you wouldn't know about that in PE.'

'Maybe. But I know about looking after myself. So I was just asking out of *concern*, that's all.'

'Your concern is duly noted,' said Ella, and raised her eyebrows.

Jo didn't flinch. 'You know you can talk to me if you've got a problem, Ell. My mum used to get drunk all the time. Me and my sister used to have to put her to bed every Saturday night and prop her head over a bucket so she didn't choke on her own puke.'

'Yes, well, there's no chance of my doing that, thank you.' She looked from Jo to Matt and back again. 'I won't keep you,' said Ella with a smile, and she strode towards the gates without looking back.

She did not need this. These...*children* pretending to be adults, with their petty concerns and their right-on credentials. Mocking her, quietly and subtly, as if they knew more than she did.

Her mother always used to say, as a way of defusing every teenage complaint, *you'll understand when you're older*. Or: *you'll think the same when you've got kids of your own*. And of course, she did. You learnt so much in that time – from the end of studenthood to the first years of motherhood. So much you couldn't know any other way.

And the *shadows*.

Nothing would make them go away.

And that evening, Ella and Bex lounged on the battered sofa, finishing off another bottle of wine between them as the TV jabbered in the corner. The floor was strewn with abandoned newspapers, glasses and bottles.

The sound and vision washed over Ella.

Her mind was in another room, with another glass of wine.

In Ella's mind, the crowded house is smoky, but she knows this cannot be right.

Back then, in the first few weeks of Ashington, she banished smokers to the patio, with some notion in mind about preserving its purity. The inside of the house is as clean and pure as Swiss mountain air; the tap of footsteps on the polished beechwood floors has a crisp solidity. The freshly plastered, cream-painted walls remind her of the unsullied surface of a new tub of Hydrena moisturiser. The dining room, where she is standing, still smells of polish, of paint, of newness.

She stands by the window, in her favourite black silk blouse and skirt, glass in hand, thinking.

A hand on her shoulder. Bex. She's shrinkwapped in a glossy blue mini-dress and evening gloves, shiny and fluid; it looks as if her body is drenched in curaçao. Sleek ice-blue boots sheath her legs from toe to knee.

'You OK?' she asks.

Ella nods, gives her a reassuring smile. 'I'm fine.'

'You seem to be neglecting your guests, babe. They're gonna start to think it's something they said.'

'I'll be there in a minute.'

'Please do.' Bex pulls a face. 'Emma's about to get off with Neil, Jeff's telling jokes about nuns and your dear husband's talking to that geeky guy about some indie band called... Stereo Cab or something?'

'Stereolab.'

'Whatever, darling. You know, when it comes to music, blokes never grow out of being students, really. It all just gets so anal. It's almost autistic.'

Ella thinks of Tom's collection of compilation tapes – two per year, all colour-coded and arranged in chronological order on a shelf in his study – and she has to agree.

'You know, you're allowed to talk about it,' Bex says.

Bex pivots on one blue stiletto heel, leaning back so that she comes between Ella and the window. Her face is just centimetres away, and blue-shadowed eyes are looking impishly at her.

Ella shrugs. 'What's there to talk about? Charlotte's dead.'

The black, leaden word thumps into the room. It slams on the floor like a lump of rock propelled by a trebuchet.

'You planted the tree,' Bex points out. 'You obviously want...something good to come out of this. But it's all still bottled up in you.' She touches her cheek tenderly. 'You can talk to me, you know.'

Ella swats Bex's hand aside like a wasp, pulls away from her. 'Don't do that.'

Bex's mouth curls into a sulky pout. 'No need to be like that, darling. I was only trying to comfort you.'

Ella looked away, embarrassed. 'I know. I'm sorry. I didn't mean...'

The door bangs open and they both jump, startled.

Jeff is there, carrying a bottle of white wine and a glass. 'Top-up, ladies?'

'Yeah, we were just coming,' Ella assures him.

'Come back and join the fray. The old room's a bit low on oestrogen. Pretty soon there's going to be football and car conversations happening, and that ain't pretty when it gets going.' Jeff slumps into a chair and pours himself a generous glass of Soave. 'Who's that guy in the blue shirt, Ell? The one you work with? God, he's boring as fuck. I can see him getting started on Road Routes To Anywhere In Mainland Britain if we don't nip it in the bud. Save us, gorgeous girls, save us!'

'Does he always talk like this?' Bex asks wearily.

'Pretty much,' says Ella, almost smiling as she sips her wine.

Jeff grins and winks. 'Love the fuck-me boots, Sexy Bexy. If you fancy walking all over me later, I'll have a window at about half-eleven.'

Bex blows him a kiss. 'You wouldn't survive a seeing-to from me, babe.'

Jeff winks. 'Oooh, I know. Some things are worth the bloody risk, though.' He touches Ella's elbow gently. 'Ciao, Ella la Bella. Don't feel left out, my darling; I fancy the pert little arse off you as well, petal, but you are my best mate's bird, so, discretion and valour and all that shit.'

Bex hands Ella her wine. 'Here. Mind that while I pop to the loo.'

'Do one for me!' Jeff calls after her.

Ella is laughing, now, leaning against the wall for support. 'I don't know how you get away with it, Jeff. Anybody else would be offensive, but you're just…you.'

'That's better,' Jeff says with a wink.

'What is?'

'You. Laughing. There's nothing wrong with it, darling. Nothing at all. Doesn't mean you don't feel…you know. Life goes on. It's the best tribute the living can pay to the dead.'

Ella looks up, and her eyes are brimming again.

'But nobody should have to do it this way round, Jeff.'

He looks down, and for a second his jokey face drops and a ghost of the real Jeff passes across a fragment of Time. 'I know, Ell. I know.'

She looks around the cavernous, minimalist dining room. 'You know,' she says, 'this is supposed to be our dream house. But sometimes I get the feeling it's really…worthless.'

'Phew. Didn't look worthless on the property details Tommy-boy showed me, love. Bloody hell!'

'It is, though.' Ella feels the frustration welling inside her. 'You know... I can't put it into words, but there's something not quite *right* with it all now. I don't feel... Ever since...ever since it happened... I've been feeling I don't belong here any more.' She gazes out at the trim lawn, the neat bushes, the summer house. 'I feel I've usurped somebody else's life, and before long they're going to come back and claim it.'

'Heavy stuff,' says Jeff awkwardly. 'Hey, sounds like you're the heroine of some bad American 70s TV show.' He mimed a big title with his open hand. *'The Impostor.* Twenty-six episodes on a Saturday afternoon. Ella Barclay has a deep dark secret – will anyone discover it or will she live to fight another day?... Starring...hmm, who'd have been you? Jaclyn Smith, maybe.'

'Oh, please, no. She was one of *Charlie's Angels,* wasn't she?'

Jeff leaps up, takes her arm. 'And with one bound, she was back in the party spirit. Come on. No more moping. Get in there and get pissed.' He sniffs her breath. 'Well, OK, more pissed.'

'I'll be there in a minute, Jeff. Honestly.'

'OK. One minute. Then I come and get you.'

Alone in the pristine dining room, she gazes in astonishment at everything which surrounds her.

The room could have come straight from a catalogue, but for the small personal touches like the curtains she has selected and the little cluster of family photos on the wall.

How did I get here? she thinks. Ten years ago we were

living in a rented hole. Now, we're...*real people*. We're grown-ups. And none of it means anything, none of it except Ben and Isobel.

And Tom, of course. She hears his laugh echoing down the hall, friendly but slightly self-conscious.

All right, she thinks. I'll do it. I'll live this life.

For now.

And now, in a gloomy Parkfield flat, Ella poured and squinted. Nothing seemed to be coming out. She shook the bottle, looked up at her friend.

'Bugger,' she said. 'Run out.'

'Trip to the offie?' Bex wondered.

'Round here? You're joking.'

'Shit, darling, now I wish I'd brought more.'

'Hang on,' Ella said. 'I did have a beer at the back of the fridge.' She staggered to her feet, and almost tripped over the huge, floppy John Lewis bag which Bex had brought in with her and which had been propped up, helpfully, next to the sofa for a couple of days now. 'What the fuck *is* all this stuff?' she asked.

'Oh, sorry. I meant to tell you. When I couldn't track you down, you elusive cow, I thought I'd better go from another angle and look for Tom. So I used my initiative. Went over to Appletree, and only found the bloody place empty, didn't I?'

'It's closed down?' Ella was confused. 'Blimey. Maybe Tom was more indispensable than he thought.' She peered into the bag.

'Anyway, there was some bloke there painting the walls, ready for the new tenants to come in. Well, when I mentioned you and Tom, he seemed to be very keen to give me all that shit. It's just junk from the office, and nobody's claimed it. I thought you might want it.'

'Thanks,' Ella said, unfurling the items at the top: an extension lead and a battered black answering-machine which looked about ten years old. The rest of the bag's contents looked dull: a couple of box files, various books and stationery items.

She left Bex sniggering in front of the sad dating show they had found on Channel 4, and went to the bedroom to plug the machine in.

The tape rewound automatically. She pressed Play.

'Hi, Tom, it's Shazia from the Waystation Hostel. Really sorry to hear about your funding, mate, let me know if—'

Shazia rambled on, sympathy mixed with vague promises to keep in touch, until an electronic beep cut her off mid-sentence.

Ella wasn't sure what she was doing, really. Or even if she was looking for anything in particular.

'Oh, hello, Mr, er, Barclay, this is Mark Lewis from the Black Community Action Forum. I was wondering if you'd still be interested in co-writing that article we talked about for Voluntary News...'

Well, maybe Mark Lewis, whoever he was, would have to do that on his own. A beep heralded the next message.

'Hi, Patrick Newlands here. Zero-eight-twenty-seven hours, sixth of September.'

Newlands, Newlands... Oh, yeah, that stuffed-shirt bloke who gave financial advice to the trustees. Ella had met him at a Christmas party once. Surely he knew Tom wasn't there any more?

'I'm, ah, trying to get hold of Tom Barclay, but his home telephone seems to have been cut off, and I'm, ah, not getting a response from the mobile. Wondered if someone could ask him to call me? I'm on two-six-zero—'

Boring, boring. She whizzed the tape forward.

And she recognised the next voice. A soft and husky transatlantic murmur. When the voice spoke, it smacked her into near sobriety.

'It's me. Look, um, I'm real sorry to bug you after we said goodbye, but I kinda think you should know I've still got your cellphone here. OK, so you haven't tried to call it yet, so maybe you don't realise. Problem is, Tom, honey, I have not got a clue where you are right now. But hey – you know where the gallery is. So if you want to come pick it up, let's, uh, have a cup of coffee and be friends for a half-hour... OK? Look, you know I'm still real sorry things had to end like they did. It was cool. It was sexy. OK, I have really said enough. That's all. Gotta go.'

Bex looked up as Ella came back into the sitting area. 'You OK, hun?' she asked.

'Fine,' said Ella curtly.

Bex did a double take, saw her friend's face streaming with tears as she eviscerated the answerphone cassette.

'Hey, babe! What's—'

'Nothing. It's really nothing.' Ella tugged the tape savagely. It was falling at her feet, a pile of brown spaghetti. 'Just remind me to listen to you in future.'

With the tape completely unravelled, she dashed the casing to the floor and stamped on it. Then she picked the whole lot up, opened the window and hurled the mess out. She watched it fall ten storeys, unfurling as it went, the shattered plastic trailing the tape. It looked like a comet. Then it hit the tarmac.

When she turned round, Bex's arms were there.

And the sobs were coming deep and hard, tearing her up, scalding her eyes and her throat and her chest.

'All right, darling,' Bex said, and hugged her tightly. 'Let it all out.'

'What's the matter with Mummy?'

The voice made Ella jump. She pushed her hand over her eyes and mouth, rubbing away the tears and mucus.

Isobel was standing in the hallway, glowering, Blue Rabbit dangling from one hand.

Ella pulled Isobel to her and hugged her. 'Nothing,' she said kindly. 'Nothing Mummy can't fix.'

'Why were you hugging Auntie Bex?' asked Isobel suspiciously. 'Are you a lesbian?'

Ella felt her cheeks filling with blood, knew her face had to be a roaring fireside red. 'Isobel! Please!'

Bex choked on her wine, spluttering with laughter. 'No, darling, your mother's never even been to Lesbos,' she said, giggling awkwardly.

Isobel gave Bex a long, serious look, one which made her swallow her giggles and look away. Bex never blushed, but now she came very close. 'I'll, um,' Bex muttered. 'I'll, just go and, um.' She retreated into the kitchen and started making a cup of coffee with a great deal of clattering and nonchalant humming.

'Darling,' Ella said, 'you shouldn't be up, you know.'

'The man's watching me again,' said Isobel.

Ella went cold. 'Where, darling?'

'Nowhere. I saw in my head.'

'Right.' Ella was relieved. 'So it was just a bad dream, then.' She started to tidy up the magazines and toys which had been abandoned on the living-room floor.

'No, not a dream. Not like that. But I don't think it is a man really, Mummy.'

'You don't?' Ella frowned. She stopped, straightened up.

'No.' Isobel paused, letting her big brown eyes fix firmly on her mother's searching gaze. 'I think it's a girl.'

PART FOUR

Survivor

'Do not assume that order and stability are always good, in a society or in a universe. Before the new things can be born the old must perish. And that hurts. But that is part of the script of life. Unless we can psychologically accommodate change, we ourselves will begin to die, inwardly.'

Philip K Dick, 'How To Build A Universe That Doesn't Fall Apart Two Days Later'

CHAPTER NINETEEN

Discontinuity

'Who were you texting?' Bex asked.

Ella quickly thumbed the Option button on her phone, then flicked it off. 'Nobody. Just seeing if it still works.'

They were on the roof. The flat, moss-covered, scabby roof of Renaissance Towers, which they had discovered by getting the clunky lift right up as far as it went. The doors had thundered open, revealing the deserted expanses of Twenty, just an open, concrete space like a half-finished sports hall. It was a shell, a building site scattered with abandoned paint pots, stepladders and pieces of hardboard. It had the wet, seaweedy smell of decay. A fine dust covered everything, and their footsteps left prints in it as if they were walking in a first layer of snow.

Bex spotted the rusty metal rungs of the ladder fixed to one wall, leading to a small steel hatchway. Cautiously testing the strength of the ladder, they climbed up it. Bex jemmied the rusty hatch open with her penknife, and they emerged into the brightness of daylight, feeling as if they were touching the sky.

There was a padlocked, bunker-like storage building, a collection of aerials and dishes on one corner, and the raised, wedge-shaped protuberance from which they had emerged. Otherwise the roof was grey and empty.

'Do you...*like* it here?' said Bex. She couldn't keep the incredulity out of her voice.

Ella smiled, leant on the parapet and blew a long, slow jet of smoke.

'I find lots of things about this life less stressful than the old one,' she said eventually. 'If that means I like it, then yes.'

'They're meant to be pouring money into Parkfield, aren't they?' Bex asked. 'The council. Supposed to be a target area. Some stuff in the paper about investment in housing and jobs.'

'You don't *believe* all that crap, do you?' Ella shook her head. 'Influential people in this city – people like I used to be – have a vested interest in keeping places like this down. I mean, who wants the bad areas to start getting good?'

'Babe, that is *so* fucking cynical.'

'Realistic, darling. Look, every city needs its bogeymen. The worse Parkfield is, the better places like Ashington and Great Lynton are going to look. Wheat among chaff. Diamonds in shit.' Ella took a long drag of her cigarette, shook her head, gave Bex a sidelong grin. 'Believe me, the middle classes *need* Parkfield as much as it needs them. When you don't have anything to demonise, what's left?'

Bex stared at her in admiration. 'You've been thinking about this, I can see.'

Ella shrugged. 'It doesn't take long to dawn on you. The authorities need this place to be a hole. They need it to have poor schools, and crap housing. They want everyone to do the fucking Lottery every week, struggle on, pick themselves up and take it on the chin. Because without the dependency culture, Bex, where does capitalism go?' She nodded, raised her eyebrows. 'Think about *that*.' She gestured expansively across the serried ranks of houses beneath them. 'I mean, look at it. Nobody's ever going to *want* to live here.'

'You told me Matt does. And Jo Tarrant.'

'Oh, yeah, the odd PC twinge afflicts people like Matty and Jojo. Kids straight out of bloody college, thinking they know all the answers. They feel they ought to live round here for a year or two. But as soon as they want to settle down and have families, believe me, they'll fly to the suburbs faster than you can say Fixed Rate Mortgage.'

Bex smiled. 'You're still the same hard bitch you always used to be. I like that.' She turned her back on the vistas of Parkfield and Cherford and gazed across the battered roof instead. 'You know, I bet nobody's been up here for years.'

'A garden,' said Ella, 'that's what it needs. A roof garden.' She leant back, shut her eyes and let the wind buffet her face, pulling her hair right back to the roots.

'So get your Lottery bid in, babe. You're in a, what's-it-called, area of urban deprivation.' Bex snorted with laughter. 'Should be a shoo-in.'

'It's the sort of thing Tom might want to do. If he was here.'

'Oh, don't talk crap, darling,' Bex snapped. 'Look, face it, he's never going to come here. He made it very clear what he thought, didn't he?'

'I suppose so.' Ella stubbed her cigarette out on the parapet with angry force. 'Oh, God, Bex, it's so fucking horrible here...' She shook her head, felt her face sinking into her hands.

Bex's arm was around her shoulders. 'Can I ask you something?' she said.

'Go on.'

'What Izzy said the other day. About being watched by a girl. It...well, I thought it would freak you out more than it did.'

Ella looked up at her friend and gave a tired smile. 'Did you?... Why?'

'Well, you know... Charlotte.'

'That's exactly why it *didn't* freak me out, Bex. When she said there was a man in her room, that frightened me. I think, with hindsight, that was just ordinary bad dreams. But if that's...' She struggled to find the words. 'If we're somehow...being watched over... I'm not scared.'

'Well, I think it's all bollocks,' Bex said with a grin. 'But then I've always been a bit of a sceptic.'

'You and Tom have a lot in common.' She paused, breathed deeply. 'You know, I went back to the house,' she said.

'The house? What, your old place?'

'Yes. Just crouched in the garden like a bloody stalker. Can you believe it?'

'What for, you idiot?'

'I just...needed to reach out and touch a little bit of the past. That's all.'

She tried to explain. She told Bex all about Henry and Sally, the perfect suburban family, and how they seemed to have slid so effortlessly into Ashington life. She didn't think they realised how bloody *lucky* they were to live there. Were they still open-mouthed with awe at the place, as they had been on the day of the viewing? Did they think twice about the beautifully kept park on their doorstep with its aviary and its miniature railway, or was that just something they expected?

Did they truly appreciate the huge rooms, the trim garden – the peace and quiet?

'There was hardly a sound there,' Ella said. 'I'd forgotten how quiet Ashington always was. You can hear the wind in the trees. Do you know, I never stood in our garden at night and just *listened* to the silence.'

And now, she never would.

'I can see that would appeal,' Bex agreed. 'You don't get much silence here.'

'God, no. There's always someone revving a motorbike, some kid bawling and screeching or a dog barking. Or DJ Dizzy Dickhead on Floor Eleven, pumping out his misogynist crap.'

'So you went back and remembered what you were missing. You poor darling. I wish you could all come and live with me.'

Ella grinned. 'It's a nice thought, but we'd be packed in like sardines.'

'My house isn't *that* small. But yeah, I take your point. I can't see Izzy wanting to share my boxroom with the Imelda Marcos collection, somehow.'

'I mean, obviously it's ridiculous,' Ella said moodily, staring at the clouds as they massed like warships over the distant silhouette of Cherford Castle. 'What am I going to do? Waltz up to the front door and tell the Morrison-Clarkes that there's been a terrible mistake, an admin error? That the house really shouldn't have been for sale, and can we please have our life back, just as soon as I've found out what the hell's happened to my husband?'

'Obviously not,' said Bex. 'You adapt. You move on. Which is what you have been doing.'

'Have I?'

She had, of course. She knew that.

Three months ago, she was the kind of person who would have raved for half an hour about an aluminium pendant lamp from Ocean. She would even – she shuddered a little now to think of this – have purchased *scatter crystals* for the house at Christmas. Nothing seemed to sum up the contrast with her former life better than the concept of scatter crystals. That she could have bought something which had no purpose other than pure pose value and frivolity made her puzzled, angry and unsettled.

There was no frivolity now. Life was pared to the bare essentials.

And in some ways, that helped to make things clearer.

'The thing you have to do,' said Bex, 'is work out where you're going to go now. What your priorities are.'

Ella nodded. 'I need to talk to Matt,' she said.

'Fiver to mind yer car for ya, sir?'

A cold and bright morning, the second Thursday in October. Matt Ryder, hefting his briefcase off the back seat of his car with one hand and supporting a tottering pile of books with the other, kicked the door of the MG shut.

He turned round, frowning, to see the source of the voice. A narrow-eyed, stocky little thug. Matt remembered his name: Shaun Moorcroft. One of Collins's mob.

'What did you just say, Moorcroft?' Matt demanded.

Shaun folded his arms, looked away for a second at the two sidekicks slouching by the graffiti-covered wall behind him. 'I said, how about a fiver to mind yer car, sir?'

'My car doesn't need minding, Moorcroft. Get to registration. And that goes for Beavis and Butthead behind you, too.'

Matt clutched the pile of books to his chest, took a firm grip on his briefcase and headed off towards the school entrance.

'Lot of dangerous villains round this place, sir,' said Shaun Moorcroft, falling into step with him. 'Nice motor like yours, anything could happen.'

Matt stopped in his tracks, swivelled on one heel and looked Shaun Moorcroft levelly in the eye. 'Lucky I've got my Rottweiler having a little rest in the back of the car, then, isn't it, Moorcroft?'

Satisfied with this retort, Matt allowed himself a little smile as he climbed the steps to the front entrance.

'Put out fires, does he, sir?' Moorcroft shouted after him. 'Clever doggie.'

It took a supreme effort, but Matt ignored him and carried on walking.

'Jesus,' said Jo, lowering herself into a chair in the staffroom. 'Oh, oh, oh.' She put a hand to her head.

'You all right, Jo?' asked Peter from Design Technology.

'Godmother of all hangovers,' she croaked.

'Paaaah! You lightweight, Tarrant,' said Dave from English. 'Egg-white and tomato juice, that'll see to it. With just a dash of Worcester sauce.'

'Nah, bacon sarnie and a pint of orange juice always works for me,' suggested Eric from Geography. 'Get some salt and vitamins back into your system.'

Jo held up a hand. 'Thank you, guys…just…please don't – OK?'

She had the feeling that there was some horrible, pungent liquid sloshing round just below her neckline, and that if she tilted herself too far it would gush out, acid-green against the brown staffroom carpet. She pinched the bridge of her nose and tried to focus. Somebody kindly gave her a cup of weak, sugary tea, and she smiled her thanks but didn't, in all seriousness, think she was going to be able to drink it.

Ella Barclay breezed in, looking annoyingly prim, trim and perky.

Jo narrowed her eyes at the woman, watching her smiling as she hung her coat on the hook, shimmied over to the group of men, made a cup of coffee with a lot of unnecessary flirty smiling and touching and, oh God, *crashing*. Did the cow always have to stir so *loudly*?

And how the fuck did she always look so good? Wasn't she the wrong side of thirty-five? She ought at least to have a few saggy bits, some wrinkles. Her new haircut, that tousled little gamine bob, ought to have been a total bloody disaster on someone her age, and yet it seemed to have taken another five years off her, the cow. That nose-stud was a fucking joke, though. How old did she think she was?

Look at her, Jo thought, tossing her head and putting her hand on people's arms. God, she even flirts with the *women*… And she isn't even a proper teacher. Glorified tour guide at the local Castle, that's all.

Oh, yes, she'd been a teacher once, according to Matt, but that was ages ago. That didn't count. Matt had talked her into this job – and Jo, for one, didn't need to speculate about his motives. Not now.

And they were looking over at her, now, and laughing. Laughing at Jo, at her state. Loving it, laughing about the boot being on the other foot, after that drinking conversation the other day.

She closed her eyes in silent fury.

The *bitch*.

Lunchtime in the stationery room. Ella's palms were flat on the warm photocopier.

She heard the door snick closed and knew, without turning round, who had come in. She also knew she was alone in there with him.

Her heart was thumping. But this time, she was clear about what she had to do.

'You've been avoiding me,' said Matt Ryder accusingly.

His shadow fell across her.

Under her hands, green light passed across the plate. She watched the numbers climbing on the digital display. 16, 17, 18, 19.

'Yes,' she said softly. 'I'm sorry.'

She didn't turn to face him. Instead, she let her gaze wander out of the window, across the flat roof to the school car park. His shiny cobalt-blue MG was there, she saw, next to Hollis's battered old Saab, someone-or-other's black Nissan and the red Fiesta which belonged to Kate from Music.

Concentrate on that. Be casual.

Matt moved closer to her. She could smell warmth, leather, tobacco, mixed with a sweet odour, a familiar one. She glanced up at him, saw his eyes unfocused and drooping.

'Had a pint or two, Matt? At lunchtime?'

23, 24, 25.

'No law against it, is there?' he responded, his usual chirpy tones roughened by smoke and alcohol. 'I've got 9G this afternoon, yeah? Need something to get me through it. If it's anything like last time, half the kids will be pissed too?'

'Students, Matthew, students. Walls have ears. Whatever would Ms Moretti say?'

'I don't give a shit what Moretti would say,' he spat with sudden, uncharacteristic vehemence. She felt his hot, alcoholic breath on her face and she found it very difficult not to pull back.

'Just concerned that you didn't get too drunk, that's all,' Ella said casually. 'After all, you've introduced me to some very strong beer round these parts.'

He pulled back, blanched. 'What do you mean?'

28, 29, 30.

Clunk.

The photocopier came to the end of its run.

'Well, maybe it wasn't the beer on its own.' She turned through ninety degrees, faced him square on, arms folded. 'Maybe, Matt, it was the double shot of vodka in each half of that disgusting bitter I drank last week. Each of those drinks that you *personally* bought me.'

The striplights buzzed.

The hot, inky smell of the photocopies crept into her nostrils.

'I wondered, Matt, why you got them in every time before anyone was due to buy a round. It seemed odd, but of course,

I was too happy and too pissed to notice.'

'I... like, don't know what you mean?'

'Oh, for fuck's sake. Is that the best you can do? Matt, I went to see the landlord and he found the part-time barman who was on duty that night. Oh, he remembered you all right.'

'Well, I go in there a lot.'

'Yes, and he wondered why you were ordering halves with a double vodka chaser each time, but he didn't query it. He wouldn't, would he? I mean, it's cash in the till. Pricey stuff, vodka.'

Matt looked away. He wasn't going to deny it now. He rubbed his nose, shifted awkwardly from one foot to the other.

'And, hey, you know what else?' Ella went on. 'It's almost odourless. How convenient is *that*?'

The hum of the photocopier subsided as it went on to standby, and there was silence in the room. Ella suddenly realised the significance of the clicking door. The latch was down. They were alone in the room and the door was locked.

'You know, the ironic thing is, Matt, you didn't bloody well *need* to spike my drinks. I'm... I was very attracted to you. I'd have slept with you quite happily on a level playing field, provided it was just the once and it didn't mean anything.'

He didn't seem to be listening now.

'All I know,' he said, leaning unsteadily in towards her, and making a grab for her arm, 'is that we had the most amazing sex the other night. The kind of thing two people...*dream* of doing. You...you were just incredible.'

'Oh, please—'

'I haven't been able to stop thinking about it. You're the sexiest, horniest, *dirtiest* woman ever to be in my bed.'

'Thank you, Matthew,' she said primly, pulling her copies from the tray and patting them together into a block with exaggerated force. 'What a lovely compliment. I do hope you changed the sheets.'

'So why the fuck have you been behaving like it didn't *happen*?' he demanded, pushing her now – actually *pushing* her, she realised with a twinge of fear.

'Matt,' she said, holding the papers in front of her like a shield and turning to face him, 'something...yes, something happened between us. When we were...both very drunk.'

'But you wanted—'

'And when I was rather more drunk than I actually realised.' She kept her voice level, made sure she was not shouting. 'Yes, it was fun, but it was also a mistake. And you used deceit and dishonesty to get me into a position where...where I wasn't *quite* sure what I was doing, if I'm honest.'

'I didn't bloody rape you, if that's what you're saying. Yes, you were pissed, but you wanted it just as much as me. It's not like I slipped you a Rohypnol, is it?'

'Jesus, Matt, do you think that makes it all right?' She shook her head, open-mouthed. 'Last of the bloody great romantics, aren't you? Look, I think it would be best for both of us, and for our professional relationship, if we considered it to be an...aberration. A one-night stand. And if we moved on.'

She had rehearsed that little speech in front of the mirror, naked (just as she had practised that speech to the Cherford

Castle funders at the heritage dinner, the speech she had never got to give). It sounded pretty good, in the bathroom – mouthed and whispered, of course, so that Bex and the kids couldn't hear. It sounded sensible and adult. Now, in the cold light of day, under the buzzing lights in the stockroom, it sounded like the trite piece of sermonising it probably was.

Matt had been staring at her throughout.

'What?' he said eventually.

'Which bit would you like me to repeat?' she snapped. 'Have I got to go through the whole thing again?'

His face was scrunched up, incomprehension and astonishment squashing it in all directions. 'No, no, no.' He started to pace up and down. 'It doesn't work like that, Ella Barclay. You don't get out of it that easily. No, no. You can't...you can't just...' He pushed his hair back, gnawed his fingernail. 'I don't want to...*move on*. I thought this was the start of something, not the end!'

She edged round him, clutching her warm photocopies as if they were a small child. 'Matt, I think we...perhaps need to have a talk about this another time.'

'No.' He walked towards her, making her take a step back against the wall. He put his arm out, palm flat on the wall, leaning over her. 'You look so sexy today.'

What was he on about? She had looked at herself in the mirror that morning and had seen a woman five years older than her. Someone with a greying fringe, tired eyes, reddened skin, breasts which actually pointed in different directions.

'Matt, I *so* do not look sexy. I've just taught four lessons, given eight detentions and broken up a riot on the top corridor.

I haven't had my lunch yet. I look, and feel, like shit warmed up.'

'Don't be stupid.' He moved in on her.

'*Matt!*'

She pushed him away, at the same time lifting up her knee so that it impacted – harder than she intended, if she was honest – with his groin.

'Jesus!' He fell against the bookcase, clutching himself, and the dislodged blocks of new exercise books in their plastic wrapping thumped to the ground around him. 'You *bitch*!'

'OK, OK.' She held up her hands, backing off towards the door. 'That wasn't fair of me. But you've got to see you're *well* out of order here. It's not on.'

'I only wanted to...' Matt winced, hauled himself to his feet. 'Fuck. You *cow*. You're as bad as Jenny was. Wanting it one minute, freezing up the next.'

'I neither know nor care about Jenny, whoever she is.'

'You're all the same,' Matt snarled, staggering to a chair and wincing as he clutched his injury. 'All the bloody same.'

Ella folded her arms and sighed exasperatedly. What was the matter with the boy? The drink situation aside, she'd gone home with him, shagged him senseless, slipped quietly away into the night and hadn't tried to call him. Wasn't that supposed to be what men dreamt of? For goodness' sake, didn't they *like* casual sex any more?

'Matt, if you've got some problems with your attitude to women, I think it's something you need to get some support with. But I don't intend to be part of your therapy.'

'You were quite happy to be part of my therapy the other night,' he sneered up at her.

'Matt—'

'When you were begging me to ram my cock into you.'

'Matt, this is *not*—'

'That's what you said. *Ram your cock into me so hard it makes me scream. I want it so fucking deep and so fucking good. I remember every word.* Do you remember saying that, Ella?'

'Please, Matt—'

'Or maybe, Ella, it wasn't you at all? Is that what you're saying? Did I have sex with your evil twin sister? Well, you'd better give me her phone number, if that's the case, because she was bloody *insatiable*.'

Ella held her hands up. 'I'm leaving. We are *so* not having this conversation.' Clutching her photocopies, she undid the latch on the door.

He was there behind her, hanging off the door, yelling after her.

'You're a bloody *slag*!'

She kept walking and didn't look back, until she had reached the safety of her own classroom. She slammed the door behind her, locked herself in and leant back against the wall, breathing heavily, listening to the distant thrum of school activity.

So – was this her answer?

Now that she knew the truth about Tom, was she ready to make her stand, to face down all her male antagonists with a new, fierce energy?

There was a time when she could not have done that.

Pudgy. Spotty. Thick, wild hair which won't do anything right. Ella MacBride spends ages in her room, reading the classics and listening to the music of Romantics both New and Old.

Everything is full of sex. She tries *Wuthering Heights* and realises that even that seems to be all about *it*, even if *it* is understated. Where do people *find* it? Boys don't chat her up at school discos. No brooding Heathcliff is going to stride into her life, and Nick Rhodes would never give her a second glance. Harriet Morecambe and Lara Teather at school have had four boys each and are now on their fifth, which doesn't seem fair.

She writes in her diary. She writes some of it to God, asking if he can please arrange for her to have a boyfriend sometime soon.

'Ella MacBride, what are you *doing* up there?' her mother calls. 'Are you going to come down and sit with us?'

At seventeen – uncertain in her body, tripping over her own shoes and peering at the world from behind new glasses – Ella looks in the mirror, curses her frizzy hair and her wonky tooth and tells herself that, come what may, she is going to Do It. She is not particularly bothered who performs the task, as long as he has the tools of the trade.

Why is it called '*losing* your virginity'? Nobody describes getting a job as 'losing your unemployment', or coming into money as 'losing your poverty'. Most of the girls at school have done it now, and they seem rather to have gained something, a kind of glow and a swagger. They walk, chew and grin with a new insouciance. (Except Lara Teather, who has mysteriously disappeared – to have an abortion, someone says.)

Her sixth-form days, though, pass without her getting close to the event.

For her eighteenth birthday, her parents buy her a Sony

twindeck radio-cassette. (Tape to tape! She's so excited. She will borrow albums off all her cool new friends at uni and record free copies.) That evening, she plays her other present on it, a brand-new tape of the Eurythmics' *Revenge*. And when she peers into the mirror, singing along to 'When Tomorrow Comes' – which isn't easy, because the swooping melody goes up and down and all over the place – she doesn't mind what she sees. Only one spot, a smooth and interesting face, a more stylish pair of wire-framed glasses and a cascading riot of wavy, black hair. Not bad, she says to herself, so why have I still not had any offers?

She is now faced with the prospect of carting her purity up to university with her, along with the books and the clothes and her Sony twindeck. Surely it will be too much to carry. Quite apart from anything else, she suspects it won't be long before her thirteen-year-old cousin gets around to Doing It, and that would never be on.

But carry it she does – invisibly, in the back of her parents' car. She suspects, as she stands in the car park and waves them off, that it shows as a bright halo, like the glow of the children in the advert who have had their Ready Brek.

Except, in this case, it's quite the opposite. It's the mark worn by the kids who haven't had their oats.

She can vote, although she has not yet. She can watch pornography at the cinema, but she has not done that either. She can marry without her parents' consent. She laughs contemptuously at this last thought, as she thumps her Athena posters to the wall with Blu-Tack.

Slowly but surely, things begin to happen. Over the next couple of days she finds people popping in to introduce themselves, probably because she often has the kettle on and plays cheerful music – *Carmina Burana* and Motown, Sinatra and Duran Duran – loudly, with the door open. Many of them are born-again Christians; she's not too bothered about that, as they are nice enough, but she smilingly declines any invitations to churches, Bible study or Quiet Breakfasts. She begins to make friends. Tasha, the girl from two rooms along, shares her musical tastes. Eddi, who is actually an Edwina ('no jokes about curried eggs, please') talks her into joining the badminton club and they soon have a regular Friday match.

She meets people in classes, at Hall lunch, at college events.

She goes to see *The Unbearable Lightness Of Being*, which is an 18 film, and she wonders if it counts as pornography. A box ticked, if so.

She irons her accent out, is careful of the words she uses. In the bar, she refers to an irritable lecturer being 'a bit of a mardy so-and-so' and wonders why everybody is looking so blank. She has to explain what 'mardy' means. Someone tells her she uses 'a lot of dialect words'. They're not dialect, she retorts angrily, they're the only words I've got.

Misunderstandings occur. She has tutorials with a nice girl called Lucy from London, and Lucy arranges to pop round to Ella's 'after dinner' on Tuesday, for coffee and a chat about their Eliot essay. So, after her midday snack on Tuesday, Ella dutifully puts the coffee-maker on to gurgle and does some notes while she waits. And waits. And, starting to feel a bit disappointed, waits some more. She eventually drinks the bitter coffee on her own at a quarter to four, watching the sun set over the quad. Later, she comes back from an evening in the bar to find a Post-it on her door. *'did try but ya weren't in. no probs – catch another time. luce xx.'* It dawns on her that, here, dinner is held in the evening, not at lunchtime. Ella would have said 'after tea'. But if she'd said that, Luce would have popped round at about four o'clock.

She fits in, though. For instance, she actually loves the rather sad, shabby college discos which don't change from week to week. A dozen wallflowers and misfits sip cider for two hours, looking nonchalant as The Cure, Bowie and The Smiths echo around a near-empty Junior Common Room. Then, at eleven-fifteen, exuberant people pile in, drunk, for the brief window between the bar shutting and the porters closing the disco down. The boys (paisley shirts, spiky gelled hair, aftershave) end up slam-dancing to 'She Sells Sanctuary' and 'Teenage Kicks'. The girls (pastels, denim, lipgloss and big earrings) prop up the wall, share cigarettes and cider with Ella and her friends, laughing uproariously while arranging a party to go on to. She gets invited along.

And things have changed. She no longer thinks so much about sex.

She realises she has three years' freedom ahead of her in a place where girls are in the minority, and so she enjoys her new-found attention. Her bed is for her own exclusive use at the moment, and she suspects that Tasha, Eddi and a few others are similarly inexperienced. She no longer has a problem with this, and, she tells herself, she can afford to wait until someone *really* fit comes along.

Tasha and Eddi, she notes, are 'dating' now. They've got little black dresses and lipstick. (Boots no.17, frosted pink.) The girls acquire leather jackets, not just black but in different pastel shades: elephant-grey, butterscotch and sky-blue. Ella, though, keeps a low profile in denim and sensible skirts. Several men are interested, but she doesn't like any of them much, and nobody gets beyond lunchtime coffee.

'There are blokes out there just *dying* to take you out to dinner,' says Tasha firmly.

'Or take you out to tea,' says Eddi with a wink.

'They're shy too,' Tasha says. 'They just don't let it show as much as we do.'

'Don't know why you packed that Andrew,' says Eddi, referring to an overeager boy in Ella's tutorial group who had been one of her Coffee Companions. 'He was all right.'

Edwina is from Sheffield, and she says 'packed' rather than 'dumped'. Ella likes the feel of the word: packing someone up, folding them away.

'Oh, come on,' Tasha groans. 'He was a *nerd*.'

What she doesn't tell them is that one of her Companions is a bit different. That cheeky PPE student called Tom, the one who impulsively kissed her on the night of the Great Hurricane. The one she likes too much. The one who lent her his New Order and Joy Division LPs (even though she hadn't heard of Joy Division and didn't realise one band led to the other). The one she's been avoiding, even though he smiled at her in the quad the other day.

Ella finally makes the loss (or gain) halfway through her second term, at the hands of one Paul Poulos, historian and fellow member of the badminton club. It is messy and unspectacular. Paul does not stay with her that night. (So, I haven't *slept* with him, she thinks.) She lies there like an effigy, arms across her cold and naked breasts, staring into darkness.

After lunch the next day, Ella sees Paul Poulos with a group of his mates sitting on the fallen beech tree outside the Junior Common Room, smoking and drinking coffee. The *Neighbours* theme bounces jauntily from the open window of the TV room. Her heart skips a beat as, folder clutched tightly to her chest, she strides in their direction. She sees Paul Poulos whisper something to one of the boys, and they all erupt into sneering, laddish laughter.

One of the boys does not laugh. Out of the corner of her eye, she sees that it is her friend from the hurricane. Tom Barclay. He stares at Paul Poulos and looks angry.

Ella scurries to the library, head down. She feels older, lighter, stranger; she does not have the urge to swagger, and there is no Ready Brek glow around her. Rather, she wants to make herself invisible.

CHAPTER TWENTY

You're The Voice

'Hello, Janie Jones show. Mike speaking.'

'Oh, um…hi.'

'Hello, there. Do you want to tell me your name and where you're calling from?'

The phone box Tom had found was high above Cherford, out on the lonely ghost-road which led to the countryside. It was a cold, empty strip of grey in the moonlight. Next to it, a wooded slope skulked on the edges of the suburbs; between the dark trunks of the pines, he could see the orange dust of the city lights. Looming above it all was the floodlit Castle on its hill, shining across the valley at him as if in mockery of their past life.

Traffic noise washed up the valley, reminding him that a major English city was down there. Directly below the slope, about a hundred-metre drop beneath Tom, was the Cherford Flyover, where endless car lights punctured the darkness, splintered into tiny flashes by the mesh of the trees.

Tom shivered, looking up and down the road as he eased open the creaking door of the phone box. It was one of the old sort, red and flaking, pungent with urine. He wrinkled his nose, picked up the receiver gingerly and gave it a good wipe with his handkerchief.

He had come to the conclusion – while lying on his back and staring at that Australia-shaped damp patch on the ceiling of his cold room – that a phone call was now urgent. And Tom, bereft of his usual contact with Jeff, knew that there was one person he could call on. A woman he felt he knew, intimately. He had heard her voice on many occasions, talking to people just like him, and although they had never met, Tom felt that she understood him.

He dialled.

The square metal buttons were cold and unfriendly against his fingertips. He knew the routine. She wouldn't answer herself – she never did at first. One of her minions, trained at spotting the nutters, screened you first.

The one he got was called Mike, and he kept asking questions.

'Hello, caller? Are you still there?'

'Yes. Sorry, yes, I'm still here.'

'Do you want to tell me your name, for when you go on air?'

Name. He'd thought this one over. There had been moments when he'd imagined that he might be Tim or Dave or Dom, just in case anyone heard him and recognised his voice, but he'd decided it would then feel like he was talking about somebody else. It wouldn't feel real, and he'd be inclined to hold back.

And anyway, he didn't know anyone sad enough to be listening to the Janie Jones Show at one o'clock in the morning.

'Tom, from Cherford.'

'Excellent. OK, Tom, as you probably know, Janie's got quite a few hot topics on the go tonight. Is it one of those particularly you've called up about?'

'Er, well, I wanted to talk about...about families. And relationships. I've got a...well, I've got a personal take on the whole thing.'

'That's great, just great. OK, Tom, give us a number we can call you back on and we'll get you on with Janie in about fifteen minutes, yeah?'

It was a long fifteen minutes. His shoulders and legs ached. He couldn't get comfortable standing up in the call-box, but no way was he going to sit down on the grubby stone floor with its cigarette-ends and its strange stains.

Not for the first time in recent months, Tom wished he had taken up smoking again. It would give him something to concentrate on right now, he thought.

He wondered what kind of weirdos had already been on with Janie tonight. It was no coincidence that her show began just after chucking-out time, and she frequently had to deal with the ramblings of the drunken and the drugged-up, the depressed and the desperate. Tom had heard her talk at least three people out of suicide on the air.

The ringing phone made him jump.

Trembling, he picked it up. 'Hello?'

'Hi, Tom, it's Mike from the Janie Jones show again. Going to connect you now, so you'll hear a record playing. When that finishes, you'll be on with Janie, OK?'

He blinked. It was starting to rain, and the big, trickling raindrops blurred the luminous outline of Cherford Castle and the scattered sodium lights.

'Hello? Hello, Tom?'

'Sorry. Yes. Thanks very much.'

The receiver began playing a crackly feed of 'I'll Find My Way Home' by Jon and Vangelis. The song was about halfway through.

Lost souls of the night. Now he was one of them.

And now she was speaking.

'Bit of a classic from the early Eighties, there,' said her sultry voice in his ear. 'Sounds great on late-night radio, that one. Hope everybody out there who's lost, abandoned, feeling a bit blue, manages to find their way home tonight... This is the Janie Jones phone-in, live across the region on 96.7 FM. OK, we're going to line one, now, and that's Tom, who's in Cherford. Tom...?'

The receiver swung like a pendulum as he backed up against the glass of the booth, shaking uncontrollably. He stared at it, the swinging, speaking black plastic thing, wondering what to do.

'Hello, Tom? Are you there?'

He reached out, stopped the phone from swinging. It smacked into his palm.

He moved to replace it on its cradle. He was going to walk away, anonymous, unheard, just another crank call for Janie to move on from.

'I'm here.'

The phone was against his ear and he was talking to her. He didn't quite know how that had happened.

The rain was thundering on the roof of the phone box, and Tom was live on air with Janie Jones.

'Tom, welcome to the show. Thought we'd lost you there for a second.'

'Sorry, Janie. I'm a first-time caller and I'm a bit nervous.'

'No need to be, Tom. As I always say, just think of it as you and me having a chat. What do you want to talk about?'

'I'm not sure where to start.'

'Beginning's always a good place... You said to Mikey that you had something to say about the family relationships debate we were having?'

'Well, yes.'

And so he started at the beginning.

He writes in an email to his parents: *Well, it's just four weeks since the birth, and already she can gurgle a bit, wiggle her toes and smile. Baby's not doing badly, either.*

He thinks it's hilarious at the time – in his heightened, coffee-fuelled, vitamin-enhanced state of being – but it loses something after he has to explain it. And later, he cannot remember if the quip is original or if he lifted it from somewhere. One of those New Man sites on the net, probably, called things like www.dadsplace.com or something, where you can go to meet like-minded souls and compete with Bob from Balham and Will from Wilmslow about how much time you are spending with your child.

He doesn't bother to tell the joke to Ella. Her sense of humour is a little unpredictable at the best of times, but her state of post-natal uncertainty sometimes makes him feel he is living with an explosive device.

He tries to joke, as well, about Ella's first fractured night in the maternity hospital. The back of the old building overlooks a pick-up spot for prostitutes, and, with the windows open on a hot night, one hears every ribald catcall and every friendly and not-so-friendly insult which the working girls trade with one another.

'Weird, isn't it,' Tom says that first night, holding Isobel in his arms and looking out on to the now-quiet alley. 'I wonder if that was deliberate.'

'If what was deliberate?' Ella asks him tersely, struggling to sit up. She scowls at him, narrowing her panda eyes and tautening her lips.

'The two images of womanhood juxtaposed. Madonna and the whore, side by side.' He grins. 'It's got symmetry. An almost artistic beauty.'

'Oh, right. A pair of old slags shouting, "Piss off out of my patch, you cow!" when you're aching with pain and exhaustion and you just want to get to sleep. You think that has an almost artistic beauty? Next time I'll let you have the baby, love.'

'Next time?' He raises his eyebrows, grinning down at Isobel as he strokes a finger along her soft, full lips.

'Yeah, well.' She gives him a shifty half-smile. 'Look, Tom, can we – and I mean both of us – can we not swear in front of the baby?'

'That's rich. I think the first words she ever heard in her life were, "Jesus Fucking Christ, that bloody hurts!" I didn't know Christ's middle name. That's an interesting one for you to ask Father Michael about next time you go to Mass.'

'It wasn't me, it was the painkillers. They gave me Tourette's.'

Tom gazes out at the glittering city, at the darkness of the hills and skies beyond, but he can only tear his eyes away from his daughter's perfect mouth for a second or two at a time.

'Weird,' he says, 'about Diana.'

'I know. The whole country's gone bonkers.'

He looks down at his daughter's peaceful, pink face and decides he's not that bothered about Princess Diana, really. Life goes on.

He's glad they've put a pink gown on her to start with. Good, that. No mistaking her for a boy. Baby Ben had been blessed with curly hair and a sensitive face, so when Tom took him out in the pushchair dressed in red, green or orange (in anything but blue, in fact) he sometimes heard him referred to as 'that lovely little girl' or 'that bonny lass'. It doesn't seem to have scarred him for life, he reflects, thinking of their son running round the park the day before, wearing a Cool Dinosaurs baseball cap, brandishing a toy laser gun and scaring the ducks. But you can never be sure.

It takes about ten days to lose the initial glow of that warm, stunned time – the days when they smile at one another and at Isobel, change Isobel, feed Isobel, kiss Isobel's head and take fitful naps whenever Isobel decrees that they are allowed. Ben trots around, Mum and Dad's little helper, fetching and carrying bowls and cotton wool, bright-eyed, adoring his little sister. It's unreal, and Tom likes the unreality.

It's like acting – they all have their roles, and they both go along with them quite happily, not thinking more than one day ahead at a time. It seems to work.

Then, Ella's playful snappiness, the repartee which always defines their relationship, seems to gain more of an edge. He asks her, one evening when his brain is numb and aching, how long he should sterilise the bottles for – is it six minutes or eight, he's just forgotten – and she jumps up from the sofa, hurls her slippers at him and tells him that he should bloody *know*, why should she have to bloody tell him? If she had to tell him all the time she might as well do it herself, and what was the point of sharing the tasks if he was always going to treat her like the bloody oracle?

He decides it's not a good time to remind her about the swearing thing. He looks the answer up in their book instead.

In the years to come, this turns out to be a good way of dealing with things he needs to ask Ella. Children don't come with manuals, but there's a host of books purporting to fill the role. Tom soon realises that, if you mix and distil them all, some drops of the Elixir of Truth can be squeezed out.

He starts to make his own little notebooks, too. Ben's favourite robot is Sir Killalot and the best band in the world is Busted. (Crossed out.) Linkin Park. (Crossed out.) Death Zenith. Isobel's best friend is Freya. (Crossed out.) Caitlin. (Crossed out.) Bethany. (Crossed out.) Freya again.

Wives don't come with manuals either. Or at least, if they do, they are all outrageously contradictory. Never mind. There are things he knows. Ella's favourite band is REM. Her favourite colours are black and white. (Crocus white. Lily white. Well, who bloody cares, it's all white.) Her favourite film is *La Dolce Vita*. (Crossed out.) *Shakespeare In Love*.

Their meeting-anniversary is the sixteenth of October.

Hurricane Day. He doesn't need to write that one down.

'Tom, that is...unbelievable. When did you last see your children?'

'About two months ago, Janie.'

'And they're...how old, seven and thirteen?'

'Eight and fourteen, now. They'll have had birthdays without me there.'

'What do you think your wife's motivation was for taking the children and moving to...well, you didn't want to say where they've moved to, but it's a council estate, yes?'

'I think she's a little unbalanced. I mean, we had a few financial worries, but nothing that couldn't be sorted out. Next thing I know, she's saying we've got to sell everything and move. She's taken the children out of their school and put them in this dreadful place, and... I just don't know what to do.'

'Forgive me, Tom, I'm a little bit uncertain about the details here. Could I just rewind and unpack a little?... You say you had some financial problems. Were they...serious problems?'

'Well, my contract came to an end and I was looking for a new job. And on the same day, my wife decides to pack in a perfectly good job and make herself voluntarily unemployed. She was earning a massive...well, she was the main breadwinner. Overnight, we were faced with not being able to pay the next mortgage instalment.'

'It sounds as if you had a real communication problem here, Tom. People don't pack in perfectly good jobs for no reason at all.'

'Well...no.'

'I think there must have been a lot going on behind the scenes at your wife's job that you weren't aware of, Tom. I mean, it's not inconceivable that there was a restructuring on the way and she knew she was going to be out anyway. It often benefits people to jump ship before they're made to walk the plank, if you get my drift.'

'I don't think it was anything like that.'

'OK... Tom, I know this must be difficult for you, but... have there been any other problems in your relationship at all?'

'Problems?'

'Well, yes. You see, when people who've been married for...how long did you say? Fifteen years?'

'Yes, that's right.'

'Well, when people have been together that long and they don't discuss important issues, it's symptomatic of other things in the relationship that need exploring, to be honest.'

'Right.'

'Are you... I mean, I assume you're living somewhere else currently?'

'Yes...yes, I am.'

'And have there been any...other strains on the marriage at all?'

'Um...'

'If I'm going to help you, Tom, you need to be straight with me.'

'There have been some...yeah.'

'Has either of you been unfaithful sexually?'

'...mm?'

'Tom? I don't know if you heard my question. I was asking you if either of you had been unfaithful within the marriage?'

'Yes. One of us.'

'I see. That'll be you, then.'

'What makes you assume that, Janie?'

'Because if it had been her, you'd have said straight away that it was her, wouldn't you? In fact, it would probably have been the first thing you came out with. Tom, trust me, I have been doing this for a while. I know when someone's holding back. So, you were unfaithful. Is that still going on?'

'No. No, it's finished.'

'Right. So it wasn't a meaningful relationship. Just a fling.'

'It probably went on a bit longer than it should have done. But yes, it was just a fling.'

'Right. Let's leave that for now. Tom, forgive me if I'm putting two and two together and making five, but when your wife decided that you had to sell the house and move, were you fully supportive of this? I mean, did the two of you sit down together and plan exactly how you were going to rescue yourselves and your family from your financial mire?'

'Um...well, my wife kind of took care of it all. I thought she was good with that sort of thing.'

'I see. And what did you do?'

'Well, at first I went to sign on the dole. I kind of thought I ought to. I mean, don't get me wrong, I was looking for other jobs, but there just didn't seem to be anything. Once you've failed somewhere, people get to find out. They don't want to know. Your name's like an unlucky charm for them.'

'I don't accept that, Tom. But again, let's leave that aside. It sounds to me as if your wife was taking emergency measures designed to deal with the immediate problem.'

'Well, I don't know about that.'

'And the fact that she didn't deal with them to your satisfaction is probably partly down to your not being as involved as you could have been.'

'Well... I suppose you could be right.'

'I think what was called for was a couple of months of

careful planning, together, while you moved somewhere temporarily.'

'Um...well, yes.'

'And instead, you vamoosed, leaving the whole damn shebang in the lurch, and letting your wife and children pick up the pieces.'

'No! No, it wasn't like that at all.'

'It certainly sounds that way, Tom. Too many people come on here wanting to blame someone for their problems, their situation, their actions. All too often, when I delve a little, I find what they need to do is take a little responsibility. Am I right?'

'Ummm.'

'Am I right, Tom?'

'I think you're bullying me.'

'You phoned the show, sweetheart. You've heard me before. You know I'm no pussycat.'

'Yes, Janie.'

'Get with the programme, Tom. Sort yourself out and get *back* in your children's lives, and sit down with your wife and talk about where the hell you're going to go! Because if you don't, Tom...'

'Yes?'

'Tom, if you don't, you might turn up one day and find your children calling another man Daddy.'

'Um.'

'Got that?'

'Yes. Yes, thank you, Janie. I've got that.'

'I bet you're pleased you called me now.'

'Actually, I am. Thanks, Janie. Thanks very much.'

'It's a pleasure, Tom. You take care now.'

'Janie?'

'Yes, Tom?'

'There's something else I haven't told you.'

'I wondered, you know, Tom. I can always tell when someone's holding back on me... But don't tell me yet. Wait until we've heard from Roxy Music. This is "Dance Away"... You're listening to Janie Jones.'

Back in his guest house, he felt tired and drained, but somehow lightened, cleansed, as if he had expelled kilogrammes of fetid shit or gallons of acrid vomit from his body. It was as if he had purged his system of toxins and would now drink nothing but water.

He held his photograph of Ben and Isobel out at arm's length and saw that he was still physically shaking. He wondered if he ought perhaps to eat something. It had been this morning, that last breakfast.

Or maybe it was yesterday morning.

He dared to let his face slide into view in the mirror.

He had never seen his skin looking so pale and undernourished, his eyes so grey and punched-looking with lack of sleep, his stubble so thick.

There was a pink Post-it note stuck to the mirror, in his landlady's handwriting. Frowning, he pulled it down and held it in front of his eyes. He tried to focus.

He read the note once, and thought it couldn't possibly say what it said. He blinked, read it again.

That was odd. Why on earth should *he* have been in touch?

The note gave no indication of what time the call had been

received, but it had to have been sometime this evening, while he was out aimlessly wandering the streets. Still shaking, he checked his watch. Five to two. No way could he call back now, when all sensible people were in bed. Even Janie Jones would be clocking off.

He lay down on top of the bed, fully clothed, and pulled the duvet tight round him like a cocoon. He stuck the pink note to his pillow so that it was the first thing he would see in the morning.

Mr Barclay, the note read. *A gentleman called Patrick Newlands has called for you: he's been anxious to get hold of you for several weeks. He needs to talk to you a.s.a.p. Please call him as soon as you can.*

Soft blackness swallowed him up. Even as he slipped into deepest sleep, he could still hear the voice of Janie Jones, there in that phone box in the middle of nowhere.

'So tell me what you need to tell me, Tom.'

'I've said.'

'You've told me her name. I don't know any more than that. Tell me the whole thing, Tom, and it might help you. Tell me. Tell me about Charlotte.'

CHAPTER TWENTY-ONE

Shadow Play

'You believe in God, Ell?'

Ella looked up sharply. It was Donna who had asked the question. Donna the Gate Mum, leaning back on the bench and blowing a jet of smoke into the air.

They had found themselves sitting side by side in the children's playground behind Renaissance Towers, little more than a patch of scabbed tarmac with three swings and a rusty roundabout, but better than nothing. Isobel was playing on the swings with Donna's daughter Larissa, the two girls laughing as each tried to go higher than the other.

Leanne hovered nearby, baby Beyoncé attached to a blubbery, blue-veined mammary. She wasn't joining in. Leanne didn't really do conversation.

'I used to be sure I did,' Ella answered. 'Now...now I don't know.'

Ella was astonished at the question. It was so long since anyone had asked her to apply her mind to anything metaphysical.

'Me mum used to believe in God,' Donna said. 'Went to

church regular. One of them whatsit, happy-clappy places.'

'Evangelical.'

'If you say so, mate.' Donna gave her a sideways grin. 'Anyway, she'd always said everything was part of God's fuckin'...design an' that. We couldn't hope to understand it. AIDs, famine, September 11th... I got really fuckin'...mad with her, y'know? Used to ask her where God was that day. Know what she said?'

'No,' said Ella, turning to face her, genuinely interested. She had always wanted to get a good answer for that one herself. 'What?'

'*God was there, sufferin' with everyone.*' Donna laughed humourlessly. 'Bollocks, innit? I mean, who wants a fuckin' God who just sits there and suffers? You want a God who can fuckin'...sort stuff out. Meant to be bloody all-powerful, ain't he?'

Ella opened her mouth, wondering how best to encapsulate the doctrine of free will and its implications, then thought better of it.

'Anyway,' Donna said, 'two year ago she were diagnosed with fuckin'...cancer, right?'

'Oh. I'm so sorry. That's awful.'

'Yeah, well. Thing was, that was it for her and God. Oh, yeah, it was all very well for other people to suffer. Children getting murdered, bloody terrorists letting bombs off all over the fuckin'...place, and it's all part of God's will. Soon as anything happens to me mum, it's like, I've prayed all me life, I've been a good Christian, I don't deserve this, it ain't fair. Turns her back on the church and tells the vicar to sod off. That was it, then. God weren't her friend no more.'

'It's an understandable reaction,' Ella offered.

'Bloody hopeless if you ask me.'

There was a silence, punctuated only by the creaking of the swings and the girls' giggling.

'Did...your mum recover?' Ella asked gently.

'Nah, she copped it. Last year.'

'I see. I'm very sorry, Donna.'

'Fuck, don't be. We wasn't exactly close.' Donna offered Ella a cigarette, which she took gratefully. 'Your mum and dad still alive, are they?'

'My father died a good few years back. My mum, well, I don't see much of her. She lives up north.'

'Get on all right with her?'

Ella thought about her mother's probing, wittering telephone conversations and her habit of rearranging the herbs into alphabetical order. She thought of Maggie's visits to the house in Thorpedale Avenue, of how she would click her tongue and plump up the cushions as soon as she walked in, then head straight for the Pledge and Cif. Of how she'd rearrange and dust the shelves while telling Ella that she ought to make sure to keep making an effort, because men, you know, they noticed these things. Subtly berating her daughter, as ever, for being a Bad Working Mother.

'Yes,' she said. 'We get on fine.'

'Good, that. Pleased for you. Gotta get on well with family if you can. They're your lifeline.' She pointed to Isobel. 'I mean, look at your Izzy. You want her to carry on bein' in your life, don't you? Not fall out with you about some stupid fuckin'...wossname. You want her to be there to bring the grandkids round to see you. To read poems out at your funeral.'

'Yes,' Ella said. She looked at Donna with a new respect. It was odd, but she rather liked that blunt way of putting it. 'Yes, you're right.'

Another silence. A dog barked somewhere on the estate.

'There was a time,' said Ella softly, 'when I almost hated God, you know.'

'Why's that?' Donna asked, interested.

She watched Isobel's curls riding the swing's slipstream. 'Tom and I, we...lost a child. A baby. Three years ago.'

Like a shadow. Always there.

'Her name was Charlotte.'

She had said it. There was no going back.

'Nice name,' said Donna.

'There were...always difficulties from the start. We were told she wasn't developing properly, that she...well, that there would be problems.' She sighed, shivered, pulled her coat close around her. 'Charlotte was born at twenty-four weeks.' Ella bit her lip, looked down. When she spoke again, her voice was little more than a whisper. 'She lived for about an hour.'

Donna said nothing. She nodded.

'We knew that was all we could hope for, but we wanted to see her... We needed to. Because of the timing, they left it up to us whether we gave her a name and a funeral. So we did. We buried her at this tiny chapel out in the country, a little place I used to pop into sometimes. When we contacted the priest about it, he was really surprised. Said nobody ever went there.' Ella smiled sadly. 'That was why we wanted it, of course.'

Donna was silent. She just nodded.

'Anyway, we were driving back home after the ceremony

and we just got this idea, both of us. It was like...synergy. It came to us both at the same time. Tom was driving, and before he even said it, I knew what he was going to do. There was this garden centre we often went past. Even though we'd never gone in there before, we knew we were going in. And we both knew we wanted this same tree, a plum tree, to plant in memory of Charlotte. We planted it in the garden of our house...our old house.'

'That's nice,' said Donna. 'Nice thought.'

Ella swallowed hard. 'Yes. The house we've bloody well had to *move* from because we both were so...so...bloody *stupid*.'

'No point blaming yourself,' said Donna awkwardly. 'Shit, at the end of the day, it don't matter where you fuckin'...live, does it? It's how much you love your kids.'

'I know. I know.' Ella drew a deep, shuddering breath, smiled and waved at Isobel. 'What made it worse,' she said, 'was the number of people who said something like, *oh, well, you've already got two, haven't you?* As if that somehow made it better. It was like we'd dared to somehow...over-reach ourselves by having another child. Like we were being punished for having Charlotte.'

'People don't fuckin'...mean it like that. They only wanna say nice stuff, like. They don't know what to say, do they?'

'No. You're right.'

'Fight your fuckin'...battles, love, and don't listen to what nobody else says. That's what's got me through twennyfive fuckin'...years in this place.'

Ella grinned. 'Wonder how many years I've got to go,' she said.

'Don't knock it, love. It's home.'

'I suppose it is,' she said. 'I suppose it is.' She glanced at her watch. 'Bloody hell, I'm supposed to be at the art gallery.'

'The *what*?'

'Long story. Donna, I'm really sorry about this, but – could you see Izzy gets back to school?'

Patrick Newlands shook Tom's hand vigorously. 'Tom, old chap. Glad you could come.'

They stood on the porch of Patrick's detached home in the market town of Great Lynton, just outside Cherford. Just up the road, beyond a line of weatherboarded cottages, a church clock was striking. Patrick looked relaxed in a cotton shirt and chinos. Tom, meanwhile, was glad he'd decided to have a haircut (albeit a budget one) and a shave. He'd also put a reasonably smart jacket and trousers on, the only ones he still possessed.

'You found the place all right?'

'Yes, fine. Great directions. I got the 33 bus from Cherford, actually.'

'Ah, yes, I always had you down as a patron of jolly old public transport. Excellent, excellent. Wish there were more like you. Come on in.'

In the hallway, Tom caught a brief glimpse of something which made his heart race and his palms sweat. But he had to forget it for now. He needed to know why Newlands had called him here.

As he followed Newlands into his lounge, he took in as much as he could: high ceiling, stripped beech floors, immaculate eggshell-blue furniture and curtains, floor-to-ceiling bookshelves packed with fashionable hardbacks and CDs. The room was cool, contemporary and welcoming, interior-designed to perfection. It was Sarah's hand, of course; Patrick's wife had a natural way with these things.

'I'll get you a drink, old chap. Scotch?'

'Oh, um, just water, if you wouldn't mind,' Tom said awkwardly, settling into one of the comfortable armchairs.

'Of course, of course. Bit early for a snifter, isn't it? Won't be a tick, then, I'll just pop to the fridge.'

A recent photo of Patrick and Sarah was on the table beside Tom, and he picked it up to have a look. She was in her mid-forties, he knew, but she looked far younger. He had met Sarah a couple of times at work events. She had the firm bust of a twenty-five-year-old, magnificent legs and iridescent skin – all testament to a stress-free life of daily visits to the gym and, he imagined, extensive applications of Oil of Olay, or something like it. And no work, of course. He found it difficult to talk to Sarah without getting very turned on.

'Here you are. Sorry I've no ice.' Newlands handed him his water in a tall green glass.

'Oh, thanks. That's fine, fine.' Tom put the photograph down. 'Just admiring the, ah, family portraits,' he said.

Newlands chuckled. 'Oh, that old thing. Yes, it's amazing what professionals can do. I hate having my picture taken. I always get bags under my eyes.' He leant forward, hesitantly, sitting on the edge of his armchair with his fingers pressed together. 'Listen, Tom, I'll come straight to the point.'

Tom sipped his water, nodded and placed the glass on the table beside him.

'Tom, have you heard of First Locate?'

He thought he ought to have done. 'Um... I'm a bit out of the loop, Patrick. You know how it is. Remind me.'

'Sure. They're a charity consortium working together to set up projects and services for refugees and asylum seekers in the Cherford region. Now, as you probably know, we haven't had a huge influx of asylum seekers here, but the word is that's going to be changing. Obviously there's going to be a bit of argy-bargy and political stuff, you know, all the usual shenanigans.'

'Getting the burning crosses ready,' Tom suggested. 'I know.'

'You've got it, old chap. Dreadful stuff... Anyway, look, bottom line is, I've been asked to head up the Board of Trustees, and that means I've got to come up with some useful suggestions as to who might manage this whole thing.'

'Right.'

Tom crossed his legs and looked thoughtful.

He tried not to let his disappointment show. So that was it. All those urgent messages, and for what? So Newlands could drag him out to Great Lynton just to pick his brains and get him to help somebody else with a career leg-up. How depressing. If he was honest, Tom could think of about three people straight off who would be ideal. He could have named them to Newlands there and then, but he didn't really have the heart.

'I mean, obviously the usual procedures have to be gone through, but my recommendation would carry a lot of weight,' Newlands was saying.

'Um, obviously.'

Tom felt embarrassed now. He just wanted to get away. He

gulped some more of his water and sneaked a look at the clock.

'So what do you think?' Patrick Newlands raised his eyebrows and spread his hands.

'Um... Look, Patrick, I'm really sorry, but I don't think I can help.'

Newlands grinned. 'Just as I thought. I told them you'd turn it down initially. Look, don't worry, Tom, I know what you're thinking. Your background is mainly working with the homeless and you think you don't have the experience. But frankly, I think your skills are ideal for this.'

Tom blinked.

Occasionally, when he was watching an American comedy on DVD, Tom would click his tongue in irritation at a joke that was delivered too fast or too inaudibly. He would stretch his hand out for the remote control to rewind and listen again, to see if the words he thought he'd heard actually made any sense second time round.

Sometimes, real life needed a remote control too.

'Sorry, Patrick,' he said. 'Run that past me again?'

In the main hall of the Centrespace Gallery, Ella lounged against the door-frame.

She recognised Phill again instantly. Cool and lissom in green velvet leggings and a red denim shirt, auburn hair tied back with a scrunchie. She was giving orders to the two guys on stepladders as they positioned a painting.

She saw her raise her hand, point over to the right.

Ella tilted her head, tried to look at her from all angles. To be objective. So what was it, what did she have? The woman's arse wasn't the pertest she'd ever seen, and her breasts were round and full, but not hyper-perky. Her face was quite pretty, Ella admitted to herself, and her mouth had a hint of wickedness about it. Overall, though, she didn't look the part of the scheming seductress.

Ella waited, watching, for five minutes, then strolled into the middle of the gallery.

'Splendid,' Ella said, looking up at the painting, her arms folded. She tilted her head and tried to gauge the piece. It was a plain, stark disc of white on a red rectangle, like a Japanese flag in reverse. 'Don't tell me. It's all about the Self.'

Phill turned to look at her slowly. 'Actually, yes. It's... Um, excuse me, but how did you get in?'

'It's stunningly simple, when the door's left open.' She raised her eyebrows at her husband's erstwhile lover. 'I don't suppose you recognise me, do you? I've come for Tom's phone.'

There was a perceptible change in Phill's expression. She reddened a little. 'Duncan,' she called to her assistant, 'take over here, will you?'

The two women, walking in step, moved over to the other side of the gallery.

'Sorry,' said Phill. 'I...didn't recognise you at first. You've...' She mimed the hair and the nose-stud, looked the new, casual wardrobe up and down. 'You've changed. You look great,' she added, pushing a stray strand of hair back awkwardly from her eyes.

'I didn't come here to be flattered, Ms Janowitz, I came here to conclude some unfinished business. Tom's mobile, please.' Ella held out her hand, palm flat, as if she was asking a Year

Nine boy to hand over a prohibited video game.

'Yes…yes, of course. Sorry.' Phill produced the small, silver object from her nearby handbag and placed it neatly in Ella's hand. 'I was gonna let him know he'd left it, but…things happened quickly.'

'Of course they did.' Ella wasn't even looking at her, now; she was thumbing the buttons, idly checking the most recent calls. 'Is he all right?' she asked, almost as an afterthought.

'Well…he was when I last saw him. But that was three weeks ago.' Phill sighed, folded her arms. 'Hey, look, don't be too harsh on him, OK?'

Ella stopped thumbing the phone, snapped the lid shut, slipped it into her pocket and fixed Phill Janowitz with her most contemptuous stare. 'I'm sorry, what?'

'I said don't be too harsh on him. He's…well, he's had a tough time. He's really missed you. And the kids.'

'Don't you tell me what to do, you fucking husband-stealing witch.'

Phill looked away, gave a grim smile and held her sawdust-covered hands up. 'OK, so maybe I deserve that. But the plea still stands.'

'I'll deal with Tom in my own way. I don't need any advice on marital relations, thank you very much. Especially not from you.'

There was an awkward silence, broken only by the shuffling of feet and the thudding of the workmen's hammers.

Ella leant on the nearest object, an elegant, up-ended prism made of what looked like mahogany. It had a steel disc half buried in each of its three smooth sides, so that a burnished semicircle of metal protruded from each face.

'Look...thanks for getting it back to me,' said Ella eventually, scratching her nose. She didn't look Phill in the eye, focusing instead on the nearest workman on his ladder. He was straightening what seemed to be a giant black-and-white photograph of a Rich Tea biscuit.

'No problem,' Phill murmured.

She nodded at the workspace. 'This your new exhibition?'

'Yeah, this is *Wotz Da Crack?* Drug-inspired, hallucinogenic art from the good people of Cherford. We open in three days.' Phill risked eye contact. 'You can come if you like. I know how much you enjoyed it last time.'

'I'll give it a miss.' Ella realised she was still leaning on the wooden prism. 'Sorry,' she said, letting go and stepping back. She inclined her head one way, then the other, sizing the wooden prism up. As a sculpture, it was a bit abstract, she thought, but at least it looked as if someone had put a bit of effort into it. The wood was beautifully finished and the metal discs shone like mirrors. 'What's this one?' she asked, pointing at it.

'Ah, those are seats,' said Phill. 'For people to sit on.'

Ella sighed. 'You know, I'm never going to get this modern art stuff.' She nodded, slipped the phone into an inside pocket.

'Oh, I may as well tell you this,' Phill added. 'I charged it up for him, and when I tested it there were three messages, all from this same guy. Patrick someone? Patrick... Newfield, Newbold? Something like that. It sounded like he was pretty desperate to get hold of Tom.'

Ella shrugged. 'Aren't we all?' she said with a sad smile.

'Well, anyway. Just thought I'd better mention it, in case it was important.'

'OK, thanks.' Ella nodded, took one last look around. 'Goodbye, then.'

She turned her back on Phill and the gallery, and walked out of the dusty, painty air into the crispness of the October day.

'Patrick, I had the wrong end of the stick.' Tom was falling over himself to apologise. 'You...you want *me* to head up this project?'

Newlands chuckled, sprawling back in his leather armchair. 'Now, I know what you're going to say. You're worried it'll be a stack of work for a not-very-impressive salary. Let me tell you, this thing is local-government funded, right? Comes under Community Initiative 47, if you're familiar with that. They're taking the money side seriously, never fear. You wouldn't exactly go hungry, old chap.'

'Rrright... Patrick, are you *sure* I'm the right person for this?'

'There you go, being modest again. Tom, everybody in the sector knows you did a *great* job at Appletree. Sure, so it all went a bit tits-up at the end, but, hey, that was just jolly old politics. Nothing to do with you. It's a risky business, and you handled the fire-fighting better than anyone.'

'Um, it's...kind of you to say so.'

'Just honest, old boy. You did miracles on a shoestring at that place, Barclay, and it didn't go unnoticed, believe me. All that invention, all that drive, all that thinking outside the box and partnership working... I intend to tell my fellow trustees all about you. And the buggers will listen, believe me. Frankly, Tom, I don't know *anybody* in the region who could do it better than you.'

'You don't?' Tom said levelly. He needed some more water. The room was going to start spinning in a moment.

'Nope.' Patrick Newlands pulled a manila folder off a nearby desk and handed it to Tom. 'Look, have a read of all that over the next day or two and then give me a call, OK? And please don't come back to me and say it's not for you, or I shall be so disappointed.'

The next few minutes were something of a blur for Tom. He remembered afterwards that he'd somehow managed to get his conversation out of first gear, to slip into professional mode and put some intelligent-sounding queries to Newlands. Then, he'd remembered to get in the required questions about the Newlands girls (one backpacking in Thailand, the other in her first term of the sixth form) and all of Sarah's charity work.

They shook hands in the hallway.

'And your darling Ella,' Newlands said, with a knowing look. 'How are things there?'

'Um...' Tom scratched his nose. 'Actually, Patrick... Well, actually, we've hit a bit of a bump. Got some chatting to do. Kind of bouncing on the old rocky road at the moment.'

He couldn't believe this. Thirty minutes in Patrick Newlands' company and he was already starting to *talk* like him.

Newlands nodded sagely. 'Comes to us all, old chap. If marriage was a bed of roses, you'd always be sneezing.' He pulled a face. 'I've no idea what the devil that's meant to mean. Anyway, you'll sort it out.' He clapped him on the shoulder. 'She's a fine woman.'

'Yes,' Tom said, nodding. And then he met Patrick

Newlands' eye and said it again. Properly, this time. 'Yes, she is. And I will. Sort it out, that is.'

'Two lovely kids, you've got. Not worth losing that, is it?'

'Absolutely not, no... Patrick, could I just ask you something?'

'Fire away, old boy.'

Tom pointed to the under-stairs shelves in the hallway, indicating the object which had caught his eye when he came in. 'Is *that*,' he said, pointing to the pink-and-yellow three-foot cube nestling behind Newlands' golf clubs, 'what I think it is?'

'Errr... Give me a clue. What?'

Tom went over, leant under the recess and patted the pink box. 'That,' he said. 'If I'm not mistaken, it's actually a Zillah Zim Magic House. Still in its packaging.'

'Oh, *that* thing. Yes, I thought Sarah had taken it down to Barnardo's, to be honest. We bought it for my niece, for her birthday. Problem was, I found out there'd been a bit of an old mix-up and her other uncle had got her one as well. Would you credit it?'

Tom shook his head in wonder. 'I suppose you know these things are like gold dust?' he said. 'I tried to get one for Isobel. No chance.'

'Of course, yes. Your little one's about that age, isn't she?'

'Patrick,' said Tom, seized with a kind of mad desperation, 'could I...could I buy this from you?'

'Oh, for heaven's sake, old man, you don't need to *buy* it. Take it. You'll be doing me a favour.'

'Are you sure?'

'Good God, yes.' Newlands leant down, moved his golf

clubs aside, picked up the box and handed it to Tom. It was bulky but light. 'As I say, we were only going to take it to a charity shop. But if you can make it go to a good home, all the better! Can you manage it on the bus?' he added as an afterthought.

'I've done stranger things, Patrick. I'll be fine.'

'Right, well...take care, Tom. And make sure to get in touch. Oh, goodness me, let me get that door for you...'

Matt Ryder had thought long and hard about his opening gambit.

He hadn't slept much, these past few days. The strange, floating, dreamlike state he found himself in was rather close to drunkenness. And cheaper. It made him feel full of bravado.

His best bet, he thought, was to ignore any pretence at making chit-chat, forget small-talk about the weather, and just to steam in as if there had been no break in the conversation from yesterday.

There she was. In the canteen.

He slammed his tray down opposite her – there was nobody else at their table – and met her implacable expression with an unflinching, wild stare.

'It won't make any difference, you know,' he said.

Ella was in the process of squeezing tomato ketchup on to her chips. She put the bottle down, sighed, leant back and folded her arms.

'What won't, Matt?'

He'd been thinking this through, and it was glorious. It all made sense. He'd got her here, in the school, where he could look at her three days a week – and, in looking at her, he could know that he'd seen beneath the tight black skirt, felt the gorgeous, ripe breasts under that gauzy top. He'd sampled the wares.

'The fact that you refuse to give me the time of day. Because I can still look at you. I can still hear you. And you know what?' He leant in close, scenting her perfume and some sort of fruity shampoo. 'I can smell you.'

'Matt,' she said, lifting her tray, 'you are being *weird* now.'

'The fact that you're in the same building,' he said, fired up now, feeling more sure of himself than he'd ever been. He was going to tell her. He was going to show her that he couldn't just be pushed around, not after he'd gone to all this trouble for her. 'Breathing the same air. That *does* it for me.'

'Matt,' she said, and he couldn't miss the tone of pity in her voice. 'Please.'

She pushed her tray aside and headed for the door, but he was following her now, past the kids, out into the corridor which linked the dining hall with the rest of the school.

'I've sat in your chair,' he said.

She paused at the swing doors, turned round with incomprehension on her face. 'What?'

'After you've gone, at the end of the day. I've done it several times. I've gone to the chair you always sit in. That big old brown leather one. And I've felt the warmth of your body coming through the leather. Just like when we—'

'Yes, yes.' She held up both hands. 'All right, I get the picture. Matt, you need help.'

'I've gone to your coffee cup after you've left it on the draining board. If I sniff it, I can smell you. Your mouth. Your body. Your pheromones. Sometimes you've left a little bit in the bottom and I can drink it, cold and wet and pungent, and it's like I'm drinking up a small piece of you. And sometimes, you leave a lipstick trace on the rim.' He realised that Ella, to his astonishment, had stopped listening and was staring out of the transparent corridor into the car park. 'What?' he snapped.

'Oh my God,' she said. 'Is that your car?'

He turned, feeling a creeping sense of horror in his body, and he saw what she meant. His blue MG, parked right by the entrance, was festooned with shaving foam and adorned with the word WANKER in bright red paint. Furthermore, the front windows had been smashed through, the glass lying in a silvery carpet across all the leather seats of the car. There were two wires hanging where his CD-radio ought to be, and the headlamp covers hung down limply, revealing blind sockets.

Matt stood there, gawping.

Beside him on the steps, Ella put a hand to her mouth. 'Jesus,' she said. 'I thought the scratch was bad enough. When the hell did they do *that*?'

Not why, or how. *When*.

Matt, unable to speak, shook his head.

The crashing impact of his lack of sleep was starting to make itself felt in his aching arms and legs. His head throbbed, making him realise he hadn't had any coffee in ages.

'And why?' she adds, not quickly enough. 'I thought they liked you!'

'Bastards,' he whispered. 'The fucking little shits. I'll kill them.'

'Now, don't go doing anything rash, Matt.'

'Don't do anything rash!' He turned on her, and she took a

step backwards. 'What the fuck am I supposed to do? I came here, in good faith, thinking I could *help* these bloody kids! Thinking I could make their fucking lives *better*!'

'I think you need to take a few deep breaths, Matt.' Ella held up both her hands. 'I realise this is a difficult time for you, and the thing to do is to avoid over-reacting to anything.'

Matt turned slowly to look at her, saw her physically recoil. He felt his fists curling, clenching, whitening. She took a step backwards.

Then he looked away from her, turned and stormed back into the school, punching the swing doors open so hard that they slammed into the corridor wall, taking a chunk out of the plaster.

'Barclay.'

Ben jumped to his feet, crushing the half-smoked cigarette under his heel as the door to the boiler room slammed shut.

A tall, familiar figure was framed in the half-light at the top of the stairs.

Ben relaxed. 'Shit, Collins,' he said, 'you gave me a fright. I thought it was a bloody teacher. I was about to have a fag.'

Collins, watching Ben intently, walked over to him, flipped a cigarette from his own packet and lit it. In the dimness of the boiler room, the flare lit his face a demonic orange for a moment.

'Go ahead,' Collins said, offering the packet to Ben. 'I ain't stopping you.'

Ben grinned, shrugged. 'It's all right,' he said. 'Actually, I ought to get out of here. It's registration in two minutes.'

The muffled sound of a bell, echoing through the

corridors above. Scraping chairs, slamming doors, thundering feet.

Collins lifted a finger, pointing up. 'Registration,' he said, blowing a jet of smoke into Ben's face.

Ben nodded, relieved. He took a step forward. 'Better go,' he said, eyes watering, trying not to cough.

'No.'

Collins's hand was there, on his chest, giving him just enough of a shove to stop him in his tracks.

'Yeah, yeah, funny man.' Ben grinned, gave Collins a playful punch in return. 'Come on, mate, we'll get seriously done if we're seen down here.'

The floor disappeared from under Ben's feet, and he suddenly felt his back slammed against the wall. The breath was knocked from him and his stomach and bowels gave a lurch. Collins's ugly, squashed face was centimetres from his own, and Collins's sinewy hands were gripping his tie firmly, preventing him from moving.

'Gaz,' Ben croaked. 'Come on, enough, mate.'

'You know, I like it down here,' Collins hissed. 'Nice and quiet. Nobody ever comes down here.'

'Yeah, nice one, mate. Can we talk about this later?'

Ben met Collins's stare as the bigger boy moved his face even closer. Millimetres away.

'Leave off, Collins, you poof,' Ben joked. 'Hey!' He raised his voice. 'Bender alert! Backs to the wall, boys, he's trying to snog me!'

Collins, who wasn't laughing, tightened his grip on Ben's collar. 'I don't like people who screw me over, Barclay,' he said.

'Shit, nor do I, mate. Tell me who it is and we'll go and put the fear of God into them.'

Collins grinned. He twisted Ben's tie. Ben felt the constriction take hold, felt real fear rising in his stomach now as his breathing became more difficult.

He was going to have to do something. Maybe kick Collins in the shins. Or knee him in the balls. Problem was, he knew how tough he was. Knew what he could take. There would only be a second, or maybe half a second, to capitalise on the initial shock, and then he'd really have to pull something out of the hat. Smack him against the wall, maybe. Or against the boiler pipes.

Collins loosened his grip.

'All right, Benny-boy,' he said with a crooked smile. 'Keep your fucking hair on. Remember who's boss, that's all.' He pulled Ben's tie straight, tweaked his ear and gave his arm a punch that was slightly too heavy to be properly playful.

'Yeah,' Ben croaked, rubbing his neck. 'Thanks, mate.'

He worried too much. Collins just wanted to remind him who was in charge, that was all. Bit of throwing his weight around. Well, Ben could cope with that.

Collins slapped his back, almost making him choke. 'C'mon, let's get upstairs.'

Ben nodded, feeling his heart rate slowing. He headed up, just a couple of steps in front of Collins.

'By the way,' Collins said. 'Your sister. Isobel. She's at the primary school, ain't she? Year Four?'

Ben stopped, turned, narrowed his eyes. 'Yeah. What of it?'

The aches in his neck, arm and ear all seemed to vanish into nothingness, swamped by a new and urgent sensation, a deep, gnawing anxiety deep within him.

Collins shrugged. 'Nothing.' He folded his arms, gave Ben his evil, cracked smile again. 'No, nothing's gonna happen to little Izzy. Just as long as you're a good boy, Benny.'

Ben stared deep into Collins's small, hard eyes. 'What?'

'Long as you're a good boy and report back to Moretti, like you're meant to, that there ain't nothing going on. That me and my boys are keeping our noses clean, and she ain't got nothing to worry about.'

Ben felt as if his stomach had turned to liquid. His heart was thudding like a wild animal throwing itself against the walls of its cage.

'I dunno what you mean,' he said.

Collins shoved him, making him take a step upwards. 'Course you do, Benny-boy. You think I'm fucking stupid? You think I'd let you into my team without knowing exactly what the fuck you've been up to all along? That's the mistake people make in this dump, Bender. They think I'm stupid. Well, I ain't.'

Ben moved back down the step so that Collins's face was on a level with his own. 'You or any of your brain-dead thugs touch my little sister and I'll kill you, Collins. I swear I'll bloody *kill* you.'

'Big talk, Benny-boy.' Collins folded his arms. 'I'd like to see you try. You fucking little posh Millmount bastard.'

Ben didn't even think. He wasn't even sure what he did with his legs, but he was aware of looping one of them round a startled Gary Collins, flipping backwards with a sudden, instinctive move and shoving him at the same time. Collins lost his footing instantly and half staggered, half fell down the boiler-room steps. He crashed into a bench of workmen's tools, sending them flying.

Ben pressed home the advantage immediately. He was on top of Collins, his hands around the bigger boy's throat.

And then the world flipped, and his stomach imploded. Ben realised Collins had physically levered him off with both booted feet. The floor, cold and hard and painful, slammed into Ben's back, and now Collins was standing over him, grinning evilly.

Time stood still. Dust hung in the air.

Collins grabbed him by the lapels and hauled him up.

'After school tomorrow, Benny-boy. Top of the field. We *finish* this.'

And he spat – a big, evil, sticky ball of phlegm, right in Ben's face – before turning around and crashing his way to the top of the stairs.

Ben followed, at a sedate pace. But he was shaking so hard he could barely force his legs to climb the steps.

Ella, with Isobel in tow, threw the last pack of frozen peas from the conveyor belt into her bag.

'Mum, I want one of these.' Isobel was brandishing a hideous plastic scythe which she'd picked up from the tacky Hallowe'en display beside the till.

'No. Put it down.'

'One of these, then,' cried Izzy, swinging a glowing pumpkin.

'Isobel, put it *down* and come and help me with this.'

Typical, Ella thought. Our ancestors lay awake, paralysed with the fear that evil spirits walked abroad to claim their souls. We, on the other hand, get kids in bin-liners and pointy hats demanding sweets with menaces. And that's progress.

'That's fifty-eight nineteen, please,' said the pale young man on the till.

She rummaged for her purse. 'Izzy, stop swinging on that rack,' she snapped.

'I'm *not*,' said Isobel with a scowl.

'Yes, you were. I saw you swinging.'

'I want a Mars bar.'

'Well, you're not having one. Especially not if you say *I want*.'

Lunchtime wasn't ideal, but she hated coming after work, with the schoolkids all hanging round nicking CDs and chocolate and sniggering at her, so she had opted to shop on her first day off this week. Being part-time had its compensations. She could have done without Isobel, but they had just come from her dental appointment round the corner, so it was easier to keep the girl with her for now.

Ella was still frantically rummaging in her handbag for her purse. 'Sorry. Just a moment.' She tried exchanging a complicit smile with the youth, but his pudding-face was unresponsive.

'I *want* a Mars bar! You're so *horrible*!' Isobel aimed a sharp kick at the Hallowe'en display and it collapsed in a clattering heap of broomsticks, plastic masks and pumpkins.

'Pick those up! *Now!*' Ella, her face blazing with embarrassment, finally found her purse and handed over her card.

Isobel snorted. 'I'm not picking them up. Someone else can pick them up. It's what they're paid for, isn't it?'

'Don't be such a *nasty* little girl.' She grabbed Isobel's wrist and tried to give her a hefty smack on the bottom, just like she used to when she was a disobedient toddler, but the girl broke free before Ella's palm could impact.

'Don't you hit *me*.'

The tone of angry challenge was new. Ella was so shocked by it that she wasn't aware, at first, that the boy on the till had swiped her card three times to no avail.

'Sorry, missus. Ya got another one?'

'I'm sorry, *what*?' Ella straightened up, hands on hips.

'It ain't workin'. Ya got another one?'

'Another one? Yes, of course I've got another one. I always carry an extra bank card around in a secret compartment of my handbag.' It dawned on her that he didn't realise she was being sarcastic. 'No,' she sighed, spreading her hands, 'I haven't. What's the bloody problem?'

'It's rejecting your card. Sorry. Have ya got cash?'

She pulled her purse open. A few coins, one note. Enough to cover less than half the shopping in the bags in front of her. 'Oh, for God's sake. This is ridiculous. Get me the manager.' She moved the shopping to a nearby chair to let the impatient woman behind her have her turn.

There followed five more minutes of embarrassed standing around, during which she had to do even more chiding of a surly, wall-kicking Isobel. Then, a girl in her twenties emerged from a back room, wearing a yellow apron with a badge saying 'Kayleigh'.

'Is there a problem?' she asked perkily.

'I asked to see the manager,' Ella pointed out tersely.

'Yes, that's me.'

'Good God. Really?... Right, OK, um... Kayleigh. This *youth* here is claiming his machine won't accept my card. Can

I suggest you try putting it through a different machine? There's absolutely no reason why there should be a problem.'

'Could I see the card, please, madam?' Kayleigh asked with a smile. Ella handed the card over with bad grace, and the girl disappeared to a make a telephone call at the back of the shop.

'I don't want to be here,' said Isobel crossly.

'Isobel, you have me confused with someone who gives a damn. Sit down, shut up and stop kicking the wall, or I will kick you. *Hard.*'

Five, ten more minutes passed. The bag with the frozen items in was already steaming slightly on the chair. Isobel sat cross-legged on the floor, sulking.

The girl Kayleigh – Ella still couldn't think of her as the manager – reappeared with a sad, slightly sympathetic expression.

'I'm sorry, madam,' she said, 'but your bank has invalidated this card.'

'What? You *are* joking?'

'I'm afraid not. This card isn't valid for transactions. Do you have any alternative means of payment today? Cash, cheque?'

'Cheque,' said Ella in relief. 'I've got a cheque book.' She tore open her handbag again.

'We'll need a separate cheque guarantee card, if you have one.'

She stopped, snapped her handbag shut. 'That's my cheque guarantee card as well,' she said, pointing to the rejected piece of plastic.

'I'm afraid, in that case, I'll have to ask you to pay in cash.'

Kayleigh tilted her head on one side and smiled indulgently.

'Oh, Christ. Is there a cashpoint round here?'

'There's one on the precinct.' She pointed out into the Hub.

A mental picture floated into Ella's mind, one which gave her a headache and made her want to flop to the floor like a puppet with its strings cut. The Hub's one cashpoint, which they'd had to walk past to get to Priceworth, had its glass smashed and a large, evil-looking crowbar sticking out of it. The nearest one now, she realised, was round the other side of Renaissance, about a mile away – and there was no guarantee it would be working.

'I'll pay for what I can,' she said. 'Let me sort things out.' She tore open one of the plastic bags, started pulling out anything which they didn't need immediately.

'I *want* a *Mars* bar!' Isobel wailed, thumping the floor with her fists.

That was it.

'*Oh, for God's sake, Isobel!*' Ella screamed.

She picked up the dismembered bag of shopping and hurled the entire lot on the floor.

The manageress, startled, jumped aside, but not quickly enough to avoid a bag of frozen peas, whose contents skittered across the floor in all directions. Ella hauled Isobel up by the corner of her school jumper and, this time, smacked her hard before she could wriggle free, once on the bottom and once round the ear.

The girl's screams shook the glass in Priceworth's windows.

'*You are not! Having! A bloody! Mars Bar!*' Ella shouted, her face livid with rage. '*Not now, not ever! Do! You Under! STAND?*'

'Let go of me!'

Isobel tried to move away, but Ella grabbed her by the upper arm, squeezing her hard so she couldn't escape. 'For Christ's sake, I have to put up with disgusting, rude *kids* all day at work. I do not expect to get cheek from you as well! *Do you understand?*'

'You're a bloody COW!' Isobel screamed.

A second later, Ella felt a sharp, angry pain in her hand as a set of small teeth buried itself there. She gasped, let go – and Isobel wrested herself away, ripping her school jumper in the process.

'Isobel!' Ella yelled. 'Come here!'

Isobel grabbed a handful of chocolate bars from the child-level display and stuck her tongue out at her mother.

Ella saw that the manageress, picking herself up off the floor amid the frozen peas, was signalling to one of her burly colleagues. Oh, *bollocks*, she thought.

'I *hate* you!' Isobel yelled, her ear still crimson from Ella's smack. 'I don't want you, I want Daddy. Why did you have to bring us here to this...this shit-hole?'

'Izzy!' Ella hissed through gritted teeth.

People all around were murmuring, pointing. An old couple at the next till were shaking their heads and saying something about children today and how people shouldn't have kids if they couldn't control them.

'It's what you always say! It's a *shit-hole*!' Isobel clearly relished the effect her words were having. To Ella's embarrassment, she turned to the people on the next till. 'She does, you know. And she says it's full of scum, and...and scroungers and criminals.'

'Izzy. Darling.' Ella lunged for her, tried to grab her arm again, but the girl was backing towards the revolving doors with her haul of confectionery.

'No! I *hate* you! You've ruined my life!'

And she turned and ran, pushing her way past the shoppers, out of the revolving doors and into the precinct.

'Jesus Christ.' Ella felt a hot, angry flush swamping her and, for a second, was tempted to let her run. But it took over. That old instinct. She tipped her purse out, threw a handful of change at the manageress without looking at it. 'Sorry,' she said breathlessly, and ran from the shop.

Jo Tarrant is emerging from the school gates when she sees it happen.

She pauses at the crossing. She's looking for something in her bag, pulling out old bus tickets, glucose sweets and tissues, plunging her hand deep and swearing.

She looks up.

Images flash across her eyes. The group of Year Ten boys by the newsagent's, not even bothering to hide their cigarettes when they see her coming.

High above, a vapour trail in the blue-grey sky, drawn by a silver dart whose shape still makes her shudder.

Rounding the corner, hooting its horn at the group of boys, comes a battered red Ford Escort driven by a shaven-headed lout, one hand on the roof and rap thudding from the speakers.

Up ahead of Jo, a small figure is running along past the row of shops, eyes ahead, not looking round. A girl with brown curls, in a Parkfield Primary uniform, sensible shoes going flap-flop, flap-flop as she tears along the pavement, running away from something, running so hard it's like she needs to get away more than anything else in the world.

And there, about fifty metres behind her and calling to the girl, is that woman – Ms MacBride, Mrs Barclay, Ella, whatever.

Jo sees the Ford Escort take the corner with a roar and a screech, and the air is filled with pungent fumes.

The primary-school girl, not stopping to look or think, runs out on to the crossing.

With a zigzag of red and a scream of brakes – or is it Ella Barclay screaming? – the car tries to swerve.

And Jo, her heart pounding, feels her bag tumbling – purse, tickets, sweets, tissues all scatter and fall as if in slow motion – as she tries to clear the distance.

There is a loud *smack* as Jo's handbag hits the asphalt.

A second later, there is only silence.

Jo stops, teeters on the kerb, unsure what to do.

The driver of the Escort, with his rap still stuttering from his speakers, flings a door open and stalks to the other side of the road, where Ella, crouched down, is sobbing uncontrollably, tightly holding on to her young daughter.

The girl, who had jumped back on to the pavement just in time, is pale, shaking, but unharmed.

'Can't ya fuckin' control ya fuckin' kids, lady?' bellows the baseball-capped youth. 'She nearly ran out in frunna me then. Almost adder over the bonnet, ya stewpid fuckin' cow.'

'Oh, shut up,' says Ella quietly, and buries her face deep into the shoulder of her daughter's school jumper.

'Some fuckin' people,' the yob comments to Jo as he stamps

back to his car and slams himself back behind the wheel. 'Shu'n't fuckin' be allowed out.'

'It wasn't her,' Jo hears herself pointing out, quite calmly. 'You were driving far too fast. If you'd hit her, it would've been your fault.'

The youth spits out of the window at Jo and invites her to do something biologically impossible. The rap is amplified another two notches, and the car leaps off again with a roar and a rattle, heading into the distance, climbing the hill back into Upper Parkfield with unchanged disregard for life and limb. The boys by the lamppost are laughing and pointing.

Jo looks both ways, then hurries to the other side of the road.

'Is she OK?' she asks Ella, and for a fraction of a second, she has placed a hand on the other woman's shoulder.

Ella looks up, her face twisted and smeared and red, and nods for a second. She wipes her nose with the back of her hand, smiles gratefully. Then she continues sobbing, clutching her precious daughter, who is now crying as well.

OK, OK, Jo thinks, feeling her own heartbeat returning to normal. So it was a shock, but it's all right now. Nobody got hurt. Anyone would think the bloody child had actually been run over. And yet here's Ella, still crying about something which hasn't happened.

Jo, now more embarrassed than concerned, hands Ella a handkerchief.

She turns away slightly, so she doesn't have to see, and goes to pick up the scattered contents of her handbag.

CHAPTER TWENTY-TWO

That's When I Think Of You

Matt Ryder was the first to spot the fight.

He was piling books into his briefcase at the end of the day, ready to scoot downstairs for his after-school History Society, when he caught sight of the boisterous crowd at the top of the field.

He'd been so drained and exhausted these past few days that he thought at first he might be imagining it. A hallucination brought on by lack of sleep.

Matt blinked, rubbed his eyes. No – they really were there. There were about forty kids, he thought, baying and clapping, waving fists and scarves at something going on behind the barrier of their bodies.

'What's happening up there?' he asked.

Kate from Music squinted across the two hundred yards of muddy field. 'Looks like a fight,' she said dismissively, finishing her mug of tea and hoisting her bag on to her shoulder.

'*Shit.*' Matt slammed his bag down. 'Come on, let's sort it out.'

'Are you kidding?' She snorted with derision as she headed

for the door. 'I've got my yoga class.'

'But it's a bloody *fight*!'

'You get too involved, Matt. It's a turf war. Let the little shits kill each other.'

Open-mouthed, Matt watched her go.

He cast his eyes around the bustling staffroom, realising that everyone else was doing their best to ignore him. Then his eyes alighted on a familiar burly figure sorting through his pigeon-hole. Bill Hollis. Of course. Mr Old School, bastion of Seventies values. Just what he needed right now.

Matt gathered his resolve and strode towards him.

'Bill, looks like a fight up on the top field. I need back-up. Will you come and help me sort it out?'

Bill Hollis looked up, his expression more interested than outraged. He seemed to consider the request for a minute, much as he would if Matt were offering him a cup of tea. Then his bushy salt-and-pepper moustache twitched like a rabbit's whiskers.

'Why not?' he said with relish. 'Long time since I got the chance to bang any heads together.'

He pulled on his thick sheepskin coat, the one which Matt always thought made him look like a football manager. Matt, conversely, took off his denim jacket and rolled up his sleeves. He threw the jacket over a nearby chair, then nodded.

'Lead on, boy,' said Hollis eagerly, cracking his knuckles in readiness.

As they hurried up the muddy field, several of the yelling pupils saw them coming and started to nudge each other and point. Nobody made any attempt to disperse, or even to look sheepish for being there.

'Looks like there's just two of 'em,' panted Hollis, red-faced as he tried to keep up with Matt's long strides. They could see the scuffling figures on the grass, now, a whirlwind of kicks and punches, rolling over and over as they fought for supremacy.

Matt nodded, eyes straight ahead, determined. 'I'll get the big one,' he said. 'You pull the other one out.'

'Right you are,' said Bill Hollis, chortling with glee as they advanced. 'God, this takes me back. Used to be able to give the fuckers a clip round the ear, y'know, back in the good old days. That'd soon put a stop to all of this bloody nonsense. Political correctness, that's what I blame. And the flaming nanny state.' He slammed a fist into his palm. 'Let's teach the little shits a lesson.'

A group of about ten large boys were at the front of the pack, waving their fists and chanting, 'In the 'ead! In the 'ead!' Their reaction on seeing Mr Ryder and Mr Hollis storming into the fray was to break into a spontaneous, sardonic round of applause, accompanied by jeers.

Matt piled in first. He wasn't surprised to see that the bigger boy was Gary Collins. He grabbed Collins by the collar, jerking him upwards and almost pulling him off-balance. Spitting, swearing and snarling, Collins flailed his arms and broke free. Matt pulled him back, but Collins slammed his shoulder into him. That winded him for a moment, making him stagger backwards.

Collins launched himself at his opponent again – but Bill Hollis already had the other boy in a firm arm-lock.

'Let me go!' the boy was screaming in insane rage. He lashed out with his feet, landing a kick in Gary Collins's groin.

As Collins doubled up with a bellow of pain, Matt Ryder, wincing, realised he recognised the boy. He knew the muddy, sweat-soaked, tomato-red face beneath the tangle of black hair.

'Barclay,' he said, clenching his fists and shaking his head.

The boy was struggling furiously, but Matt noted with satisfaction that Bill tightened his grip and didn't let him go. Bill had once boasted, Matt recalled, that nobody had ever fought free of one of his arm-locks.

Ben Barclay spat.

Matt ducked the sizzling bolt of phlegm just in time.

'Oh, dearie, dearie me, Barclay,' said Matt Ryder softly. 'You've done it now.' He raised his voice, turning on the crowd of onlookers. 'All right, you lot, show's over, yeah? Get yourselves home or you're all in detention, right?' He looked down at Collins, who was still on his knees, writhing in agony. 'And Collins, don't be a big girl. Get up.'

There was a ripple of derision from the onlookers.

'Sir, you're so *masterful*,' called a girl's voice.

'Ooh, you're scary, sir!' added another.

Matt blanched. He felt the playing field tilting under his feet, and clenched his fists. Any second now, he was going to punch someone himself.

'*All right, enough!*' Bill Hollis's sergeant-major voice boomed out, echoing off the cliff of the school buildings as if amplified by a megaphone. He let Barclay go, shoving him aside. Matt thought the boy would make a run for it, but he didn't. There was a sudden, palpable silence as Hollis strode forward, his stocky body exuding menace. 'There's nothing to see any more! You have five seconds to get yourselves off home, you bunch of vultures. Starting now. *Five!'*

Several of the girls hoisted their bags and began to slink off. Others followed, shaking their heads and looking over their shoulders. The boys looked nervous, but nobody wanted to be the first to comply.

'*Four!'* Hollis bellowed.

Some of the boys, too, were now breaking off from the pack.

The crowd of bigger louts stood their ground, laughing and chewing, until Hollis looked them squarely in the eye.

'*Three!'*

That was enough. They'd stayed long enough to show their bravado, but at the end of the day, people didn't argue with Hollis. He was about the only member of staff who was actually feared.

'*Two!'* bellowed Hollis.

The boys turned, albeit with a marked show of reluctance, and headed back down the field towards the gate. A couple of them straggled, lingered a few metres away, laughing and pointing at the muddy, tattered figures of Ben Barclay and Gary Collins. However, Bill Hollis only had to advance a few steps to make them pick up their pace and disappear towards the main gate.

'One,' Hollis said quietly, with an air of satisfaction, and slammed a meaty fist into his palm again.

Matt, who had been watching this impressive display with an increasing sense of powerlessness, now rounded on the nearest target – Ben Barclay.

'You really are in trouble now, Barclay,' he said through gritted teeth.

Ben rubbed a hand across his forehead, smearing trails of mud and blood. He folded his arms across his ripped school shirt and nodded down at Collins. 'Oh, yeah? What about him, sir? He's the one who's been pinching dinner money from little kids who can't fight back.'

'Oh, so you decided you'd be Robin Hood, did you, Barclay? How public-spirited of you.'

'Just thought it was about time he picked on someone who'd give him a run for his money. *Sir*.' Ben grinned insolently.

Matt extended a finger at Ben's grinning face. 'Nobody makes fun of me, Barclay. I'll have you excluded for this.'

Ben laughed derisively. 'See if I care, Ryder. This place is a fucking Borstal. You're welcome to it.'

Matt actually took a step backwards as if he had been punched. He felt fury coursing through his veins, a fury born of frustration and anger and impotence. 'You think you're too good for this place, don't you? You and your damn *mother*.'

Ben took a step forward. 'What the hell do you mean?'

A firm hand thumped on to Matt's shoulder. Bill Hollis.

Matt realised Hollis was making it look like a gentle gesture of support, but there was no mistaking the iron grip of the older man's fingers, pulling him back, slowly but firmly. At the same time, Hollis had rounded on Ben Barclay, one finger extended, until the boy unclenched his fists and took a step backwards.

'All right, Mr Ryder,' Bill Hollis said, his voice uncharacteristically soft. 'Why don't you go and inform Ms Moretti about this...incident? I'll keep my eye on these two young delinquents.'

For a moment, Matt hesitated.

Bill Hollis glared up at him, narrowing his eyes. 'This needs to be sorted out through the proper channels, Mr Ryder. I'm all right here. You go and get Ms Moretti.' Bill opened his eyes wide. '*Now*, please,' he said, and his tone was unmistakable.

Matt Ryder felt his fists and his jaw slowly relaxing. He met Barclay's cool, insolent gaze and reminded himself that the boy was going to be punished.

Whatever happened.

'Yes,' he said, rubbing a hand across his tired eyes. 'Yes, of course, Mr Hollis. I'll go now.'

And he set off towards the main school building again, feeling Ben Barclay's mocking gaze on his back all the way.

Isobel folded her arms and scowled, staring at the stain on Miss Thompson's classroom wall. She kicked her legs back and forth and refused to look at Miss Thompson, who was asking her the same question over and over.

She didn't know why Mrs Brooks, the classroom assistant, needed to be there either. She was just sitting, watching, with her hands folded on the table and her head tilted to one side.

'Isobel,' said Miss Thompson gently. 'I'm only trying to help you.'

All teachers were old, of course, but Miss Thompson seemed less old than most. She was a Miss, for one thing, and there weren't many of them. Most of the Parkfield Primary teachers were called Mrs, although one or two of them would only answer to Ms as a rule. Isobel wasn't sure what a Ms was.

Miss Thompson had spiky corn-coloured hair, dangly

earrings and big blue eyes, and wore patched jeans and multi-coloured tops. Sometimes she wore T-shirts with the names of bands on, although it was never anybody Isobel had heard of.

'Isobel,' said Miss Thompson, 'I just want to know about this bruise.' She took Isobel's hand in hers and pulled back the torn pullover sleeve to reveal the ugly, yellowing mark on the girl's forearm. 'Did someone...hurt you?'

'No. I did it myself.'

Miss Thompson and Mrs Brooks exchanged a look which Isobel couldn't read.

'Well, the problem with that, Isobel,' murmured Miss Thompson kindly, 'is that I find it hard to believe. I'm sorry, love. I'm not saying you're lying. I just think you might not be telling me the whole truth for some reason.'

Isobel pulled her hand away, pulled the pullover sleeve sharply down. Why did they have to keep getting it out? She didn't want to show the nasty bruise to anybody. If they just left it, then it would go away.

It had only been an accident. That time in the supermarket when her mum had got so cross that she'd grabbed her really hard. That was the day Isobel had almost got run over. And when she called her mum a cow. She was more worried about them finding out about that than about the bruise. Could they put you in care for calling your mum a cow?

If nasty old Ms Harris hadn't seen it when she was getting dressed for gymnastics, then nobody would have known about it anyway. And now, here she was, sitting in a classroom having to talk about it, when she wanted to go home.

'Isobel,' said Miss Thompson. 'You're not in trouble. Please understand that.'

Isobel folded her arms. Silence, she had found over the past few weeks, was a good answer to anything she didn't like.

'Nobody's cross with you. We just want to find out...well, we want to be sure nobody's hurting you.'

What did they mean? She felt confused, angry.

'Is everything all right at home?' Mrs Brooks asked.

She bit her lip.

She knew what they were trying to say.

She wasn't going to tell them anything.

Because if she told them, then it would all come out, and they'd think her mum was no good as a mum, and her dad would never come back. And that would be it. For ever.

It was cold at the gates and Ella had brought a flask of coffee. Donna sidled up next to her and nodded. Before Ella could say anything, Donna had flipped out two cigarettes and had passed one to her. And now, Ella was pouring her coffee and sharing it with Donna.

'What happened to your bloke, Donna? Did he just bugger off?'

Three weeks ago, she'd never have dared ask that. Now, though, she and Donna had developed a wary mutual respect.

'Yeah. Fucker.'

Ella nodded. 'Were you married?'

Donna narrowed her eyes at her, but Ella offered her the coffee cup again, smiled, and Donna took it with an almost friendly nod. 'Yeah,' she said, 'we was married.'

'Divorced?'

Divorced-beheaded-died, divorced-beheaded-outlived, went the sing-song voice in her head. She shut it out.

'Yeah. Two year ago.'

'You got custody of Larissa and Kyle automatically then?'

Donna blew a jet of smoke before answering. 'They don't fuckin'...call it that now. Lawyers. They call it fuckin'...residence.'

'Residence. Right.' Make a mental note of that, thought Ella, and hope I never need to use it.

'But yeah, I mean, they always give it to the mum.' Donna made a dismissive noise. 'The wankers,' she said.

Ella frowned. 'I don't understand. Your bloke – your husband. Did he contest the custody – I mean residence?'

Donna looked at Ella as if she were mad. 'Contest it? Why the fuck would he? He's laughing himself stupid, the prick. Life goes on as fuckin'...normal for him.'

It dawned on Ella – stupidly late, she told herself – what Donna was saying. 'He didn't want the children.'

She narrowed her eyes again. 'I was drinking like a bloody fish back then. Even tried to make meself look a bit more scruffy, like. More like a slapper. They just kept tellin' me what a good mum I was. And I'm there thinking, what the *fuck* do I have to do to get 'em taken off me?'

For a moment, Ella was too shocked to speak.

'I mean, they always land 'em on the mum, don't they? Unless you're a fuckin'...junkie nim...nimbo-wotsit.'

'Nymphomaniac,' supplied Ella.

'That's the bugger. You're right good with words, you. Yeah, you gotta be one of them before they'll give the kids to the dad.'

There was a pregnant silence.

Ella turned towards the gossiping group a few metres away,

then, drawing heavily on her cigarette, eyes stinging, she looked back at Donna again, searching her face for any sign of a joke.

'You really mean it?' Ella said. 'You didn't want them?'

Donna looked at her pityingly. 'I ain't been out at night for six fuckin'...years, have I? Never get a minute's fuckin'... peace, do I? And him, he's with some tart, boozin' it up, livin' the life of fuckin'... Riley. He don't care.'

'But they're your *children*,' Ella protested. She heard her own voice, croaking and choked, wondered why her eyes were prickling. It had to be the cold.

'I know,' Donna said with a shrug. 'Fuckin' joke, innit?'

'No. No, it's awful.'

'You're all right. I mean, your Izzy, she's a good kid, ain't she? Does what she's told, does her fuckin'...homework and that. Don't go out round the fuckin' estate till all hours.'

'I should hope not,' said Ella, shocked at the very idea. 'She's only eight.'

Donna gave her another of those pitying looks which she had come to know so well. 'I've seen 'em so many fuckin'...times,' she said. 'New here, just like you. Give it a year and you'll be busting to get rid of yours an' all.'

'Never,' said Ella defiantly, and ground her cigarette-butt into the pavement with a powerful anger.

No, Isobel and Ben were, astonishingly, not allowed to go and join the other children in the traditional Parkfield activities of throwing stones at cars, taunting pensioners and pushing lighted rags up people's drainpipes. Something had been lost there.

Ella always used to be outside after tea, even on schooldays.

On the street where she had grown up, there would often be five, six or seven children 'playing out', as they called it. It spooled in her mind on sunny, slightly jerky cine-film with no sound (Ella throws a ball to Kerry, who laughs as Jason falls over, while in the background, Natalie wiggles in a bright blue hula-hoop).

There was silence for a few seconds, and then the sound of the school bell rang out across the playground.

'Sorry if it upsets you,' said Donna. 'With...what you told me an' that.'

Ella shrugged. 'It's your life,' she replied awkwardly.

Donna had stopped listening. She was looking over Ella's head into the playground. 'Look out,' she said. 'This might be trouble.'

'Why's that?'

'Thompson. Deputy head.'

Ella turned round and saw the spiky-haired Lisa Thompson bobbing across the playground towards the gates. She was looking a little uncomfortable and rubbing her ear as if she didn't really want to be there. Her eyes were searching the crowd of mums, and suddenly appeared to alight on Ella.

Ella took a step backwards.

'Mrs Barclay?' said Lisa Thompson briskly, holding out her hand.

'Yes?' Ella replied, more sharply than she intended.

'Could I have a quick word inside?' she asked, hugging herself against the cold wind.

'What's the problem? Where's Isobel?' Ella felt panic rising in her stomach.

'I think we should talk about this inside, Mrs Barclay,' said

Lisa Thompson, her smile fixed and her hair rippling lightly in the wind.

Behind her, Ella heard Donna doing an exaggerated, comic wince and a tutting sound.

'It's...really nothing to worry about, Mrs Barclay,' Lisa Thompson explained as they hurried along the corridor. 'Just something we need to talk about. Isobel's just down here with one of our classroom assistants.' Miss Thompson opened the nearest orange door and gestured for Ella to go in.

Ella stepped inside.

The classroom was empty.

One of the desks was lying on the floor, its contents scattered. Ella swooped on the strewn books and picked one up. 'Isobel Barclay, Y4', it said in neat, familiar writing.

Ella whirled around, her heart thudding.

'Is this some kind of joke?' she demanded angrily, but Miss Thompson was still outside the room, talking urgently with a red-faced classroom assistant who had just come sprinting up the corridor.

Ella ran to the door.

'I couldn't stop her,' the classroom assistant was saying, her face hot and flustered. 'She just ran out. She called me an old cow, threw that desk over and ran!'

'Oh, Jesus.' Lisa Thompson cast a helpless look at Ella.

Ella could have responded with any number of sarcastic retorts, but she quelled the panic and anger rising within her and reached for her mobile. 'She won't get far, will she? Everyone knows everyone on this estate.'

'I'll tell the police to keep a look-out,' said Lisa Thompson, hurrying in the direction of the office.

Ella was already striding off, thumbing her mobile into action. It became apparent to her a second later that it was ringing already.

'Yes?' she snapped, as she hurried back out into the grey daylight. She cast her eyes back and forth, scanning the crowds of kids and mums as they dispersed outside the school. 'What?' she said, as it became apparent that the voice on the phone was that of Liz Moretti, and that she wasn't calling about anything to do with Izzy. 'He's done *what*?' she exclaimed. 'Oh, Christ. Liz, I do not *need* this now.'

'...!'

'Well, yes, I know it's very serious, but I've got a bit of a crisis on right now.'

'......?'

'Yes, it is more serious than that, actually.'

'......'

'Liz, they're boys, aren't they? Boys get into punch-ups now and then. Please just sort it out. Give him a bloody detention or something. I *cannot* be there right now.'

She thumbed the mobile off and stood in the middle of the precinct, oblivious to the kids streaming past her, to their shouts and comments. She was *thinking*.

A car, she thought. I need a *car*.

Two minutes later, she was back in the Secondary building, pounding up the steps to the staffroom. It was almost deserted, but a handful of people looked up half interestedly as she burst in. She strode over to the window where Jo Tarrant was deep in conversation with two other teachers.

'Where's Matt?' she interrupted.

They all turned to look at her. Jo closed her eyes slowly and deliberately and put one hand on her hip.

'Actually, Ella, we were having a *conversation* here,' Jo said, not bothering to mask her irritation.

'Where's Matt? Tell me! I need to borrow his car.'

'How the hell should I know?' Jo snapped. 'You seem to know more about where Matt is than I do these days.'

'I think he does History Society tonight,' someone offered.

'Didn't he go and sort out a fight or something?' someone else asked.

Ella tutted in frustration. She didn't have time to track him down. She charged over to the pigeon-holes, knocking over a chair in the process, and, finding Matt Ryder's, began leafing through it in desperation. Nothing. She hurled the papers on the floor.

Then she saw his jacket.

His battered denim jacket was hanging over the back of one of the armchairs. She grabbed it, plunged her hand into one pocket. Nothing. Into the other pocket. Her fingers closed over a key-fob.

She pulled the keys out with a brief growl of triumph and threw Matt's jacket back on the chair. Then she grabbed a piece of paper, plucked a pen from the nearby desk-tidy and scribbled a note. '*Matt. Really sorry, but I've had to borrow the banger. Will bring it back, honest. Dire, DIRE emergency.*'

She was about to put it in his pigeon-hole, then she paused. There was always a chance he wouldn't check it, of course.

She folded the paper in four, ran over to Jo, grabbed her hand and pressed the note into her palm.

'Jo. Will you please, *please* give this to Matt, OK?'

Jo looked from Ella down to the square of paper and back up to Ella again.

'*Please*, Jo! You'll be doing me a big favour.'

'Yeah, yeah. All right.' She slipped it into a pocket, tutting audibly and with undisguised bad grace.

'Thank you.'

'Yeah, you're bloody welcome.' Jo muttered, but Ella was already running from the room.

'Come on, come *on*.'

She is finding the MG heavy going. She doesn't like being this close to the tarmac, and it makes her feel especially insignificant beside the buses and lorries which are thronging the roads now.

She has been driving round and round Parkfield for half an hour. She has to have covered every street on the estate, she thinks desperately.

Where in God's name is Isobel? She can't possibly have got any further, not with Thompson and the other teachers looking for her as well.

The mobile trills.

Where the hell is it? There, on the dashboard.

Heading down the hill, away from the estate, she struggles to control the car with one hand as she reaches for the phone. Still ringing insistently, it is just out of reach.

As Ella indicates to come off the Parkfield road, she stretches for the phone and manages to grab the loop of the strap with her fingertips. And then she looks up to see the bulk of a white delivery van heading straight for her.

* * *

Upstairs, at the staffroom window, Jo Tarrant pressed her nose against the glass and wondered what to do.

She took the note out of her pocket, half unfolded it, then shook her head. She didn't fancy reading it.

Instead, she crumpled it into a tight ball and hurled it into the waste-paper basket. Then she grabbed her jacket, hoisted her bag on her shoulder and headed out of the staffroom, a superior little smile haunting her lips.

On her way down the stairs, she was almost knocked over by a dishevelled man carrying a large, pink cardboard box.

'Hey, watch where you're going!' Jo snapped.

'Um, sorry, sorry.' On the halfway landing, they eyed each other warily.

'Can I help you at all?' Jo asked.

The man looked wildly from side to side. Jo thought he looked a bit crazy, as if he hadn't had much sleep. His dark hair was tousled and his eyes were red-rimmed, and he hadn't had a shave in several days. Jo stared in puzzlement at the box he was carrying, which sported a big, flashy logo made up of two Zs interlocking, next to a cartoon of some Barbie thing or other. She thought it looked vaguely familiar, from Saturday morning kids' TV or something.

'Can I help you at all?' Jo repeated. 'Are you looking for someone?'

'I need to find Ella,' he said, gabbling. 'Do you know where she is?'

Everybody wants Ella, thought Jo sourly. 'Ella MacBride? You've just missed her, mate.' She waved towards the car park. 'Raced off on some mad mission about twenty minutes ago.'

'Oh, *shit*,' he said, and let the big pink box drop on the landing with a loud thud. Then he sat down on it, head in hands, and gazed blankly into the distance.

Jo was starting to have a suspicion. 'Um...do you know Ella, then?' She stuck a hand out. 'I'm Jo Tarrant. I work with her.'

He looked up, smiled bleakly. 'Tom Barclay. I'm Ella's husband.'

Jo grinned, folded her arms. 'Blimey. You took your time. Been round the world and back, have you?'

He glowered at her. 'I don't know what she's told you, but I wouldn't believe half of it if I were you.'

'Well...yeah. Not getting involved, mate. Anyway, I'm sorry, but you've just missed her.'

'Right. So you said.'

He didn't seem about to move.

'Look,' Jo said awkwardly, 'you can't sit there all night. The cleaners need to get round, for one thing.' She leant down, peering at the box. 'What *is* in there, anyway?' she asked.

'It's a Zillah Zim Magic House,' said Tom, looking her in the eye for the first time.

'Oh.' Jo was none the wiser.

'I bet you're sorry you asked, aren't you? Don't worry. If you haven't got kids, you won't understand.'

'Rrright.' Jo decided not to pursue the matter. 'Look,' she said, 'do you fancy a cup of tea in the staffroom?'

He looked up, smiling gratefully. 'Actually,' he said, 'that would be nice.'

* * *

The white van thunders past, almost scraping the MG, blasting her over and over with its horn. The driver is shaking his fist and yelling at her, but Ella, thumbing the phone as she joins the dual-carriageway ringroad, doesn't even bother shouting back.

The little car is picking up speed, now, and she can feel it starting to get a better grip on the road.

She knows it's illegal to use the phone in the car like this, but she doesn't care.

'Yes?'

At first, she doesn't recognise or understand the voice jabbering in her ear. It is one that she feels she ought to know, and yet does not.

'She's what? *Where?*'

'......'

'I'm sorry, you'll have to speak up. Sally who?'

'......'

'Oh, my goodness. Of course. Of course she would. Why the hell didn't I think of that? Is she all right?'

'......'

'Thank you. Thank you so much.'

'......?'

'Yes, yes. Absolutely. I'm on my way now. Thank you. And thank you for getting hold of me so quickly.'

She thumbs the phone off, throws it aside. It hits the passenger seat, bounces, clips the gear-stick and falls to the floor on Ella's side. She doesn't notice.

She has already gone too far around the ringroad, she realises, and the traffic is building steadily now that Cherford's usual three-hour rush-hour is gearing up. Buses, vans, lorries, cars, all of them higher up and bigger than her, and all of them more powerful than her, are making her feel even more vulnerable in the battered sports car.

She eases up a little on the accelerator as she takes a left by the warehouse-flats on the riverside.

Then, joining the flow of traffic out to the west, she heads up on to the three-lane bridge and joins the flyover, ready to hit the route out to the suburbs. Back to Ashington.

The call is from Sally Morrison-Clarke. The woman Ella watched a few days ago with a fluffy pink baby on her shoulder. Sally and Henry, the new owners of 28 Thorpedale Avenue. Sally, this afternoon, happened to look out of the lounge window while feeding the baby, and saw a schoolgirl, silent and sullen, on the swing in the garden. Outraged, she tapped on the window, but the girl ignored her. Only when Sally went outside to confront the girl did she vaguely begin to recognise her, and to realise too that the girl was in a state of distress.

Izzy. Izzy. Izzy.

What the hell have I done?

Ella checks the rear-view mirror and decides to risk overtaking the school bus. Up, up, up the speedometer climbs.

The bus, a great thundering beast with a rusty Seventies chassis, belching smoke in all directions, is not going to give up without a fight.

Ella brings the MG alongside it. She is giving it everything she has got. Come on, *come on.* The road is about to go down to one lane. She has to get past it. Finally, the bus seems to ease back to let her past, and she nips into the space.

Approaching the Westview crossroads, now, the point

where she has to go straight ahead for the Ashington road.

The lights are green.

She steps on the accelerator.

Behind her, the bus looms large and green and ugly in her rear-view mirror. She wishes it would drop back and give her a little more space.

The lights at the crossroads flick to amber.

Fuck this, Ella tells herself, and takes the MG as fast as it can go through the lights.

Leaving the bus behind, she grins in relief, glancing up at the dirty block of green as it drops back in her rear-view mirror.

A half-second later, she looks back at the road in front of her and sees the sleek, white double-decker coach emerging from a side road. Straight in front of her.

She swings the wheel. Slams her foot on the brake pedal.

The brakes, old and worn and unserviced, scream.

And the silver block of the mobile phone is jammed between the brake pedal and the car floor.

The double-decker coach clips the side of the little blue MG, sending the car spinning in a half-circle across the road.

The coach screeches to a halt, while the MG, still propelled by its momentum, smashes bonnet-first into a pillar-box on the verge. Its bonnet erupts, steaming, and the battle-cry sound of a horn booms upwards and outwards into the skies of Cherford.

Behind, the green bus has slammed on its brakes.

Its tyres grip the road

  it is screaming

  its ancient body tries to pull itself back as it closes in on
the MG

  closing in

  the space between it and the helpless, marooned MG

  growing smaller

  closing in

  and smallerandsmallerandssmallerand

CHAPTER TWENTY-THREE

The Dying Days

The room is silent, apart from the steady pulse of a heart monitor.

He is perched on a plastic orange chair beside her bed, his hands clasped so tightly together that they are white. Outside, night has fallen. The city is coming alive, the people are coming together.

The man and the woman are sliding apart.

Something is ending.

'I never meant for any of this to happen. I don't know why it did. Why didn't we do something earlier, Ella? Why didn't we talk?'

Beep.

Beep.

Beep.

'Christ, I don't even know if you can hear me in there. I can't even see your face. Jesus... I came straight away. I did. That girl brought me. Your friend, from the school. Jo. She's really worried.'

Beep.

Beep.

Beep.

'The children are with Bex. I've phoned your mother and she's on her way too. Bloody hell, maybe I shouldn't have told you that. She'll come in here and start plumping up the pillows, I expect.'

Beep.

Beep.

Beep.

'It's dark outside, Ella. I can't see anything, really. Just darkness. If you can hear me, can you just...do something? Move your hand or...something. Anything.'

Beep.

Beep.

Beep.

'I don't know why you had to go to that awful place. I couldn't have lived there, with you and the children. I would have felt like such a bloody failure.'

Beep.

Beep.

Beep.

'You know, I just haven't known what to do with myself since...since Charlotte. Spent the last three years getting drunk with Jeff and talking about women. It's all so fucking meaningless.'

Beep.

Beep.

Beep.

'Ella, please do something. Squeeze my hand.'

Beep.

Beep.

Beep.

'It's even darker out there now. I hate the night. Hate it.'

Be-e-e...p.

'Ella?'

Beeep –

Bip-bip.

'Can someone come?'

Bip –

Beep-bip

'Hello? Hello? Please, somebody! Quickly!'

Beeeeeeeeeeeeeeeeeeeeeeeeeeeeeeeeeeeeeeeeeeeeeeeeeeeeeeeeeeeeeee
eeeeeeeeeeeeeeeeeeeeeeeeeeeeeeeeeeeeeeeeeeeeeeeeeeeeeeeeeeeeeeee
eeeeeeeeeeeeeeeeeeeeeeeeeeeeeeeeeeeeeeeeeeeeeeeeeeeeeeeeeeeeeeee
eeeeeeeeeeeeeeeeeeeeeeeeeeeeeeeeeeeeeeeeeeeeeeeeeeeeeeeeeeeeeeee
eeeeeeeeeeeeeeeeeeeeeeeeeeeeeeeeeeeeeeeeeeeeeeeeeeeeeeeeeeeeeeee
eeeeeeeeeeeeeeeeeeeeeeeeeeeeeeeeeeeeeeeeeeeeeeeeeeeeeeeeeeeeeeee
eeeeeeeeeeeeeeeeeeeeeeeeeeeeeeeeeeeeeeeeeeeeeeeeeeeeeeeeeeeeeeee
eeeeeeeeeeeeeeeeeeeeeeeeeeeeeeeeeeeeeeeeeeeeeeeeeeeeeeeeeeeeeeee
eeeeeeeeeeeeeeeeeeeeeeeeeeeeeeeeeeeeeeeeeeeeeeeeeeeeeeeeeeeeeeee
eeeeeeeeeeeeep.

Bip

CHAPTER TWENTY-FOUR

There Is A Light That Never Goes Out

The sun is a loose, orange blob behind the cityscape, nestling among the clouds like a giant poached egg.

The car Tom is driving is a creaking Vauxhall Astra with rusty hubcaps. It's not old, but not that new either. He brings it to a halt beside the ornate, wrought-iron gates above the city, and turns, smiles at the back seat.

Ben and Isobel are there, side by side, both in a nondescript school uniform of steel-grey jumpers and charcoal trousers and white shirts. They are looking at him expectantly.

'Could you pass me those flowers, please, Bizzy?' Tom asks gently.

His daughter reaches behind her, pulls the big, wrapped bunch of flowers from the parcel-shelf. Tom nods his thanks.

'I won't be long,' he says. 'You'll be all right here, won't you?'

Ben looks at his little sister, who looks back at him, uncertainly at first. Then they nod and turn back to their father.

'Yes,' says Ben. 'We'll be fine.'

Tom shuts the car door behind him as firmly as he can without slamming it. His feet crunch on the gravel as he approaches the gates. They squeak, and leave a powdery red deposit of rust on his hands.

He walks purposefully through the serried ranks of graves. An elderly couple are tending some flowers at one of the gravesides which he passes, but otherwise he sees nobody.

It doesn't take long to find the one he is looking for.

He has been here enough times, after all.

He stays about ten minutes, letting the last rays of the sun sink behind the distant hills, gazing moodily at the clustered, orange clouds. He is thinking how chunky they look, like slabs of orange chocolate or pink Cornish pasties. How solid they seem, and yet in a matter of minutes they will have dissolved, re-formed, scattered.

He smiles sadly, stroking the clean marble of the gravestone in front of him.

Odd, to see his own surname on there. It reminds him that he'll have one of these, one day.

He shakes his head, stands up, hears the gravel crunching loudly in his head as he returns to the gates.

Back at the car, Ben is playing some hand-held computer game and Isobel is just staring moodily out of the window.

'OK?' Tom says, sliding back into the driving seat.

Ben looks up, smiles briefly.

'Izzy?'

She turns, and for a second he looks into familiar eyes. Then they glaze over again, becoming the eyes of a girl heading rapidly into confusion, into womanhood, eyes he cannot reach. She smiles, but there is no depth or warmth to it.

'Yes, Dad.'

'OK. Let's go home.'

He stands at the kitchen sink of the small terraced cottage they now call home. Somehow, the draining board has yet again become encrusted with ground coffee. Well, he knows who to blame for that.

Tom!

Calling his name.

Of course she is.

She's always calling his name, these days. She usually has to call it twice, but by the time she gets to the second time, it sounds as if she has been calling him for half an hour.

Tom, are you there?

He smiles at the way the voice echoes in his head.

He pours a glass of water and makes his way into the dining room.

A tall, dark figure is standing by the french windows, dressed in something black and loose, leaning on what looks like a stick.

'I thought I'd pre-empt you,' he says, leaning against the door-frame. 'Is this what you wanted?'

The figure at the window turns.

'How kind.'

He hears her voice, but does not see her lips move.

She moves quickly over to him. She is propelling herself efficiently, using the crutch she has been given. She is moving much more easily these days, her leg healing fast.

Smiling, she eases herself into a chair with Tom's help, leans the crutch against the table and takes the glass in her left hand. She is not left-handed, but her right hand, unfortunately, is still bound tightly in plaster and a pristine white sling.

'Anything else I can get you?' Tom asks.

'No, thanks... You were late getting back. Did you take the kids somewhere?'

'Oh, no,' he says, sitting at the table and starting to leaf through the newspaper. 'I just went to put some new flowers on Mum's grave.' He looks up at her, smiles briefly. 'It's been a while, after all. I feel I've been neglecting things there.'

'You have,' says Ella. 'Still, look on the bright side. Could have been me in a hole up there too – couldn't it?'

Ironically, it was the worn brakes on Matt Ryder's MG which saved her.

If they'd been efficient, she could well have come to a halt two seconds earlier, right on the crossroads, directly in the path of the oncoming coach. It would have pitched straight into her on the driver's side.

As it was, she took a second longer to brake – a delay added to by the presence of her phone beneath the pedal – and the coach had no more than clipped her, spinning the car off the edge of the road and out of the way of the traffic behind. This included the green Cherford District bus, which was quite unable to stop as quickly as the driver had hoped and ended up juddering to a halt on the other side of the crossroads, thankfully without injuring any passengers.

The first person at the scene of the MG had found Ella gripping the wheel, unable to let go. She was sobbing hysterically, a curtain of blood across her eyes.

A large, ugly gash on her forehead was the source of the blood, one which was later revealed to be deep enough to require stitches, but nothing like as bad as it looked.

And then, somehow, she had lost consciousness in the ambulance.

She had no recollection of anything at all after slamming her foot on the brake pedal and feeling the MG slip from her control. She did not even know how close it had been that night in the hospital when her supposedly 'critical but stable' condition fluctuated, and a brisk, efficient army had surrounded her, hurting her to save her, jolting her body with electricity in order to wrest her back into life.

And back, fighting all the way, she had come.

Bruised, battered, shaken, weakened.

But alive.

She could not imagine what her children, her mother and her husband – yes, even her husband – had been through in those lost hours. She was grateful not to have been aware.

And now, weeks later, with her spirits regained and her body healing, she had to face another problem entirely.

Life had been given back to her.

She now had to decide where Life was going to go.

'Jesus! My fucking *back*!'

Bex thumped the enormous blue stone tub on the front doorstep and emerged from behind a tangle of foliage and fruit. She winced and straightened up, rubbing her lower back.

On the threshold, Tom and Ella stared at what she had brought.

Then they turned and looked at one another, and back to Bex again, who was running a hand through the sweat-soaked spikes of her blonde hair.

'Well?' she said in between gasps. 'You know what it is, don't you?'

Dumbfounded, Ella nodded.

'How did you...' Tom began.

Bex held up both hands, palms flat. 'Don't bother thanking me. Thank Henry and Sally. Those lucky people who got your old house.' She folded her arms, grinned. 'You see, I don't think they know the full picture, but then they wouldn't, would they? Somehow, they've realised that your little plum tree is worth a hell of a lot more to you than it is to them. And when they realised that, they wanted you to have it. Ain't that sweet?'

'You told them,' said Ella, eyes widening in realisation.

Bex shrugged. 'Well, you might say that, babe. I couldn't possibly comment. You remember that time up on the roof?' Ella nodded. 'You were telling me about going back to the house, touching a little bit of the past. Then a couple of days later I found a handful of plum stones in your coat pocket. So I'm a bit smart, me. I put two and two together. Decide to go and, well, be a bit cheeky.' She gestured at the tree. 'And it paid off.'

'How...how did you get them to...?'

Bex spread her hands. 'Hey, I'm persuasive. I can lay it on thick when I want. And anyway, they're nice people.'

'Bex, you're a marvel,' Ella said, and hugged her tightly.

Over Ella's shoulder, Bex gave Tom a superior, mocking look. He had to turn away.

And then, just as a tearful Ella and Bex disengaged, another familiar figure was making his way up the path, waving a four-pack of Stella.

'Hey, John Thomas, as I live and breathe!' Jeff shouted. 'And the lovely Ella. And, good God, it's sexy Bexy. Haven't seen you for ages, love. How you keeping?' Jeff slapped Bex on the bottom and peered down at the plum tree. 'Well, I don't have a tree,' he said apologetically, 'but I do have beer. Will you still let me in?'

Ella nodded at Bex. 'Better ask my landlady.'

Rebecca Lydiard had been in bed with her young accountant friend, Nick, on the day of Ella's car crash. Despite his being a recent recruit into Bex's world, Nick had been left to mind the house while Bex took charge of Ben and Isobel. Tom, after all, could barely be trusted to get himself to the hospital. Bex had slipped into Nick's life with ease, and with the kind of mercurial delight for which she was renowned.

Every man Bex slept with ended up worshipping her, as Ella well knew, but this one seemed to have it worse than most. He did flowers. He did chocolates. He did expensive dinners at the best restaurants in Cherford.

After Bex spent a whole weekend having fervent sex with him – punctuated only by a visit to her recuperating friend in hospital – he asked her to move into his flat. And Bex, to her astonishment, heard herself agreeing. And so it was that Bex found herself in need of some tenants for her house.

'Sure, Jeff,' Bex said. 'As long as you keep your hands to yourself,' she added with a flirty smile.

'I'm sure I'd have to join the queue for a grope, Rebecca. Anyway,' Jeff said to Tom, breaking open a can there and then on the front doorstep, 'got to tell you, mate, I've been discovering the older woman in the past few weeks.' He stepped over the threshold. 'Three things, Thomas, you shouldn't leave too late in life – a pension, a prostate check, and sleeping with a woman who's old enough to be your mother.'

'Why don't you come in, Jeff?' Ella said with a languid smile.

He gave her a peck on the cheek. 'All right, Ella love. You're looking well. As well as can be expected, anyway.'

The telephone rang, saving Jeff from a caustic response. Ella picked it up as Jeff and Tom disappeared into the kitchen, talking animatedly about Joanna Lumley.

'Hello?'

'Ella, darling, it's me.'

'Hi, Mum.' Ella signalled to Bex, who grinned and pulled her up a chair.

'Are you resting? Is he looking after you properly?'

'No, Mum, I've actually been up a ladder fixing the guttering. Then I went out and got the week's shopping for the entire family before putting up some shelves.'

Bex sniggered, signalled that she was going to make some tea. Ella gave her the thumbs-up.

'Well, there's no call for sarcasm, Ella. It's very *low*. It doesn't make you sound modern or clever.'

'No, Mum.'

'Everyone's been asking about you, you know. I saw Helen Sandford the other day. You were in infants' school with her

Robert. You remember little Robbie Sandford? The one with the allergies, who went to Holland to be a farmer.'

'I don't have the slightest recollection of him, Mum.'

'Oh, don't be silly. You used to play doll's houses with his little sister... Annabel, was it? No, Angharad, that's right. She's living somewhere posh down south, now. Got a great job working in the financial sector, I think. Two children and all that long way from her mum. Don't know how she copes.'

Of course, thought Ella. The woman's son is in Holland but it's the daughter somewhere in the Home Counties who shouldn't have moved away, who should be feeling guilty. Nothing changes.

'Anyway, are you looking after Rebecca's house? It was *very* kind of her to put you up at such short notice. I always thought that girl was a bad influence on you, but maybe I've misjudged her. There's a little bit of Christian charity in everyone, it would seem. I hope you're remembering to thank her properly.'

How old am I? Ella wondered.

'Oh, and have you *seen* the television news today? That man saying they're going to be giving primary-school children lessons in how to be lesbians. I thought they'd banned that sort of thing now. I mean, can you imagine? It's no wonder they don't find time to teach them how to read and write, what with having to fill their heads with all this nonsense. I hope you don't have to teach any of that. Still, you're out of that now, aren't you? That teaching lark. I was never sure about it, especially in such a *rough* place. It's an ill wind, as I always say.'

'Sorry, what is?' Ella interjected, but the moment had gone.

'I mean, the more I hear about the world, the more I'm convinced it's all going to pot. It's like waking up one morning and finding that someone's declared that night's going to be called day and day's going to be called night. Just like that, and there's nothing you can do about it. If you try to make a stand, you're between a rock and the deep blue sea. I suppose you think it's all perfectly all right?'

'Er... All what's perfectly all right, exactly?'

'Well, I don't know why I bother. You're obviously not listening. All I can say is, you'll understand when you get to my age.'

'Yes, Mum,' said Ella wearily. 'I'm sure I will.'

And she sank back into the chair, closing her eyes, letting her mother's prattle wash over her.

'Auntie Bex,' said Ben, handing her the spade, 'why do you swear so much?'

Bex grinned. 'Fuck knows,' she said. 'But don't you try it. You'll get chucked out of your new school.'

The three of them – Ben, Isobel and Bex – bent down to examine the hole Ben had dug in the small vegetable patch in the back garden.

Ben wrinkled his nose. 'I wouldn't be bothered,' he pointed out, but he couldn't help smiling as Bex met his gaze.

Auntie Bex was nice, he thought. His friend Will would call her a crazy chick. In fact, she gave him the same sort of feelings as some of the girlfriends Will's dad had to stay. He tried not to look at the low-cut top she was wearing.

Bex pulled her gardening gloves off and threw them aside. 'Oh, come on,' she said. 'It's got to be better than Parkfield.'

She rummaged in the earth, smoothing out the hole. 'Now that's a good hole,' she said. 'My earth's good for fruit. Your mum's tree ought to do well here.'

'How long can we stay here?' asked Isobel.

Bex sighed, smiled. 'Well, to be honest, quite a while, I think. Nick and I are talking about travelling round the world for a year. Get to see a few places before settling down, you know. I've always wanted to visit the Pyramids.'

'One of the Seven Wonders of the Ancient World,' said Ben. 'The only one left standing.' He blushed, feeling he ought to justify himself. 'We did a project on them last year.'

'Blimey. You'd be handy in our pub quiz, mate. Shame you're too young.'

'I can drink Coke,' he argued with a grin.

'They have to let you in first. Still, plenty of time for all that. Shall we get this bugger planted, kids, or what?'

Bex hefted the tree and they eased it into the earth. Ben felt a thrill, as if they were connecting with the planet itself; adding to the landscape, creating something new. It was the first time he'd ever done that.

They smoothed the earth around it. Isobel squatted down and patted the rough trunk of the tree. 'Take care, Charlotte,' she said in a soft voice.

Ben hefted the spade over his shoulder in what he hoped was a macho pose, and went to stand next to Bex. A light drizzle had started to fall, hazing the air.

'Do you suppose they're OK in there?' he asked, nodding to the dark figures of his parents, who were having a lively, hand-waving conversation in the illuminated window of the kitchen.

'They'll be fine,' she said. 'Give them time.' She glanced

down at him. 'So, have you forgiven your dad?'

Ben was hoping nobody would ask that, because he wasn't sure yet if he knew the answer. He shrugged, and narrowed his eyes.

Auntie Bex half smiled and put an arm round his shoulders. He tried not to go red, and tried even harder not to look at her cleavage.

'It's OK,' she said. 'You don't need to answer that yet.'

'I don't think he's—' Ben glanced at Isobel, but she was busy peering round the tree and murmuring softly to it. 'I don't think he's a *bastard*, if that's what you mean.' He said the word self-consciously, as if it were from another language.

Auntie Bex smiled wryly. 'No,' she said with a sigh, 'he's not a bastard. He's just a bloke.'

Ben narrowed his eyes at her. 'What's that supposed to mean?' he asked.

'You'll find out. And not before long, I expect.'

'You two said a rude word.' Isobel scowled up at them. 'I heard you.'

'Do your mum and dad still have that swear-box?' asked Auntie Bex. 'Used to cost me a bloody fortune when I came round.'

'No.' Ben smiled at the memory. 'Mum had to raid it to pay the milkman off when we moved from Thorpedale Avenue. I've not seen it since.'

'Just as well,' Bex murmured, gazing at the animated figures in the window. 'They'd probably find themselves using it quite a lot in the next few weeks. Come on – let's go back in before we get soaked.'

CHAPTER TWENTY-FIVE

Definitely Maybe

Finally, there is this.

'Why did you fuck her?' asks Ella.

It catches him by surprise. Why does she have to bring that up? Why now?

They are up above the city in the Millennium Park, and it is a lovely Sunday afternoon in early February. It is cold but bright, and the playground is swarming with children. Ben and Isobel have rounded up enough for a game of five-a-side football on the vast expanse of grass. Ella is sitting delicately on a park bench, a magazine held in her good hand. Her eyes are protected with sunglasses; she has seen little daylight these past few weeks. Tom is surveying the distant woodland with his binoculars.

'Who?' he asks, not turning round.

He knows who, but he has to say that; he's playing the game, because he has never formally been accused of adultery and has never actually had to deny it, even though they both know it took place.

'You know perfectly well who I mean, you git. That...woman. The one with the dreadful taste in art and the unnecessary amounts of bangle.'

'Oh, her.' He lowers the binoculars to polish them.

'Yes. Her. You know, I often wondered if it might be her. The way you said her name was a bit of a giveaway, or it would have been if I'd been paying attention. Pausing. Checking yourself. Making sure you hadn't betrayed anything.' She sighs. 'I mean, you mentioned lots of people, all the time, but with her there was always that little...breath. Like a look over the shoulder. Inaudible sigh of relief. That sort of thing.'

Silence for a moment.

'So come on,' she says again. 'Why?'

Deep breath, Tom, he thinks.

'Usual sort of crisis, I suppose. Someone being in the right place at the right time. Tapping into this sort of...directionless wandering I've been feeling.' He smiles sadly. 'A bit about you and me, a bit about Charlotte. I reckon some of it was just post-September 11th millennial angst.'

'Oh, for God's sake. That's such crap, Tom. You're the only man I know who could blame his infidelity on international terrorism. As excuses go, that's right up there with The Dog Ate My Homework, that is.'

Down the hill, a blonde mother tugs on the hand of a reluctant toddler, trying to get her to climb back to the path after investigating some flowers. It doesn't escape Tom's notice that the woman has quite incredible breasts underneath a very tight sweater.

He puts the binoculars back to his eyes again.

'Anyway, it's digging up the past. We said, when we moved into Bex's, that we weren't going to do that. Going to move on, we said.'

'Yeah, I know.' Ella sighs. 'I just didn't want you to think you were getting away with it that easily.' She folds her arms, puts her head on one side. 'And I don't think you've said sorry. No, in fact, I'm absolutely bloody certain you haven't said sorry.'

'I did.' He rubs his nose, feeling defensive. 'I spent ages talking to the children.'

'Yeah, and...?' She sounds unnecessarily accusing, he thinks.

'Oh, right.' His gaze meets hers briefly. 'I'm sorry, Ella.'

She gestures – a multiple sweep of the palm, like a magician. Inviting more. Eyebrows up, head on one side.

He sighs. 'OK, OK. I'm sorry... I'm sorry I ran out on the situation. That I left you on your own among the Great Unwashed. All right? Is that good enough?' He pauses, has an ironic thought. 'You seemed to manage, though. You seemed to settle in quite well.'

'Oh, thanks, Tom. In fact, I'm thinking of getting a job in Priceworth and changing my name to Sharon.' She sighs, shakes her head. 'Well, it was like getting blood out of a stone, but I suppose it's better than nothing.'

'You slept with someone too.'

He keeps his voice and the binoculars level. He's not sure how he dares, but he'll give it a try. See what she says.

'I did?'

It is definitely a question.

'Oh, I don't know his name,' Tom murmurs. 'I don't even

know anything about him, beyond the fact that he was at some conference you went to about four years ago.'

'You think what you like, Tom. I've not got a clue what you mean.'

He thinks he hears her voice change tone; almost as if she has relaxed for a second, as if she were holding her breath, tense for a moment, and has now allowed herself to relax. Surely that cannot be the case. He dismisses it.

'Of course you haven't.' He allows himself a superior smile, then lowers the binoculars again. 'So do you want a divorce?'

She snorts. 'Good God. Not particularly. Why, do you?'

'Not particularly,' he agrees.

'Good.'

'So let's leave it, then,' he says.

'What?'

'Referring to...stuff. If you want shot of me, then fine, dig it all up, smear it all around, kick me till I bleed. But if you don't – and if we want to make things right again for those two little precious ones over there – then leave it, OK?'

She does not answer.

'You've had the chance to boot me into touch,' he goes on. 'And I'd have understood if you had. I really would. But no, you chose...this. Whatever this is going to be. And if you choose this, you give up the right to the moral fucking high ground, right?'

She still does not answer.

'Right?' he persists.

'I'll think about it, Tom,' she says with acidity.

There is another long silence.

'Look, things aren't just going to go back the way they

were, Tom. Just because we're still married.'

'I know that.' He's annoyed that she should feel the need to say that. Trying to make sure she is still in control of the conversation. It's all on her terms.

'We've got an awful lot of thinking to do.'

'We've got two children,' he says. 'I don't want them to get hurt any more.'

'OK, so don't bugger off at the first sign of trouble. That's really what they need, isn't it, a father who's spineless?'

'I wasn't spineless.'

'Oh, no. You just thought you needed some "space". Well, guess what, Tom, so did I. Except I wasn't fucking well going to get any.'

'I would have come back,' he says.

'Oh, yeah. Eventually. When I'd worked myself stupid and got us a house somewhere slightly more salubrious than Parkfield, you mean. Then you'd have ventured to poke your nose back round the door and remember that you had two children, would you?'

'I never forgot them.' He knows there is anger in his voice.

She is quiet for a few moments.

He tries to see if he can change the subject.

'You know there's a house for sale round the corner from Bex's?' he asks. 'It's small, no garden, but it's pretty nice. We could afford it.'

'Oh, yeah, until Patrick Newlands gives you some more bad news.'

'That isn't going to happen, Ell. The First Locate project isn't a two-bit charity like Appletree. It's funded for five years under a major-league Government initiative to help asylum seekers. It's not the sort of thing that gets the plug pulled unless a lot of very important people want to end up looking very stupid. OK?'

'I know. You've told me again and again.'

'Well, it seems like it doesn't sink in,' he remarks.

'I know. I'm sorry. I suppose I can't quite get over your having been given such a responsible job on a plate,' she adds with a slight sneer.

It hurts, but he ignores it.

'That reminds me,' he says. 'Be careful about when you give notice. You squeeze as much sick-pay as you can out of them before you quit. I know it may not be ethical, but it's what anybody else would do. The last thing you want is to have to go back to that fucking place.'

'What makes you think,' she asks quietly, 'that it's the last thing I want?'

That makes him turn round.

'You're not serious? Ell, you're not going back to that God-awful school?'

'Why not?'

She is serious, he's thinking. Jesus Christ, look at the set of her jaw. I'll never talk her out of this one, the stubborn cow.

'Bloody hell. You obviously took a lot of brain damage from that bang on the head. Read my lips. I'm *working*. We can afford to live in Birchwoods. Thanks to the loucheness and generosity of Auntie Bex, we're renting on a nice street and our children are in an OK school. What *possible* reason could you have for wanting to carry on teaching at that...hellhole?'

'Well,' she says, 'that *hellhole*, as you call it, is the only place I've ever worked where I felt...where I felt I could be me. I'm not going to sit on my arse all day, Tom. I'm going back there as soon as I'm out of *this*.' She waves her strapped-up arm at him.

'You're mad,' he says.

'Maybe,' she agrees. 'But maybe I've learnt you have to be a little bit mad to cope with life. Maybe it helps.'

She pushes off the arm of the bench, and staggers uncertainly to her feet.

'Hey, hey, be careful.'

'Tom, will you *please* stop fussing?'

She scowls at him, pushes her hair out of her eyes. She has let it grow again, since the accident, jaw-length. It's dark and fluid like it used to be, but she's given herself a quirky streak of blackberry-red in the fringe, and she's kept the nose-stud. He glimpses, briefly, what will be the one lasting physical legacy of it all. The thing which will remain long after her wrist is out of its sling and back in action.

The scar.

No longer livid, not even especially wide, but long; an extra ridge across her forehead, like a permanent worry-line. She will bear it, they have been told, for the rest of her life.

Ella doesn't seem to mind. She got off lightly, she claims.

'Come on,' she says.

They begin to make their way down the incline of the path. They have to pass the blonde mother with the inquisitive toddler. Ella gives her a smile, which she returns.

Tom smiles too, although it is a slightly different character of smile, and the young woman knows this, as she doesn't show her teeth when she smiles at Tom. He's used to that. Women can be funny creatures.

As they go past, Tom turns, treating himself to a brief glance at the woman's denim-clad backside without either her or Ella noticing. It's something to share with Jeff later on – thoughts on horny mothers in parks and how much they might be up for it.

He hears his wife calling his children's names. Eyes swinging to the front again, he allows himself a wicked grin.

She may do something about the scar, she thinks. Get it seen to. It probably wouldn't be the most expensive operation in the world.

Yeah. If they're ever back in that private-school, aluminium-bowl, scatter-crystal, beechwood-floor, terracotta-vase bracket. How bloody likely is *that*?

They have to pass the blonde mother with the inquisitive toddler. Ella gives the young woman a smile, which she returns.

She knows Tom sneaks a look at the girl's backside when they've gone past. She knows he's brought binoculars so that he can look at all the fit young mothers while pretending to be doing a more innocent kind of birdwatching. Somehow it doesn't bother her as much as it should.

'Give them a shout,' she says over her shoulder. 'Ben! Izzy!'

And they walk on, separate but together. They walk on into the sunlight, towards their children.